THE RED FLOOR

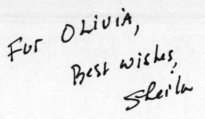

*For OLIVIA,
Best wishes,
Sheila*

The **RED**
FLOOR

SHEILA KINDELLAN-SHEEHAN

Véhicule Press

Published with the generous assistance of The Canada Council for
the Arts, the Book Publishing Industry Development Program of the
Department of Canadian Heritage and the Société de développement des
entreprises culturelles du Québec (SODEC).

Cover design: David Drummond
Set in Adobe Minion by Simon Garamond
Printed by Marquis Book Printing Inc.

LIBRARY AND ARCHIVES CANADA CATALOGUING IN PUBLICATION

Sheehan, Sheila Kindellan
The red floor / Sheila Kindellan-Sheehan.

ISBN978-1-55065-315-1

I. Title.

PS8637.H44R44 2011   C813'.6   C2011-901220-0

Published by Véhicule Press, Montréal, Québec, Canada
www.vehiculepress.com

Distribution in Canada by LitDistCo
www.litdistco.ca

Distribution in U.S. by Independent Publishers Group
www.ipgbook.com

Printed in Canada on 100% post-consumer recycled paper.

For Patricia Morley

Author, professor,
mentor, beloved friend
January 2009

List of Characters

THE DUO

Caitlin Donovan: 34, nudging 35, finds herself in the role of counselor and protector

Carmen DiMaggio: 33, normally sane, unlucky at the slots, takes a gamble on love

MONTREAL ARISTOCRACY

Douglas Henley: 61, ultra-wealthy potentate, a powerful influence in Montreal and in his daughter's life

Robert Tyler: 37, entrepreneur, Jessie's husband, and a man in flux

Jessie Henley: 34, self-assured, still her father's girl who dotes on her son

Justin Henley Tyler: 8, the boy with everything

THE NEIGHBORS

Steve Sharpe: 36, his first impulse is doing the right thing, without considering the consequences

Donna Sharpe: practical, a lioness where her son is concerned

Colin Sharpe: 8, breaks family rules and finds himself swimming in deep water

Susan Sharpe: 14, often forgotten in the crisis

MAJOR CRIMES: THE TEAM

Jean Geoffrion: 50, Lieutenant-Detective, cowboy trim, master of interrogation at the top of either the hard or soft game

Denis "Moitié-Moitié" Bertrand: 47, Lieutenant-Detective, his expertise is speech analysis and he doesn't miss much, ever!

Pierre Racine: Montreal chief coroner, a man who treats the dead with gentleness and dignity

Doug Hoye: a lawyer with a difficult client who refuses to heed his advice

Mike Fortier: 79, a retired shotgun veteran of Montreal Major Crimes, a no-nonsense old cop who can still track a clue or a suspect

Chapter One

CARMEN DIMAGGIO planned the next five hours with the tight focus of a gambler. Tentative plans to meet her best friend Caitlin for the last outdoor concerts of the Jazz Festival would change if the balls tumbled in her favor. The buzz and the sudden burst of hope she felt as soon as she'd driven her Mini onto the Bonaventure Expressway were gamblers' hooks. At her keno machine, she dissolved into the game, free from anxiety, real and perceived. There was no pull towards self-analysis, to where she was heading in her life, to the man she hadn't found, to the Italian family obligations, to Caitlin's dissection of gambling. Carmen might hit seven out of seven a few times!

Her heart hammered when she turned onto avenue Pierre-Dupuy and drove across Pont de la Concorde onto Île Notre-Dame. The casino was minutes away, and the city itself and Old Montreal were behind her. The Biosphere, site of Expo '67 to her left, the casino just ahead, beckoning like a silver cake, deceptive diversions to the money she'd lost over the years. To a gambler, every visit was a new beginning.

Carmen parked, hurried into the casino and turned right on the first floor. Grabbing her machine near the wall, she expelled a satisfied breath of air as she sat down. Reaching for the first twenty from her purse, she bent down and tucked the purse at her feet, fed the machine, tapped the 'play' button and waited to hear the sound of thunder, the roar that would multiply a win by four. She began with quarter shots that didn't pay, straightened up on her stool and switched to three-quarter shots. Playing her usual seven numbers, the closest Carmen came to a win was a measly 48 quarters. Carmen began to tap the 'play' button insistently. The machine was cold and dismissive. The air around her began to close in like the claustrophobia of a holding cell. Her shoulders sagged with loser's depression.

It took Carmen one hour and eleven minutes to lose $100. It was 11:43 a.m.

The familiar knot of Sunday gamblers didn't seem to be faring any better. The older woman in a beige suit was reaching into her purse, the leather-jacketed blonde woman, whose husband thought she was out shopping, sat staring at her screen, an old man was tapping his right foot. Carmen scooped up her wallet. The drink cart was nowhere in sight. Ordinarily, she would not have left her machine. It might turn hot at any unguarded second and give it up to a stranger, but she was in no hurry to lose her last hundred dollars. Another machine might bring her luck.

Making a beeline for the *L'entre-mise* deli one floor up, she ordered a minestrone soup and a smoked meat sandwich. No sooner had she enjoyed a small slurp of hot soup, than she heard the words, *'Si vous me permettez?'* and M. Fortin, carrying a hat with a small red feather like the one her father had worn eons ago, sat down at her table and pulled his chair closer to hers. M. Fortin had cared single-handedly for his wife Suzanne until she lost her battle with cancer. But from that point on, the seventy-eight-year-old told anyone who'd listen how he intended to be with his Suzanne as soon as he could arrange the details of his suicide. His penthouse had a private balcony, but he hadn't chosen to jump. No dignity, he had told her and her mother a month ago. What about the Pont des Îles right here at the casino, Carmen had wickedly suggested. He'd smiled knowingly, grasping her arms, *'Trop froid!'* Carmen had never met a merrier presumptive suicide and didn't believe M. Fortin for a second. She rolled her sandwich in napkins, smiled guiltily but got to her feet and left the old man. *I'm not up for the latest news on his suicide plot.* Carmen wanted to get back to the machines.

M. Fortin brushed imaginary dust from his hat, cupping it in his hands as he walked back to his own machine. He noticed the man who had his eyes trained on Carmen and turned his swivel stool to have a better look.

He was standing not ten feet from Carmen, leaning against the back of a keno machine, his arms akimbo, his head tilted to one side and his right foot crossed over the left. Tall and tanned, masculine and confident, serious dark brown eyes and a prominent chin saved him from the usual handsomeness. M. Fortin saw that his white cotton shirt rolled below the elbows, the gold, slim-faced watch, the linen pants and tan leather shoes were expensive and carefully chosen. The old man's cheeks pinched with envy. His youth was gone, but he trusted his eyes. In that casual and leisurely pose, M. Fortin saw a predator, smooth and dangerous.

Two croupiers coming on shift spotted the man. The younger voiced their common thought. 'The pick-up artist is back again! It's amazing how he zones in on women. Never leaves alone. Lucky for the casino the guy doesn't gamble.'

'Doesn't have to,' his partner answered, smirking.

Chapter Two

THE FAMILIAR CALCULATED come-on had been honed to a remarkable pseudo innocence. He waited until the young woman had taken a long look into her empty wallet. He knew what she was feeling— failure, as gray as the river outside, and waste, time that was void and lost. The buzz had evaporated. Her money was gone. At this disadvantage, she was ready to be taken. Robert Tyler walked to Carmen's side and whispered in her ear. 'I can drop $50 into your machine or I can take you for an early dinner at Nuances or I can kiss you and know I'm in heaven.'

Carmen's cheeks flushed. His breath was warm on her ear. She dared not turn. His presence was potent; she smelled his aftershave and her belly felt a jolt of nerves, deep and low. It was also disturbing and arrogant. Ghosts from her past appeared—men who had broken her heart. Still she didn't move. A second later, covering her mouth with her hand, Carmen tried to conceal a smile. Was it just last night she'd begun to worry about calluses on two of the fingers on her right hand from too many solo games?

Turning, she answered, 'I've been playing three-quarter shots. I should take you up on all three of your offers!' Carmen had lost today, but she could play a good game and she was tired of the tension of loneliness.

Robert made no reply. The silence between them seemed natural but charged.

'I'm kidding! I'm meeting my best friend at the Jazz Festival.' She scooped up her purse and her self-respect and as she stood realized she was only a foot from him. He hadn't moved.

'I *wasn't*.'

Carmen saw a self-satisfied easy smile and a looseness to his body that was depressingly seductive. She sensed a moan at the back of her throat. *This is a pick-up. When will I learn?* She took a deep, deciding breath. 'You know you're attractive, but I …'

'Let fate decide.' Robert fed the keno machine a $50 bill. 'What numbers do you play?'

Carmen leaned down to the machine and punched them in. Her hip touched his. Her belly went hard.

'This is your machine, play for us.'

What's the harm? Talk about arrogance! Carmen bet one quarter at a time. On the fourth play, she hit her numbers, all seven of them, to the roar of thunder. Three thousand, two hundred quarters! An $800 win! *Holy shit!* Her fingers tingled; she closed her legs tightly.

Robert ran his hand across her shoulders. 'You owe me $50. How's that for an entrée? You take my breath away when you blush. I'll settle for a drink.'

'One Singapore Sling.'

'I can handle that.'

Carmen checked her watch. She still had time before she met Caitlin at the festival. Fate was double-shifting. They found themselves on the elevator alone.

As soon as the door closed, Robert stepped up close and kissed Carmen on the mouth. He didn't pull her to him. His palms spread against the wall above her head, and his body rubbed slowly and rhythmically against hers. His tongue probed with a gentle insistence that compelled her to respond.

Carmen might have thought of the elevator scene in *Fatal Attraction* but her mind had ceased to function.

Robert did not touch her breasts. All he needed was his mouth and the slight teasing pressure of his groin. 'You taste like a summer breeze.' That was all he said.

Struggling with the embarrassment of groping in an elevator, Carmen had no defences had he chosen to do just that. A year of celibacy had not been her choice. Her need was raw. The door opened, and he took her hand and led her to a table.

M. Fortin had followed the couple until they stepped into the elevator. *Mon Dieu*, does *mademoiselle* not know we can see everything through the glass walls of the elevator?

Carmen tried to focus, but an ache that reached deep into her thighs blanked her thoughts. Her breath was ragged.

'I'm staying at the St-Sulpice on St-Denis. Spend the night with me.'

The night. The words weren't even large, an article and a noun. Their implication travelled up from her belly to her brain. Her single word was hoarse and banked by experience from old regret. 'No.' Carmen looked into his eyes. Was that a flash of anger that she saw? It left as quickly as it had appeared. Intensity took its place. She felt a sudden need to justify herself. 'I'm meeting a friend. I told you that.' A shiver shot up her back. Who was she afraid of, him or herself? Her body throbbed.

'I think I might want you forever.'

Might! A tentative whim? Carmen had an answer for him. 'I'm not up for *tonight* anymore. I should go. I don't even know your name.'

He reached across the table and covered her hand with his. 'Robert.'

Carmen took the money from her purse. 'Here, this belongs to you. I don't feel right taking it.' Indignation aside, a carnal urge tingled in her thighs. The hair on her arms began to rise. She saw the joint absurdity of lust and reason and feared she'd break out in screams of laughter. *How do I allow these things to happen?* Yet she lingered. She always had without understanding the why of it. Carmen always played the same machine. In a sense, the same men played her. Unable or un-willing, she didn't change either routine.

Robert's eyes darkened. He was not a man who tolerated contra-diction, stated or implied. To ease into the encounter, he smiled and his face softened. 'Let's begin again. I watched you for awhile. I saw hope and not greed when you played. I watched it dashed in your face. I know what it feels like to be on the outside.'

Carmen stood in silence. Robert said nothing further. In the silence, they met in a wordless connection. In such come-on moments, her life had a feel to it she accepted. Outside of them, Carmen chose not to explore their root causes where she might find her own sense of inadequacy or frustration. She lived most acutely in the moment.

'Please sit back down and put the money away.' Robert reached across the table and took her hands in his. She felt their warmth travel down her veins and arteries when her blood raced.

'I do have to meet my friend.'

'How about dinner tomorrow night? Can you trust me with your first name and number?'

You're too good to be true! Are you married? 'Carmen.'

'There's passion and music in that name.'

'Here's my business card.' It was a slip on her part, a lapse due to flattery and pride in her new title at work, sales manager.

'Let me take you to your car at least.'

In the indoor parking lot, Carmen walked briskly and unsteadily to her Mini. Robert was faster. When he kissed her again, her purse dropped to the cement floor. When she picked it up, Robert was gone. *Why did I give him my card? I don't even know his last name. He knows where I work. It's the erotic charge. It's been so long.* As she drove out of the parking lot and off the grounds, Carmen heard her own groan of uneasiness that arose from repeating patterns. The trail went all the way back to a church on her wedding day and a groom who never showed. Its lesson was clearly written, but Carmen didn't read it. At work, she knew intuitively when a client wasn't a serious buyer and she moved on to one who was. At the casino and with men, reason was a no-show, like the groom. The ride, and the possibility of where it might lead, seduced her. The plonk of the coin drop, the electric nerve that sparked when Robert's mouth was on hers, they were speed bumps that got her on the coaster. So far the rides ended with an empty wallet or a broken heart, but Carmen waited for the next one that might not leave her dangling. Robert might be the man who took her with him.

She wouldn't share Robert with Caitlin. Heading to the Queen Elizabeth Hotel to park as Caitlin had suggested, she could well imagine her friend's admonition. *A pick-up at the casino, are you out of your mind? Didn't we both resolve to turn our lives around?* Frankly, she was doing Caitlin a favor by joining her at the Jazz Fest. Pop/Rock was her thing. When your best friend is a university professor, everything is analyzed. She didn't want Robert picked apart. She'd do that herself.

The Jazz Festival, a hallmark of the Montreal summer scene, was Caitlin's stakeout every year and she wasn't alone. The event was always well attended by world-renowned musicians and a mass of appreciative fans. It was without equal on the North American scene.

Hurrying out of the underground parking at the Queen E., she saw Caitlin had beaten her to Cathcart Street and was waving her down. *I have to keep my mouth shut.*

'Hello, you! Busy day down in the city. I'm not sure I'll make the

Mory Kanté concert. Maybe we can just walk around and inhale some of the last jazz party of this year. You look too happy to have lost.'

'$800!' Carmen's eyes flashed.

'You're treating!' Caitlin looked closely at her friend. 'What did you lose though?'

'$200.' Carmen turned away. The thought of Robert flushed her cheeks a second time.

'Are you hiding something?'

'I'm just buzzed about the money.' Carmen ruffled her hair. The ride was on.

It was a signature of evasion Caitlin recognized. She'd wait. She had enough pride for that. Carmen couldn't keep a secret. Polar opposites, in appearance and temperament, they knew one another better than sisters. That wasn't always good, even in the mundane. Caitlin got rid of her birthday cards the next day—Carmen kept her shrine going for a month. Nonetheless their mutual pact had endured six years. Caitlin would get Carmen out of trouble. She was her champion. In return, Carmen would keep her professor friend laughing or crying or running for her life, depending on the situation. On either end, the capital gains were good, the losses held to a minimum. In the larger issues, they differed. After the untimely deaths of her husband and brother, Caitlin shunned risk. Carmen couldn't function without it. At times anxiety for Carmen quickly turned to irritation. Until Caitlin threw herself back into her own life and grappled with it, she sometimes enjoyed being the silent personification of caution and censure for her friend. That was the reason Caitlin knew whatever Carmen was hiding was troublesome.

Chapter Three

THAT NIGHT ROBERT LAY IN BED, mulling over the sudden change in his routine. Trysts, affairs, or whatever one wanted to label such transgressions, were to him one-act plays. As lead actor, he was the lover he wanted to be that night, seductive, alluring, mysterious or passionate. The burden and the insecurities of the mundane were left back at home. It was a free-for-all. It was licence, a walk-away. It was ironic, he thought, that such passionate, insulated hours fell victim to familiarity like everything else in life.

He balled a fist in his hand. His routine was smooth. He hadn't counted on making a mistake. He ought to have moved in on Carmen before he saw her face when she lost the last of her money. The vulnerability he'd caught in her eyes, pure and innocent, had reached under his skin. He remembered what it was to be clean. It was exactly eleven years ago. He was twenty-six years old then. He turned on his side to brush that thought away and the thought of what had transpired in the intervening years. An hour later he was still awake. In the beginning, he'd been guilt-ridden. The minute the sex ended, Robert wanted to go home. He was more solicitous with Jessie. He held private board meetings with himself and made resolutions to change.

But time dried up his guilt. In that period, he blamed Jessie who'd taken him in as an add-on to her life. He deserved that spurious thrill of having a woman listen to his story, fawn over him and wait on his call. His double life sustained his need for stability at home and excitement and escape where he found it. Changes he hadn't counted on occurred in the past year. He began to see Jessie as the adulterer in their marriage. The attachment to her father had robbed him of a wife. Her doting on Justin, their only child, had shut him out. Jessie had widened their estrangement. She was the real adulterer. The more Jessie moved away from him into her own life, the less he found in his affairs. His own story began to bore him. He could see the end of the affair on the first night. Life flattened.

Robert sat up in bed, balancing himself with his hands. He didn't turn on a light. He felt the ache and he knew what it was. He needed someone to be with *him*, to be on *his* side. Maybe someone like Carmen. He lay back and drifted off.

Carmen was distracted when she got home. Serious questions banging against her brain never had a chance to surface. Before she knew what she was doing, Carmen was grinding the sheet between her legs till she fell asleep and knocked one of her pillows to the floor.

When the 7:00 a.m. alarm went off and the radio turned on to Q92, Carmen woke bleary-eyed and fought to extricate herself from the sheets. The shower didn't do its usual wake-up job. Padding into the kitchen, she drank hot coffee. Her dark hair gave her the next trouble. The dampness of the early morning cost her time drying it. *He probably won't call.* The bed was a mess that would have to wait till tonight. Driving along Highway 13, she blasted music and shook herself awake.

It was Monday morning. Shielded by their dividing cubicles, the four co-workers took their time to come to. At nine, a note arrived by messenger. It was printed so well that Carmen thought Robert had typed it using a font she didn't know. When she realized the script was his, she ran her finger over it: *Dinner tonight at Toqué, 900 Place Jean-Paul-Riopelle, Montreal International Commercial Center in Old Montreal, at 8 p.m. One favor, take a cab at my expense. Parking is a hassle. Robert.* There was no cell number or last name. *Still no way to contact him! I won't go. Then again, what can happen at Toqué, at one of the city's ultra exclusive eateries? One thing is certain, if I go, I'm driving.* Each second thumped, and she watched the minutes stretch their sixty seconds.

In her apartment, as she stood in a hot shower, her arms trembled. She closed her eyes tightly against the sting of the hot water. *What am I doing?* Trepidation did not induce sanity. It never had. In the grip of lust, Carmen chose her best black dress and gold jewellery and party shoes. When she opened the front door, she froze. Pink roses with a second note: *I'll be waiting for you. Robert.*

Carmen rushed back into the apartment. Perspiration spotted her forehead and underarms. *He knows where I live!* She stood in a slow wave of sweat. *I want to go. How sick is that? How lonely.* She tore off the sweaty dress. Out came the wet towel and the deodorant and the splash of coconut perfume and on went another sleek little number. Carmen picked up the phone and spilled her story to Caitlin. 'I don't need a sermon.'

Caitlin didn't say anything, once her weapons were taken from her.

'I wanted you to know where I'll be.'

'Don't go back to his place, Carm.'

'Gotta go. Toqué, remember.'

'Dinner only!' Caitlin shouted into a dead line.

Cab it! Sure, I'd have no wheels and have to take money from him a second time. Carmen wasn't so cocky when she drove onto St-Antoine, searching for parking. A car nearby pulled out, and Carmen slid slowly into the space. *I'll pop out to feed the meter and break the tension too.* Before she got out of her car, Carmen checked herself out in the car mirror, played with her hair and checked her mascara. She tried her best sexy walk, putting one foot directly in front of the other, which she felt gave a gentle sway to her hips. One heel caught in a crack and she almost took a header. She straightened up quickly and looked around quickly to see how many people had noticed.

On the other side of the street, Robert had seen the stumble and he inadvertently reached out for her before he caught himself. He saw too that Carmen had driven down. He liked that, showed she *was* different. Allowing her time to recover, he jay-walked across the street and came up beside her. 'Glad you made it.' He leaned over to his left to meet her eyes and smiled.

Carmen's nerves knotted immediately. 'Hi!' was the only word she could get out. In the block of uneasy silence, she did manage to see his single-breasted tan blazer and matching tan shirt, one button opened at his neck, with a solid brown silk tie casually loose. His tan pants were narrow. Her kneecaps quivered. *Maybe…*

Unsettled because Robert was walking so close to her, she forced her voice to work. 'How did you manage to get a reservation here?'

'Always easy when you know people. Here we are. I saw that you parked. If need be, I'll take care of the meter.'

His self-possession excited and irritated her. A ripple of nerves ran up under her breast. She could almost feel his hand there. *I'm out of my league. Toqué? I could never come here.*

As soon as they were seated, her bravado fell like a spoiled soufflé.

Robert smiled and kept his eyes on hers. He leaned across their table. 'We could skip dinner and go…'

'I'm Italian. We don't skip food.' There was a sharp ache in her stomach. Carmen wanted to reach over and pull Robert into her.

He burst out laughing. It was the third time Carmen had tugged at his heart. He was right about her. 'Well then, trust me to order?'

'Go for it!'

When the foie gras terrine and small berries with balsamic vinegar arrived, Carmen saw only Robert's hands, strong and masculine, rounded at the tips. The duck supreme with baby turnips and carrots, topped with puréed strawberries and licorice sauce, had her squirming on her chair. She closed her legs tightly. The Beaujolais stoked the fire in her belly. Infected with passion and food, Carmen looked away, trying to keep her mind from images of tomorrow. When she did speak, her words echoed past humiliating and shameful times in her life. At least there was growth in these thoughts that surfaced before the damage was done. Her voice was weary when she spoke. 'Robert, I shouldn't have come.' Carmen felt a sense of pride.

He spoke softly but firmly. 'Can't we just enjoy tonight?'

'It's not a question of tonight. It's what comes after and what you won't tell me about yourself. I don't want to end up sneaking around like some truant or to get caught in the mess of tears and self-disgust left behind.' Her words did not echo her thoughts. The pull-back routine was part of it.

'Dinner then. No strings attached.'

For the first time in my life I don't care about food! The duck can wait. She saw the corner she had just walked into. Taking back her words now would expose her as an airhead and an idiot.

When she looked up at Robert she realized she might as well have spoken out loud. Robert was smiling. The duck got the worst of it. Carmen tore into the young bird with a wicked vengeance. After all, they were both losers. Licorice sauce soon dribbled from the side of her mouth. Trying not to laugh, Robert handed her his napkin. Carmen took it and asked for more sauce. The evening was a disaster, she thought bitterly. Why let a good dinner go to waste? It wasn't a pretty sight she was giving Robert. At the first chunk of duck, she'd conceded defeat. And now, the duck was already complaining in her stomach.

'I hope you don't end up with indigestion.'

'Hot water and sugar.'

'What?' he asked.

'The Italian solution. No jokes about my eating. Italians can't laugh at themselves.'

He waited for her to finish. 'I've had a delightful time. I can't recall the last time I saw a woman really enjoy her food. You're a character. At least, let me walk you to your car.'

When they reached the Mini, Carmen slid onto the front seat. Robert kept his hand on the passenger door. 'Can I sit with you for awhile?'

Bloated and palpably sad, Carmen answered, 'It's open.'

The Mini was suddenly filled with bodies, the dead duck included. Robert leaned over and kissed Carmen, and she fell against his shoulder. 'I ruined tonight.' He didn't reply. His hands grazed her breast and his mouth covered hers. *Oh God, I could come right here.*

'I want to see you tomorrow night at my place,' he whispered as he got out of the car.

In the end, words didn't mean much, not hers anyway. Carmen drove off in a wet daze.

Chapter Four

FOR CARMEN, THE DAY flew by. *St-Sulpice at eight. I'll have dinner waiting.* The delightful boutique hotel was just the place for secret getaways. On her drive down to Old Montreal, the caution she should have felt evaporated. The old hotel, a vintage building with a limestone façade had been renovated. The awnings had been changed, the door and windows had been replaced, and the garden was something entirely new. Her knees wobbled on her way to Number Four. At the rasp of the lock, Carmen took a deep breath.

Robert reached for her hand and led her through the suite to the lovely garden in the back that was part of the old seminary. He kissed her then and drew her close. Carmen forgot about caution and questions. She felt his mouth all over her. Fumbling with one another, they managed to get back into the suite. Her apprehension and alarm dissolved. His flesh glistened with sweat and mingled with hers. With every thrust, she felt the power of reckless abandon and the spread of release in every orgasm.

On a small table in the living room, the poached salmon and creamed vegetables shrivelled.

In the crush of sex, it seemed to be a silent pact that there'd be no words. Around two in the morning, Carmen reached for her clothes. 'It's late. I have to go.' The firm grip of sex was already fading, and isolation grew in silence.

Robert helped her into her clothes, and dressed quickly. He didn't want her to leave. 'I know you want some answers. I have a business meeting in Toronto. Come with me Friday night. I'll send a cab for you, buy the tickets and make reservations at the Royal York. We'll have time and I'll tell you about myself then.'

Like the food, something in Carmen shrivelled.

'Think about it. I'll call you Friday morning before work. I have a lot to tell you. Explanations take time, Carmen.'

She didn't answer.

He kissed her again and walked her to her car. Suspicion began to pool in her brain.

On the Decarie Expressway, her eyes teared. *He wants me to fall in love with him so I won't be able to walk away.*

Her answering machine was flashing when she got home. She walked by it. Four hours of sleep was all she'd manage before work. The flashing light tugged at her conscience. 'Dammit!' She called Caitlin.

'Thank God, you're okay! I couldn't just go to bed and forget about you... Do you have a last name?'

'No.'

'Did you do the nasty?'

'Guilty. Five counts. It's been a year, Caitlin. That played into the mix.'

Sermons were out of the question because Carmen's propensity for risk had her foot in the stirrup for another ride. Had she still been in her twenties, Caitlin would have pounced on her with morals and lessons in a period of obstinate certainty. In her early thirties, edges gave way. Her brother Chris had followed the rules, waited for green lights. What had happened? A drunk driver blew through a red, ran him down and left him to die alone on the side of Sherbrooke Street, a block from her home. Losing her only sibling had left her frightened. Caitlin threw herself into her classes at Concordia University and bordered herself behind a fierce independence. Risk and excitement she left to Carmen. From a safe distance, Caitlin got caught up in them. In the end, Caitlin watched out for her friend as Carmen did for her. What other options were there?

'He wants me to go away with him to Toronto for the weekend. He promised to explain things when we're there.'

'Are you actually thinking of going?' Disappointed and furious that Carmen would even entertain such a trip with a man she didn't know, her tone was grim.

Carmen ignored it. 'I'd like answers.'

'At the risk of heartbreak and perhaps worse?' Her tone was now definitely contemptuous.

'You don't know that,' Carmen answered defensively.

'I know you.' And she itched to add, 'I'll be picking up the pieces.' That'd be nothing new for Caitlin. Headstrong and professing her hard-fought independence, she'd walked away from the second man she loved. Pieces, she had made their acquaintance. Caitlin was at that tedium every day. Carmen recovered quickly from her debacles. *God, what an idiot I was!* That cleared the table for her. True to her profession, Caitlin mulled over failures.

Robert Tyler showered and changed quickly, a ritual he always followed, before checking out of the hotel. It was second nature now to slip back into the familiar persona Jessie knew. He left the alluring lover at small hotels. In the beginning, he'd marvelled at how easily duplicity could be hidden and with such little effort. People saw what they wanted to see, he learned early on. After his very first affair, he felt Jessie would see his guilt, but she hadn't. She never looked closely enough over the years to find traces of satisfaction that sometimes clung to him. People wore masks to fit a variety of situations. He heaved a sigh. His disdain for Douglas, the man who had commandeered his marriage, was disguised under a mask of respect. When the specter of guilt bothered his heart, Robert consoled himself with rationalization. He wasn't blazing new trails, shifting from lover to husband. That road was well travelled.

He drove home to a luxurious house on Roselawn Crescent in the posh borough of Town of Mount Royal. After the predominately English of Westmount and the French of Outremont, the Town of Mount Royal was the third golden star of Montreal. Here, the English and French happily co-existed. When he reached Rockland Road in TMR, Robert cut his speed. He didn't want to add to the six demerit points he'd already lost. He turned off the lights on his late-model, black Porsche as he drove onto the cobbled driveway. The gray stone house, mid-century style, was remote, impregnable, and imposing even in this wealthy area. A stone wall ran along the right side and on the left a high decorative wrought-iron fence was partially hidden by landscaping. Yellow canopies that hung over triple-glaze windows were gently lit by blue halogen lamps imbedded in the manicured shrubbery. Yellow begonias grew in thick, carefully tended clusters in the front of the house. The double mahogany front doors were decorated by heavy brass knockers and matching double doorknobs. The back property was kept private by a thick twelve-foot cedar hedge. A pool with a Japanese waterfall took up half the yard.

Inside, the house itself was dark.

For a while, Robert sat in the car, staring up at the house where he felt he was almost an intruder. Slumping forward, he dropped his head on the steering wheel, swept by an overwhelming depression and a keen contempt for the whole family set-up that had immobilized him in his own life. How could he have seen the trap at age twenty-five at a time when he was certain of everything, especially hope? The young entrepreneur and the beautiful Henley daughter! Success was their right. Jessica came from money. He'd made his, starting his business from the one-bedroom apartment when he was twenty-three and working nineteen-hour days, seven days a week. *There's no need for a prenup! I want the marriage contract to say we will share everything acquired during our marriage equally.* That was how Jessie had phrased it. What did he know of the trusts the wealthy set up for themselves to protect their lifestyle and their equity?

Reluctantly, using the remote, he opened the 'whisper-quiet' double garage door and parked beside Jessie's Mercedes. He had no fear of waking her. They didn't sleep together, her idea five years ago. *You move all night. Anyway, it'll be more romantic, like dating!* Walking quietly, he went down to the basement that included, beside his own impressive masculine ensuite, a home theater, a billiards room, a pool table, two Apple computers, shelves with expensive games, a dart board, a marble chess set, a wall of his own books and finally, an impressive wine cellar.

In the dark, Robert stripped and threw himself into bed. Tonight, he had been touched by something genuine that both saddened and heartened him. The sex had been what he expected of first-time encounters, but it was that look of hope, that simple stumble, that held him. Robert didn't articulate that night that he wanted out of his marriage, perhaps he had for a long time. It is often the simple truths we miss. He wanted to be needed. In Carmen, he'd seen a vulnerability he could support. He tried to isolate something that Jessie or Justin needed of him. He couldn't pinpoint anything. Before he fell asleep, he remembered that Jessie was taking Justin for his first golf lesson at the private Beaconsfield Golf Club on the West Island, site of LPGA tournaments. Lunch in Westmount with her father, Douglas Henley, was always a delight for both Jessie and Justin. His majestic mansion had a panoramic view of downtown Montreal and the Saint Lawrence River. The game room for his grandson was state-of-the-art. Justin seemed to feel more at home with his grandfather than he did with him. Robert shook off the thought to keep his emotions in check. He had the house to himself today for business he could conduct from home and a few things he had on his mind.

Hope had existed at the beginning. He'd met Jessica at the Mount Stephen Club where he'd taken his first big client to celebrate. Located in the heart of Montreal and founded in 1926, it was once the estate of George Stephen, co-founder and President of Canadian Pacific Railway. Back then, the area was known as the Golden Square Mile, the wealthiest residential downtown neighborhood in Canada. Jessie was descending the club's fabled oak staircase when he spotted her— a tall, leggy, blonde with a self-assurance that had nothing to do with men. Jessie had dominated the room when she walked into it, and filled it with a contained sexuality. He fell for her that very night. Back then, he had loved Jessie with a fierce passion. Back then... Robert had cheated on Jessie in the second year of the marriage, mostly because he was the third spoke in the Henley wheel. Jessie and her father were the 'A' team. At first, he cheated for revenge, then habit that spilled into his own need.

Before he dropped off, he thought of Toronto and a new chance he'd begun to create for himself. He slept past eleven. The note was the first thing he saw when he walked into the oversized kitchen. It was on the white marble island, propped up by a glass of orange juice. An array of brass pots hung above the counter. *We should be back by three at the latest. Justin is yours tonight. I'm out with Dad. J.* Piqued by the implication that Justin wasn't his on other days, he ripped the note to shreds and felt like leaving them for *J.* to find but thought better of the juvenile taunt. He booked two business-class tickets on Friday night at eight to Toronto.

His company sold moderately-priced and high-end souvenir items, mostly pewter, and had a net worth of $16 million, thanks in part to big contracts from major airlines hosting anniversary or sports events. China was moving in on his market. It was a good time to sell and concentrate on real estate. He had no intention of equally sharing what he'd made on his own, not after he'd supported Jessie and the house and gotten nothing in return. Douglas protected the family fortune so that Jessie had nothing to share with him in the event of a divorce. The trust held the deed to the house though he paid the bills. Two prospective buyers for his company had come forward, both Chinese. Robert needed half the sale to be hidden and the money banked in Belize where there was no extradition, but this manoeuvre was delicate and would take time. There was excitement and power in his scheme. Carmen was another matter. Carmen was in his head because he needed another spark.

Wearing a pair of white cotton cleaning gloves, he carried the vacuum with him upstairs into the master bedroom. Walking on the plush carpet would leave footprints. The safe was cleverly hidden behind a wall unit of drawers in Jessie's closet. Robert had stumbled onto the combination seven years ago when Jessie had asked him to run up and get her wallet in her night table. His hand had brushed against a plastic strip, taped to the back panel of the drawer. He'd bent down on his knees to investigate. At first he thought it was a company serial number. When he took a second look, he recognized the numbers: Justin's birthday, her father's and the date of her mother's death.

He knew where the safe was. He felt a surge of power when he ran the digits and swung the door open. In the beginning, they'd joke about *her* little territory, her secret documents. During their marriage, he'd waited for her to include him, but Jessie said she deserved some privacy. If he asked about the contents of the safe, he became an irritation and a minor intrusion. On occasions when Jessie was out, Robert ran the combination to the safe now and again to see what she was hiding from him. Money was never the goal. He felt no guilt about the subterfuge. He was deeply insulted he had to resort to such means. Robert felt worse about this sneaking around than he did about cheating. Tonight, he discovered a new file folder. He put the rest of the pile back carefully into the safe. He stood quiet and irresolute for a moment before opening the folder. Then he read the two documents with great care. Nothing in the set of his shoulders revealed his thoughts. He'd learned long ago to keep anger inside, but his breaths were deep and long. He replaced the documents, closed the safe, turned on the vacuum, erased his footprints and left the inner sanctum. When all was secure, he laughed bitterly and bit his bottom lip.

Chapter Five

JESSIE HENLEY DIDN'T BOTHER to slow down as she sped along Beverley Avenue onto Dumfries in the Town, and home. Her name and smile had gotten her out of numerous speeding tickets in a borough that had a very strong police presence. A trill of excitement vibrated around her. Jessie was tall and tanned and had changed from her golf clothes into a soft white cotton suit that revealed her décolletage and her assured femininity. A gold thin-face Cartier watch on her left wrist lay beside a pink breast cancer bracelet. Her Paris sandals set off the suit. 'Hey, buddy, are you going to be alright with your father tonight?'

'Why can't I go with you?'

'Your grandfather and I have work to do. Your father has to see you sometime, and I won't be late.'

Justin turned away from his mother and stared out the window till he got out of the car. He felt awkward with his father. Tossing a football wasn't that much fun. His father threw the ball hard, and Justin missed it most of the time. His grandfather had taught him chess. It didn't help the bonding of father and son that Justin bore no resemblance to his father. He was blond like his mother and had the Henley chin. His hands were too big for his body, just like his grandfather's. Whatever his father wanted from a son, he didn't have it. That was the last thought Justin had when the car came to a stop.

They found Robert at the pool. He'd made Jessie his concoction: fresh mint, ice cubes, a touch of lime, Floc de Gascogne mixed with a *rosé*. He was sipping cognac. 'The duo is back!' There was a hint of hostility in his voice, but he kept it disciplined. He saw nothing different in Jessie when he studied her face. Since he had no intention of revealing what he'd discovered, he looked over at Justin. 'How about a pizza at La Pizzaiolle, Justin?'

'Extra pepperoni?'

'You got it!'

Justin gave his mother a weak smile.

Jessie took a few sips. 'Thanks for this, Robert. How was your day?'

'We're losing more accounts. The Chinese can produce the same work at a quarter of our cost. That means more lay-offs in both plants.' It was a clever way of setting up the lower price he'd tell her he got for the company. If he walked away with ten million, he could live with that. Battling the Henleys in court would prove costly for him.

'You'll work your way out of it. You always do. Listen, you guys enjoy yourselves. I won't be late. I have to shower and change.' Jessie gave Robert a quick peck on his cheek, threw her arms around Justin until he wiggled free, laughing. She was at the patio door when she called back. 'By the way, what time did you get in last night?'

'Business. Some of these guys could go all night.'

'Be good, both of you! Justin, to bed by nine. You have a riding lesson in Hudson tomorrow afternoon.' And Jessie was off.

Justin and Robert watched Jessie till she disappeared. The boy hiked his shoulders, uncomfortable being alone with his father. Robert and Justin were always stuck with re-entry on occasions when they were together. The easy banter Justin enjoyed with Jessie and her father disappeared. Robert didn't much like the kid Jessie and Douglas had spoiled rotten. Justin got whatever he wanted and he could pretty much do what he wanted. 'What about a little football before the pizza?'

'It went into the pool the last time, Dad.'

'I'll stand at the pool; you take the hedge.' *Riding, golf and chess! What kind of shit is this for a kid of eight who can't catch a football and doesn't want to learn! I quarterbacked the McGill Redmen for two years. My own son should be able to throw a ball.*

When Justin was born, Robert felt he had something of himself now, a son bolstering his side, an ally to help pull away from Douglas, to be a family. It hadn't worked out that way. From the start, Jessie's attachment to Justin was boundless. When he could crawl, Justin followed her like a puppy and still did. Douglas doted on his grandson as though *he* had orchestrated the birth.

Robert and Justin walked out to the back lawn and took up their positions, like a lopsided duel. 'Ready?'

Justin raised his arms. The spiral slipped through his hands and caught him on the shoulder. He fell back and winced. Then he kicked the ball into the hedge before throwing it back at his father. His toss wobbled, and Robert had to take a few steps forward to catch it.

'Keep your eye on the ball and close your hands tightly as soon as you feel it.'

'I hate football.'

'When you make your first catch, you'll feel differently.'

Rubbing his shoulder, Justin turned away, out of the path of the next throw, and said, 'I'm hungry. Let's eat.'

Robert was about to say, 'Forget the damn food. Learn to catch a ball! Everything isn't going to be given to you in life. Some things you have to work for.' When Robert saw he was wrong, he gave up. Justin would never have to struggle for anything. They walked to the Town center, to the converted railway station that was now La Pizzaiolle. Justin walked ahead of him, listening to music. The place was popular and they weren't the first to arrive. 'How about eating outside, Justin?' Neither Robert nor Justin looked over at the Pierre Elliott Trudeau Rose Garden that was in full bloom across from them in the Town circle.

'I like the second floor better.'

Robert tried to think of one thing he and Justin could agree on and came up short. He ordered his pizza with sun-dried tomatoes, not the mounds of pepperoni Justin was devouring. 'How was the golf lesson?'

'Okay.'

'Do you like the game?'

'It's harder than it looks. Mom can really hit a ball. She's a natural, Dad. I saw other guys looking at her when we were just hitting balls off a hill.'

'How's the pizza?' There wasn't much conversation after that. Back home Justin went up to his room and Robert got caught up on his newspapers before he headed to his suite. A little after ten, the phone rang. 'I'm on my way. Shouldn't be long. Justin's in bed, I hope?'

'Should be.'

'Didn't you check on him?' There was rising irritation in her voice. 'It's the only night you have him.'

'He's eight, Jessie. I'll check on him now.'

'Alright.'

Justin wasn't in his bedroom. Robert called out to him. There was no response. He called louder. Nothing. The traditional chandeliers throughout the house, that Jessie had insisted on, cast unsettling shadows on the walls. He turned on the pool lights and ran out back. 'This isn't funny, Justin. Your mother won't find any of this amusing.' His voice had taken on an anxious edge. He glanced at the shallow end of the pool. Suddenly, the air was thick. He spotted Justin lying on the bottom, his hair gently swirling around his head. Robert jumped in and pulled him out. His legs shook as he hurried up the in-pool stairs with Justin in his arms. Sweat soaked his eyebrows and ran into his eyes. 'Help! Help! Someone call the para-medics! Help!' Robert's voice was unrecognizable. 'Oh my God!'

Quickly he lay Justin on the flagstone, turned his head to one side and began CPR. In-between, he screamed, 'Help! Help!'

A light in the house behind his went on. 'Is that you, Robert?' Martin Bissonnette called.

'Get help! It's Justin! Please get help!'

Other lights went on.

Justin's blue eyes were half open and vacant, his lips were slightly parted. His legs lay across one another. His chest bounced like rubber each time Robert pumped it. His blond hair was plastered across his forehead. Robert forced air into his mouth with every breath he took. Martin and his wife Louise appeared with a blanket. Robert kept pumping on the small bundle of flesh and bones that had stopped moving. Working frantically, he looked back at Louise.

'Let me help!' Robert waved her off though Louise was a cardiac surgeon. She didn't insist. Looking down at Justin she knew that he was dead. The boy looked very small. She stepped back with her husband and imagined Justin in Robert's arms. She thought of the Pietà.

Robert kept working. 'Spit out the water, Justin. Just for once, do what I want! Listen to me!' He was shrieking and slapping the boy's cheeks.

The quiet residential crescent was suddenly ablaze with flashing red lights and wailing sirens. A fire truck was first on the scene. The police and the ambulance arrived together. Two constables stayed out front to prevent neighbors from trying to get on to the property.

Jessie slowed down when she saw the commotion on her street. There were so many flashing lights, she couldn't pinpoint the source.

A cold fear clutched her stomach when she discovered it. Jessie accelerated the rest of the way and jumped from her car, leaving her door open. When a constable tried stopping her, she screamed, 'I live here!' She ran through the gate.

Robert had to be physically taken off Justin who was then lifted to a gurney. The law in Montreal was to get drowning victims to the nearest trauma hospital and if need be to pronounce them dead there. Justin's arm had slid off the gurney.

Every muscle in Jessie's body spasmed. Her universe broke into small sharp pieces. In agony, she watched dumbly as Justin was wheeled past her. Her body jammed when she saw his arm. She couldn't move. She couldn't go to him. What did erupt was anger. In the next instant, she flew at Robert hitting him with ferocious punches. 'What have you done?' The cruelty and accusation were unmistakable.

Robert gripped her wrists. Then she began to kick him. 'Jessie, I didn't even know he was in the pool. Go to the hospital with Justin.' He let go of her hands and Jessie slapped him hard across the face.

'One night! And you couldn't take care of him!' Jessie turned and ran after the ambulance. She grabbed a constable. 'He killed my son! My father is Douglas Henley. A crime occurred here tonight! Call in the proper authorities.' There was a note of challenge and shock in her accusation. Jessie screamed back at the officer. 'If you don't already know, find out who my father is!'

A paramedic held out a hand for her and she climbed into the ambulance as it raced off to the Level-1 Trauma Unit at the Montreal General Hospital on Cedar Avenue. Jessie held Justin's hand, kissing every finger, tasting the chlorine. She couldn't look at the feverish attempts to resuscitate her son. She could not bear the blow that would tear her heart apart, that Justin's life, so barely lived, was gone. A cutting jab of pain beat against her ribs as though they too were cracking. Décarie and Ville-Marie Expressways flew by. Until the ambulance turned onto Cedar Avenue, Jessie rocked back and forth wailing, 'Please God, please God, please God…'

Chapter Six

Constable Brossard called Jean Geoffrion, her lieutenant,-detective, at the North Division on Crémazie Boulevard East in Montreal North. She knew he was *sur le gun*, on 24-hour duty. Brossard knew her job and gave Geoffrion the pertinent facts: a drowning in an exclusive residence in TMR, only the husband and the victim, his eight-year-old son, were on the premises at the time. She added, 'The wife claimed a crime has been committed and pointed to the husband. That's the reason for the call. She said her father is Douglas Henley.'

'Is there a possibility the wife is simply accusing her husband of negligence? This might be a tragic accident.'

'No, Sir. She was hysterical, but serious about the accusation.'

Geoffrion knew very well who Douglas Henley was. 'Minus the prison term, Henley's up there with Conrad Black. He's also a major contributor to the Montreal Police Force and every political party in the province. He has the power of a premier in Quebec. Freeze the scene, look for possible witnesses, question the neighbors, don't allow anyone to contaminate the scene, and leave the husband for me. I'll send down the crime techs. I'll be there in less than an hour.' It was his habit to arrive at the crime scene once it was secure and the evidence bagged and sent to the police lab. Geoffrion called his partner at Major Crimes at Place Versailles on Sherbrooke Street, in Montreal East, Lieu-tenant-Detective Denis Bertrand. They were on the 24-hour stint be-cause they liked to work the seven-to-three shift together.

'Is the boy dead?'

'According to a physician neighbor who was at the scene. Taking him to the Montreal General was procedure. They'll pronounce the victim there.'

'Jean, what's the husband's name?'

'Robert Tyler.'

'Begin to question him. I'll do background. We can't discount suicide, so I want whatever we can get on the boy. Get some of that from the neighbors tonight. I'll alert Pierre Racine at Parthenais. He'll want to break the routine and be present when the body arrives at the morgue. We can work together and off one another with Tyler. Douglas Henley's grandson! Lots of scrutiny. We don't want a lawsuit.'

'We're up to the challenge, Moitié.'

'Never said we weren't.' He could hear the mounting excitement in Geoffrion who generally assumed and took the lead. Geoffrion was a *pure laine*, an expression for old stock French Canadian. As such, in Quebec, he thought he was entitled to top billing so he'd set high career goals for himself. Lieutenant-Detective sat well with Moitié. Glass ceilings, he knew, were triple-glazed and hard to break. In his niche, he had acquired his own personal techniques. As the second on their cases, he worked the background and he sniffed out crusts under the table. He often slipped under expectations and surprised himself and Geoffrion. In fact, their solve totals were just about equal. The 'big boss' knew this team covered every angle of their cases and he knew the men were competitive. Together, they were a good mix.

Geoffrion and Bertrand had come up through the ranks together. Geoffrion did not fit the stereotype of a pot-bellied, cynical, donut cop. Geoffrion was fifty, as trim as a cowboy, as clear-eyed as a recruit and a master of interrogation. He was happily married with two sons. His job and family drew equal attention. In fact, he saw himself as *un directeur* of the Montreal Police Force.

Bertrand, "Moitié–Moitié" as he'd been dubbed by the homicide cops, was three years younger. Although he was born in Montreal North, his father was Haitian and his mother Québécoise; hence the nickname, "half and half." He came by his soft, fluid swagger and bubble ass naturally and he wore the best threads on the sixth floor of Place Versailles. He was a bachelor who looked thirty-five. His short brown curly hair, boyish appeal and easy way worked to his advantage. Suspects sometimes made the mistake of thinking of him as *their* ally, or concluded that he was not as sharp as a white bread cop. Geoffrion himself had learned that Moitié, to use his abbreviated tag, ate macaroni pie and sugar cake and sipped Mauby instead of coffee or coke when he was at his desk, and had razor-sharp pick-ups he respected. Together, they headed up the Major Crimes. The men looked like hunky suburban husbands.

With this information, Moitié alerted the 'big boss,' the police chief, waking him out of a sound sleep.

'I've met Douglas Henley and his daughter Jessica at different events. You and Geoffrion work the case. Henley is intimidating and meticulous. Be prepared, but don't allow Henley to take control. I've read he dominates his business empire. He made himself the center of the events I attended.'

'Yes, sir.' Moitié left his office and walked down the hall to Central Filing, the room that stored computer documentation. For a moment, he wished he had the total information access granted to the chief coroner. He sat at the computer and got to work.

Robert hadn't made any attempt to follow Jessie to the hospital. He sat alone at the back of the pool inside a yellow and blue gazebo, staring out at the water. Dumbly, he stared at the police crime-scene tape that wound up the bottom steps of the pool and then around the whole area. When a police tech picked up a towel and put it into a plastic bag, it was the first time Robert had noticed it. He had disassociated himself from what was unfolding around him. In and out of shadows, police with flashlights moved back and forth and spoke in low tones to one another, but not to him. He saw lights in each of the three homes that bordered theirs. He waited for someone to approach him, but no one did. Did that young constable believe Jessie's accusation?

Finally, a tall man in a suit walked toward him.

'Mr. Tyler, I'm Lieutenant-Detective Jean Geoffrion. This is a very difficult time, but you know that I'll have to ask you a few questions.'

Robert met his eyes. From the very first statement, he felt he was a suspect. 'Have you news of my son?'

'I'm waiting for the official call.' Geoffrion noted that Tyler had not used his son's name.

In the trauma room behind Emergency on the first floor, the team's feverish work was slowing down at a nod from the chief surgeon. 'Call it.' He left the room to talk with Jessie who stood rigidly against a wall. Terror and anger held her in a vise. As the surgeon approached, Jessie grabbed her cell and stabbed in her father's number.

Douglas Henley heard an indiscernible strangled scream. Had he not seen the ID, he would never have known it was his daughter. 'Jessie!

What's wrong? What's happened to you?'

Her scream grew to a higher pitch.

The doctor took the phone and turned away from Jessie to spare her further pain. She seemed to dissolve. 'Mr. Henley, this is Doctor Faigan at the Montreal General. I regret to inform you that your grandson drowned in the family pool tonight. The trauma team did what we could, but he was unresponsive when he got to the hospital. He had no pulse, respiration or pupil reaction. I'm sorry.'

'Justin?' Henley winced at the sudden shaft of pain and shock.

Faigan related the circumstances. 'We did everything possible...'

'That hardly matters now.' His voice was thin and bloodless. Henley's throat began to constrict. 'I'm minutes away. I want to talk to you. Tend to my daughter.'

The surgeon tried to hand the phone to Jessie, but she was beyond seeing him. He put it on a seat beside her. 'Your father will be here shortly.' Faigan felt the young mother didn't want him near her. He headed back to the trauma room. 'Clean up in here. Douglas Henley is on his way. He was a major contributor to the oncology wing.' The nurses worked silently and quickly. Faigan had other patients, yet he knew he had no choice but to wait for Henley and try to explain once more that his grandson was dead. Breaking procedure he brought Henley's daughter Valium.

Jessie stared at him as though she'd never seen him before and ignored the medication.

Faigan had discovered a small contusion on the right side of the child's forehead and another on the same side below the collarbone, but he would disclose this information once Douglas Henley arrived. The young mother was in no condition to hear any of this.

He was turning away when a voice, cold and deliberate caught the physician off-guard.

'Justin couldn't drown. He floats like a top. I've tried to pull him under in fun, but I swear his body's inflated with air or helium. Justin knows he's not allowed to swim alone.'

He looked over at Jessie, but her face had hardened into stone.

Douglas Henley rarely revealed his emotions. Jessie and Justin were the sole exceptions to that hard and fast rule. Once his driver let him off at the hospital, Henley strode past the smokers outside and into Emergency. He moved with the authority of a man who ran prosperous, multinational corporations. Jessica's fine features were a reflection of her father's more than her mother's. Henley's light brown hair was combed straight back from a strong forehead that bore an old hockey scar at the hairline. He was a handsome man at sixty-one. That night, his steely blue-gray eyes were cold and unyielding. A black cashmere sweater and and light gray pants revealed a body as taut as a distance runner's. A nurse rushed after him and tried to ask where he was going, but he dismissed her contemptuously. He'd come for the truth about Justin's death and he had the means and determination to acquire it. He didn't need a nurse delaying him.

Henley saw his daughter, but he also saw a physician, standing just outside the trauma room, talking to a police officer. The hospital was familiar to him. He was a director as well as a generous contributor. He went directly to the men. 'I'm Douglas Henley, Justin's grandfather.'

'My condolences,' Faigan offered.

'What happened?' As he listened to the surgeon, a vein at his temple bulged and throbbed. 'Where's my son-in-law? He should be here with Jessie.' When Henley heard of his daughter's accusation, he did say, 'Jessie had reason to feel Robert was negligent. My grandson was in his charge.' When he learned about the bruises, he was resolute. 'Do what's necessary, but permit my daughter and me some time with Justin before anything else is undertaken.'

'Of course. This was a young boy, and boys have all sorts of bruises. It's common for the spouse who was with a child at the time of his death to be blamed by the one who wasn't. As a physician I thought I should tell you that.'

'I want answers. I don't want to hear the obvious, that boys have bruises. I want to know its cause. Your take on responsibility is of no interest to me. Am I making myself clear?'

'Perfectly.' Doctor Faigan didn't utter another word as Henley walked off.

The officer backed away and called Geoffrion.

'Accompany the van to the morgue. Advise me if the Henleys follow. Moitié will meet them there.'

Jessie saw her father approach, but she didn't collapse in his arms. She stayed frozen against the wall. Her father took hold of her shoulders and pried her gently into his embrace. 'Jessie, I'm so sorry. Let's go to Justin. He's alone in there with strangers.'

Jessie tried to pull away, but he held her tightly. 'Take my hand.' He steered his daughter into the room, but she looked away from the stationary gurney.

'I can't.' Jessie dug her head into her father's shoulder. 'I won't.'

Henley looked at the two physicians. 'Leave us.'

Henley, pulling Jessie by the hand, guided her to Justin. A wrenching sob doubled her over. 'Jessie, kiss your son goodbye.'

Jessie's eyes fell on her only son. It was difficult to tell that Justin was beyond danger or harm. Had he not been in a hospital, one would have said he looked like a sleeping angel. His blond hair had dried and his cheeks were tanned. One of his small hands was closed in a fist, but the other was open and free. Only his eyes, slightly open and glazed, betrayed the sad appeal of death. But Jessie didn't see that. 'Is he really dead?' Her whispers floated above Justin. It was the only statement she made before she covered Justin's face with kisses. Henley held his daughter up or she would have fallen to the floor.

Chapter Seven

IT WAS TIME TO QUESTION Tyler in depth. Geoffrion entered the gazebo. 'Mr. Tyler, I need your account of tonight's events. It would be easier if we went to my office. There'd be fewer distractions. It's best if you drove with me. You're still in shock.' The pink polo shirt Tyler wore hadn't yet dried and clung to his chest and arms. His dark hair was dry.

Robert kept his eyes on the pool. 'I should go to the hospital. Jessie's right. I should have been more vigilant. I never even checked on him until she called.'

Tyler's immediate account of the drowning was important, particularly if the case became a criminal investigation. 'An officer will drive you back home. The sooner we can establish this tragedy was accidental, the better for your family.' Geoffrion wanted the home searched, with special attention to Tyler's clothing. He didn't want to give Tyler a chance to get rid of anything. If this was indeed a crime, he'd staged it as an accident. Depending on the time of death, Tyler had without doubt already hidden incriminating evidence, but he guessed it was still in the house. His wife's accusation must have surprised him. Geoffrion thought of the bruises he'd discovered from the hospital call.

'What could I say that would bring my son back?'

Tyler had asked the question, looking down at his shoes. The man wasn't emotionally flat, but he was a hard read. Geoffrion wanted him back at his division. He might persuade Tyler, as a means to exclude him from any part in the death, to undergo a body search that would reveal scratches on him. In the yard, he was protected by shadows.

Robert might be suffering from shock. But inside his head anger, dread, grief and guilt swirled in a frenzy. When he saw the cop enter the gazebo, he looked at him warily. Jessie's accusation brought bile to the back of his tongue. What she and her father could do with their influence, the people they knew in the right places, the ears they could bend, the markers the old man could call in, all of it could have him arrested and whatever else came after. Henley had the arrogance that money built. Robert's shoulders began to shake and he looked around as though he didn't recognize the gazebo. He had to take some action, begin with his version of the events. He thought of Doug Hoye, a lawyer friend he could call, but that would arouse suspicion.

'My shirt is wet. My shorts too,' he said as he rose. 'I'll change but I prefer to talk here. I want to be home when Jessie gets back. I don't want the house empty.'

Geoffrion couldn't force the issue. Tyler had lost his son tonight and he wasn't under arrest. He had to work the evidence and wait for it. 'We can talk in the living room.'

Robert's knees were rubbery and he held the railing on his way downstairs to change. Geoffrion followed him and Robert knew he couldn't object. He wished he had another chance to see the safe to be sure that he'd left no evidence behind that showed he'd gained access. With this cop shadowing him, Robert had no chance of that. The airline tickets were on his computer behind two firewalls and safe for now. When he could, he'd call the buyers in Toronto and see what he could come up with there. He'd call Carmen if he had the chance before Friday, but not from any home phone. Right now, he had to clear himself of suspicion. If he could just talk to Jessie... What was Justin doing in the pool anyway?

Geoffrion walked back up to the living room with Robert. He took out a pad and a recorder.

Robert's nerves began to pop. He felt rushed and unsteady in his thoughts when he sat down. Geoffrion set the recorder at his side. Things were moving so quickly.

'I hope you don't mind. This is procedure to protect us both. Please recount the events of last evening after your wife left the house. There is no live-in help, I take it?'

'Sylvie finishes at three.'

'Why did your wife go out tonight?'

'Something with her father.'

'What time was that?'

'Before five, I think.'

'Where was Justin at that time?'

'He was with me. I suggested we toss the football out back, but Justin didn't want to.'

'Any particular reason?'

'His exact words were, "I hate football."'

'And yet, you both tossed the ball anyway.'

'I felt my son should learn to throw a ball at least. Jessie has him in golf and riding, her old man's stuff. Nothing wrong with golf or horses, but Justin hates—hated,' he corrected himself, 'hockey as well. I wanted him to be a little like me, I guess. None of that matters now.' Robert stopped talking and had a good look at the cop when he leaned forward and increased the volume on the recorder. He seemed to be in his late forties, maybe fifty, with prematurely white hair. Robert caught a whiff of the gel he used on it. The fine hairs on his hands were bleached from the sun, veins popped up in a few places and his nails were cut short. The black band of his Swiss Army watch was worn at the edges. His tie had a food stain that made him seem more of a man than a cop.

'How long were you out back with your son?'

'One spiral.'

'Pardon?'

'I threw one spiral to him. He missed it, and the football caught him on the shoulder. He kicked the ball and quit. It's hard to know that the last thing I did with my son hurt him.' Robert rubbed his eyes and the bridge of his nose. 'He wanted to eat so we walked to the old train station and had pizza.'

The shoulder bruise. 'Was he angry about the football throw?'

'He was busy devouring his double pepperoni pizza.'

'Did he say anything?'

'He spent his time watching the flat-screen TV mounted on the wall behind me.'

Geoffrion asked the next question quickly as though it were a cast-off. 'Did you get along with your son?'

Knowing what Jessie would say, he offered up the truth first. 'He picked sides early for a kid. He chose his mother and grandfather. Jessie was enraptured with him at birth and that never changed.' Robert tried to rein himself in, not go too far.

Geoffrion thought Tyler knew what he'd just given up. He respected the smart move. 'When you got back home, what happened?'

'Justin holed up in his room. I went down to my suite.'

'You don't sleep upstairs then.'

Robert stuck both legs out and crossed his feet, filling up space. Nothing in his life would be private. The physical separation from Jessie and Justin didn't reflect well on him. He felt a prick of resentment at the loss of privacy. The cop saw him now as the family outcast. Any comment on his part would smack of the underdog at some point. The detritus that followed Justin's death would open sour, painful secrets.

Geoffrion left that point till later. 'So, you don't know what he was doing up there?'

'Playing games on his computer. That's what he generally does.'

'You didn't go up to check on him?'

'Jessie coddles him. At nine, I called up and told him to turn off the lights and get into bed because he had an early riding lesson in Hudson.'

'What were you doing?'

'Checked work on the computer, shot some darts, got caught up on the newspapers, dozed off for a while. That's it I think till Jessie called.'

There was nothing in the statement that could be verified. Geoffrion had carefully noted how few times Tyler used his son's name and distanced himself from the boy. There were no tears either.

'Did you hear anything from outside?'

'Not with triple-glazed glass. It blocks out most noise. Obviously, my son snuck out for a swim. He'd make sure he was very quiet.'

'Tell me what happened when you went up to check on your son.'

'Jessie called to say she was on her way. Her father lives in Westmount. I went to my son's room, but he wasn't there. I called throughout the house. I think I said, "This isn't funny, Justin!"'

'How soon did you think of the pool?'

'A few weeks ago, a young boy drowned in a family pool. I had a sick feeling, quite suddenly. I turned on the lights and ran out back. I spotted him and thought he was swimming underwater to hide from me. His hair was moving. But he wasn't. I panicked. I jumped in and pulled him out.'

'How did you lift him out?'

'It all happened so fast. I reached under him and lifted him to the side of the pool and hopped up myself. I screamed for help. I turned his head to the side and began CPR immediately. I kept screaming for help and I think I was screaming at Justin to wake up. A neighbor called for help, I think, while I worked on Justin.'

'Did you by chance hit his head trying to get him out of the pool?'

Robert folded his arms tightly around his chest. He pulled his legs in and began gesticulating with his hands, with his palms held up. 'I scooped him up. I don't know if his head struck the side of the pool. I don't think so. His head was in the crook of my arm. I can't be sure… I don't know…'

Shifting gears again, Geoffrion asked, 'Was your son "down" as the kids say about anything? Would you know if something was bothering him?'

Robert rubbed his forehead with his fingers. 'God almighty! He devoured a pizza and two cokes in record time. He got everything he wanted, except for being able to throw a spiral, and he wouldn't kill himself over that. Besides, I've read that suicide by drowning is almost impossible. Even if that were a remote possibility, he would never have chosen the shallow end of the pool. He was smarter than that.'

Tyler's first reaction to the loss of his son, Geoffrion felt, had been the subdued shock. If he did take his wife's accusation seriously, his demeanor did not reflect that. He had admitted the young boy was closer to his mother and grandfather. That might well be the reason he felt distanced from his son, even in death. In the detective's expertise, that wilful separation pointed to guilt on one level or another. It was his job to discover to what degree. *Accident or murder.* One bruise had been explained for now. His sergeants had been up to the boy's room, but hadn't gone to Tyler's quarters. Geoffrion thought better of his idea. He'd wait for an official warrant. Henley had given the go-ahead for a search, but Tyler's private quarters were another issue. He didn't want to spook Tyler while he kept up the pattern of not using his son's name. Did he not realize his response had moved him closer to becoming a suspect?

'Mr. Tyler, you'll have to come to the North Division for a formal statement and further questions, perhaps tomorrow.' For Tyler, the tragedy itself was ended. His son was dead. For Geoffrion, the file was unfolding. When Geoffrion stood, he didn't roll on his toes and reveal the potential he thought this case might have for him and his future.

He was pleased he was the lead with Tyler. If there was a solid case here, he had the prime suspect.

Robert didn't move from his chair to let Geoffrion out of the house. He had no idea if the detective was coming back. Outside, lights still flashed, cops spoke in small groups. Robert got up and watched the police from the windows behind drapes. He wanted to see Justin's room, but he hadn't the energy to walk up the stairs, or to go down to his own suite. He went back to the chair in the living room, unaware of the room itself, of the fine art that surrounded him. He kept his eyes on the front door, waiting for Jessie.

The room began to oppressively close in on him. Guilt crept around the edges of his body into his pores, guilt for failing his family, guilt for everything. An involuntary spasm rocked his chest, and he jerked up and sat rigid.

Chapter Eight

ONCE JESSIE LEFT THE TRAUMA room, Justin's hands and feet were bagged for evidence before the body itself was tagged and wrapped in white plastic, covered with a sheet and brought to the basement to a waiting van that would take it to the morgue.

Jessie did not give in to her father's wish that they leave. 'I'm going to the morgue, Dad. I don't want him to be all alone down there. I want to see him one last time before…' Her sobs were deep and dry. 'Before…'

'I'll go with you, Jessie.' Henley informed Doctor Faigan of their intent, and the surgeon called the morgue to advise the staff of their arrival. Faigan had to run after the Henleys because they had walked away from him. 'Excuse me. The chief coroner will meet you at the front entrance of 1710 Parthenais. He will be waiting for you.'

The Henleys ducked into the limo without responding.

The chief coroner was a lawyer who had accepted his recent appointment at Parthenais with professional enthusiasm. When he was called about Henley's grandson, Pierre Racine dressed with care in his best brown-striped suit and dark tie. He was fastidious about his appearance. His small glasses made him appear like a professor or an owl. He knew the depth of the tragedy, for he had lost a niece the summer before to drowning, but he also felt the sense of importance that accompanies meeting powerful men. Racine was a cultivated man who spoke impeccable French and decent English. At the front desk, he conferred with the admitting officer. 'I will meet Mr. Henley and his daughter, but I feel we should dispense with the electronic search. I will take full responsibility.' He would spare the father and daughter the delay of emptying what they carried onto a metal tray, signing in and the proffering of IDs.

Taking the elevator to the morgue, Racine informed the techs of the arrival of the family. 'Carefully but promptly, weigh and measure the body. Then remove the plastic as soon as possible for the viewing in the external examining room. Keep the door to the hallway closed.

I don't want the family further upset. Expose no more than the head and the neck.' After checking on these particulars, he left.

As legal holder of the corpse, no examination on the body could be performed without his permission. Racine would request all medical files on the young boy to assist the autopsy. 'My clients are the dead,' he maintained. Crime lab analyses and the results of the autopsy, both final reports, came to him. He'd make the final determination on the cause of death. It was also his decision when to release the body to the family. Tragedy saddened him. The preventive aspect of his position satisfied him most and levelled out the rest of it. He was proud of such changes as mandatory seat belts and his work on compulsory bike helmets.

It was very early morning as he waited outside the front doors for the Henleys. Racine felt a sudden need of fresh air. He intended to be present at this autopsy. He nodded to Denis Bertrand who was heading toward him. '*Bonsoir, Monsieur.*' Racine was formal and never used Bertrand's tag.

'*Bonsoir, Pierre.* Would you permit me to use your office to question the Henleys? It would be much easier for them than having to drive to my office at Place Versailles later this morning.'

'*Bien sûr.* Allow me first, however, to ask them some preliminary questions about their boy.'

'*Naturellement.*'

The limo glided up the driveway to the front door. Father and daughter got out of the car quickly. Racine immediately saw in Douglas Henley an air of authority, but something else too he well recognized, a sad recognition and an air of defiance that mortals exude when death enters their lives.

Introductions were made quickly. Henley glanced at Moitié disapprovingly. 'You're the man in charge of Major Crimes?' Henley spoke with an influence born of success and a measured scepticism. He wanted the top men on this case, not someone like Moitié. 'Where's Geoffrion? He's the lead on this case, isn't he? He should be here.'

Moitié bristled at the inferred racial put-down. 'I have nineteen years experience. I hold the position of lieutenant-detective because I earned it.' He wielded his authority when needed. 'Detective Geoffrion and I are partners.'

Henley, not accustomed to being met head-to-head, nodded with a measure of respect.

'Would you be so kind as to accompany me to my office? We will proceed to the viewing area very shortly,' Racine said, leading them inside the building to the elevators. Douglas Henley and Jessie, Racine and Moitié rode to the sixth floor in silence. Had this been another office or another occasion, Henley would have evaluated the panoramic view of the city the wall of windows afforded. City lights blazed though the humid air. The cross on Mount Royal was the first landmark Henley saw for it stood guard on the mountain. Jessie's thoughts were focused inward. She wanted to see Justin. She and her father refused to sit but stood squarely in front of Racine's desk, a move that forced them all to stand.

'The pathologist has given me a few questions. Is there a family history of heart problems?'

'No!' Jessie stepped forward and stared down Racine.

'Was your son asthmatic?'

'No!'

'Was he taking any kind of medication?'

'No!'

'Were there prescription drugs he might have found? Kids are curious.'

'This is a waste of time. Justin wouldn't sneak into my room. He wouldn't want my birth control pills. The Ativan I occasionally use is in a drawer.'

'I know this is very difficult for you, but is there a chance of school drugs, experimentation, something like that?'

'Justin's eight years old! He couldn't drown.' Jessie slipped back and forth between the present and past tenses. 'He's been swimming since he was two. I've tried to tell the other officer. We used to joke that his body was made of cork because he could float for an hour. Even when I tickled him and made him laugh, he wouldn't sink in the pool.'

Moitié saw an opening for his questions. 'Miss Henley, you made an accusation at your home. Do you really suspect something worse than negligence in this tragedy?'

Jessie looked quickly at her father for a clue. An eye signal the two other men did not pick up, told her not to go further. Her knees buckled and her father grabbed her. To manipulate Moitié, Henley barged into the question and took the lead. 'My daughter does suspect Robert is implicated in the death of Justin. Although Jessie was under great stress when she made this claim, she did not make it frivolously. It warrants an immediate full investigation and don't waste time.

'Mr. Henley, rest assured that we are fully capable of…' Moitié meant to underscore his comment with authority but he never had the chance.

Firm in his pride of place, Henley continued as though he hadn't heard him. 'I have what you need to know. Robert and Justin did not bond, not in the usual way a father and son do. I may have been the cause of that. For whatever reason, the boy gravitated toward me. Robert buried himself in his company and didn't pay much attention to the boy when he saw what was happening. That's curious in itself.'

Moitié cracked his fingers. *The arrogance!* He caught the power play Henley must have engineered with his son-in-law because it was not dissimilar to the one he was using with him.

Henley didn't miss the cop's take on his monologue. He wanted his attention and he'd gotten it. Triumphant, he continued speaking as though he were the detective. 'Robert's early family life was difficult. I won't bother with that history now. You're the detective. Dig up whatever else you need on that front.

'To Robert's credit, he set goals for himself when he was a teenager. He worked three jobs to put himself through McGill. He started up his own company with nothing. Jessie could have had any man she wanted, but Robert's independence and his determination attracted her. That's what you need to know of my son-in-law. Carry on from this point.'

'How do you know all this, Mr. Henley?' Moitié's eyes narrowed. Bullies disgusted him. He'd known plenty when he was young, still did. *If Robert Tyler was involved, he'd chosen the wrong target.*

'I wouldn't permit my only daughter to marry a man whose background I didn't investigate. Actually, the man who did the work is a retired Montreal detective himself who can still ply his skills. I have to admit my son-in-law is a quick study. Robert saw that my flesh and blood come first. Justin and Jessie are all I have. He might have been under the impression that marrying into the Henley family was a free ride. It didn't take him long to discover his misconception or to develop an antipathy for anything Henley. You should start there.' Henley didn't bother with Moitié's title.

Concisely and unhesitating, Henley built Tyler up and cut him down by smoothly insinuating a motive for murder into his monologue. Throughout, Moitié's eyes, dark and keen, hadn't blinked. 'Thank you for this information.' He turned away without further acknowledgment.

Why did Tyler wait eight years? What was the tipping point? Moitié had many more questions but he'd bide his time till after the autopsy. The rich had layers he'd come to appreciate. Moitié worked a file with facts. He'd wait for the autopsy results and the neighbors' contribution to this complex situation. He'd taken an immediate dislike to Henley. He'd seen the easy treachery in the rich man that cronies missed, or chose to miss because they needed him.

Chapter Nine

IN THE BOWELS OF PARTHENAIS, a white van turned into a long rectangular garage in the back and stopped. Two techs in whites waited to receive it. The body of Justin Henley Tyler, bound in white plastic, was lifted onto a steel gurney. At its center, the gurney was moulded into the shape of a body to prevent the corpse from slipping off as the gurney was wheeled along a hallway to a weight scale and then measured. From there, the body was wheeled into the External Examining Room a few feet away. Everywhere the walls were gunmetal gray. On the left below a large magnifying glass was a wooden gurney covered with a sheet. Shelves were stocked with labelled bottles and gray canisters, syringes and cotton. Two drawers contained the implements for the first tests. In sharp contrast, the floor of the examining room was a bright red, as was the door.

The techs cut off the plastic, covered the body with a white sheet and rolled it to the right side of the room beside a two-foot-high cheap green curtain that covered the only window. Its color did nothing to soften the blow behind it. Justin's hair was brushed off his forehead. The sheet was drawn back to the shoulder. A call went out to the coroner.

Racine saw the red flashing light on his phone and knew what it meant. 'We can go down now.' The three rode down the six floors in the coroner's elevator in silence. When the door opened to the morgue, Jessie froze for a moment, but then dumbly followed the coroner as he led them down a narrow, gray corridor. Her father tried to take her arm, but she dodged the gesture. Racine bristled when he saw a door to one of the two fridge rooms ajar enough for Jessie to see the double rows of fridges. Her gasp was a half scream.

'We don't have to do this, Jessie.'

Jessie's moan was quiet, even weary. When the coroner stopped beside a wall before they reached the end of the corridor, Jessie grabbed her father's arm. She saw the window in the center of the right wall. She saw the curtain behind it. A few techs stood at the end of the corrridor, waiting for a glimpse of her. Racine kept his hand rigid at his side and motioned them to leave. They disappeared. He guided Henley and his daughter closer to the window and he tapped on it. Henley threw his arm around his daughter. The tech pulled back the curtain. Jessie fell forward against the glass, her palms spread wide, her cheek against the pane. Like Orpheus, Jessie had come to see her loved one, to reach Justin beyond the frontier of the dead. When she saw him still and quiet, it was as if he died a second time. Her hand flew back and made a fist, but her father caught it in mid air. 'Why are you so calm, Dad? You know as well as I do that Justin couldn't drown! He might have been struck by a car or fallen off his horse, but he wouldn't drown. Don't you see that? Don't you?' Her voice was an accusing shriek, a mother's final defiant wail. Jessie looked around her and shivered in this colorless gray world until she saw the floor and recoiled. The floor was red, like blood. The smell of the plastic used to wrap the dead followed her out and stuck to her skin. Her boy was gone.

Jessie was wrong about her father. He wasn't calm. Henley took his daughter's hand and pulled her away from the curtain. 'It's time to go.' Jessie's strength dissolved. She looked back at the window all the way to the elevator, but the curtain had been drawn. When they reached the main floor, Henley spoke. 'Detective Bertrand, stay with my daughter. I want to speak to M. Racine.'

Racine moved out of hearing range. Henley first gave the coroner his private number. 'I want the results as soon as they are made available. You call me, not my daughter. There is no gentle autopsy, but I want my grandson's body treated with the utmost dignity. I'd like you present. My daughter is not a hysterical woman. Something is wrong here. I want your best pathologist to discover what that is.'

'You have my word. Every body in Parthenais is treated with dignity. Your grandson's will not be an exception, but the rule. I will be present.'

'I want far better than the rule. If there are specific tests the government doesn't cover because they deem them unnecessary, perform them. I will cover the costs.'

'I understand.'

The detective had his first clue. The mother wasn't denying her son's death. It was the manner of it that she refused to believe. Mothers knew their children; he'd learned that over the years. He was certain Geoffrion had further details gathered from the scene. For the moment, he'd wait for the preliminary results of the external exam.

Robert tried to see Justin's face as he tossed him the football, but his mind refused to look back. The only image he saw was the side of Justin's head, darkened by the night, bouncing on the concrete as he worked to revive him. The bounce wouldn't go away, he could feel it. Was that where the bruise had come from? Was that it? Something else suddenly clanged in his head, the tumbling cylinders of the safe. If Jessie discovered he'd seen its contents, he was lost. Robert jumped from the chair, on his neck a sheen of perspiration. He'd worn gloves— he always had. The drawers slid out easily but also left two depressed marks in the carpet. Once he'd read the two documents, had he been as careful? For this terrifying moment, Robert was impervious to the loss of his son. Standing ramrod still in the middle of the living room, he steeled himself for what he must do.

He had to get back upstairs and check. If he'd left any trace of himself in that room, the police had a motive. It was four in the morning. Outside the air was misty. From the kitchen window he could see the police were still there. If Geoffrion came back into the house and discovered him on the second floor, he'd say he had to see his son's room. If Jessie and Douglas came home while he was upstairs… Robert rubbed his eyes and he rapped his temple. He had no choice. A second later, he was running up the stairs back into the bedroom. He couldn't chance a light. He could make out the unit. With great care, he walked very close to the wall across the carpet. Using his hand, he felt he could erase his footprints on his way out. The unit should be flush against the wall. Kneeling, his fingers caught the edge of a rounded hole. With his right shoulder, he pushed the unit half an inch and felt the hole. It was snug.

The brief flush of success morphed to terror. He heard voices he recognized. Scurrying backwards, he gave a quick swipe to the last of his footprints. He ran to the end of the hall to Justin's room. He was about to toss the clothes he found on the nearest chair, but he thought better of that idea. He slumped into the chair, laid the clothes across his knees and waited. The t-shirts and shorts felt like leaden weights on his knees.

'Well, where is he?' Douglas's voice was a torrent of angry emotion. Robert didn't move or answer. Justin's screen saver had kept his attention riveted to it. A photo of Justin with his four-iron followed three other photos as they captured his swing. He appeared so young, so determined. His blond hair blew in the summer breeze. His limbs were bony. *He must have put those into his computer yesterday.* No brain can absorb the transition from life to sudden death, the hopelessness and the finality of it.

'His car's still here. Maybe he's out back.'

Jessie didn't follow her father out to the pool. Sullen and quiet, she climbed the stairs, her hands balled into fists like small animals ready to pounce. Color drained further from her face as she reached Justin's room. She felt no pity for Robert when she found him in Justin's room. 'Get out! You couldn't take care of Justin; you didn't bother to check on him. How dare you touch anything of his now! Get out.'

Robert stood uncertainly and gently put the clothes back on the chair. He made a move to Jessie.

'Stay away from me.'

'Jessie, I'm sorry, if I could change...'

'Stop! He's gone. Nothing you say matters now. Never set foot in this room again.' Jessie pulled Robert the rest of the way out and slammed the door behind him. She punched Robert on the back under the shoulder blade, and he winced.

'Enough!' he shouted and turned to face her. 'How the hell could I know he'd sneak out to the pool? You told him he had to get up early today, so I never expected something like this. But he was a kid, for God's sake! Kids disobey.'

Tears burst from Jessie's eyes and spread across her cheeks. 'How can you talk about Justin in the past tense so easily?'

'Couldn't Justin have fallen from his horse or been struck by a car while you had him? I'm sorry. What else can I say? Don't ever hit me again, Jessie.' Robert knew Douglas would be back in the house any minute. He wasn't about to be clobbered by both of them. He tried to touch Jessie, but she slapped his hand away.

Jessie wheeled around so that her face was inches from Robert's. 'Tell me, how could "our floater" drown? Justin's been swimming since he was two! Why didn't you see him out in the pool?' The volley of questions didn't stop. 'Why didn't you take one minute and check on him? Why? That's what I need to know! Why? How could Justin drown a few hundred feet away from you and you knew nothing! Did you kill Justin?'

'Are you out of your mind?'

Jessie had already left Robert and bolted down the stairs. Robert went after her. Douglas stood at the bottom of the stairs. 'Douglas, I know that Jessie is overwrought, but surely you understand this was a terrible accident.'

'The question is, why aren't you, Robert? You were entrusted with Justin's life!' Henley's mouth grimaced with anger and danger.

'Douglas, for God's sake!' The two men faced one another. Their bodies pulsated with animosity. 'You can't possibly think I...'

'Possibly? I'll find out exactly what you did last night. Bet on that! Jessie has lost her only son. I've lost my grandson, the male Henley heir. *Sorry or I should have* won't cover this tragedy. I've just begun with you. Now get out of my sight!' Every word carried with it an oppressive threat of violence.

'I live here, Douglas.' Robert spoke softly for effect and control.

'In the basement.'

The secrets of the safe kept Robert from further comment. He needed time to gather his thoughts.

Chapter Ten

PIERRE RACINE DONNED a white coat to assist in the initial exam and the autopsy of Justin Henley Tyler. The coroner watched as the head pathologist aspirated the young boy's eye for the toxicology report. The eye is the last part of a human body to die, so it is the best place to harvest evidence of drugs. Next he aspirated the kidney and the femoral artery. The hands and feet, which remained bagged in plastic, were not touched. That exam would take place in the autopsy room directly behind them. A large magnifying glass was pulled from the wall. The search for external wounds began. The two bruises were already marked. The pathologist raised the boy's arm and examined every part of it. He continued the procedure for the other arm, the trunk and the legs before the body was turned over. He examined the heavy bruising very carefully at the small of the back. This discoloration was caused by pooling blood after death. The mouth was checked for foreign objects.

'There can be evidence of bruising beneath the skin that we can't detect. We should take the body to autopsy.'

Racine agreed and helped wheel the gurney into a bright yellow room where two other techs were waiting. The body was lifted to another table under strong lights. The process of searching and cutting and weighing began in the hope of finding answers.

The Sharpes, Steve and Donna, were the Tylers' neighbors. For a good part of the night, they had stood together quietly at the back of their driveway with their fourteen-year-old daughter Susan and watched the unfolding tragedy. Their son Colin was Justin's best friend. Three or four times, Donna had gone to Colin's room to see if the commotion next door had awakened him, but her son was as sound asleep as only the very young could be. *I won't wake him. He'll learn about Justin soon enough.* Donna wanted to take Colin in her arms. She was grateful to have her son still with her.

When the Sharpes were questioned by the police, there wasn't much else to say. Steve spoke with the constable. 'We're busy people and quiet neighbors. We don't infringe on one another's privacy.' The Sharpes' home, perhaps not on the grand scale of the Tyler home, was nonetheless impressive. 'We have dinner together once a year, wave at each other from our driveways and share small talk. Colin would know more about them than we do. The boys are in the same class at LCC, Lower Canada College. Jessie spends a lot of time with her father and Robert spends long hours at work.' He listened to the next question.

'How did they get along?'

'I suppose about the same as most of us who've been married twelve years or more. Good days and a few bad days.'

'Did you hear or see anything around the pool tonight, sir?'

'No. You can see our house is tall. I'd have to be on the roof to see anything. Donna and I were in the family room on the other side of the house. I'm certain you've noticed that special care was taken in the construction of the homes. Privacy was a central issue. We heard nothing until the ambulance and police arrived.'

'Mrs. Sharpe, can you think of anything else?'

Donna looked at Steve. He hiked his shoulders. 'Well, Jessie and Justin are—I guess I mean *was,* for poor Justin—very close to his grandfather Douglas. At times, I felt sorry for Robert. That might just be my take on things. I'm only saying this because when the boys were here, Justin didn't mention his father. He'd talk about his mother and grandfather. Still, Justin never said a mean thing about his father either.'

'Is Colin up?'

'He's still sound asleep and I don't want to wake him.' Tears filled Donna's eyes. 'Little boys shouldn't die or have to face the loss of a friend. What an awful time for the family! Excuse me. I want to check on Colin.' When she looked into his room, Colin was still asleep. There was a soft tap of her heels on the oak floor as she left the room.

Colin rolled over. He was wide awake.

Robert knew that Henley was a dangerous adversary who didn't need the law. He had power beyond it and he was deliberate. Bristling with humiliation and fear, Robert made a strenuous effort to contain his anger. 'Douglas! Let's sit down together. Justin's death has shattered all our worlds. I'm so very sorry.' Jessie sat beside her father. 'I know you gave birth to him and he meant the world to you, and to you too, Douglas.' Robert sat alone with his hands on his knees. His knuckles were white, much like his face. He used the momentary icy courtesy that Douglas was allowing him. 'It's a horrendous accident, and I take full responsibility for not checking on Justin.'

'What was he doing in the shallow end? You know he always swam in the deep end.' Jessie leaned forward, her face contorted in awful pain. Robert instinctively moved further back. Anger and grief supported Jessie. 'What did you do to Justin?' The accusation shot across the room like a discharged bullet. 'You never loved Justin, not really, not the way I did. When did you ever want to spend time with him? '

The last question gave Robert a weapon of his own and he used it. 'How could I ever have found that kind of time? From the moment he was born he was yours. You blocked me out. I didn't mind that so much because I told myself it was your first child. When you supplanted me with Douglas as his surrogate father, you closed another door. For awhile, I even thought I could live with that too because I was busy with the company. Then you and Douglas made it pretty clear I didn't count. Why did you choose that route, Jessie? The cops know I live in the basement. Kind of symbolic of my situation, don't you think?'

'Enough! Robert, Jessie is no fool. If she suspects foul play, she must have a good reason, and I've already told you I'll find out what that is.'

Robert locked eyes with Douglas. 'I'm appalled at both of you.'

For the next few minutes, the three sat in sullen silence.

'Robert, I will use every ounce of my power to investigate the circumstances of my grandson's death. I will dig into every hole of your life. I will discover every secret personal matter.'

For a second, a spasm of anger and contempt creased Robert's face. And then he gained control. 'What reason would I have to kill my own son?'

'Only you know, for now. Have you ever gained access to Jessie's safe?' The question slipped out in the heat of the moment.

Robert's heart leapt. 'You mean Fort Knox, Douglas? Is there more that I should know? If the police get warrants, it might well be your secrets that are exposed. Money can't prevent tragedy. Jessie, your son drowned; Douglas, I don't know why, but he did. I'm sorry. I was just thinking about something you said in our second year of marriage. I wanted more from you, to be a part of your life. Do you recall what you said?'

Jessie looked away irritably at the change of subject. Tears streamed down her face. Douglas was listening.

'You said a bit of me was better than none of me. That's all you ever wanted. I should have left you back then, but I thought you were kidding. In time, I saw you only wanted a "bit" of me and that's only when it suited you.' Robert felt a profound pity for them both and for himself. 'Jessie, had you left me some room with my son, things might have been very different. He might have known I'd be a soft touch and asked me to swim last night, and I might have been there to supervise him.'

Jessie collapsed and wept loudly, calling out her son's name.

Henley stood up in a posture that suggested he had made a decision. He announced, 'I'll tell the police they're free to search the house, except for the contents of the safe. If there is something that incriminates you, Robert, better they find it now. If they don't, rest assured I will discover, in time, what occurred here tonight.' Without another word, he walked out to the pool area. Henley knew the autopsy would take a few days, but learning from Geoffrion that DNA results could take months was a real disappointment.

Robert felt himself shrink into something smaller than himself. 'I'd better shower and change my clothes. If you can, you should too. Our days will be long and hard.' Was there anything of Carmen around, a number, anything? Damn! Her business card. He hurried downstairs the minute he was out of sight. Would the cops actually search his quarters on the hysterical rant of his wife? What evidence did the police have to go on, except the fact of his presence at the scene of the accident and his attempt to rescue his son? He found the card and eyed the shredder by the side of his desk. Jessie would pick up the sound and come after him in her present frame of mind. He reached for his box of various business cards, lifted the pile and slid the card to the bottom.

Robert went to the window and watched Henley conversing with the cop Geoffrion as if he and his power were anodynes that could soothe the pian of a sudden death.

The man had walked in and taken over. Had he not seen the documents, Robert would have flung his best volleys at him, but he and Jessie could produce his motive for murder. As long as they held that card, what could he do? *Bastard! Your insatiable desire for control ruined your daughter for a normal relationship. Then you went at Justin. You think you've protected them, made them strong. You've destroyed us all.* Robert's rant had no safe place to go.

After the police left, he'd take a walk and get out of the house. If Henley intended to hire his old crony, the retired detective, he wouldn't have had the time to set that plan in motion yet. Without a doubt, Henley would set himself up in this house and run the investigation. Had Jessie thought about the safe? If she hadn't as yet, any minute she would. She'd check it and her papers carefully. Had he made a sloppy error in replacing the two documents? He hadn't been himself, after he'd read them. Would Henley inform Geoffrion about the safe? This family guarded their privacy. If police came up with hard evidence, Henley might then reveal the contents of the safe, but not now. He was in no rush to air family secrets. In any event, Robert had to leave the house, at some point the next day.

Carmen deserved to know he couldn't make the Toronto trip. Using his cell was out of the question. At the Town center, there was a red phone booth, fashioned in the British style with a gold crown at the top of the cabin. He hoped it functioned. Thoughts buzzed in his head. It was Thursday already. Their flight was Friday. Robert was not about to cast suspicion on himself, not with Jessie and Douglas working against him. He'd do what he could about Friday.

An unnatural stillness filled the spacious living room, broken only by Jessie's lament.

Chapter Eleven

DONNA AND HER FAMILY had gone back inside their home. At the moment, she was stacking blueberry pancakes on the breakfast table. Steve was squeezing oranges on a designer countertop—used pieces of Douglas fir salvaged from a chalet up north in Ste-Agathe. Susan was working at the marble island, slathering cream cheese on St-Viateur bagels. The table, near the match-booked rosewood cabinetry, was already set.

After seventeen years of marriage, Donna and Steve had begun to resemble one another. Both were dark-haired and tall. At times, they were mistaken for brother and sister. They worked out at a Nautilus club and both were buffed, sculpted and toned. This was not their usual morning breakfast. Sustenance was needed today, comfort food that stuck and filled up the holes. Something wasn't right. Colin should be hurtling down the stairs because he could smell pancakes a mile away. Donna went up for Colin. In the doorway of his room, she saw that he had pulled the blue sheet over his head. *He must have gotten up during the night. He knows something bad has happened.*

Donna crept over to the side of his bed and sat beside him. 'Colin, I think you're awake.' When Donna began to pull the sheet off her son, it was soaked at the top. 'Colin, I guess you know. Son, turn over, please.'

Very slowly, Colin obeyed. His eyes were puffy and red. He was chewing the nail on his thumb. Colin was neither big nor small for his age. He was bony, and his knees were sharp. When his mother hugged him, she could feel the outline of his ribs. His dark unruly curls sometimes made him appear even younger than eight. His mother loved his shy, crooked smile.

'What is it, Colin?'

'Please don't get mad at me.'

'Why would I be angry with you?'

'I should have stayed with Justin.'

'What are you saying?'

'We snuck into the pool last night.'

'How did you get out of our house?'

'By the garage door.'

'Steve!'

'You were with Justin?' Colin began to cry as his father rushed into the bedroom. 'The boys were in the pool together last night.'

Steve knelt by his son's bed and laid both hands on the boy's shoulders. 'Start from the beginning, Colin.'

Colin was shaking. 'Is Justin dead? Dad? Is Justin dead?'

'What happened last night?'

The parents listened as words, chewed up by sobbing, tumbled out. 'Colin, get dressed. We have to speak to the police, Son.'

'Am I in trouble for sneaking out too?'

'Never mind that now, just dress.'

Donna didn't want to go back to the police, but Steve was determined.

In a few minutes, the family walked across their driveway and waited in a knot together while Steve went to look for the police who were still in the back of the house with Henley. 'Officer, may I speak to you?' Henley followed Geoffrion.

'One of your officers interviewed our family last night. We live in the house next door. I have just learned that my son and Justin were swimming in the pool last night.'

Henley's face set into hard lines that clearly revealed his age.

'I must talk to the boy with a parent present,' Geoffrion said, following proper procedure. He turned on his heel, piqued that this new twist hindered rather than helped the lead he'd chosen to pursue. Henley made a move to follow. 'Mr. Henley, you cannot attend this meeting, but I will keep you informed.'

'Please come to our home.'

Geoffrion permitted both parents to be present. The young boy's shoulders were heaving. 'Justin invited you over, is that right?'

A nod and a sob.

'Colin, I am recording our talk, please answer for me.'

'Yes.'

'You swam in the darkness so no one would see you?'

'Yes.'

'Tell me what happened next.'

'We swam mostly under water 'cause we didn't want to make too much noise, just racing and stuff. Justin was beating me. He always wins.'

'Did Justin hit his head while you were with him?'

'I don't know. It was dark.'

'And then…'

'I wanted to go home. I didn't want to get into trouble, but he said he wouldn't invite me back if I left. I called him a bad name and I took off.'

'Did he try to stop you?'

'Yeah, but I swam away from him and hopped out.' A shot of fear crossed Colin's eyes.

'Did you have to kick at him to get out of the pool? I see you have a few scratches around your left ankle. Did Justin try to grab hold of your leg?'

Colin looked back at his father before answering. 'I kicked him a little on his hands and I hopped out.' Colin crossed his feet, hiding the left foot.

'Was Justin still in the pool?'

'Yeah, he was giving me the finger.'

'Was this the first time you boys had snuck into the pool?'

'No.'

'I'm sorry about your friend.'

Colin began to cry hard. His whole face contorted into sudden grief.

Geoffrion believed kids lied best. They could eyeball you and lie without a single twitch. He knew from experience—he had two boys of his own. The giveaway was the sudden rush of tears they couldn't control, like Colin Sharpe's.

'I should have stayed.' The boy continued sobbing. 'He'd be okay. Pool rules: don't swim alone. Are you going to arrest me?'

Steve reached for his son. 'That's enough, Detective.'

Geoffrion turned off the tape recorder. 'Try to follow the rules from now on, Colin. You see now what can happen.' *Version number one.* The case had begun to take shape: the football bruise—he believed Tyler on that one, the boys in the pool—the kicking. Colin Sharpe knew more than he'd told this morning, but none of this information had final answers: How had Justin Henley struck his head? How had he drowned? What lay behind the wife's accusation? Geoffrion didn't alter his take easily. Tyler remained his prime interest.

Henley was waiting for him as he made his way back to the victim's home. He listened, calculating every word. A small decompression in his face began to occur, but it didn't last. 'The boy left Justin alone in the water?'

'I'm afraid so.'

'Do you believe the boy's story?'

'I will question him again.'

'Do it immediately before the parents shut you down! My grandson is dead.'

'Sir, permit me to do my job. The boy is not up to further questioning right now.' Geoffrion ignored Henley's sudden fury.

As the men stood there, a summer wind rose and instinctively, they looked at the sky. 'I have to tell this news to my daughter.'

Chapter Twelve

WHEN HENLEY CAME BACK into the house, he found Jessie where he had left her, fragile and weeping on one of the four couches. If anything, she seemed more remote, lying on her side, staring at the far wall, in a fog of disbelief.

Robert was alone downstairs, slumped in a burgundy chair with his legs splayed in front of him. The frenzy of his thoughts and concerns had evaporated, and like Jessie, he too was lost to the numbing of death. He knew he'd find no solace up on the main floor, so he sat and fingered the football.

Henley went to his daughter and sat beside her. 'You don't have to answer, Jessie, but you must listen. Last night, Justin and Colin snuck into the pool together. Apparently, that wasn't the first time. They'd been in the pool when you were with Justin as well.'

Jessie didn't stir, but she had heard.

'The boys had some sort of scuffle. Colin might have kicked Justin while they were in the pool. Detective Geoffrion doesn't think Colin told him everything. He'll question him again. The boy says Justin was fine when he ran home. Have you heard what I said?'

Jessie sat up. The rigid set of her shoulders and the shock in her weary eyes told Henley she had. Jessie rubbed her cheeks with the palms of her hands. When she finally stopped, he saw the start of red welts. Her accusation against Robert began to fester at the edge of her thoughts. Without the energy to ascribe any conclusion or to forge an apology, she dropped back down on the couch. In ordinary times, Jessie wasn't one to waste energy on apologies. She just moved on. 'If Robert had checked on Justin just once...' Her body shuddered.

'Honey, we have a reputation to maintain. We can't appear to be going off half-cocked, accusing Robert until we have something to go on.' There was an edge to his tone. He paused, waiting for his daughter to respond. When she didn't, he continued, 'From what I've learned, Justin might have drowned when you were home. No parent has eyes in the back of his head. Colin Sharpe might be involved. Terrible accidents occur. We have to wait for the autopsy results. If the pathologists find evidence of foul play that in some way points to

Robert, I'll move heaven and earth to see that he's brought to justice.

'I'll need your help with the safe when you feel up to it. I assume only the new will was in it. You didn't put the other document with it, did you? That should never have left your safety deposit box.' He studied his daughter who turned her head into the couch, and he knew that she had. 'Even with that, Jessie, we have no proof that Robert was able to get into it. He doesn't have the combination. Don't give him any reason to think that we suspect him of any such thing. I want to be absolutely certain of his culpability, if there is any. Mike Fortier will do a sweep of the room. If there is something there, something disturbed, he'll find it. I'll call him right now. Actually, use the guest room tonight. Let's keep your room free of unnecessary activity. For now, we should all try to eat something. It's been a while. I'll call Robert up to eat with us. You two need to talk. Until we know differently, I want to present a solid family front. Now, Jessie, I want you to go down and get Robert.'

'I can't.'

'Yes, you can. You have to be strong, Jessie. We both need to discover how Justin died, how our boy, who could swim a full length under water, drowned.'

The Sharpes had their arms around Colin when Geoffrion left. They headed into the kitchen. Steve sat his son down in front of a cold stack of pancakes. 'Colin, it's just your mother and me here. We want the truth.' They seemed oblivious to their daughter Susan who was with them. The growing clarity of their involvement in the tragedy filled them with dread.

'He's not sure, Steve.' Donna hovered behind Colin.

Colin began to squirm.

'Mom says you were crying most of the night. How did you know that something had happened to Justin?'

'I got up and I saw all the police cars.'

'How did you know it was Justin?'

He hiked his shoulders. 'I don't know.'

'Why were you crying if you didn't know for sure?'

'Steve, Colin is upset as it is.'

'Son, if you're old enough to disobey the rules, you're old enough to tell us the truth.'

Colin began to cry in earnest, wiping his nose with his hands before Donna passed him a Kleenex.

'I saw the police at the pool, so I figured it was Justin. He was disobeying the rules.' Colin hung his head.

Donna glanced at Steve in a silent plea to stop the barrage of questions.

Colin's voice rose in volume. 'Why should I be in so much trouble? I just wanted to get home.' Colin kicked the table leg and cried harder, wiping his runny nose again with the back of his hand. 'I kicked him 'cause he was grabbing at me.'

'Was he giving you the finger like you said when you looked back?'

Colin shook his head from side to side. 'I just ran.'

'Why did you lie about that?'

'He always gave me the finger when we didn't do what he wanted. He said it wasn't like he was really swearing 'cause he wasn't using words. I figured he was doing it then. Am I in trouble? Did I kill Justin?'

Susan had backed up against a wall and hadn't uttered a word. Donna, suddenly aware of her daughter's presence, said, 'None of this leaves this room. Susan, stay with Colin, and both of you eat something. Use the microwave to heat up the pancakes. I want to talk to your father.'

In a minute, the children heard the bedroom door slam. Global fear, political corruption, the economic collapse and recent police shootings in the city had eroded belief in authority figures. She wasn't the only mother who saw herself as the first and last defence of her children. The change had occurred gradually over several years. She'd defend her children's side of things against teachers and other parents and now police. Borrowing from Carl Schurz, *my country right or wrong*, Donna substituted children for country. If Colin was wrong, *she'd* set him right. Whatever had happened to Justin had been accidental. She was in no mood for Steve's altruism. 'Don't hammer your son into the ground!'

'Colin's not responsible for Justin's death, but he lied to the police. That detective will figure out you can't see a finger in front of your face when the lights are out at the pool. We have to set a good example. His best friend died. I won't have him lying and us backing him.'

'And then the police will wonder what other lies he's told. His involvement will get all around LCC He'll be the boy who either killed Justin Henley or the boy who left his best friend alone in a pool to die. Kids bully one another. We'll have to change schools. He'll carry the guilt around for the rest of his life, and it might well destroy him.'

'Justin must have hit his head. The detective asked about it. If they find marks on the body consistent with a foot, who do you think they'll go after? Geoffrion will be back. Colin has to tell the truth to help himself. Can't you see that?'

'Text messaging and cyberbullying are things you and I never dealt with as kids. Their world is complicated and sometimes horrible. I know you're right, but what do you think Jessie would do if the reverse were true? He's my baby and that's all that matters to me.'

Chapter Thirteen

From the moment Jessie had seen the fragile, lifeless body of her son who she loved more than herself, the amalgam of vengeance and grief worked together to keep her from total collapse. After her father told her what he had learned from the Sharpes, Jessie's vision began to tunnel and her bones felt soft.

Henley stayed outside the room as Jessie tried to pull herself up from the couch. For the second time in many years, he knew what it was to be helpless, to be vulnerable in a situation that called for healing. He had known that angry despair when his wife died. Jessie was his only blood, the only living person he loved, his heir, the person he trusted, and yet he couldn't bring Justin back to her. He could buy and sell companies and people with them, but Henley couldn't turn back time. He could donate hospital wings, but he couldn't take on death. Those who have cared for terminally ill loved ones knew that helplessness and that despair. A rueful gaze that passed between father and daughter reflected their isolation as Jessie walked away from her father.

Sylvie had arrived and was quietly making breakfast in the kitchen, but Jessie couldn't have told anyone she smelled hot brewing coffee because she didn't when she reached the door to Robert's quarters. Every fiber of her body worked to get her down the stairs and into his room. Robert knew by the lightness of the footsteps that it was Jessie. Without a word, she sat in a chair across from Robert. His scalp tingled and grew hot. Her eyes, reddened and puffy, were still razor sharp blue and unforgiving. 'I've been trying to figure out why Justin never liked any of the things I liked as a kid. He didn't much care for me either.' Robert hadn't gotten up for Jessie and he was still fingering the football.

Jessie swallowed a gagging lump of raw pain and groped for an answer. Robert's words had built a meager connection between the two. She didn't shrink from it, she met it head on. 'No one can compete with Dad. He can make anything happen.' These were the first kind words Jessie had spoken to Robert since the tragedy.

Jessie couldn't face another kind of assault or offer an appeasement on that front. 'The Sharpes spoke with the detective. Colin was in the pool with Justin last night. It wasn't the first time they had snuck into the backyard together. There's a chance that Colin might have kicked Justin…' Hot tears streamed down her face. 'Might have kicked him… He wanted to go home, but Justin wanted him to stay.'

Robert put the ball down and sat up. Relief flowed through him. He felt its warmth deep inside. Its comfort quickly cooled. 'He was still in my care. Jessie, I didn't think he'd get back up since he had that early ride today.'

'The boys had also been in the pool on nights when I was in charge… but I would have checked on him. I would have done that.'

'I was also trying to figure out what I'm doing down here.' Jessie didn't hear a word he said because Robert had turned the topic to himself again.

'If you had only gone into Justin's room, just once, he might still…'

'Be alive…' Robert buried his face in his hands.

'You should come up and eat with us.'

'I can't be with either of you right now. I feel badly enough on my own. You came very close to accusing me of killing our son. I'm going to take a walk and clear my head.'

'Eat something first.'

'I can't, just like you can't apologize because you still hold me responsible.'

Jessie sprang up, and Robert leaned back into his chair, prepared to ward off another blow.

'One goddamn check and you couldn't take the time!' Her voice raged high and shrill.

'Don't you think I know that? Think about this though. You might have gone up to his room three or four times in a single night, but Justin still might have gotten past you and still drowned.'

'You bastard! You're missing the point. He never had a chance with you because you never went up, not even once!' Her last word was flung at Robert like a sharp stone.

'Leave me alone.'

Henley had come down when he heard the screaming. 'Both of you stop it!' His voice was sharp but controlled. 'Robert, come up and eat with us. We all have to gather some control.'

'Douglas, right now, I have to get out before I explode.'

Jessie flew by her father after Robert. Bitter, hot tears coursed down her cheeks. 'I wanted to say...' When Robert didn't turn around, her face hardened into white hot rage. The perfect oval face quite suddenly forecast age and its accompanying misery.

Robert was quick, intuitive and angry. He knew Jessie might have wanted some kind of confession just to accommodate her desperate need to shovel her pain onto him. He slammed the front door. Both knockers shook. The police were gone. That was one good thing, but the yellow tape was still there. The Sharpes' house was quiet. As soon as he turned the corner, he began to run. At Beverley Avenue, he turned right and continued toward the Town center. His throat burned and he was gasping but he didn't stop until he reached the site of the new condo construction in the hub of the Town center. At Pizzaiolle, he stopped and slumped, gulping air. The restaurant wasn't open in the morning. *Double pepperoni!* He saw the two phones at the glass railing above the tracks, but someone might recognize him if he made the call from there. He wondered if he'd been followed. Had Douglas already reached out to one of his many cronies?

For the next twenty minutes, he stalked through the rose garden, past the tennis courts, to the Town Hall and kept a lookout. There was no one behind him and no car following him. When he passed St. Peter's Anglican Church, he crossed the circle and headed for the red phone booth that appeared much more impressive and unique to the city at a distance than it did close up. Graffiti spoiled the already gritty windows, the front door was gone and grime stuck to the wall. The royal crest looked out of place. At first he thought the phone might not be operational, but it was. After a few deep breaths, he stepped quickly inside the booth and called Carmen's work number and asked for her.

'Carmen DiMaggio!'

'It's Robert.'

'Robert? Hi! This has to be short because I'm not supposed to take personal calls at work.' Carmen was about to tell him she had decided to go with him to Toronto, but she never had the chance.

'Toronto is off. My son drowned last night. I can't talk. I'll call again when I can.'

'What?'

Approaching laughter and footsteps forced Robert from the booth. With a set determination, he went back home. This tragedy wasn't about him. *So much never happened. Now it never will. I wanted to get Justin a black Lab because I'd always wanted one. Even had the name picked out, Cool.*

The buyers in Toronto would understand and give him a week, at least. His company had to be sold. There was no question of keeping it now. He wished he could talk to Carmen, to explain everything to a sympathetic ear, but he couldn't take that risk. *Strange,* he thought, *I've always been alone, even as a kid.* For the present, he had a role to play back home and he would do his best. Robert wasn't ready to leave Roselawn Crescent. To forestall another attack, he went out to the pool area and sat on the grass close to the tape, near the area where Justin had drowned. Markers and chalk lines told him the scene had been processed by the police. The bottom of the pool where he'd found Justin was beyond his sight. When he thought of last night's events, he bit the inside of his lip and dropped his head.

He didn't hear Jessie approach. She didn't sit down with him, but stood to the side behind him. 'I might never be able to …'

Robert jerked around and got to his feet. 'If our positions were reversed, I'd have trouble too, but I hope eventually I could forgive you.'

'Come and eat.' Jessie knew Robert was following her, so he couldn't see her face. It was forbidding and taut. Her father's words rang in her ears. *He mustn't suspect anything.*

Robert felt the invitation might be a ruse. He knew something of masks and deception.

When Mike Fortier heard his phone, he cursed. He had just gotten into the shower. At seventy-nine, with a bum leg that had been shot out during a bank robbery way back, he couldn't get to the call before the ninth ring. His thigh was burning today, and his hip cracked as he limped to the phone. Both hurt like buggers. His burly voice betrayed none of the pain he was feeling. 'Hello?'

'Douglas Henley, Mike.'

'Let me find a chair.' Fortier knew that Henley was Montreal aristocracy and carried the aura that went with it. He had met the man years ago at the Royal St. Lawrence Yacht Club and a friendship developed though they had nothing material in common. 'You shoot from the hip, Mike. I admire that.' Barrel-chested, strong as an old bull, he had a decent head of white hair, broad shoulders and hands the size of George Foreman's. Apart from the pronounced limp and the leg brace he kept hidden, Fortier looked every bit the imposing presence he was thirty years ago, a man cocked full of energy, confident and secure. He'd also learned a long time ago not to interrupt anyone, Henley in particular. With so many months in recovery over his years on the force, he'd learned patience. Taking five bullets had taught him that. Fortier knew what blood meant to Henley and he waited for a few seconds before he responded. Thirty years ago when he wore a badge and carried a shotgun, he could never stomach the death of a child, or spousal abuse. On the job, he'd take care of things before he brought the perp in and booked him. Nothing in the intervening years had changed his mind. 'There are no words, Douglas. How can I help?'

There was silence again while Fortier listened. 'I can't obstruct an investigation, but there's no harm taking a look at the bedroom since you haven't spoken to the badges about it. I'm not forensics; you know that. Keep your daughter out of the room.'

'Already thought of that.'

'Give me a couple of hours. Traffic on the Metropolitan Express-way is a nightmare.'

'I'll be waiting. Here's the address…'

'You're talking to a cop. We know how to get information.'

'That's what I need.'

'After you're through with the room, I want you tailing my son-in-law. You may have to break a few rules, Mike. I want everything.'

'I can break rules within the law. I have a good relationship with loopholes.'

'I mean everything.'

'I hear you, Douglas.'

'You'll be well compensated.'

'Rule 14: never turn down a buck, but fair comp is good enough.'

Chapter Fourteen

CARMEN CALLED CAITLIN at lunch from her car for privacy. Before that call, she'd made one to the St-Sulpice Hotel with a story that she'd left a favorite comb behind a few days ago. The suite, she was told, had been cleaned and no comb was turned in. Presently, it was also occupied. Carmen didn't think Robert would be there, but it was worth a try when she had nothing else to go on. She wasn't expecting Caitlin's support and she didn't receive it.

'If he calls again, tell Robert you don't want to have anything to do with him. He's married, as we suspected, and has, or had, a child. His son is dead. Most likely, he won't call you again anyway. We're not kids anymore. He picked you up at a slot machine. It's a low common denominator to begin with. I'm harsh because I'm trying to protect you, Carm. All you have invested here is a few nights.'

'I'm not twenty, but I want to know what happened, why *us* in the first place. For all we know, he could be a single parent.'

'He was holed up in a hotel for a hook up, and you were it. Let it go.'

'I can't. I'll hear him out.'

'We're getting nowhere, Carm, so I'll change the subject. I just got back from my parents' place. Talk about an averted crisis. Earlier this morning, poor Monsieur couldn't walk. Mom and Sophia were in tears, thinking the worst. The vet came to the house and gave him a cortisone shot, and the little guy was up pirouetting a few hours later.' Monsieur was a pug the family had adopted along with their wonderful cook, Sophia Argento. He was a character who loved to dance in the privacy of his home on the Boulevard, but was as snooty as a proper Westmounter when he was taken out for a walk. Monsieur was not fully aware of his importance to the Donovan family. He had been taken in at the time Caitlin's brother had been killed. The pug kept Chris's memory close by association. The fact that he did such lovely pirouettes and had brought joy with him was an added bonus.

'How long will the cortisone work?'

'Nobody wanted to know.'

'Gotta get back to the old grind.'

'Give your situation some thought.'

71

'I will.' When Carmen was back at her desk, she finished up a quote and made some cold calls. It was a sluggish afternoon work-wise. She much preferred a busy day. Slow days got her thinking. Carmen made another call to block it. It didn't work. Looking around at her colleagues, she saw hard-working women in their forties, some with kids and partners and others single and struggling through the daily grind. *It's a struggle for everybody. It's easy to say I should wait for the right guy, but the fact is I have no one right now. Seeing the right guy doesn't mean he sees you. Apart from the sex and the adventure with Robert, I felt he liked me, that we connected. I was myself with him. I wasn't wearing the usual first date mask. He might be leaving his wife if he has one. If the whole thing was a pick-up, why did he invite me to Toronto and promise to tell me about himself? The thing is, I want to know.* Carmen was good at making things fit.

Wrong choices, wrong men! Can any one of us change? Fear began to grow in her head that at thirty-three, almost thirty-four, she might just have hit the *Minski Point*. Had she passed her best marketing phase, staring at the time when she'd have to settle or end up alone? Had she been dating when Robert approached her, she'd have been flattered but would have blown him off. He'd come along in her lean period. Thoughts that were coming close to the truth of her loneliness were interrupted by a call from her best customer who wanted two grilles. Her company manufactured the security grilles found in many shopping plazas, banks and medical centers. Carmen made the sales and wrote up the quotes. She turned off the danger switch and got to work.

Robert needed a strong drink before he sat down with Jessie and her father. Sylvie had backed right out of the room when Jessie, with Robert trailing, came into the spacious and bright eating area. Henley didn't look up but kept his eyes riveted on Justin's empty seat. Robert headed for the bar and tossed back a neat whiskey before he sat down. Overcome with a need to compensate for his neglect, he offered to take care of the funeral arrangements. 'It might save you both additional grief.' He looked over at Jessie's stricken face. Her cheeks were blotched with tears, and her lips twisted in anger aimed directly at him.

'I've called the church and Mount Royal Cemetery. We have the family plot there.'

'I appreciate that, Douglas. I was thinking of the funeral home itself, the announcement and the clothes…'

'Please stop!' Jessie pleaded. 'Justin was alive last night. It's too soon.'

'Jessie, you should take something and get some rest. Robert, I'd prefer to take care of things.'

Filled with a rage of his own, he did not give Douglas or Jessie the slightest indication of his indignation. He spoke quietly. 'He was my son too, Douglas.'

'Considering the circumstances…' Douglas began.

Robert got up from the table. His eyes narrowed. 'When you both hear that the boy next door might…'

'Colin!' Jessie hissed. 'You don't even know the name of his best friend.'

'… that Colin might have played a part in this tragedy, I won't easily forgive either of you. You mistake yourself for God, Douglas, but I don't. I'm grateful that Justin didn't drown when he was with you, Jessie.'

'Robert! Sit down, please. Try to empathize with Jessie's grief. Justin was her only son and my only grandson.'

'Are you suggesting he was nothing to me?' Something inside Robert died, ended, like the closing and bolting of a door with him on the outside. The two of them sat there like baying jackals, waiting for him to flinch. The Colin link would change nothing. He could never expect vindication. *Wallow in your suffering…* He was about to harbor worse thoughts, but he stopped there. He dropped his head onto his arms and he shook. He opened his eyes to look at his hands. They were shaking too.

'No, I'm not, Robert.'

'You have so much money that you've never had to look at the world from the outside. You don't have to because you own everything around it. Do what you will with the arrangements, you did just that with Justin's life, but I'll be there. Bank on it.'

'Robert!' It was Jessie calling, but he didn't turn around before he went downstairs. There was an edge of gentleness in her voice, but he closed the door behind him. When the doorbell rang, he heard it, but he was already tossing back another whiskey while looking for the Toronto numbers.

Henley whispered, 'Jessie, I need your help with Fortier. You know your bedroom. I'll stand watch to see that Robert doesn't surface. I'll signal you on your beeper if he does.' With that comment, Henley went to the front door. 'Mike, we have to be quiet. Robert's in the basement. Jessie will take you up.'

Fortier took a look at the thickly carpeted stairs and wished he could lose thirty years. Under his meaty hand the railing wobbled as he used it to hike himself up the stairs. He cursed the stairs in his own condo every day. Jessie was about to open the door when Fortier put up his hand to stop her. He motioned her to another room. Once they were both inside with the door closed, he sat down heavily on a chair, and Jessie pulled hers closer to his. 'Jessie, I hope you remember me.'

'I do,' she said. Her voice was hollow. Anger was her sole support.

'Accept my deepest sympathy. Now, I need to ask you some questions before I take a look at the room. Robert is your husband. Why doesn't he have access to the master bedroom? These are personal questions and I'm sorry I have to ask them.'

'Different working hours and poor sleepers. I thought it was best for both of us that he set himself up downstairs…'

'He still has access then. I mean the door wasn't locked.'

'No, of course not. We're still intimate and we use both rooms.'

'Now, there's a safe you want me to see as well as the room.'

'Yes.'

'As far as you know, Robert had no reason to be in the bedroom yesterday?'

'That's right. Sylvie vacuums the carpet every day, and I was only back in there after Justin…' She dissolved into tears, rocking back and forth.

Fortier sat and waited for his next question. 'Robert has never had the combination to the safe, is that right?'

'Yes.'

For an instant, Fortier felt a genuine sympathy for Robert. He himself came from struggle. His mother, whom he'd idolized, had single-handedly raised five boys. She never kept secrets and she'd swipe the back of the head of a son who tried. 'Was it always this way between you two?'

Jessie had caught the veiled criticism. 'I'm a private person. I have things I don't feel I have to share. Robert has safety deposit boxes that I haven't seen, for his work I assume.'

'Has he ever made any visible attempts to get into the safe before?'

'He's joked about it. I knew he was hurt that I kept things separate from him. But the answer is no, not that I know of.'

'The combination is memorized then?'

'Well, yes and no. I know it, but I also had it punched out on a plastic strip that's taped to the top of my night table drawer. The drawer is deep. The installer suggested that arrangement. He said burglars would assume it was the serial number for the set.'

'What you're saying is that Robert might have come across the combination.'

'There's a slight chance.'

'What's in the safe that would prompt Robert to murder his own son?'

Blood drained further from Jessie's cheeks. When the thought occurred, it struck with such force, Jessie doubled over. 'My God, if Robert killed Justin, I'm partially to blame. I should never have brought the documents home. What have I done?' Her tears were insistent and hot on her cheeks.

Fortier waited again.

'I'm sorry, Justin. I'm sorry, Justi…'

The old cop ran his hand through his hair and adjusted his hearing aid. 'I need to know.'

Every word Jessie spoke was a hand holding Justin under the water. 'I changed my will. I left everything to Justin, but very recently I added a codicil that I felt was of little significance. I didn't want to give Robert a reason to contest the new will. Robert had his business. If Justin predeceased me, which seemed improbable to me, I left half of my estate to my father and the other half to Robert. I didn't have a chance to get to the bank. That's the reason I used my private safe. Oh my God! What have I done?' Jessie covered her mouth with both hands and folded in two, groping with the unforgiving court of truth.

Fortier felt an instinctive pity for her, but he had to persevere. 'You said documents. That's only one.'

'What?' she moaned.

'The second document?'

Fortier's question pulled Jessie back and tortured her. She looked over at the door, terrified that Robert might burst through it. 'Years ago, I had two brief affairs. I think Robert has had his share, but I don't know for certain. We never discussed sexual infidelity. Our marriage wouldn't have survived such an exchange. Robert is gorgeous. Women must have made advances to him. But my indiscretion at the time of my pregnancy is the issue, isn't it?' Jessie moaned and covered her face before she could go on. 'A document, stapled to the back of the will, says that Justin might not be Robert's son. Justin has—had— my features and none of Robert's, but there was still a 50-50 chance Justin might be his. I never took further steps to find out. The other man involved was married with a family and has since moved overseas.'

'Why did you keep this information if you didn't intend to investigate it?' Fortier saw the spurt of irritation and anger in Jessie's eyes. This was none of his business, he knew that, but he felt he had to ask the question.

'Marriages dissolve. I wanted that document as leverage. Robert might not be his father, but he raised him and was the only father Justin knew. The courts would take that into consideration and they can be unpredictable. I would never have allowed Robert to take Justin from me or share custody with him.'

'That wasn't a strong possibility. You were his mother and your relationship was good.'

'Insurance. There are all sorts of fathers' rights motions in courts. Laws can change.'

'If Robert got into your safe, you know that this information…'

'…gave Robert his motive to kill my son,' Jessie whispered morosely. 'I know what *I've* done. I want to know what Robert has done.'

Fortier was, not for the first time, glad he had no money to speak of and that he was not part of this unenviable world. The power, entitlement and manipulation that went with money stuck in his craw. The rich were forever manning their barricades, waiting for the barbarians. He'd happily stick with his DVDs of *The Godfather, The Sopranos* and *The Wire.* These papers had set her son and her husband up for a fall. 'Robert was disinherited, for all intents and purposes, and Justin might not be his. These are two powerful motives if he found the combination. The case cops will have to be informed.'

'My father wants to wait for the results of the autopsy. We also want to know more about our neighbors' son. My father won't reveal any of this private matter prematurely. Our lives are complicated and passionate, we accept that and we will not open up our private lives to public scrutiny.' Jessie seemed to be speaking from a script her father had written.

Fortier knew enough not to probe that monstrous, calculating script. 'When did you put these papers in the safe?'

'Three days ago.'

'Robert might have planned to be alone with Justin. Did he offer to take care of Justin last night?'

'No. He forgot I had asked him to.'

'Let's take a look at the room.'

Chapter Fifteen

MOITIÉ LEARNED ABOUT Colin Sharpe from Geoffrion. At 8:30 the next morning, both detectives sat with Coroner Racine in his office, six floors above the morgue. 'I have a preliminary report. The chief forensic pathologist will continue testing. For now, we can rule out suicide. The TOD was between eight and ten last evening. We found no evidence of drugs or sexual assault. COD is officially suffocation and *hypoxia* (lack of oxygen), drowning. The young victim was a healthy specimen. The gastric contents were consistent with an earlier meal that was fully digested. I received the victim's medical history and there was nothing remarkable about it.

'The small contusion on the right shoulder is consistent with being struck by a football. The contusion on the forehead, above the right eye, was consistent with photos of the concrete pattern at the side of the pool, leading us to conclude that the victim struck his head against it ante-mortem. The contusion itself was not the cause of the death. At most, it might have confused the victim. Immersion in water, the CPR and other efforts on the victim post-mortem rendered trace fibres of no assistance. From the victim's nails, we extracted skin specimens, too minute for definitive matches. Pool water washed the better part of them from the nails. DNA tests will be done, but you both know results can take months. Examine both people who had contact with the victim for scratches.

'Two findings led us to conclude there are grounds for an official investigation. There are subcutaneous bruises on the top of both shoulders. Whether they were made with feet or palms to hold the victim under water is being studied. We also found bruising behind both large toes. Such injuries might be the result of the victim trying to push his head above water. It is the pathologist's belief that the victim drowned in the shallow end of the pool, and the suspect used the floor of the pool for leverage. Once the victim was deprived of oxygen, unconsciousness and death occurred quickly. That's the reason we sometimes refer to drowning as the silent death. We are handling this file with the utmost discretion and will continue to do so.'

Geoffrion discussed what he had learned from Colin Sharpe.

'Each corpse reveals its secrets to us,' Racine commented. 'The shoulder bruising is this story. Getting the truth from the victim's young friend is significant. You already know there was an altercation. I understand you are considering the father, but discovering the motive for a father to murder his own son will be an arduous task and a very sad one indeed. I will inform you immediately of any new development. I cannot rule the file criminal until you extract the truth from this Colin Sharpe. If the young boy is responsible, you both will probably determine there was no intent on his part. For the time being, the file will remain listed as an official investigation. Douglas Henley will no doubt call my office.'

'Tell him only that the case is under official investigation and results are still pending.' Moitié was firm. The two detectives left the gray building and conversed out front near the sidewalk on rue Parthenais. 'Jean, I grew up in Montreal North! I know what kids can do. Rich kids are no different. Interview Sharpe at the Crémazie Division.'

Geoffrion thought for a second. 'Alright, a kid is dead. One parent, not both, can attend the interview. They might contact a lawyer, but there is nothing we can do about that. I'll make the call now.' Geoffrion walked over to his car and got inside before he contacted the Sharpe home. Moitié left him alone. 'Good morning, this is Detective Geoffrion. Am I speaking to Mr. Sharpe? Good. I'm sure it was a difficult night for your family. Until we can manage the details of what occurred last night, we must continue the investigation. We would like to speak to Colin again, for the record, down at the Crémazie Division at one o'clock this afternoon. You can be present for the questioning.'

'We may come with lawyer,' Steve said nervously.

'Your call, Mr. Sharpe. Basically, we require a formal statement. All we need are the facts, Sir. Here's the address and use the intercom. I'll come down to meet you.'

Steve's neck was slick with sweat as he listened. Since discovering that both boys had been in the pool, they hadn't known whether to call Jessie and Robert, so they hadn't intruded. Donna knew the phone call from the police was coming, so she jumped when it rang and stood nervously beside Steve until he put down the phone. 'I told you this wasn't the end of it. I called Harvey Wasserman who said he'd come with us if need be, but his presence will make the police think Colin's guilty of worse than he's already admitted to.'

'Did he have any suggestions about Colin's lie?' she asked hopefully.

'He couldn't advise Colin to lie. He did say that the lie is testament to the fact that Justin was alive when he left him.'

'What are we going to do?' Donna collapsed onto the nearest chair. She clutched the armrests, and her fingers were white.

'Where's Colin?'

'He hasn't left his room. He's up there lying on his bed.'

'The detective saw the scratches and Colin admitted kicking Justin. Come up with me and we'll go over what Colin should say in the interview.'

'So you're admitting we're in trouble.'

'I'm agreeing with you that Colin is our only concern.'

Colin's room was a clutter of posters, toys, games, the LCC mascot, Guitar Hero and the new Nintendo Wii, the whole system bundle. The walls were blue and red, the comforter was navy with streaks of red and the pillow cases were red. It wasn't difficult to figure out the boy's favorite colors. In this loud, busy decor, Colin seemed lost and much smaller than an eight-and-a-half-year-old. Coaching the boy wasn't an easy task, and there were many *but you saids* until Colin had his story down. In her present state, Donna agreed Steve should take Colin into the interview.

'I'll wait outside the interview room, but I'm not staying home.'

To his surprise, Robert fell asleep for a little time before the present woke him and he sprang up in bed wide-eyed and edgy. While Fortier was studying the master bedroom, Robert took a long shower in his quarters. The bathroom floor was antique pine, finished to such a hard surface that water was no threat. Two white sinks were surrounded by the same wood and framed by a slate-blue accent wall. In the middle of the room, an immense white square bath sank into a square block of wood. Even the glass shower door showcased a wooden stall. A white toilet was set off by itself under a modern acrylic painting. Suggestive of a modern Roman bath, any hint of a woman's presence was abscent. The room was all hard edges—edges that could cut into skin if one was careless.

Robert couldn't pinpoint the exact second as he dressed when a nauseous wave of panic began its roll deep in his stomach. With the death of Justin, guilt and blame ate away at both parents, judging them, condemning them, damning them. Shock bound the couple together in their failing marriage. Robert could not hear anything that went on upstairs and yet it was the absolute silence that began to gnaw at his stomach. He quickly finished dressing. Jessie and Henley had cut him off again, but he was not going to remain exiled like this, away from contact. He'd get out. Something above him made him pause, forced him to stand quite still, paralyzed before he was able to move.

By the time he reached the main floor, he caught Fortier on the last step on the main staircase and Jessie waiting for him on the landing. Henley was standing by the grandfather clock. A simple darting look among the three carried the full weight of their condemnation. Robert knew immediately who Fortier was and what the retired cop had been doing. He had met the retired detective on the family yacht a year ago. His breath left him. Clasping his hands behind his back, although they were balled into fists, Robert shifted his own sharp gaze on Jessie. He spoke quite steadily although the muscles around his mouth tensed. 'Will you go as far as manufacturing evidence against me, Jessie?' His legs felt hollow, but he turned and left them standing guilty in their tight conspiracy.

Chapter Sixteen

The Sharpes left for their one o'clock appointment.

'The police should have scheduled this meeting in the morning. Look at the mess on the Metropolitan. We'll be lucky to get there in one piece. Did you see what that eighteen-wheeler just did? That bastard could have run us into the cement wall!'

The Metropolitan Expressway, especially the elevated stretch from the Decarie Expressway to boulevard St-Michel, was the bane of all Montrealers, cowboy drivers most of them, who sat fuming and honking in stopped traffic, inching forward a foot or two, and then found themselves cut off by the more reckless of the lot. No one with any sense wanted to be anywhere near this crazy mess at lunchtime.

'Take it easy, Steve, and language, please. Get off at the St-Denis exit and use the service road.'

'Did you see that idiot? Alright, we're off the damn thing. Keep your eyes glued for St-Hubert. We have to make our turn under the expressway after it.'

Donna was in the back seat, hugging Colin who had his head against her shoulder. In the car, silence grew and intensified once Steve had negotiated the turn, spotted the gray building on the corner and driven onto the parking lot beside the police division.

Steve leaned back over his seat. 'Remember what I said, Colin. Tell the detective that you think you saw Justin give you the finger, but it was too dark to tell. Then, son, it's not really a lie. Repeat that for me.' The boy sped through his lie. 'Slower, remember that.'

The large front doors were open. Once the family was inside, every other door around was locked down. It was almost as though they were standing inside a vault. Donna felt hot and cold and, when the room tilted, she grabbed at it for support. 'Donna! You'd be better off at home.' The hair on the back of Steve's neck rose as he spoke into the intercom. 'This is Steve Sharpe. I've come to see ….' The family stood together, eyeing the doors suspiciously, hoping they'd stay closed.

Geoffrion and Moitié came down the stairs together, opened the door nearest the intercom and greeted the family. Geoffrion shook hands with them. 'Thank you for coming down. This is my partner, Detective Bertrand. If you'll follow me, we have a room on this floor.' The questioning room was large enough not to cause claustrophobia. It was sparsely furnished, a small conference table such as one might see in a school, with chairs around its perimeter. There was nothing on the walls. The detectives sat across from Steve and Colin. Donna had been led to another room. 'Colin, don't be nervous. This is a recorder and it's nothing to worry about. It's a tool to remind me of my questions and your answers, so I don't forget. Detective Bertrand and I want to find out as much as we can about your friend's drowning, that's all.' Geoffrion had handed the kid off to Moitié. Tyler was his target.

Colin began to squirm, tapping a chair leg with a nervous right foot.

'The first question isn't hard. Was Justin your best friend?' Moitié decided on a soft approach. He knew the kid was a hand-off. He liked coming from behind, fleshing out the unconsidered facts that Geoffrion might overlook in his zeal for the quick solve that was his trademark. Moitié's easy way worked well with kids. He was a natural with them.

Colin had been rehearsing his answer, so this question spooked him. He wanted to give the one he'd rehearsed and get it over with. His two large front teeth appeared massive because his eye teeth had just broken the gums. 'I guess. I mean sorta.'

'Maybe not your best friend, but still a friend.' Moitié began subtly to play with his silver dollar, slipping it nimbly from one finger to another. He had the feathery fingers of a basketball player.

Colin followed the coin and then nodded. 'My best friend lives in Westmount, and I have other friends in school.'

'You have lots of friends, I guess.'

A little smile broke out on the boy's face. 'Yeah.'

The silver dollar worked with kids, won them over. Steve scowled at Moitié. He saw that the cop had played his son.

Geoffrion had seated himself so that he could see under the table. Colin rarely moved on his chair, but both knees were shaking wildly.

'The night you both went out for a swim, you did a pretty good job of sneaking out of the house.'

A second smile began to curl Colin's lower lip, but when he looked over at his father, it died. 'I guess.'

'What made you want to get back home?'

'I didn't want to get into trouble.' He was happy to see his father's approval.

'But Justin didn't want you to go.'

'He was always the boss of everything.'

'Was he a bully? Believe it or not I was bullied when I was a kid. It was no fun. It was pretty tough.'

Steve opened his mouth to protest, but Moitié shook his head.

'Sometimes.'

'You told him you were going home.'

'Yeah, and he called me a baby and I'm not! I just swam away toward the ladder.'

'But he swam after you to stop you.'

'Yeah.' Colin corrected himself. 'Yes.'

'I'll just check the notes Detective Geoffrion gave me, Colin. You're being a big help to us. Justin caught up and grabbed your ankle. That's when you kicked him, right?'

'He wouldn't let go.'

'You had to kick him to get away. You wanted to go home.'

'I kicked with both legs and he let go. I didn't even use the ladder. I hopped up and ran.' There was the triumphant air of a kid who gets to the top of a hill first.

'Where did you kick Justin?'

'I don't know, his hands, I don't know.'

Moitié asked his seminal question quietly, suggesting it wasn't very important. He began to work the dollar again. 'Did you look back and see Justin give you the finger?'

In a panic, Colin shot his head around at his father. His eyes were as round as saucers. The investigators knew the next sentence would be a lie. The giveaway was that simple. 'Yeah, but I'm not sure if I saw the finger. It was too dark, but that's what Justin always did.' Wide-eyed, Colin looked quickly back at his father for approval.

Moitié knew that Colin had just lied. He scribbled in his notebook.

'You said you saw it the night Justin drowned.' There was not even the hint of accusation in Moitié's mellow voice.

'I thought I did.' Colin squirmed from side to side on his chair.

'What size shoe does Colin wear, Mr. Sharpe?' The sudden shift caught Steve off-guard.

Before he could object, Colin answered. 'Four and a half.'

'Thank you, Colin. We'll need a photo of the scratches.'

Geoffrion had his digital ready.

'I want to speak to our lawyer first.'

'That won't matter, Sir. We can get a court order for the photo. We have probable cause.'

'But you're just about accusing my son…'

'We are not, Sir. We are collecting the facts just as we would if the victim were your son. Now, can we have the photo?'

Colin was crying, but he'd taken off his boat shoe. Moitié told Colin he'd done a good job and waited with Steve and Colin while Geoffrion went for Donna. Moitié dropped the silver dollar into his breast pocket. He shuffled his feet. Bullying kids never felt good. He didn't feel any guilt either. A boy was dead. That mattered to him. He'd made progress. That's what counted.

The family rushed out of the building. Steve punched the roof of his Jag and left a slight dent. 'They think…'

'Let's go home, please.'

'Did I kill Justin?' Colin stared up at his father.

'No, you didn't,' Steve shouted.

It had begun to rain. The sky was a grizzly gray, more like a November sky than an afternoon in the middle of a hot summer. All three were drenched before they were safely inside the Jag. Colin was crying quietly in the car. 'I shoulda obeyed the rules.' Steve shot a worried look at Donna. He could feel the drumming in his chest.

'I'll shoot the photo over to the crime lab,' Geoffrion said, not without a note of disappointment. Had he tossed off the kid too soon? Given Moitié the better file? He hated curve balls. First and foremost, he was a good cop and he was honest. 'The kid lied. We might have more here as well.' Both men steered clear of early deductions that clouded the mind and prevented it from clearly assessing new evidence. These men had arrived at this knowledge by trial and error. 'Crime might be able match the shoulder bruises with the kid's foot.' It might have been easy for rookies to conclude that Sharpe was their case, but these detectives were anything but amateurs.

'You were tough on the kid.'

'No choice. Had to break up the memorized answer.'

Geoffrion reminded his partner of Tyler. He didn't want his case veering off sharply from the vic he'd chosen and he set it back on course. 'We have to get the husband down here for questioning. We'll need photos of his palm and we'll check him for scratches as well. Something was off when I spoke with him the night of his son's death. The wife was certain he was involved. We don't know yet if her accusation is based on fact or anger. Certainly, it might have been the wife's accusation that had him off-center, but it could be something more. The neighbors say Tyler wasn't around much with his son, but both Henleys were very present in his life.'

'You were at the house. Contact the wife and ask if we could go out there and talk to her today. We need a broader sense of things. Let me speak to Racine first to see what, if anything, the family knows about the autopsy. This won't take long.' Moitié got through quickly. 'Has Douglas Henley called, Pierre?'

'He has, and I informed him that we are investigating the death of his grandson. He asked when the family would be able to claim the body. I told him we needed a day or two.'

'Good. Keep me posted on any new finding, Pierre.'

The Henleys and Fortier sat grim-faced in the dining room. Waves of overwhelming grief had hollowed Jessie's heart. Justin's face, the one she had seen behind the green curtain, moved down from her brain into her mind's eye. Even with her hands on the table, she couldn't stop them from shaking. Nausea swirling in her stomach forced her to take very deep breaths to keep the vomit at the bottom of her throat.

'Jessie, you should lie down,' Douglas said softly.

'I can't, Dad, not till I know. I have to know.'

'Douglas, without forensics, what little I've spotted is not enough for an arrest. You need the crime techs in the room. The small depression on the carpet and Jessie assuring me that she opens that panel out fully are not enough. The documents were in order. Robert may never have been in the bedroom. Yet I don't believe in coincidence. The timing of the new will and the paternity question are significant. Robert never asked to be alone with Justin, that's of importance too. If Robert's innocent, those documents represent a monumental betrayal. Investigations expose all the flaws and secrets. Are you ready for that kind of scrutiny?'

'I wanted to wait for news of what went on with the Sharpe boy,' Henley reiterated.

Jessie had put her head on her hands. She was past hearing.

'What would you do, Mike?'

'Once a cop... I'd want it all out there, but my warts have all been exposed, so I'd have nothing to lose. You're in a different situation.'

Geoffrion called. A state of alert went up around the table. Henley took the call. 'My son-in-law is not here at the moment.'

'It's your daughter we want to see this afternoon, if possible. I'm certain you appreciate the urgency.'

'I agree, but my daughter is overwrought, so she can't give you much time.' Henley snapped the cell phone shut and said the police were on their way.

'I shouldn't be here when they arrive. As old as I am, my mug is still on walls. You don't want to run the risk of the suits recognizing me. I'll get to work on Robert. You have the initial book on him. If he has any secrets, I'll sniff them out.'

'I'll pay well for anything you find.'

'I know that, Douglas. I've lived too long. Money doesn't mean much to me anymore. Give me what you feel I'm worth. All my guys are gone, but me. Been to most of their funerals. Nothing like a cemetery to keep you grounded. It took me awhile to figure out what counts. It ain't money. I'll be in touch.'

Henley went to Jessie as soon as Fortier left. 'If you're not up to seeing the police, I'll take care of things.'

'I can't just abandon Justin.'

'You're so tired. Lie down on one of the sofas until they arrive.' The rain had suddenly stopped. Jessie liked the house cold, but Henley went to fetch a light blanket anyway. By the time he got back to her, she was asleep. He set himself up in a chair close by. He thought about the two documents. No matter how discreet the police wanted to be, someone would leak the information. Jessie's trust, the money itself, the ownership of the house, the country home at Gray Rocks, the apartment on Fifth Avenue in New York and the Boca home in Florida would all become the grist of public knowledge. Guarded family business and his estimated worth appeared vulnerable as well. For a man who had diligently protected his privacy, the idea of prying eyes, loose tongues and censure by the common herd was odious. He shifted uneasily on his chair and waited.

Chapter Seventeen

As Robert drove along Autoroute 13 towards St-Eustache, he saw how Jessie and Henley had purposely isolated him. *They'll frame me for murder.* He punched the wheel. Bravado pumped up the other half of that thought. *I was careful. What can they prove? It's not as though I've never been in the room. We had sex last week. Let them try to set me up. They'll get nothing. I don't even know when Jessie put the will in the safe. It could have been over a month ago.* Robert remembered his second, hurried dash into the bedroom that night.

Blood pulsed in his neck and he rubbed it because it hurt. *The odds are on their side.* He was already in the past tense. *The friends we had were theirs, never mine, like the house and Jessie and everything else. Even Justin wasn't mine. Jessie cut me out of her will! They made certain I'd have none of their money while they were alive. That's cold, deliberate Henley management.* He thought of the countless nights, the wasted years with faceless women, the nights he spent working on his business that paid for the house he didn't own and the family that wasn't his. What a ridiculous notion it now appeared to be, to have thought at the beginning that he'd become a member of the Henley golden tribe!

In one of his lengthier affairs, he'd kept the woman on a string for three years. For all that time he believed he brought excitement into her life. She was a tall, French beauty employed by the federal government—a dedicated separatist who worked for an independent Quebec. He smiled when he recalled she didn't appreciate the paradox. In the end, she was the only woman who ever left him, or invited him to a last gourmet dinner so that he could pick up articles he had at her apartment. When he saw the shoebox with his toothbrush, aftershave and some other incidentals he couldn't recall, shame wormed its way into his heart. At the end of all his tawdry affairs, after he had broken into women's lives, rummaged through their hearts and left when the sex dulled, in the end, there was nothing, not even friendship. That afternoon as he drove, he knew he was utterly alone without a single ally.

Robert never admitted to himself that he didn't just like women, he needed them. He felt stronger in their company. If the events of the last two days hadn't occurred, he might not have made the drive. He was parked close to Carmen's business and flipping open his cell because he was scared. 'I'm across the street. I have to see you and I'll pay for your time lost.'

A casino pick-up. 'I'm in the middle of an account.'

'I wouldn't ask you in any other circumstance. Please. I meant every word I said.'

Carmen looked at the time and saw that she still had two hours. What could she tell her boss? An emergency had come up, dock her the two hours. What if he had shown up at her apartment? Get it over with, that's what she had to do and that wasn't possible over the phone, not when he just lost his son. *I want to know.* Carmen went to her boss, freshened up in the bathroom, knew this was another bad move, and walked out the front door to meet him.

He got out of his Porsche and called to her. 'I'm over here.'

Carmen drove her Mini the short distance. She didn't want her colleagues to witness the so-called emergency. The change in Robert was dramatic. His eyes were dark from fatigue and desolation, and his face was drained of color. She read defeat and sadness in his posture. Had she passed him on a street, Carmen might not have recognized him. Shock at seeing him like that kept her silent.

'Can we go to your place?' There was such need in his voice that Carmen almost acquiesced to his request. 'There's a St-Hubert restaurant around the corner. You have to appreciate...'

'I understand.'

'I'm very sorry about your son.'

'Come with me in my car.'

'I'd rather take mine.' Carmen saw he wasn't pleased.

'Alright, I'll follow.' Inside the chicken restaurant, they found a private corner and ordered sandwiches and wine so they wouldn't be disturbed.

Robert told Carmen about Justin, his wife and Henley. His story wasn't complete because there wasn't time and he didn't want to scare Carmen off. He didn't share what he had found in the safe. His words collided or imploded in broken sentences and aborted phrases. The ideas contradicted each other or ran parallel and didn't connect.

Carmen said nothing. Robert had taken her hand, and instantly her arm was hot, and the heat jetted into her belly. The one-sided conversation was in a dimension that frightened her, but she didn't hear much of it. It was the heat that she felt kneading the inside of her stomach until she pressed her hand against it. In this strange confusion, she finally managed to get her mind back up to her head. 'Why are you here?' Had she said that? Was that voice hers? Was there a safety valve in her heart she didn't know about?

'I'm not making sense, I guess.'

Reluctantly, Carmen eased her hand away. It was warm and damp although the a/c kept the place downright frigid. Once she had her hand back, she began to feel cold and afraid. They had not touched the food. It lay between them like a fence. 'I was just a pick-up, Robert.' *You can't come and hide with me just because you're scared.* Carmen could have said those words, but she wasn't that brave.

'At first, that's true. Let me try again, but I can't sum up my life in a few sentences. I'm not a great person. I won't stoop to the usual excuses, *poor me*, or *no one understands me*. I did marry for love but I wasn't drafted for the Henley team, Douglas and his daughter Jessie. At best I was Robert Tyler, the water boy. I went elsewhere, but nothing lasted. I wasn't looking for long-term anything. My infidelities, like most, are what they were, low runs and calculated games. They filled a void and I felt I was entitled to them.' Robert looked away. His own self-knowledge suddenly disgusted him. Carmen was looking at her hands when he turned back. 'I saw something better in you the first night we met. That sounds trite, but that's the truth. There was something about you that I didn't want to use and discard. That's why I didn't push for sex like I usually do.' He reached for her arm, but Carmen pulled it back.

'It wasn't even a chance meeting. You planned everything and you left me with no way of reaching you.'

He ignored her comment. 'You had such a sad look on your face when you kept losing at keno. You took me back to a better me. Then you tripped going to the restaurant.'

Her cheeks flushed. 'You saw.'

'I wanted to scoop you up in my arms... When I was a kid, I found seven large beer bottles. I carried them to the corner store and a few feet from the door, I tripped. I didn't know what had happened at first. When I saw the pieces of brown glass, I knew I'd lost all my money. A man saw what had happened and gave me a buck. That's why I gave you the $50. I saw myself in you.'

It was a struggle for Carmen to get her balance. She liked what she'd heard, but the truth was there as well. 'Your son is dead, Robert. You have a wife. I don't belong here.'

'Please give me a few more minutes. I wanted time in Toronto to explain my life to you. I was going there to sell my company that I built from nothing. I wanted to start again. I know this is all very fast, but real chances don't often come by. Don't walk away from one. You can take your time.'

'Your son is dead.' Those words closed the door for Carmen. 'You shouldn't be with me.'

Robert grabbed both her wrists and held them too tight. Carmen winced. He spoke between his teeth. 'I know Justin drowned in our pool, I know I should have checked on him. I never thought he and his friend would sneak into the pool when the lights were out. It's dark as a bitch out there because of this massive hedge. Don't you think I know that?' The muscles in his face flared and tightened. 'My wife is suggesting I murdered him. Jessie and her father, the gazillion-aire, are trying to frame me, for Christ's sake! They'll go to any lengths to bury me.'

An uncontrollable shiver shook Carmen. *Why would your wife even think you murdered your son?* Carmen edged back against the booth. What had Robert said earlier? Too much had come out of him, his company, the money, the trust, the exclusion… Henley? She'd heard the name, but it never connected for her. If that family had blocked Robert from their money, why would his wife even consider murder? He had no motive for such a heinous act. What monster could kill his own son?

'My father-in-law had a retired homicide cop snooping around today, looking for something they could use against me. Isn't that remarkable? And I have no one, not one fucking living soul but you who might give a damn!' He let go of her and folded up as though he had no more energy.

Carmen wanted to get out and drive far away from Robert, but there was a final question that she felt compelled to ask. That Robert was more concerned with himself than with the loss of his son unnerved her. Shaken, pulled into the chaotic trauma of lives she didn't know, Carmen dared to ask, 'Robert, did you love your son?'

He looked up and regarded her closely, keeping his eyes on hers. A muscle in his jaw spasmed and he rubbed it out with the palm of his hand. 'I'd hoped you'd take my side.' He didn't reveal that Justin was probably not his son. His shoulders deflated. 'I guess I've forgotten how much I loved him when he was born.' He smiled sadly. 'Justin chose his side early and it wasn't mine. He probably didn't choose it. Jessie and Douglas channelled his route. Money can bulldoze its way through a father and son. I could never compete with the two of them. Justin didn't even look like me. He was blond like his mother. How much can you love a son who's happiest when you're not around? I've never told that to anyone.'

Carmen looked down at the shrivelling chicken sandwiches; the white bread had curled, and the lettuce had brown ridges. The pasty gravy had curdled. Sliding across the seat, she reached back for her purse. Robert got to his feet first and barred her way. 'I've never opened up to anyone before,' he said heavily, unaccustomed to asking favors of anyone. He hadn't expected objectivity or perception. He'd come for her support, but he found a woman who was unexpectedly real. His longing for her grew. He needed someone to care about *him*.

'Robert...'

He stood aside. 'You have reason not to trust me, but ...'

'I never fully realized, till now, how lucky I am to have a friend like Caitlin in my corner. We don't always agree, but we're there for one another.' It was as though these words were private thoughts and speaking them was accidental. 'Go home, Robert.' He made no move to stop Carmen as she rushed out the door. He stood forlornly as she left. Seconds later, he ran to the door and caught sight of Carmen as she drove out of the parking lot. It was easy to see that she was heading back to work for the last hour.

Robert went back to the table and ate half his sandwich, drank a glass of cheap wine and washed up in the bathroom. Twenty minutes later, he was parked outside Carmen's apartment. It was a small red brick building with only eight floors. The outdoor parking would make Carmen easy to spot when she came home. After he checked the time, he sat back and waited. He knew what was going on at home and he didn't want to be there. Behind Carmen's strength, he saw her loneliness and her need. Carmen had connected with him—he'd felt it. Robert couldn't face the days ahead alone. His move on Carmen was lopsided, off line, even presumptuous. He knew all that, but he also felt an irrational hope as he sat waiting for her. He could not face possible obliteration in the coming days without a single witness for the defence. As the minutes passed, he felt only the vaguest guilt for employing his venal charm. It was a persuasive habit.

Chapter Eighteen

STEVE SHARPE CONTACTED Wasserman as soon as the family was home. 'No, Harvey, it didn't go well. Unless they were idiots, the detectives knew Colin was lying. I'd rehearsed the answers with him, but Colin was nervous and gave himself away. They took his footprint, Harvey, and a photo of the scratches.'

'I know you're all very upset, but keep in mind that this was an accident, and your son is eight years old.'

'His mother is a nervous wreck worrying about him and about what will happen when he goes back to school in September. Sometimes the bullying is worse at private schools. His name will be tainted for the rest of his life. He hasn't said a single word since we got home. What about a lawsuit?'

'Let's not get ahead of ourselves. You did say that Colin wasn't certain where he kicked his friend. Are they questioning anyone else?'

'Robert, the father.'

'That's something. I gather his son was in his charge. Adults are responsible for the supervision of their pools. This Robert is looking at negligence. Regarding our case, Justin invited Colin over. As I read it, neither Colin nor Robert is guilty of deliberate negligence. The file reads as a tragic accident, but it's the police and the coroner who'll determine how far they want to pursue fault before presenting their findings to the crown prosecutor.'

'They must have a large mark or marks somewhere on Justin's body or they wouldn't have taken a photo of Colin's foot. Donna warned me not to go next door and admit anything, to think first of Colin. She was right all along.'

'You did the honest thing, Steve. Reverse the picture and ask yourself if you'd appreciate this father admitting the truth to you?'

'Ethics come with a cost.'

'Think of the damage to Colin if you'd told him to lie. These boys were friends after all.'

'We're still in a mess.'

'Sit tight. Don't speak to the neighbors, don't speak to anyone. Don't try to dig out the absolute truth from Colin. He might not know it, and prodding him is not in his best interest. Call me if you need me, no matter the time. I'm your lawyer and friend.'

Donna was in Colin's room. He'd pulled the sheet up over his head and was curled up in a fetal position. Donna knew her son. She'd given up a good job in computer programming to stay home and raise him. Colin wasn't telling them everything that happened. He revealed his mistakes in bits and pieces. Over a year ago, he had come running into the house to say a neighbor's dog was hurt. Three weeks later, he admitted the husky had gotten loose and rushed both Justin and him. The boys had thrown rocks to protect themselves. One of them had hit the mark. She felt Colin knew where he'd kicked Justin. That was the reason Donna would never ask him or allow him to reveal another part of that. Colin was alive. It was his life that mattered. Justin's, sadly, was lost. The hole was too dark to think of Jessie. This family had to survive. That's what Donna was thinking when she finally nodded off. No one had slept the night before.

Henley was out in the solarium, relying on the intercom to announce the police. Since Justin's death, he hadn't left the house on Roselawn. When Jessie awoke, she wondered what she was doing asleep in the living room, and in the middle of the afternoon. For a fleeting second, Justin wasn't dead, but only for that second. When Jessie felt a weight on her eyes and tried to rub it away, she knew. Her eyes were swollen almost shut and they were caked with the salt of dried tears. Crossing her arms across her chest, she cried again, rocking against the back of the sofa until her eyes burned and hurt to touch. When she managed to open her eyes, she saw that she was alone. Seizing upon a notion that only a talk with Colin could offer her any solace, she got to her feet uncertainly. Colin had been with Justin just before he… Jessie was at the front door before Henley saw her. Distraught and in the same clothes she'd worn the night Justin drowned, she was in no condition to leave the house. Her blond hair was tangled and matted at the side of her head. Her steps were tentative, but her intent was clear.

'Jessie, where are you going? Honey, the police will be here any minute. Perhaps you should shower and change, if you're up to it.'

'I need to talk to Colin.'

Before Henley could say another word, Jessie opened the front door. He caught up to her on the front steps. 'Come back inside with me. We can't be talking to the Sharpes when the police are investigating. Damn, there's the unmarked car.' He pulled Jessie inside.

She whirled around. 'I won't wait long. Justin is dead, Dad. He's dead! I have to know what happened. If Robert had anything to do with my boy dying, I'll see to it he pays for the rest of his life. But if he didn't… if Colin is responsible…I have to know how my Justin drowned.' A prominent vein cut a diagonal line across her forehead. 'Can't you see that, Dad? You're my father, back me up!'

Henley refused to lose control. He would not permit family secrets to be exposed when the situation did not yet warrant it. 'Don't offer anything up before we know what the police have learned. If Robert didn't get to the documents, your whole admission is a moot point. The fact that you live apart in the same home is awkward for both of you. I'm devastated myself, but if Robert is involved, our own investigation must be thorough, not rushed or haphazard. Rushing in with unfounded accusations is not the answer.'

'This isn't business. Justin is dead.' The three words had become her mantra. 'Doesn't Justin's death mean more than our damn privacy? I don't understand your calm, Dad.'

'I'm not calm. I'm fighting to exercise restraint for both of us. I know Justin is dead.' Color drained from Henley's face. He took Jessie's hands in his. 'Just trust me, Jessie. I'll do what's necessary with Robert, but not in the heat of passion.'

'I am in the throes of passion. My son is dead!'

'You're also a Henley. Remember that too.'

The doorbell rang. In the afternoon, Geoffrion had a better appreciation of the luxurious home. 'Could you park your car here, Moitié?'

'How well would my Sorrel or white rum drinks fit in here? Anyway, I prefer my semi-detached. The newlyweds argue through the walls until well into the night. They know I'm a cop—doesn't faze them. I like noise and people. I guess that's why I'm a cop. It's never quiet. Imagine having only one child in a place this big!'

'They don't even have one now, but I could get used to living here. I have plans for my life.'

'Yeah, I know, but I prefer the trenches. I like getting dirty.'

When Henley opened the door, the men stopped talking. 'Come this way.'

Sylvie had stayed past her quitting time when she was told that the police were coming to the house. Jessie hadn't the will to move, so she sat leaning heavily against the sofa for the support she sorely needed. The suits sat across from Jessie while Henley chose a single wing chair. When Sylvie set up cups, coffee, glazed lemon cake, plates and forks, Jessie glared at each of the men, daring them to touch anything. It was a hollow victory.

'Miss Henley, we know this a very difficult time for you,' Geoffrion said.

'You have no idea until you lose a child.'

Henley got up and poured himself a cup of coffee. The careful control Jessie was attempting to muster cracked when Henley took the first sip. If her father had slapped her in the face, Jessie could have borne the pain, even welcomed it. She was no church-goer. That practice had fallen off when she was sixteen. Yet she clearly heard Christ's words, *Could you not but watch one hour with me?* How could her father sip coffee when the most precious part of her life was gone? When her beautiful little boy had been cut up into pieces? How were family secrets more important than justice for Justin? In thirty-five years, she had never once crossed her father. This abandonment drew Jessie further into her torturous journey. She trembled with pain and rage and added her father to her list.

'Are you alright, Miss Henley?'

'What have you learned?' Jessie did not look over at her father. She'd tell these cops whatever helped Justin.

Moitié took over because he had met the Henleys at the morgue. 'The coroner did tell your father...'

'Tell me.'

'We are officially investigating the death of your son.'

With the uttering of those words, Jessie was stricken with a new shock. Justin's death was not an accident. Her son was a victim. That word *victim* cut a strip of flesh from Justin and she felt her heart tear. There would have been more comfort had he drowned, had a hand in his own demise. *Victim* meant he was cast down beneath the water because he didn't count, tossed aside like refuse. 'Colin Sharpe? What happened between the boys?' Her voice was cold and cutting.

'We have questioned him. Forensic study is under way.'

'I want details.' Jessie was unaware that tears coursed down her cheeks and fell from the sides of her jaw.

'We can disclose minimum details, but nothing specific in an ongoing investigation. You do know there were bruises on the body, but none serious enough to cause death. The two boys scuffled, and we are investigating that.'

'Did Justin suffer?' Jessie's voice was very quiet.

'There was no evidence of strain on your son's face. The pathologist said death occurred quickly.'

'I wonder if Justin called out for me.' Jessie put her hand over her mouth.

'Neighbors did not report hearing any voices that night.' Moitié allowed a welcome pause before he went ahead. 'We're here, Miss Henley, to ask you about your husband. Is he home?'

'No, he's not and I'm glad of it. Was it Robert you came to see?'

Henley tried to make eye contact with Jessie to calm her, but she steadfastly refused to look his way.

'Actually, we have a few questions for you.'

'Ask them.' The red floor flashed in her mind. Her nostrils pinched at the remembered smell of plastic.

'We will have Mr. Tyler in for questioning, but first we wanted to ask you why you accused him of a crime in the death of his son.'

Jessie hesitated.

'We understand that you blame your husband for not taking better care of your son that night. That emotion is natural and common in such tragedies. You also said that your son's death was a crime and you implicated your husband. Do you remember that allegation? Detective Geoffrion took your words very seriously.'

'Very clearly.'

Henley got to his feet, walked over to Jessie and stood so close that she felt the heat from his legs. Poetry and the Bible were not Jessie's favorite subjects, but Eliot's words came unbidden to her ears. *And time for a hundred indecisions/And for a hundred visions and revisions/Which a minute can reverse.* If she spoke the truth, broke the seal of family privacy, she'd lose her father's confidence, which was the cornerstone of her life. She had never had to stand behind her own words without her father. What if Robert hadn't seen anything?

What if he had? A more sinister thought wormed its way into her ear. Judgment struck and it was severe. Foolishly depositing the documents into the safe instead of her safety deposit box meant Jessie had contributed to the loss of her Justin. If she had taken better care… A low guttural moan caught the men by surprise.

Moitié looked over at his partner and waited for a full minute before he put the question very simply. 'What prompted you to make such an accusation?'

Chapter Nineteen

CARMEN WENT BACK to work to regain her balance. The minute she started up her car, she regretted walking away. What if Robert was telling her the truth? Her heart pounded; her thighs ached. *Get a grip!* But she didn't. A longing burrowed its way into her. A business cold call didn't help. Writing out a long quote didn't help. A long call from her best customer helped quiet the fire, so Carmen kept it going with small talk. The work day ended; the longing followed her to her car. *It's been a year, for shit's sake!*

Turning on her Bluetooth, she called Caitlin. Her voice was rushed and she stopped making sense in a minute.

'Carm, slow down. Robert came to your office?'

'Yes, yes and…'

'His wife is accusing him of murdering his son?'

'She's trying to frame him.'

'What did he want with you? You barely know him. This isn't a case on *Nancy Grace* that you get wound up in while you're safe in front of your TV. It's a real life story from an adulterer who may be endangering you by pulling you into his mess.'

'I know I sound like a raving idiot, but I also know he's attracted to me and he trusts me.'

'Trusts you? He wanted to unload, Carm. The real point is, why would you trust him? He's lied to you from the outset. He's desperate for an ally. You don't have to be it. Men are attracted to you. That's nothing new.' Caitlin knew enough not to fan the fire and went to the finish line. 'You did the right thing by walking away. He might have dragged you into this terrible and frightening affair. You're probably in the regret stage, but that's just you. Don't go there! I'm not trying to be mean, but he picked you up, he hid things from you, his son is dead, and his wife's making allegations against him. Henleys! They're a powerful family. My father's done legal work for Douglas Henley. Robert might well be innocent in the death of his son, but he might also be a murderer.'

'That's enough. You wouldn't think the worst if you'd seen him.'

'Don't be carried away by his drama. He told you he's had other affairs. He knows exactly the kind of woman who'll fall for him. Why choose to be one of them? Why take a chance? How about I come over tonight? You need someone to keep you on track. To change the subject, Monsieur is completely pooped. He reminds me of my grandfather, a real show-off! At his last St. Patrick's Ball, Granddad danced around the floor and drew applause. He laughed, regaled the guests at his table with his stories, and collapsed the minute he got into the limo and for the next week moaned and groaned. Like Grandad, the little pug had to do his pirouettes and now he's out cold.'

Carmen hadn't heard much. Caitlin's unsympathetic tone hadn't helped. At that moment, although she loved Monsieur, she didn't give a rat's ass about his pirouettes. Life was tough for everybody.

'Are you there?'

'Yeah.'

'I'll be there at 7:30. I don't trust you to be on your own. Be good. See you then.'

Turning down her street got her mind off Robert and onto her leaking faucets that kept her awake at night. Towels under them, closing the bathroom door—nothing had worked. Drip, drip, drip was Chinese torture. Maintenance better have come because she was in no mood for 'drip.'

Robert had followed a tenant inside the apartment and he waited inside the main door. Drip was her central thought as she opened the door. His mouth was on hers before she actually saw him. He held her in a vice that she didn't fight because she was afraid and she wanted to be held. 'Carmen, I won't stay. I didn't mean to frighten you.' He let go of her. 'What we felt was real; what I said was real.' Then he was gone, and Carmen stood shaking for a few seconds before she ran up the four flights of stairs. Carmen never ran anywhere if she could help it. She left exercise to Caitlin. Grabbing the portable, she stabbed the memory number. 'He got into my building!'

'Get out of there! You'll sleep at my house tonight.'

'I can't! It'd take me two hours to get to work, from Westmount to St-Eustache.'

'I'm coming out then. Don't open your door for anyone, not even for 'drip,' the maintenance guy. I have my own key.'

'Thanks, Caitlin.' When the phone rang a minute later, Carmen grabbed it thinking it was Caitlin.

'I didn't mean to scare you. All I'm asking is that you not write me off. I'm not a stalker or some wacko. I know my son just died, Carmen. With my wife and father-in-law putting the screws to me, I'm wound up and off balance. Everything is in chaos right now. This person is not me. I'm as uncertain as you. I keep seeing my son lying on the side of the pool. Justin never got a second chance when I tried to revive him. I saw first-hand how quickly life is lost, no matter how hard I worked to keep him alive. I want one more chance to change my life, one more than my son got.'

Robert sounded as desperate as Caitlin had just said he was. Carmen dropped the phone. The plastic backing flew off, and the battery bounced out and fell to one side, still attached to red and black wiring. Still shaking, she ran to the door and double bolted it. A single fact didn't change. She wanted Robert. She wanted to believe him. When she flopped down on her yellow sofa, grabbing both knees, she was already crying. *What the hell is wrong with me? How did I let myself fall so goddamn quickly?* Answering those questions could devastate Carmen. Why had she kept on gambling when she always lost? Why fall for men who played her and dumped her? Who would want to admit she needed risk to escape her own life? Admitting her internal wiring had been set up wrong might well destroy Pandora's gift. If hope was lost… Carmen hid from the longing that frightened her and pushed her on. After Robert left, introspection was the last thing she wanted. It was easier for Carmen to keep on crying.

There was no swagger left in his walk when he left her building. *What a royal fuck-up! I've frightened Carmen. Why the hell did I go into her building?* When he reached his Porsche, the phone was ringing. From the caller ID, he saw it was Alex Chong from Toronto. The buyers had made a decision or they wouldn't be calling, because they knew about the death in his family. He grabbed the phone. It was better to know where he stood.

Chong apologized for the timing of the call, but he felt Robert would want to know their decision in case he decided to seek other buyers.

Robert waited for the bad news.

'We are still interested but not at the suggested price. The crisis in the economy and the cash placement you requested both factored into our counter offer of $14 million.'

Robert had no time to go hunting up other buyers. Financial institutions were not lending freely. The immediate outlook for the economy was bleak, and its resurgence was probably a few years away. 'Tell your partners I accept the offer, but I can't fly to Toronto before next week.'

'Drawing up the papers will take time. Next week is fine. You have a solid company and we feel we can work well with it.'

'That's good to hear. My heart and sweat went into it.' *And you just pocketed two million dollars, Chong!*

'We will await your call.'

Robert had chosen to live his life in chunks from every day. His focus had always been the vehicle just ahead of him. When that focus broadened, he saw the detritus of a life he had ignored. The company was gone, Justin was gone, Jessie had turned her back on him and now Carmen was afraid of him. He couldn't start the car. He punched the wheel repeatedly until he yelped in pain. For the first time since Justin's death, Robert felt the weight of all the water in the pool on top of *him*. Was that what Justin had felt when he couldn't break the surface of the water? Was he lost in the fog of a dark watery grave? Did he know he was dying? How utterly alone he must have felt. Robert pushed against the headrest, still gasping because he could feel Justin drowning. The water was seeping into him.

I've gone at my life all wrong. Why didn't I make friends? Since year two of my marriage, when I saw where I was, why didn't I just walk out? Didn't I want better than that? The chicken sandwich sat heavily in his stomach and gave it the full weight of soggy lettuce and too much mayo. What he needed was a shower and a change and support. He dreaded being alone. He had to make Carmen understand that he needed her. He couldn't fight the Henleys and the cops alone. Someone who believed him and wanted him, that's what he needed. He saw that Carmen wanted to do both. He'd understood that longing in her. In himself, he didn't dare intuit a simple truth. He was afraid. Robert shifted on the car seat. *I can't allow Jessie and Douglas to ruin me.* With that sudden thought, Robert started up the car and drove home.

Jessie's accusation and the old cop's appearance forced him to be doubly cautious. He hesitated before he used the remote for the garage door and drove inside. He paid the mortgage. He had every right to be in the house. Every goddamn right!

Chapter Twenty

'MISS HENLEY, WOULD YOU like *me* to repeat the question?' Geoffrion asked, taking over the questioning, positioning himself as the primary.

Henley's grip on his daughter's shoulder tightened. His stance was no longer confident as he stood crookedly. 'When can we have Justin's body?' As soon as Jessie uttered the question, her eyes soaked with tears. 'I never said goodbye. I want Justin's swimming trunks!'

'Mr. Racine will call, but I think it might be tomorrow or the next day. Rest assured you will receive your son's effects once the forensic testing is complete.'

Every word sounded the reality of Justin's death and renewed her determination to find the person responsible. Jessie dropped her head. 'I changed my will.' Henley's grip tightened a notch, but Jessie rotated her shoulders to get away from the vise.

Geoffrion caught the dangerous glare from Henley. He was the cop responsible for tearing into the private life of one of Montreal's most prominent families. Henley had the power to exact the price for the intrusion. Geoffrion didn't look at his partner. He'd made the break. He held his ground and waited.

Jessie looked back at her father, pleading for forgiveness or understanding, but his eyes were trained on Geoffrion 'I left the estate to Justin.' Those six words provided a definitive motive for murder.

Every nerve began to buzz an alert. This might be the high profile case that would further his career! Geoffrion struck with a volley of questions before the mother changed her mind. Moitié scribbled notes.

'All of it?'

'Yes.' There was not a whiff of guilt. 'Robert has his company.'

The case turned. Geoffrion was spiked, but his outward demeanor appeared calm. 'Did you inform your husband of this change?' His voice didn't betray a hint of alarm.

Henley had left Jessie's side and now stood a few feet in front of Geoffrion, his physical presence a sign to stop the questioning.

Henley had lost control of Jessie. 'No, I saw no point, but I placed the new will in the safe in the master bedroom a few days ago.'

'And he has the combination, of course.' Geoffrion stepped out of Henley's path.

'No, he doesn't.'

The room grew silent. It took time for the implication of the statement to seep into each head. Galvanized by what he was hearing, Geoffrion knew from experience he had one detail, incomplete, perhaps even distorted, of a complicated life. It was his job to piece the details together because he also knew Jessie Henley was providing him with a motive. Her son was dead. Geoffrion had to discover who these people were and how their son died. He was not about to get ahead of himself, certainly not when he felt he had a solid file.

Moitié, who was escaping the immediate pressure from Henley, had time to sum up the emerging file. *Husband's sent to the basement, even if the place is luxurious. Then he's disinherited from multi-millions in favor of his son, unless his son dies.*

Geoffrion charged on. 'Has the combination to the safe been changed recently?'

'No.'

Henley turned back to Jessie, relieved. She hadn't revealed the question of parentage, the most damaging information to the family name.

'Was the combination kept in the house?'

'Only in one place.'

'Accessible to your husband?'

'He'd have to have come upon it by accident. It's hidden in the master bedroom. We did go in to check the safe, but other than that, the room has been closed off.'

'Good, I'll have the crime techs here tonight or tomorrow morning.'

All four people heard the opening of the garage door. Even whisper-quiet doors made some noise. The sound was muted, but it was unmistakable.

Robert hustled down to the basement where he showered and changed. The unmarked car in the driveway alerted him to be prepared for the gathering upstairs. As he shaved, his reflection startled him. The skin on his face seemed to hang, black bags had settled below his eyes and when he held out his hands, they were shaking. He wouldn't have recognized himself. With nervous effort, he got his facts in order.

I used gloves, got the documents back as I found them, vacuumed, went back along the wall and smoothed out the carpet with my hand. What can they find? He rubbed his hands with the almond oil he used every day. *What can they find?* Then he knew. Had he left fingerprints when he'd found the combination a few years ago? *Shit!* Jessie had asked him to get something from the drawer, so he had an excuse for his prints being on the drawer. Had he left prints near the combination? He had no defence for those. How long were prints viable? He rubbed his hands with more almond oil before he left.

When he appeared at the french doors, Robert scrutinized the gang of four. He began to work his defences. 'Jessie, I'm sorry I left. I had to get out. I kept thinking of what you told me. If I had made one check on Justin, he'd still be alive.' There was an anxious dread in his voice. There was room beside Jessie, but he'd find no welcome there. He sat on an empty sofa to her right and rubbed his palms together, trying to slough off the tension that he felt mounting. His palms were slick with oil.

It was Geoffrion who rose and had the dubious honor of making the introductions. 'Mr. Tyler, Detective Geoffrion. We met last night. That's Detective Bertrand, my partner. Again, accept our sympathies. We've been going over the events of Wednesday night. Actually, we were waiting for you.'

'I'll help any way I can.'

'We would like you to come down to the North Division on the corner…'

'I know where that is.'

'Good. We need a formal statement. Your young neighbor was down this afternoon.' Geoffrion wanted to get Tyler in the box, skipping the questioning room, without setting up red flags. 'As I advised the Sharpes, and now you, you have the right to an …'

'I don't need one. When would you like to do the interview?'

'We're finished here. Could you come with us now, Sir?'

Robert scoured the faces around him. He was a target of the investigation or the cops wouldn't have suggested the immediate interview. *Those were my rights! Shit!* He couldn't back down now. He was usually adept at concealment, but the spurious skill abandoned him. The air he breathed was dense. His suspicion of them all stretched and grew. 'Justin was my son. Of course, I'll do anything I can. Jessie and I both want to know what happened.'

A silent communication passed between the detectives. They had followed the shifting emotions that Robert couldn't hide from experts. Tyler would be a challenge.

'I'll get my wallet and follow you.' Robert wanted to be certain he had Doug Hoye's number. *Don't volunteer or theorize.* He didn't need Hoye for common sense.

'Sir, it would be easier if you came with us. Traffic is miserable at this time. We'll use the siren and get there a lot quicker and an officer will drive you back. A perk of the job.'

Robert smothered a gasp. Henley had come up beside him. 'We want to know what happened to our boy. Robert, I'm sure you'll make this easier for Jessie rather than having her worrying about you or waiting up all night.'

Robert tried to smile. 'Are you going to cuff me?' His attempt at humor didn't come off.

'Of course not! If you'd prefer your own car...' Geoffrion was good at mental games, better at keeping suspects off balance.

'I'll go with you, but I need my wallet.' Robert's legs were stiff as he left them. *I can't call Doug now! Dammit to hell.* Riding with the police meant he'd already given up a measure of control. He watched Henley close the front door.

'Donna! Robert was just driven away in a police car. Let's hope some of the pressure is off Colin.'

Donna tore down the stairs. 'Justin's death has to have been an accident. We can't even go over there and offer our condolences to Jessie. Thank God we still have our son. Would you go up there and get him out of bed and washed? I'll see to dinner.'

Standing over the bed, the lump under the sheet appeared very small. With one swoop, Steve pulled the sheet back with one hand and scooped up his son with the other. 'Colin, I know this is a tough time, but you have to be brave for all of us.' He carried his son to the bathroom and set him down beside the shower. Colin stood statue still and dropped his head like a rag doll. Steve turned on the shower and stripped the clothes from Colin, who hadn't moved. He guided

Colin into the shower and closed the thick glass door. 'You don't want me in there to wash you, Son. Get to it!' Under the shower spray, Steve couldn't see that Colin was crying.

As he wrapped a towel around Colin, he saw a livid scratch on his shoulder. 'What happened here?'

Tears burst from Colin's eyes. 'Justin wouldn't let me go. He grabbed at me and called me a pussy, so I kicked him real hard with both legs. Did I kill Justin, Dad?'

'No, you didn't. Justin drowned. Did you hold his head under water?'

'No.'

'Then you didn't drown him. Look at me when I'm speaking to you, son. Don't talk to anyone else but me. Don't tell any of your friends about this. Do you understand me?'

'What about if the police ask me some more questions?'

'If the police ask us to come in again, we'll have a lawyer with us.'

'Am I going to go to jail, Dad?'

'You're not going anywhere. What did I just say?'

'Not to talk to anybody?'

'That's right. Let's go down and get something to eat.'

'Okay, Dad.'

Chapter Twenty-One

THE INSTANT THE CAR DOOR closed, Robert felt he'd been cuffed like a suspect. Without Hoye's representation, he'd have no intermediary during the interview. The questions would come right at him and he'd have to respond, even if he used monosyllables and gave up little information.

'We know this tragedy has been a devastating experience for you and we do appreciate this cooperation.' Geoffrion wanted Tyler calm and unsuspecting.

Sure you do. Robert's clothes began to constrict. His socks felt tight. He sat on his hands and tugged at his pants. Things got worse when the police used the siren on the Metropolitan Expressway as the car leap-frogged through a horrendous maze of traffic. Cars on either side were only a few feet away from the back window. Curious motorists and passengers eagerly peered into the car, zoning in on Robert. Being caught on some camera phone and posted on YouTube or some popular blogger's board terrified Robert. His company deal would fall through, to say nothing of the damage to his reputation. He shielded his face with his hands. *These assholes knew this would happen when they suggested I go with them in their car.* Dialing down the ambient traffic noise amplified his hurried breaths. *Why didn't I see this coming?*

Moitié called the division and spoke in French while Geoffrion did the grunt work of driving. Robert did hear that they'd make due. *Already a complication.* He'd seen celebrities duck down in back seats to escape cam shots. Ducking hinted at something to hide. Robert was not about to give these homicide cops freebies. His relief at finally exiting the unmarked car didn't last.

Inside the gray building, the cops were all business. 'Mr. Tyler, unfortunately the interview room is being used. We'll be obliged to use an interrogation room, and I'll leave you in the good hands of Detective Geoffrion. As soon as we conclude the interview, an officer will drive you home. We are all here for the same reason, to bring closure to this tragedy. Again, my sympathies, sir.' Moitié unlocked a steel door and, with a remarkable agility, sprinted down a steep flight of stairs. Geoffrion and Robert followed at a much slower pace. Robert felt a twinge behind his left knee and thought it might buckle.

Moitié set himself up in the video room beside the interrogation box. He'd grabbed a cold Mauby and took a deep slug. Every nerve ending remained on alert. He'd analyze every word and every gesture while he videotaped the interview. Later he and Geoffrion would study what they had. Moitié did not want Tyler to suspect his presence. He closed and locked the door.

Directly behind the interrogation box were 14 cells: a common cell, one padded cell and 12 single cells. The duty cops had been alerted. The desk officer who scanned the video screen of all the cells had ordered all doors on his side shut. Then he began to eat his pizza and guzzle Pepsi. Robert would be unaware of his surroundings behind the interrogation room. He'd never know, at least not tonight, about the intake room, adjacent to the cells, where suspects signed themselves in at a computer, gave up their personal belongings that were then stored in numbered lockers against the far wall, and then led into another room for their prints and mug shots. He'd never see the suspect in cell 9 pacing up and down.

When Robert stepped into the interrogation box, a windowless 8x10 room, he gritted his teeth. The white table was a piece of Formica, fitted into the wall and supported by only one leg. The two swivel chairs were red. The walls were bare. Robert spotted the tiny microphone on the green wall in front of him. He didn't see the one near his knees under the table, the one that could catch a mumbled whisper if his head fell in dread or despair. Geoffrion closed the door behind them and a blue light flashed above the door to alert other detectives that the room was in use.

Geoffrion took out two sheets of paper. One had the notes from the first exchange with Robert, the other was blank. Robert saw the other chair had an armrest; his didn't. With his feet, he rolled his chair closer to the table and rested his elbow on it. 'Well? Let's get on with this.'

'I was going over the notes. Let's start at the beginning.'

'I see the microphone.'

'As we told the Sharpes, the recording protects us both so that facts are clear.' Geoffrion had studied law for three years, so he knew a few tricks. 'The evening began with football in the backyard.'

'That's right.'

'The ball struck Justin on his shoulder.'

'He missed the catch. We decided on an early dinner.'

'You told us Justin hated football. Did you know that before you asked him to toss the ball around?'

'If you're suggesting that I taunted my son, I didn't. I wanted to teach him to throw a spiral.'

In the video room, Moitié caught the quick flash of anger.

'You had pizza with him for dinner. You said he was more concerned with the TV on the wall than talking.'

'Pretty normal for an eight-year-old.'

'You sent him to bed early.'

'I assumed he was playing computer games. I did call up and tell him to turn off the lights and hit the sack because he had to be up early for a riding lesson. You have all this.'

'How would you characterize your relationship with your son?'

Robert sighed and his guard fell an inch. What had Jessie told these cops?

For the first time, Geoffrion saw more than the flat emotional response or the lack of real engagement that he had exhibited the night of the drowning. 'Sir?'

Robert felt a reluctant respect for this cop. Perspiration beaded on his forehead and pooled under his arms. He looked up and saw that air was pumped into the room, but not enough. 'You've spoken with my wife and father-in-law. Haven't they given you enough?'

'For the record, I want to hear from you. Your take will differ or coincide with theirs. Either way, I want a good picture of your son. You were his father.' Geoffrion's last sentence was his bait.

'For the record, my son was a momma's boy, and his grandfather gave him everything he wanted.'

'It's your relationship that I'd like to know about.' Geoffrion noted Tyler had yet to call his son by name.

'They didn't leave much time for my son and me. I got used to that. My company took up a good deal of my time as well.'

'Was there a particular reason you didn't go up to your son's room to check on him the night he drowned?'

'The kid had to be up very early. It didn't occur to me that he'd sneak out. I feel tremendous guilt about that.' Robert turned away from Geoffrion and rubbed both eyes. 'My wife has reason to be angry.'

Geoffrion saw the genuine anguish of a preventable death. 'You didn't hear the boys in the pool.' Two Naya water bottles were on the table near the wall. Geoffrion reached for one, opened it and took a hefty swallow. With a gesture he offered the other to Robert who followed suit. If Tyler left the bottle behind, they had their palm print. If he took it with him, Geoffrion figured he'd need a court order for prints. To conceal the ploy, he ignored the bottle Robert was using. Geoffrion also got a good look at Robert's arms because he was wearing a polo shirt. He saw no scratches.

'No. I was busy on my computer and other things. My mind was elsewhere. The house is very sound-proofed.'

'When your wife called, you did go up to check.'

'And I searched until I found him.'

'To the best of your recollection, recount the events that took place when you saw your son in the pool.'

'I jumped in, grabbed Justin and lifted him up out of the water. I screamed for help and began CPR.'

Tyler had said his son's name and had shortened the distance between his son and himself.

'Did he strike his head?'

'I don't know. I was panicking.'

'Do you have any idea if your son was still alive at that time?'

'No.' Robert rubbed his temples. The room was close. He began to breathe heavily again.

'Did you grab him by the shoulders at any time?'

'I don't know. I pushed him away from the edge of the pool when I lifted him out of the water.'

'By the shoulders?'

'I might have.'

'During CPR?'

'I might have.'

Tyler's calm was back and it irritated Geoffrion. On the whole, Tyler was a cool customer. 'You've suggested that you and your son were not close.'

'Not my doing, but I didn't try correcting anything either. Guilty on that front.'

'Were you and your wife close?'

'You're asking me this because of Jessie's accusation.'

Geoffrion waited.

'We manage. Jessie's very devoted to her father. They're a formidable pair and territorial.'

'A prosperous and prominent family.'

Robert sat up. 'I married money, but I had to make my own. I have my own business.'

'Was there friction in the family?'

'No more than in any other family.'

'Did your wife tell you she had executed a new will?'

Every nerve in Robert was on alert. 'No.' He'd give up nothing.

'Do you know the combination to the safe in the master bedroom?'

'Fort Knox? No. It's a well-guarded family secret.'

'Your wife named Justin as her sole beneficiary and left the will in the safe a few days ago.'

Robert's head rolled back and he laughed hard. The sudden dramatic sound bounced off the four walls. 'The Henleys at their best! At least now I know why Jessie is out to get me.' Robert understood perfectly the purpose of the interrogation, because that's what this was. He got to his feet. 'I'm leaving and I'll grab a cab.' Robert stood, impatient for Geoffrion to open the door and lead the way out. He left the bottle behind.

'A moment, sir. There's more. Something you should know.'

Robert had no intention of sitting down again. He turned and stood glaring at Geoffrion. 'Well?' His glare didn't have much behind it. *What else can there be?*

'Miss Henley added a codicil to the new will.'

In an instant, a sour perspiration flooded his body. He'd stopped reading after seeing that Justin was Jessie's sole beneficiary. The nerves around his spine tightened like claws.

'Are you alright?'

'Get on with it.'

'In the event of Justin's death, you'd be back in the will.'

Jessie's nailed me with a prime motive. His thoughts scrambled wildly. When he could speak, his words were bitter and desperate. 'Douglas Henley will make certain I never see a penny of their money. Besides, Jessie will change her will now.'

The oblique family criticism was not lost on the detective. That was the only real mistake Tyler made in the interrogation. The answer and laugh were rehearsed, Geoffrion thought. The laugh couldn't conceal the bitterness behind it. *Tyler knew the question was coming. He didn't know about the codicil. Must have missed it.* Geoffrion wasn't finished with Robert Tyler. No matter what Tyler had just said, the codicil had given him a motive for murder.

Chapter Twenty-Two

As THE STEEL DOOR closed behind him, Robert began to run along the service road. He ran across rue St-Hubert on a red and was nearly struck by two different cars. He didn't notice. Foul language, he felt, revealed a limited vocabulary. Sometimes though, these words were far more apt and real than their politically correct neighbors. *Fuck! The old cop was snooping in the bedroom. Now these bastards know about the safe and they'll send experts. If Jessie had told these cops Justin might not be mine, I'd have been arrested. Another motive!* He bent over gasping. When he saw the reason for his release, he stood up and hooted. *Thank God old school reputation means so much to Jessie and Douglas.*

Not a single cab passed, so he continued running till he saw an ESSO station where he called for one. He cursed that he'd left his cell phone at the house. When he got home, he'd confront Jessie. He'd had enough. He'd also have to find a way of getting back into the bedroom. If the crime cops found trace evidence, he'd say he was in there recently. When Jessie went up to the room, he'd follow her. The cab finally arrived, and he flopped onto the back seat and leaned over and took off his shoes. His socks were soaked with sweat. It was one thing to hear Jessie's accusation; it was quite another to know she was taking steps to prove it. *I can play dirty. Jessie doesn't know that.* The interview began to replay itself. As Hoye had advised, he hadn't theorized, or explained much, or added supposition. On the whole, he felt he had acquitted himself rather well. Geoffrion had to believe what he'd said about the codicil and the money he'd never see. *Jesus! It's his job to see through the muck of things.* He clenched his fists when he suddenly caught his amateur's blunder. *Shit! The bottle!* He'd seen that ploy on *Law & Order* many times.

When the cab pulled into the driveway, Robert saw that Henley was still there. *Dammit! Will he ever go home? If Jessie and I had some time together, we might have a chance to talk to one another. He's like a plague in our lives, a chronic disease. A wealthy man's child is always under his control.* He couldn't order Henley to leave because the house wasn't his.

* * *

Geoffrion immediately went back to the box and picked it up by inserting his pen into the empty water bottle and dropping it into a plastic bag which he then labelled. Moitié waited for his partner in the video room. He had opened the door for him because that room was also small. He broke into a smile when he saw his partner with the bag. 'You have the palm print, Jean. That's something, but you noticed how Tyler covered himself with his *I might haves*. Do you want to brainstorm here or go up to your office?'

'Let's go to my office.' He waited for Moitié to gather his notes. The two men were in sync and had mostly black names on the murder board and not the usual red for open files. Moitié used the LSI Scan technique in the video room and when he himself interviewed subjects. Although its creator, Avinoam Sapir, had his critics, Moitié believed in the efficacy of the scan. The Laboratory for Scientific Interrogation, LSI, held the belief that body language was a second-rate technique. The scan purported to determine a subject's truthfulness or deception, what the subject was concealing and whether he or she was involved in the crime. In simplest terms, the scan studied the subject's choice of tense, nouns and pronouns in the belief that guilty subjects followed a common pattern. For example, a guilty subject often employed the present tense because he had to concoct his alibi. He used pronouns, not nouns, to put distance between himself and the crime. He might begin with the name of the victim but change the pattern to a pronoun for the same reason.

Geoffrion held fast to body language. When the men reached the office, Geoffrion sat in his usual chair. The oblong desk was clean with ample room for their notes. The wall was framed by Geoffrion's diplomas. The room was bright and clean and new. As a lieutenant-detective, he enjoyed a corner office with a large window. All his computer equipment was new. There was one family photo on one side of the cabinet. 'I'll begin because I had the first interaction with Tyler the night of the drowning. The facts we have should be tempered with the wife's accusation that interfered with the normal run of his emotions at such a time. That said, we're not dealing with the usual grieving father. According to neighbors, the wife and he himself, the relationship with the son was not close. However, this crime was not premeditated. We learned the wife set the babysitting night which he had apparently forgotten.

'Generally, Tyler's emotions are flat and controlled. I heard only one or two moments of genuine anguish and they appeared to be for the wife more than the son. That might be manipulation. Here's a man who married wealth and got none of it. Had a son and lost him to the wife and grandfather. He's detached, but bitter. I think he knew about the new will; that he was waiting for the question. What does he get out of killing his own son? That's the question.'

Moitié laid his notes on the table and polished off the Mauby. 'Motive is always the key. We can forget about tense. His answers were disciplined and short. He used his son's name only once. He chose pronouns. In fact, he even referred to his son as *the kid*. That's about as far away as you can get. Cold for a father who's just lost his only son. He was terse and judgmental about Henley and his daughter. What he said in the interrogation was truthful generally, but guarded. What Tyler told us about his family revealed more about himself. His relationship with his son, his wife and Henley set himself up as the man behind the fence. *I got used to that.* We have men doing background checks on him. We should discover how Tyler filled the void. Was he withholding information? I'm back to your question of motive. Why kill the kid? He'll never get anywhere near their fortune. He won't win his wife back. The only answer is vengeance. Tyler wanted to inflict pain. But why the son? Why not Henley? That would have made more sense.'

Geoffrion was a little ahead of his friend. 'I'd like to know what was in the original will and what made Miss Henley change it and cut Tyler out. Did he get into the safe? Was there something else in it that prompted him to kill his son? Did the boy do something to him that night? What could an eight-year-old do to cause his father to murder him? Tyler wasn't lying as much as he was withholding. The Henleys are holding back information too. It's a good start.'

Moitié wouldn't let Geoffrion forget about Colin Sharpe. 'If the lab techs come up empty, we're back to the kid. Next round won't be as easy for us. Both suspects will be on their guard.'

Chapter Twenty-Three

CAITLIN SHOULD HAVE listened to Carmen and avoided Highway 13 that now seemed under perpetual construction. It was down to two lanes as she inched her Beetle forward beside a concrete pylon while keeping her eye on the tailgater who was riding her bumper. Apart from her concern for Carmen, she had a genuine fear for her own life until she finally exited the expressway and drove along boulevard St-Martin. By the time she reached Carmen's front door she was definitely edgy. When she saw the pizza box, she was furious. 'Carmen! Did you just open the door for this pizza?'

'I had no real food. You love Juliano's pizza, so I took a chance. I made sure it was Tony before I buzzed him up. Sit down and have a slice. I have diet Coke or wine.'

'Wine, and don't try to distract me with food. I've come out here to protect you from yourself and this Robert. If I know you at all, you're less afraid now than you were. You've fallen for him, and there's excitement thrown into this mess. You don't have to tell me that either.' Caitlin stopped her lecture and began to eat. The wine went down easily.

Carmen ate half her slice before she responded. 'You're right on all counts but one. I am afraid, and being attracted to Robert complicates everything. If I had a contact number, I'd tell Robert that I don't want to see him until ... until I don't even know what to say. Until your son is buried, until you leave your wife, until her attempt to frame you for your son's murder is quashed, until I have your phone number. I could go on.'

'Don't. Consider what you've said. What sane woman would become involved with a man under any one of those conditions?'

'Except for meeting him those two nights when I didn't know anything, I've avoided Robert as best I could. He's the one pursuing me. He knows where I work and where I live. The whole connection is one-sided. Other than what he's told me, I know nothing about him really. I checked the obits and didn't see anything about the death of a young boy.'

'You don't know whether anything he told you is true! If all of it is, you don't want to be dragged into court as the other woman. You two were an item before his son died.'

'What if he's telling the truth about the frame and leaving his wife?'

'Don't fall backwards, Carm. What if he did murder his son? Then he's a monster.'

'He said he needs someone to give a damn about what happens to him and he's fallen for me too.'

'He needs a hideout.'

'Caitlin, you're not an A+ in relationships of late either. Look what happened…'

'On point there. But this Robert is potentially dangerous.'

'I wish I could talk to him and get the truth.'

Their ideas began to run to non-sequitors, so they stopped talking and got back to the pizza and wine. Carmen's backup cell phone vibrated a few inches on the table in front of them, and she grabbed it. 'It's Robert.'

'Don't answer it!'

'He'll leave a message.'

'Then you can hear it.' They waited for three minutes before Carmen went to her messages to see if Robert had left one. She listened and then she passed the phone to Caitlin. *I never meant to frighten you, Carmen. I want to talk—I have to see you.* 'He might come here tonight. I'm glad I'm here with you. Turn off your phone. Let's finish eating and take in a movie. That way we won't feel like hunted prey, and he won't be expecting you to be with anyone when we get back.'

'What if he's outside right now?'

'Damn! You're right. Have you taped anything interesting?'

'You said you'd watch Hitchcock's *The Birds* with me.'

'That'll calm us for sure.' For the moment, they were protected by a locked door, four walls, a silent summer night and their friendship.

The Sharpes wanted to barbeque after their interview, to get out of the confines of the house, but thought better of it. Donna made a salad and heated up a chicken casserole and garlic bread. Colin's hair was still damp from the shower, and the dark curls were tangled because he hadn't combed them out. He sat at his place, beside his sister, quiet and fragile. Susan, usually a steady-stream talker, had become as quiet as her brother. 'We all have to eat to keep up our strength.' Donna tried to create a sense of unity, but no one was at ease.

Colin took a bite of the bread and tried to swallow it. His face turned an ugly white and he bit his lower lip to check a jet of vomit. His eyes teared as he got to his feet. The sudden vomit spray stained the Italian tile and seeped into the pristine moulding around it. Leaving a small trail behind him, he ran upstairs crying and choking.

Donna was on her feet before Steve caught her. 'Let him go. We're both hounding him. Sit down and let's get a few things straight. He can hear us, by the way, so let's keep this quiet. I blundered with the police, but today I thought I helped Colin, made him a little more secure. This subterfuge isn't helping him. Colin's still hiding something and it's gnawing at his insides. He's eight years old, Donna. He can't starve and hide for the next couple of years. I asked him if he held Justin's head under water and he said no. I assured him that he wasn't responsible for Justin's death. They were friends, and the boy is dead. We haven't helped him with that trauma. Maybe we should begin there. Kids get past things faster than we do.'

'He hasn't slept, he's withdrawn and he's vomiting. We're not helping him. I'll make a peanut butter and banana sandwich and get him into clean clothes.'

Fear suddenly evaporated the slender rapport between the couple. It was everywhere around them.

'The police took his footprint?' Donna forgot about the sandwich and the clothes.

'I'm sorry, alright? I never dreamt there was anything more than the kids sneaking a swim. Wasserman will delay any other meeting with the police. I won't let anything happen to Colin.'

'You already have.'

Henley and Jessie knew Robert was back home, but he hadn't come up yet. Henley was not a man to indulge himself in grief or dwell on errors of judgment. He was a man who knew when to shift gears. After the contents of the will had been disclosed to the police, he stepped into the next trench with an adroitness few of his peers possessed. Once the police left, Jessie was about to ask her father for his forgiveness, but he took the initiative. 'What's done is done, Jessie. Robert is officially a suspect. I understand your reasoning, but we must remove the parentage document immediately. I won't submit my good name to ridicule. Don't turn away from me, or ever entertain the thought that Justin was not an integral part of my life, treasured and loved. That said, your disclosure has created a serious problem for us. Our immediate concern is what the police refer to as a 'no-knock' warrant which would give them access to the explosive contents of the safe.'

'We've been told to keep out of the room.'

'Never mind those orders. Go up now, take out the document and bring it down to me. If the crime techs get here first, it becomes their evidence. I won't allow our lives to be splattered on the front page of every rag in the city.'

'What if I'm right about Robert?' She threw that gauntlet at her father's feet.

'There's a great deal of discovery before we're back at that point. If things come to that, you have my word that I'll do right by Justin. Now please get that document.' As soon as Jessie left, Henley called his executive assistant at home, because it was past business hours, advising her to make the arrangements with the Mount Royal Funeral Complex and to see to it that the family mausoleum was prepared for the coming days. He knew, though it meant travelling back and forth, that Jessie wanted the service at St. Peter's Anglican Church in the Town.

'I'll take care of everything, Mr. Henley. Don't concern yourself with this. I'll see to the flowers at the church and the funeral home and all other necessities. Will you be selecting the casket yourself?'

For a moment, Henley the grandfather couldn't utter a single word.

Julia Hanson waited patiently.

'I'll see to the obituary and the music and the casket. My grandson was only eight years old, so the floral arrangements…'

'I understand. I share your grief.'

'I appreciate that, Julia.' Henley was still on the phone when Robert appeared at the door of the living room for a second and then went to the kitchen. Henley wasted no time. He headed upstairs and waited outside the bedroom for Jessie to hand him the document. When the couple reached the kitchen, they saw Robert out in the solarium drinking coffee. 'No doubt Robert is furious and he'll be back in here in a minute. We want to keep our talk civil. Have you considered that Robert's only offence might be simple negligence? That Colin Sharpe is more involved?'

Jessie had no chance to respond because Robert had joined them. 'Thanks for just taking off on us!' Jessie gave no quarter or mercy to Robert.

'Douglas, I'd like the opportunity to speak to my wife alone. Is that possible?'

'I have nothing to hide from Dad. He can stay if he wishes.'

'Jessie, let's talk things out. Douglas, give us a break.'

Jessie pulled out a chair and sat down. 'I don't suppose I can avoid this.'

Robert poured himself another cup of coffee and poured one for Jessie, which she didn't touch. When he heard the front door close, he knew they were finally alone. He wrapped his fingers around the cup and ran his thumbs around the rim. He looked over at Jessie, but she was morose and indifferent. Keenly aware that she had a sheet of paper that could go a long way in convicting him of murder, the steam of his intended confrontation evaporated. 'I will be sorry for not taking better care of Justin for as long as I live.'

'Haven't you said something like that before? It doesn't matter now and it didn't matter then.' Her words were cold and meant to wound.

'Well, I'll continue repeating myself since I feel what I say doesn't matter. For the record, if you had looked away for a minute and Justin had died accidentally, I would forgive you. Take one second to digest that thought.' Robert's fingers on the cup had whitened. 'I don't want to hear that I didn't bond with him. Since you pretend to like the truth so much, be honest and admit you and your father stole my son from me on the day he was born. How many times did I complain about that? It wasn't easy to be pushed off to the side. For the record, remember that wasn't the first time Justin had snuck into the pool late at night, so he did it when you were taking care of him. Of course, you would have checked on him, but you couldn't have checked him every minute! He might still have drowned under your patrician nose!' Robert was shouting and he had risen to his feet.

'Stop! Will you just stop!' Jessie slammed her hand down in a cold fury, but she was crying.

'Stop? Stop? You don't know anything about the word! It wasn't enough you accused me of being involved in our son's death the night he died. You supplied this evidence and had it sprung on me in an interrogation room! Do you know what it feels like to hear that your wife has cut you out of her will in front of a homicide cop, salivating to get my reaction? I wanted to shout in his face that the will didn't change much. Like Midas, the Henleys sit on all their money.'

Jessie got to her feet, took one step and stood inches from Robert's face. 'You got into the safe, didn't you?' she shouted back.

Robert grabbed Jessie and held her tight. She pounded his back with vicious blows, but he didn't let go until she had worn herself out. 'I'm sorry, Jess. Why can't you believe me? You own the house, and the money, and directed the way we lived our lives, but grief doesn't belong to you alone. He was my son too, for Christ's sake!' He released her and turned away.

Jessie caught her balance. 'You got into the safe, and the crime techs are coming tomorrow and they'll prove it,' Jessie hissed at his back.

Robert was grateful Jessie couldn't see his face. Instead of leaving, he did something that took him by surprise. Encumbered by the burden of the last few days, he sat back down at the table. His head fell forward onto his arms. His shoulders began to heave. The sound of his lonely weeping was agonizing because it held the pain of accumulated injuries.

Jessie froze and listened. When she could move, she laid a hand on Robert's shoulder.

Mentally, he rubbed both hands together. It was a single if short-lived victory.

Chapter Twenty-Four

ON THURSDAY NIGHT, Colin's parents were sick with apprehension and they slept uneasily. Colin waited for their angry whispering to stop. Caitlin and Carmen slept with an eye on the phone. Henley slept in the house on Roselawn Crescent to protect his daughter. He'd had clothes and other necessities driven over. Jessie laid awake with her own guilt Why had she used the home safe? Would Justin be alive if she'd taken more care? Robert lay atop his sheets reviewing both sallies into the master bedroom. When could he actually say he was last there? What could he safely say he had touched in the room? He needed a clear head.

Robert continued his review. *I used Sylvie's cotton gloves and took a new pair from the box and replaced them. Sylvie's a big woman. Her hands must be the same size as mine. I folded the gloves before replacing them halfway down the pile.* What if the crime techs figure out gloves were used? Does cotton leave lint behind? Robert felt a sigh of short relief. *Sylvie must clean the room. She could have left that trace, but the cops might then examine all the gloves. Can they get my DNA from the inside of the gloves? Did I wipe Jessie's prints from the safe when I was there? I was careful not to smudge the surface, but all the same...*

He wondered if the old cop found the carpet indentation. Was that the reason for the crime techs' visit? With no opportunity to get back into the room, he'd have to rely on his furtive actions and hope they were well concealed. His body was sweaty and sticky, everywhere but his palms. He reached for the tube of almond oil on the bedside table and pressed a dollop into one palm and rubbed his hands together. Abruptly, he stopped. He smelled his palm. He ran his nails against the palm of the other hand. His body stiffened. A spasm in his neck took hold. He couldn't swallow without a cutting sharp pain. It hurt to breathe. *Try to breathe slowly.* He rubbed the constricted muscle gently, and the pain began to ease. His terror was easy to understand. He'd used his hands to smooth out the carpet along the wall. He'd left a trace of oil on the carpet and inside the gloves.

On business trips, he used sleeping pills. At four in the morning, he swallowed three.

* * *

The techs from the Montreal crime lab presented themselves at the home promptly at eight Friday morning. Henley led the two men upstairs. Jessie watched from the guest bedroom down the hall. They stepped into white plastic suits with hoods and boots. They wore white masks, goggles and gloves. *Laboratoire* was printed on the back of their suits. The men carried their blue equipment trunk into the room, officially froze the scene with tape, shut the door behind them and went to work.

A few minutes later, the phone rang. Robert had showered and changed and decided to be more involved at home. He had the call before Henley. 'Yes?'

'Mr. Henley?'

'I'm Justin's father.'

Henley had picked up another line. 'Robert, I have this.'

'Mr. Henley?'

'Yes.'

Robert listened in on the extension.

'Some test results are still pending, but I am able to release the body this morning. If you've chosen the funeral home, I will make the call for you. They come for the remains.'

'Mount Royal Funeral Complex.'

'The Complex will have the remains this morning. The director will contact you. I'll give him the necessary information. As soon as my report is finalized, I will contact you, sir. Courage in this difficult time!'

'Thank you for your assistance.'

'I am at your disposal.'

Robert stood on the landing and called up to Henley. 'I want to be part of the arrangements.' Involving himself was his best means of regaining control and of keeping tabs on the progress of the cops.

Henley had already closed Jessie's door and was relaying the news as gently as one could in such circumstances.

A scream broke the uneasy quiet of the Sharpe home. 'Steve! Come quickly!' Donna was tearing off pillows and sheets, throwing open cupboard doors, dropping to her knees and shouting the name of her son when Steve ran into the room. 'Colin's run off!'

'Have you checked the kitchen or the family room?'

'Colin?' they shouted as they ran through the house. Susan joined the search.

'He's not here!' Donna's eyes were wild with fear.

'We have to call the police. He might be in danger.'

'You said to leave him alone. And now he's run off!'

The master bedroom afforded a good view of the pool and solarium. One of the techs, curious to see its size, glanced out a window and saw a boy lying at the side of the pool. The boy was motionless. He was well aware that another youngster had drowned in that pool a few days ago. He ran from the room and shouted down the hall for Douglas Henley.

Henley stepped from Jessie's bedroom enraged. 'Must you shout! Don't you realize what…'

'Sir, there is a young boy lying by the side of your pool.'

'A boy?' Henley repeated, confused. He hurried down the stairs with the tech. Robert ran ahead out to the pool.

Colin Sharpe had fallen asleep, but he jerked up when he heard his name. 'I didn't want to kick Justin, but he wouldn't let me go home!' The side of his face was creased with the pattern of the flagstone. Half his curls were dusty. He shouted again, 'I never meant to hurt him, but he scratched me and he wouldn't let go. I didn't want to get into trouble, so I just kicked him.'

Henley felt no pity for the boy. His grandson was dead. He looked down at the boy with disdain.

Robert knelt and tried to console Colin. It was already warm and humid, but Colin was shaking violently. Robert ran to the beach hut for towels and covered Colin with them. 'I'm not supposed to talk to anybody but Dad, but I didn't start the fight. Justin wouldn't let me go home. He wouldn't… Did I kill Justin?' Colin began to heave and sob, trying to make the adults understand he wasn't to blame.

The two people responsible for his grandson's death comforted one another by the side of the pool at his feet. Henley would not have trusted himself with a bat. Formidable, he bought and sold companies, influenced the stock market, moved people around the country, but at that moment he was powerless to redress Justin's death. Henley loathed the word *if*. The word stank of failure and often great loss. If Robert had checked on Justin, if Colin had obeyed the rules—there was no sustenance in adverbs. Small words were vacant and without purpose. Henley was far from through with Robert.

Jessie had come out back but kept her distance. She feared she might attack Colin if she went any closer. She shouted angrily, 'Why did you come into our pool? Why didn't you stay where you belong?'

'Come on, Jessie. It was an accident,' Robert said, trying to calm his wife.

The tech listened and would relate what he had heard to the lead detectives on the file.

'Why didn't you stay home?' Jessie kept at the boy, but the fire of her rage had gone out.

No one phoned the Sharpes. No one had to because the parents were out searching their yard when they heard their son shouting. The parents ran to the wrought-iron fence and pleaded. 'Please open the gate for us.'

The boy fell silent when Robert set him down on a lawn chair. Robert looked over at Jessie before he went to unlock the gate. Henley had gone to her. Jessie stepped over the tape and looked down at a marker on the bottom of the pool. 'It's not good for you to be here right now, Jess.'

Colin closed his eyes and turned his head away from all of them.

Donna and Steve showed no less strain than Jessie. Their meeting was awkward. Donna ran to her son. Steve spoke to Jessie. He didn't dare touch her. 'We're devastated by this tragedy. Donna left Colin in bed on Thursday night. We never knew he got out of the house. There are no words for your loss.'

'If Colin is responsible for Justin's death, we will…'

'They're little boys, Jessie.'

'My little boy is gone.'

'Donna, we should leave.' Steve went to his son and carried him home in his arms.

Neither mother had spoken one word to the other.

A colloquial truth says, 'No one is right for very long.' Henley and Jessie felt the queasiness erupting from a possible misjudgement. 'Geoffrion should be told what just happened,' Henley announced, searching for better footing. Jessie's eyes stayed on the marker.

Robert ran into the house and asked Sylvie to take some water out to Jessie. The second she was out of the house, Robert went to her box, snatched the gloves and stuffed them in his pocket. He'd get rid of the evidence as soon as he could. Colin's outburst should vindicate him, but with the police in the house, how could it? If they found traces of the goddamn oil on the carpet, nothing had changed. Henley had shown the cops where the combination was hidden. The bedroom was the key. Jessie's second document was the deadbolt of his prison cell.

Chapter Twenty-Five

'COLIN!' STEVE PLEADED too loudly, 'What did you tell the Henleys?' He set the boy down in front of them.

Donna was livid. 'You and your bloody principles that told you to choose right over family.'

'Stop yelling!' Donna and Steve, stung by such agony in the young voice, stopped their tirades. The threesome collapsed into a vulnerable knot of frightened souls. Under their own power, they got to the kitchen table and sat down, a parent on either side of Colin. Exhausted and powerless, they held onto one another. For a few minutes the room was quiet. Susan sat on the stairs crying quietly.

The police had driven Robert away for questioning. Perhaps all wasn't lost. 'Wasserman knows more about these things than we do.' He got no response when he left the room. Wasserman was talking to a client. 'Tell Harvey this call is urgent.' Steve sat by the phone for five minutes before it rang. 'Harvey, I apologize for the intrusion.'

'What's happened?' There was a note of alarm in Harvey's voice.

Steve closed the bedroom door. 'Colin's falling apart. He snuck out of the house and went over to the neighbor's pool. He told them everything and threw in that he might have killed his friend Justin.'

'My client will understand that I have an emergency. Can you all come to my office?'

'Right now, Colin feels best in the fetal mode. Your office and the size of your desk would put him over the edge. I'll pay the extra cost to have you come here. I have no alternative.'

'We'll work something out. I owe you many referrals. Give me 45 minutes. In the meantime, hydrate Colin, get food into him. Breaking down is as much physical as it is psychological. Colin will function better if he feels stronger.'

'Forty-five minutes?'

'Should be.'

Steve made grilled cheese sandwiches. Susan poured chocolate milk for the whole family. 'Son, we're in this together. Mom hasn't eaten for a long time. Would you help her, Colin?' That approach worked, and it drew a feeble nod of approval from Donna. 'Harvey's coming here.'

It was vital for Jessie to know what occurred during the last moments of Justin's life. To get those answers, she had aimed her vengeance at Robert, fully determined to exact a life sentence. Colin's admission unbalanced her and scuttled her aim. The sole dreadful certainty was the death of her only son. The moments before he died were clouded now and uncertain. Jessie wanted to wreak injury and justice on the guilty party. That arsenal shielded her from her own unfathomable pain. In such confusion, that pain penetrated the shield and seeped into her heart. Henley felt it when he held Jessie back from the water. He felt it when she crumbled to the ground in spite of him holding her.

Robert had watched from the window. He ran to her side when she fell. 'Douglas, let me take care of her. You have that other work. I'll help you get her inside.'

Henley saw the white van was still parked out front, but he left the house to prepare for the drama of the funeral, a three-day play that gave solace for minutes and left behind its solemn pomp, the void and the finality of incalculable loss. Jessie's world would grow silent, the raucous, boisterous, clamorous noise of young Justin forever gone from it.

Robert carried Jessie back to the living room and went to pour her a glass of sherry. When he handed it to her, she took it. 'I might…'

If only Colin had come over sooner, the techs might not be there. Robert felt the thud of his pulse and he dreaded what they might discover. Trying to exude calm he didn't feel, he did his best to console Jessie. 'Colin doesn't alter the fact of my neglect.' In that quiet moment with Jessie, Robert almost believed that Colin had cleared him of any offence. He rubbed Jessie's arm and she didn't pull it away. The sherry and fatigue worked together. Jessie fell asleep sitting up. Robert laid her down and covered her against the chill of the air conditioning. For a while, he sat watching her, wondering what had gone wrong between them. He thought of the stream of betrayals, especially the one he'd just discovered. *How ironic that Jessie is sitting so close to evidence that could ruin me!* Slipping his hand in his pocket, he pushed the gloves further down near his crotch. *Did she ever tell the birth father? He had a son he never knew and now he's lost him. I had a son who wasn't mine and I reared him.* He was in no position to judge her infidelity.

He knew he had to get out of the house and dispose of the gloves. Geoffrion had been called after Colin's fiasco. He could show up at any minute. Sylvie poked her head around the corner. Robert signalled that he wanted to talk to her. He followed her into the hall. 'Sylvie, I have a little work to do. Jessie should sleep for a while. Would you sit with her so that she's not alone when she wakes up? I should be back before one. I'm hoping she'll sleep till then.' Sylvie took up her post, and Robert collected a few things and left. With luck, he should arrive at Carmen's workplace before she went out for lunch. She had to know about the neighbor's admission, had to understand that she had nothing to fear from him.

The tragedy had taught Robert that he wanted trust in his life and a woman who loved him. It highlighted the emptiness of the life he'd led. If the kid next door contributed to Justin's death, Jessie would still never forgive him his part. *I wonder if she ever told Justin. Was that the reason he never had much use for me?* None of that mattered now. Jessie would gravitate to her father, and Justin's ghost would haunt the house. This thinking, of course, was predicated on the cops' lack of discovery and the Henleys' abhorrence of anything skeletal.

Robert loved cars. Like most men, he knew their stats. In fact, he could tell you what each of the ten neighbors around his home drove and what each car said about its owner. That was the reason he noticed the five-year-old tan Buick parked six doors up as he passed it. The car didn't belong. That or Jean-Guy and Hélène had hired new help. With other things on his mind, he let the car go. His plan was simple, get rid of the gloves and call Carmen from across the street. *You don't have to come out to see me. I don't want to frighten you, but I want you to know that the boy next door...* Once she heard that bit of news, Carmen would meet him and they'd talk. Next week, he'd have the money to begin afresh. The money was his because he'd earned it.

Robert was making Carmen his chance because he didn't want to be alone. He needed support, or something to hope for. He wasn't about to rush Carmen. Taking their relationship slowly was actually a necessity. His mood was buoyant, even hopeful, until he remembered the water bottle with his fingerprints. In all the ensuing crises, he'd forgotten about it. Jamming his foot on the gas pedal, the Porsche roared out of the right lane and sped down Highway 13. Robert hadn't been paying attention, so he checked his rear-view to be sure he hadn't cut some poor slug off. Other cars had pulled out as well. That was the reason he didn't see the Buick three cars behind him.

'Can't teach an old dog new tricks, but by God, they remember the ones they once learned,' Fortier snorted.

Chapter Twenty-Six

HENLEY HAD THOUGHT long and hard when he stood looking at Justin's closets of clothes, trying to select which would hurt Jessie the least when she saw her son in a casket. He'd considered a closed casket, but he knew Jessie desperately needed that final contact. For many months, the image of her son at the morgue and that of the child lying quietly in a box of polished bronze would eclipse the living pictures. His smile, his laugh, his whining, his coltish limbs, his unruly blond hair, his hands, clean and dirty, his quick kiss on her cheek and the smell of a young boy, would retreat behind those two pulsating images. With time, the mosaic of Justin's eight years would flesh itself out, but now the pain was everywhere.

Henley knew his grandson despite all his activities and the sportswear that went with them. He wasn't much different from boys who had much less. Justin wanted to be like everybody else. With that thought, he chose his school uniform and a small lion, the LCC mascot. In the back of the limo, while the driver was still on Rockland Road, Henley opened the suitcase and touched the clothes. *Uniforms! How they evoke the sublimity of youth!* Justin running into his home, a flash of blue and white and gray, shouting about something new and exciting. Henley saw the knot of his red tie, scattered with tiny blue lions, yanked open, half the blue blazer caught behind his school bag, a leg of his gray pants snagged on one of his black polished shoes. But mostly, Henley remembered the pristine white shirt flagged beneath a flawlessly beautiful face and Justin's blond hair damp at the edges and eyes, expectant and bursting with life.

He still held the clothes as the limo turned left onto Côte Ste-Catherine Road, and for the turn onto chemin de la Forêt. He folded the clothes before they reached the Mount Royal Funeral Complex. Since he had decided to restrict the funeral service at the church to close personal friends, Henley had asked his assistant to secure three rooms at the complex for two days. The largest he reserved for Justin and he wanted it kept quiet and solemn for Jessie. In the second, he planned to have one large photo of his grandson flanked by blue roses.

Henley considered pictoral memory books or video tributes tacky. People could talk in this room and gather in the next room as they wished. He did not want to hear friendly greetings or the hint of laughter anywhere near his grandson. Jessie should be in peace for the last time she would see her son.

The funeral director assented to these wishes, received the suitcase of clothes and told Henley he had the instructions for the flowers and had called McKenna Florist. He furthered assured Henley he would take great care with the other arrangements. The two men discussed and agreed on the smaller details. As Henley left the Complex, he felt the lifeline Justin's existence had extended into his own life sever. When his wife Leslie died, apart from a grief that he carried for years, Henley was aghast that death had dared to enter his life. He felt violated and angry, and worse, he was afraid.

For that reason, most of all, he had shored up Jessie's life and guarded her with a ferocity he didn't know he had. When Justin was born, Henley exhaled and gloried in the birth. Parentage didn't matter. Justin was of his flesh and blood. He would carry on the heart of the family. Jessie and the boy were his treasures. Henley had not sought another wife because he'd found his joy, a gift one discovers only once in this life. Sex and friendship with women came with firm limits. No one could ever take Leslie's place. She was his first love and she had given him Jessie. Now Justin would go to Leslie and he hoped he'd find peace. Once the Henleys were a team of four. Now they were two.

With an effort, Henley cleared his head and remembered that the tech had called Detective Geoffrion. 'Give it more speed, Richard. I have business at my daughter's until things are cleared up. We'll need groceries there. Sylvie can go with you on the errands.'

'That's fine, Mr. Henley.'

When Geoffrion got the news from the tech at the Tyler home, he stood quietly disappointed for a few moments before he called Moitié. The letdown didn't hinder his work or its goal. He was first a homicide cop. 'I'm still waiting on forensics. Nothing new there. What the lab rats find at the house will require additional time as well. Call the Sharpes. If this file closes with the neighbor, we have to interview the boy ASAP, but my guess is that the family has lawyered up. Drownings are always sticky files. Remember the one last summer. We both felt the boy had been drowned, but we couldn't prove it.'

'This is a different file. Let me get back to you. I'll make that call.' This kid was his bait, and Moitié was not about to pull in *his* line. The crack here was the kid's age. Geoffrion was keen to focus on Tyler. The kid's age didn't deter Moitié for a second. He knew he had something.

The tone at the Sharpe home had changed. 'Steve Sharpe. Yes, Detective Moitié. We've been expecting your call. I'll put our lawyer on.'

'Harvey Wasserman, Detective. I understand, but Colin is in no shape for an interview at this time. I've spoken to the boy. Nothing additional was said at the Tylers.'

'I believe he added he might have been responsible. He used the word 'killed,' didn't he?'

'The boy was hysterical. He hasn't slept or eaten. Whatever he said was exaggerated and cannot be taken at face value.'

'A boy is dead, sir.'

'We know that.'

'Tomorrow at eleven, please have the boy back at our office.'

Wasserman wanted the last word. 'If his health permits.'

'See to his health today. Tomorrow at eleven.'

Wasserman lost his chance. 'Steve, we have no choice but to go, but I'll be with you and direct the questions Colin should answer and block the ones I feel he shouldn't.'

'What are we looking at, Harvey?'

'You did say the husband is under investigation, right? Let's not discount that.'

'What's the worst outcome for Colin?'

'The drowning was an accident, precipitated by an argument begun by the victim. It was a scuffle that turned tragic.'

'Stop with the analysis. What's he looking at?'

'He's not going to jail, Steve. Worst case scenario, counselling with Family Services is my take. We're talking about two eight-year-olds, good friends at that. First off, we are not sure of the extent of Colin's involvement. Their tests won't be ready, trust me.'

'He almost admitted killing the boy!'

'I can defend that hysterical outburst as exaggerated grief. Let me do my job tomorrow.'

'Donna was right when she said this will get out.'

'They can't publish his name, if that's what you mean.'

'The kids know each other. With their iPhones and texting, they'll have the word out faster than CNN.'

'Let's not get ahead of ourselves. If you have to make changes, you'll make them. My words are inadequate because words always are. Your family will recover. This trauma won't last. I promise to do the best I can.'

He nodded dully. 'Colin's not big for his age.'

'That's to our advantage.'

'I mean he'll be brutalized by the kids when he goes back to school. Justin was popular, a kingpin among his classmates. I should never have taken Colin to the police the night Justin died. We should have pieced the facts together first.'

'That's the past; can't undo it or change it. Work with what we have and stay positive.'

FORTIER COULD GIVE LESSONS on surviving surveillance. Sitting across the street from the Porsche and brown brick one-level office building, he took a swig of the blended fruit juice he'd made himself. On the passenger seat he had a hiker's pack of nuts and dates and dried fruit. Even way back, he never needed to blow smoke, and rode rough-shod over partners who did. He didn't lose sight of the Porsche when he reached for the drink with one hand. His eyes were trained on the mark. He knew that Tyler was on his cell.

Carmen's phone rang at one minute after twelve. "Unknown Caller" could mean it was her landlord, telling her he had installed a new washer in the faucet, or it could mean it was Caitlin who gave out as little personal information as possible, or it could be Robert. Carmen was curious. She took the call. 'Hello!'

'It's me. Please give me two minutes.'

'I'd rather not.'

'Please, two minutes.'

'No more than two.'

'The police have learned the boy next door who snuck into the pool with my son played a part in the tragedy. Their investigation is off me. I'm not a jerk or a stalker, Carmen. I meant what I said about starting my life over. I've told you more about myself than I've told anyone else. Did you find out who the Henleys are since I told you?'

'Yes.'

'That was the reason for not giving you a number to reach me. I want you to think about giving us a chance. Take the time you need. For the next ten days, I'll be very busy. I've sold my company because I want a new life. I'm outside your office right now. Before I go, I'd like to see you, but if you're not out in a minute, I'll leave.'

Robert's proximity startled her. 'You're outside!'

'I'm leaving in a minute.'

Robert's world was dizzying. She hadn't said goodbye. Had he miscalculated with Carmen? When he saw her walk outside, he let go of the wheel.

Fortier put the juice bottle down. 'Bingo.' He took out his camera, an old Canon, like the old fossil himself, which still performed near the top of its game. He got a full frontal of Carmen and waited to see what transpired. Robert had good taste; he had to give him that. The thirtyish woman was tentative, stopping about ten feet from Tyler. Fortier was puzzled.

'I'm here.' Robert had been hard to miss.

'I've thrown a lot at you, but I'm not stringing you a line about leaving my marriage, or about you.'

'You don't know me, Robert.'

'If I weren't serious, you'd be long forgotten. It's not just someone on my side now. I'm sorry about the neighbor, but at least the truth is freeing me from an outrageous accusation. I'm here to tell you to take the time to weigh things. I knew I could love you from the moment you lost the second hundred dollars. Everything around me is in chaos. I know I'm not the person you met at the casino, but this is still me. Don't give up on me.'

Carmen took one step closer, but stopped. 'You've been dishonest. How can I trust you now?'

'From the moment I opened up to you, everything I've said is the truth. You have to admit that, right? You have a contact number, but let me call you. You can appreciate what my house will be like for the next week.' Robert took a step closer. 'I won't keep you, but how about a hug before I go?'

Carmen blushed. She knew something about spiders and webs. 'A short one.'

Robert took her into his arms. Her blood raced when she felt his hands on her arms. His breath caught, but he let her go. 'Take the time you need, but don't give up on me.' He left Carmen standing on the driveway, got back into his car and started it up.

'Jackpot! Might not be the mother lode, but it is a hit.' Fortier took another photo of Carmen before he packed up his equipment and drove off after Robert. It was easy because the Porsche had already stopped at the curb. He wanted more on Tyler before he gave anything to Henley. *Let the family get through the funeral. This woman could be just a friend. A hug is only a hug. But there was something in the way she looked at him that tells me there's more here.*

Robert called Carmen again. 'Thanks for listening. I can smell you.'

Carmen blushed. *What if Robert is for real?* Her heart raced. She ran her hands over her arms where Robert had touched her, laughed uneasily and waved him off. A niggling thought persisted. *Why isn't he grieving for his son? In his own way, maybe he is. At least I have time and a name. He drove out here to see me.* Carmen stared up at the cloudless sky and smiled. *That's something.*

Fortier was thinking the same thing.

Robert was thinking the same thing.

Caitlin called soon after, and Carmen knew she'd be in for a sermon.

'Hi you! Checking in to see that you're alright, no sightings, no calls. You have me worried, Carm. *Anyhoo*, I don't want you to be alone, so you're coming to my place tonight. If you like, we've been invited to my parents' for Sophia's lasagna and homemade bread. Dad's home for once. He and Mom haven't seen you in a while. Monsieur will love the company. You can judge for yourself how the injection's working. We're not Italian, so if you don't want that, we can go out. After dinner, let's hit Crescent Street and change your ideas. There's always something going on there. I don't want you in any danger, so I'm in my protection mode. I just offered you food, why aren't you cutting in?'

Carmen didn't reply at once.

'What's happened?'

The story didn't take long. To Caitlin's credit, she listened without interrupting. 'Let me have it,' Carmen said, waiting for the onslaught.

'I teach ethics, but I certainly could pull down a doctorate in relationships. I'm still in recovery from blowing my own. Eat your lunch and get back to work. Let's talk tonight.'

'Thanks for not jumping on me. Food? I'll be there. See you at seven on the Boulevard or Wood?'

'It's easier to go straight to my parents' place.'

'Alright.'

* * *

When he figured that Tyler was driving home, Fortier dropped back a few more cars. No sense in taking a chance Tyler would spot the tail.

Robert saw that the lab rats were still at the house. *Have they come up empty or found something?* The hope he'd just felt burst. *Shit!* He used foul language again when he realized he still had the gloves. To further his chagrin, he saw a blue trunk in the hall and heard voices in the sitting room. *At least I haven't used the oil today. Have to lose that too. Jessie doesn't smell much with her sinuses. She might not know I even use the stuff.*

Henley came out to the hall to meet him. 'Robert, the police have taken our fingerprints, a precautionary thing. They're waiting to take yours. It won't take a minute.'

'I was with Jessie in the bedroom last week. Of course my prints are in the room. I live here.'

'They've printed Sylvie. There's nothing to this, Robert. How about cooperating?'

Shit! Robert had hoped they'd forego the investigation. 'I have nothing to hide.' His bowels began to loosen when he thought of the drawer.

Jessie and Henley left Robert alone with the tech who had the ink pad and a white print sheet ready. Seconds later, Robert took a cloth from him and wiped his fingers. His print sheet was slipped into a plastic evidence bag. The power of a single print! That was something Robert had never given full weight to until that minute. How easy it was as a film buff to watch culprits down though the years arrested because they'd left a single print on a murder weapon. A smudge of tiny swirls sent these characters to their ungodly deaths. Robert had joined that group of men and women. He prayed and bargained that he hadn't left his prints on the underside of the drawer. He handed the cloth back to the tech and waited alone till the men had left the house.

When he rejoined Jessie, Henley was gently telling her about the arrangements. Her body had folded against his. Whatever sorrow Robert had felt for Jessie dried up when he put his hands down on the print pad. Joining them, he listened because he wanted to know about the funeral. He waited for Henley to finish. 'I would have liked to have been involved. Nevertheless, you've handled everything very well as usual, Douglas. The wake is Sunday and Monday with the funeral on Tuesday. Would you like me to call LCC?'

'My executive assistant has already seen to that. Julia has asked the principal to invite only Justin's classes if they wish to attend. I don't want a carnival atmosphere.'

Jessie must have taken medication because she didn't say a word.

'Douglas, I don't know whether Jessie can hear me, but I want both of you to know that you've humiliated me. Colin Sharpe's full confession might not be enough to dissuade you from pursuing me, but there are limits. When Detective Geoffrion told me about the will, I wanted to say it was no great surprise! I could have gone on at my expense, but at yours as well, but I didn't, out of respect. Jessie and Justin were my beneficiaries. Interesting isn't it, Douglas? My point is that I've been cut out of your money all along. The will is a minor slap. The embarrassment of being told about the will by the police was a major blow.'

Jessie's eyes opened slightly.

'Was there something else in the safe that I should know about?' It was Robert's turn to catch their reaction. He could go on and vent his fury, but they had him handcuffed with the second document. Henley stepped forward. Every line in his face deepened. Robert held his ground, but he didn't ask another question.

Chapter Twenty-Eight

WASSERMAN SPOKE TO BOTH parents calmly. 'We have to marshal our defence and answer their evidence. A little boy's guilt over a fight is not a definitive admission of guilt, however it was made. If the footprint matches a significant area on the body, we'll address that situation when it comes up.'

'How?' Donna asked. She forced a stoic calm to settle on her.

'We'll want to know the location of the print, whether there was one print or two, things like that.'

A small witness had crept halfway down the stairs and listened to every word.

'The crux of their case is whether or not Colin turned back and saw Justin after the altercation. If Colin saw Justin's head above water, well, that's in our favor, big time. That response is something I have to cover with Colin before we meet with the police. What concerns us now is clearing your son.'

'I know what the boys at school can do even if you clear Colin.' Donna's calm evaporated.

The small witness crept back to his room and curled up in bed.

'Have no communication with the Henleys or Robert Tyler or anyone else for that matter, not even your parents at this point. The fewer people who know about our defence, the better. Colin shouldn't be left alone. We don't want any more impromptu excursions. I'll be back tomorrow at nine. I'll go over things with Colin then. Get some rest. You both look like the walking dead.' Wasserman broke the Jewish stereotype. He was blonde, and 6' 2" with what Blacks call a 'bony white ass.' He untangled his legs from under the table before he got to his feet. 'Who caught the case?'

'A Geoffrion and a Bertrand,' Steve answered.

'Hmm.'

'What?'

'Top men, both of them, and pit bulls.'

'That's just great,' Steve said dejectedly.

'That might work in our favor. They don't screw up and they're fair. That's what we want.'

Wasserman seemed to have relieved some of Steve's panic. Donna couldn't believe her husband was that naive. 'Harvey's a lawyer. He cares about billing hours. He has to be positive.'

'When did you become such a cynic?'

'Thursday morning when you took Colin to the police.'

The pending excitement about Robert did not prevent Carmen from feeling the awe that always accompanied a visit to the fourteen-room gray stone mansion that sat comfortably on the north side of The Boulevard in Westmount. In Montreal, this 'suburb,' a city onto itself, bridled at the very word. Here, quite separate but still an integral part of Montreal, reside the well-heeled gentrified citizenry. English money and power hold sway in this distinct society whose subtle snobbery is a fact of history. Yet there was nothing subtle or reserved about Caitlin or her mother Maggie who had made Carmen family.

As soon as she pulled into the driveway, Monsieur took up his position behind the huge oak door, wagging his tail and giving off a breeze. There was no need for Carmen to use either brass knocker because Monsieur announced her presence with his familiar bark. *Caitlin must know how lucky she is to come from all this! I never thought I'd ever get inside one of these places.* Chris, Caitlin's younger brother, sprang to mind. Five years ago, a drunk driver had killed him. Carmen bowed her head. *Wealth doesn't mean much in the end.*

'Hello stranger!' Like Caitlin, Maggie was tall and Carmen was in her arms before Monsieur had a chance to perform half a pirouette. 'It's been well over a month, but I'm sure you haven't forgotten the tantalizing aromas from Sophia's kitchen. When I told her you were coming, she heated up her meatballs and she has a care package for you to take home.'

Carmen beamed. 'Sophia didn't have to do that, but I won't refuse it. Has she tied it up in her famous knot?'

'The same. One pull on the right ear and the bag opens without a fuss.'

Monsieur was nuzzling Carmen's ankle. She knelt down and gave him such a good rub that he went belly-up for a tummy rub. 'How're your kids at school, Maggie?'

'They're teaching *me* everything I can do on my iPhone. Other than making me feeling old and behind the times, the kids are fine.' Maggie sensed her husband's presence before she turned to him. 'Guess who's here for dinner?'

Maggie and Frank Donovan were a striking couple. He was tall and patrician. Maggie was gregarious and energetic. 'Good to see you, Carmen. You haven't come for my legal advice, I hope?'

Caitlin had just joined them, but she'd heard her father's comment and cut in quickly. 'Dad's kidding, Carm.'

Carmen knew their personal code and laughed. 'We've been on the straight and narrow, Frank.'

'Car men!' Sophia appeared at the door, drying her wet hands on her apron. She dragged out Carmen's name so that it sounded as though it were two words. Hugs were exchanged. The good company and the Italian dinner made for a fine time and too many irresistible calories.

Carmen hated to leave when Caitlin signalled that it was time to go. 'Bye everybody!' Monsieur began to sulk as they left. He had expected a full night of attention and he wasn't going to get it. Carmen parked on Wood Avenue behind Caitlin. Before any thought of Crescent Street, they talked in Caitlin's living room, curled up at either end of her sofa. 'I'd like your take on Robert, Caitlin.'

'If Robert's been truthful, I agree, things appear hopeful, but divorces take time, especially when you're involved with someone like a Henley. His wife's lawyers could stall. Are you willing to wait on the sidelines? Robert's mourning a son and he feels guilty about his death. Healing could take time as well. You helped me after Chris died, so you know what kind of time I'm talking about. '

A thought came back to Carmen.

'Carm?'

'Robert isn't mourning his son, not that I've seen. That bothers me. At first, I thought his wife's accusation blocked his grief. His wife and father-in-law literally hijacked the boy, so Robert said he and his son were never close, but just the same…'

'That's not normal. You only have Robert's side of the story. He has a lot of baggage, and the trunk in the Mini isn't big enough.'

'Yet he sold his company. He wanted a new start, all before the tragedy.'

'Carm, who goes ahead with something like that when his son has just died? Who pursues another woman at such a time?'

'I hear you, but if this boy next door is responsible for his son dying, at least I don't have to be afraid of him.'

'He may still be under suspicion and he's still married. You have time, Carm, take it and protect yourself. You have to learn how to do that. This isn't some crazy lark!'

'I've already…'

'I know. That's your baggage. You might not be able to carry it.'

Chapter Twenty-Nine

EARLY SATURDAY MORNING, before their second interview with Colin Sharpe, the detectives conferred with Racine and then called the crime lab. They had requested overtime after Colin Sharpe's outburst by the Tylers' pool. 'What do we have, Pierre?' Moitié had begun with the coroner and he kept the lead.

'The pathologist did discover additional bruising behind two of the fingers on the right hand. No cuts, just bruising.'

Geoffrion checked his notes. 'Sharpe said he thought he kicked the victim on the hands. That corroborates his version. He said he used both feet. He might have kicked the victim more than once.'

Moitié was more interested in the shoulder bruises and asked Racine what he had on those. He liked the Sharpe kid for them. Kids that age horsed around and fought.

'They appear on both shoulders. Detailed photos have been sent to the crime lab for comparison against the footprint and the palm print you men had from a water bottle. The interesting aspect is that no fingerprints were found around the shoulder bruises. If the father drowned his son, he had to hold him down like this.' Racine held his hands out straight, fingers on a line with his palms. 'He used pressure from his arms to hold the boy down. The shallow end, when the body was discovered, suited his intentions. The victim's feet touched the bottom of the pool. That gave his murderer leverage, a backboard if you will. The victim had nowhere to go. Had the father attempted to drown his son in the deep end, the boy could have escaped his hold by swimming down deep into the pool.

'If the neighbor kicked the boy and connected on both shoulders, the victim might have struck his head, become disoriented, swallowed water and panicked. It was dark. Drowning occurs very quickly as I have told you. The boy drowned in shallow water. Crime lab has established a body moves and shifts in water, but very little when there is no current as we have in a pool. Where you found him is where he died, give or take a foot or two.'

Geoffrion remembered something. 'His mother said that he hated shallow water. He either pursued Sharpe as he tried to get out of the pool, or his father lured him there. Does Crime have anything for us?'

'I suggest you call,' Racine said as he left with his notes.

Geoffrion did just that. 'Geoffrion. Jocelyne Thibeau, *s'il vous plaît.*'

'*Un instant.*'

'*Ici* Thibeau.'

Geoffrion wasted no time. He began with the shoulder bruises.

'We are performing analyses as we speak. Unfortunately, the size of the youth's foot and the size of the adult's palm are remarkably close. The contours of the images we lifted from the victim's shoulders are not definitive. We will continue to analyze for comparison points. We require a count above five.'

'What about the prints in the bedroom?'

'We have five sets, one belonging to your suspect.'

Geoffrion's hopes rose with caution.

'On the safe?'

'Not the set you want. Two actually, both Henleys. We did find slight smudging.'

'He could have used gloves. Trace evidence?'

'Pending. Takes time.'

'Damn.' He had held back on his last question. 'Inside the drawer?'

'We have Tyler's prints on the night table.'

'Near the combination?'

'Prints inside the drawer, but none on the numbers themselves.'

'Shit!'

'Detective!'

'I could say worse.'

'Be patient, we still have work to complete on the drawer and other areas in the room.'

'You know where to reach me if you come up with anything.'

'Always do.'

'Be nice if we had a solve in a day like *CSI Miami*. We might well be looking at months! In the meantime, we could ruin a kid's life this morning.'

'Why are you leaning toward Tyler so hard?' Moitié wanted to know. 'We learned what Henley had on him. No record, successful in his own right, no history of abuse. From all accounts, he's a decent guy.'

'He knew I was going to ask about the safe. He was waiting for the question.'

'Doesn't mean he got into it.'

'We know the house is held in trust, but he pays the bills. He's in this situation for twelve years. Then he learns he's been cut out of the will. We now know he was a beneficiary in the first will. Has to have been a blow, but he pretends it's nothing.'

'He has money himself.'

'You're dodging my point, Moitié.'

'I'm not. You've added your own agenda to it. That's the problem. Look at the other side. The victim bullied Sharpe. He fights back to get home. He's lied to us; we know that. Then he begins to lose it, comes close to confessing he killed his friend. Kids kill. Don't intend to, but they do. We've seen it. Open your eyes, Jean! If you'd grown up in Montreal North, you'd know first-hand what little monsters kids can be. Colin Sharpe is a little rich kid who'd probably gotten everything he ever wanted.'

Geoffrion didn't pursue Moitié's dig at his agenda. Miscalculation for him was worse than failure. He got back to the file. 'Two 'spects and they both look good. Let's get back to the office and prepare for the kid.'

Saturday morning, Robert had fixated on the gloves. *The crime rats are gone. If I toss the gloves, Sylvie might discover she's missing a pair.* When he took them from his pants, they were badly creased. He'd have to get rid of them with the almond oil. Eating breakfast out was the answer. He'd leave the stuff in a bathroom and shove all of it down to the bottom of the trash can. His office and storeroom were located on Hymus Boulevard in Pointe Claire. He'd drop in first and then go eat at Chez Cora in the strip mall near by. It was always crowded. That meant refuse and prompt disposal. He dressed quickly, told Henley he had to go to the office and would be back in a few hours. Leaving the house wasn't difficult. Since the question he'd posed to Henley went unanswered, there had been almost unbroken silence between the two men. Henley hadn't bothered to tell Robert the obituary was in *The Gazette* and four other papers.

* * *

Fortier had been parked at his post on Roselawn since eight. His bum was relieved when he spotted the Porsche backing out of the garage.

Robert was already regretting his words to Carmen. He would have liked to have eaten together. He needed human contact. The tan Buick caught him off guard. It was Saturday after all. Hired help didn't work weekends as a rule. The oil and gloves were in the pocket of a light jacket on the seat beside him. Was that a cop in the Buick sniffing around? He was becoming paranoid, he knew it. Sweat flowed from his pores. *If that's an unmarked car and that cop has a warrant…* Robert turned right on Beverley and parked in front of a blue van. Then he waited.

Henley sat alone quietly with Justin's obituaries in front of him. He checked the color photo in each paper. The one he had chosen had been taken outdoors at his Westmount home. The copies were good. Henley carefully read the texts which appeared in *The Gazette, The Globe and Mail* and *La Presse.* It was odd, he thought, how one could proofread a text without touching its substance. The first word of the obituary had stalled Henley. 'Tragically,' 'accidentally,' 'suddenly,' each word was an end in its own right. He chose 'suddenly' because he felt the word was gentler, more private. It also hid the enormity of the great pain that lay behind it. Henley had taken great care to reveal what he felt was necessary and to protect what was private domain. The obit took up a quarter of the page. The last line, however, was personal, borrowed from Shakespeare, who had plumbed the depths of loss. It gathered together the grief and the question of a family who had lost a child. *Did heaven look on / And would not take (his) part?* Henley left only one copy opened for Jessie to see.

He rose from the table, unsure and unsteady. Assuming the role of a reactor, waiting for events to unfold rather than causing them was alien to Henley. Justin's death had diminished the iron strength of his grandfather, had brought him down to the common herd, to a place he didn't understand.

Upstairs, Jessie stood under the shower spray, using her right arm against the stall to support herself. She had not showered since Thursday morning. More than being physically unable to get herself into the shower, it was wrong, she felt, to go about quotidian tasks when Justin was dead. The profusion of life that he had brought into the house was gone, the space he claimed was vacant and the silence he left behind was filled with police and doubt and anger. Stepping from the marble stall, she walked haltingly to the window and looked down at the pool. *After the funeral, I'll have it drained.*

Chapter Thirty

SURVEILLANCE HAS steadfast rules. Never allow the mark to get behind you, maintain your distance, and keep the mark in your sights. Fortier adjusted his 95-buck Grand Prix cap and began his tracking. As soon as he turned onto Beverley, he saw that the Porsche was nowhere in sight. *He thinks he's made me.* With a slick U-turn, Fortier drove back to his parking spot, turned off the engine and hunkered down. He knew what to expect if his hunch was right. It was his turn to wait. He was the expert.

Robert sat on alert for seven minutes. The Buick didn't pass him. He stalled for another two. *There's only one way to figure this out.* Robert eased out and drove around to the other side of the crescent. His house stood at the head of the road. Robert would have to drive past his house and begin a right turn in order to see if the Buick was still there. It was a chance he had to take. First though, he shoved the jacket under the front seat, no sense advertising evidence. Approaching his house, his muscles tensed. He nosed around the corner. The Buick hadn't moved. Emboldened by this discovery, he didn't bother turning around and going back the way he'd come. Instead, he drove past the Buick a second time.

Fortier had high-tuned his hearing aid. He heard the Porsche pass. The game was back on. After this tail, he'd retire the car because it was tainted. Tyler'd recognize it. Henley would set him up in a rental.

The Sharpes had been up most of the night. The parents had taken turns sitting outside Colin's room. No one had opened *The Gazette* that morning. Donna prepared oatmeal, scrambled eggs and toast with orange juice, milk and coffee. 'Colin, we are all with you today. Eat up, you need your strength.'

Colin wore chino pants and a blue polo shirt that hung on his shoulders. He was listless and detached as he pushed the oatmeal around the white bowl with his spoon as though it were alien food or poison. When he began to drop egg into the oatmeal, Steve intervened.

'Colin, this is a hard time for the whole family. Eat the food your mother's made. We're here to support you but you have to hold up your end.'

Colin kept pushing the oatmeal. It was lumpy now. He looked over at his father and back at his food. He began to jam the oatmeal into his mouth, tucking it in his cheeks. Bits spilled out the side of his mouth.

'I didn't say all at once. You'll choke.'

Colin continued his jamming, but more slowly. His cheeks were so hollow Steve could trace the lumps of oatmeal as they built up in his cheeks. 'Swallow! You're not a baby, Colin. Help us out here!' He swallowed with difficulty. One mouthful had gone down.

Susan had learned since the crisis began to accept the fact that her parents wouldn't notice her much, even when she was sitting at the table with them. She crawled into her own shell and listened to her music.

Wasserman arrived and worked with Colin on the crucial questions and drove the family to the Crémazie division. He didn't trust either parent at the wheel.

The detectives were ready for them and led the party to the interview room on the first floor beside the parking lot. A water pitcher, glasses, a copy of the obituary, notebooks and the recorder were all on the table. After the introductions, the questioning began. Moitié brought the family up to date. 'I'm sure you have seen this!' He handed Steve Sharpe the obituary. 'Good morning, Colin. I know this questioning is very hard for you. But it's my job and Detective Geoffrion's job to speak for Justin because you know he can't speak for himself and tell us what happened. We don't believe you meant to hurt your friend. Are we right so far?' Moitié's friendly *I'm on your side* approach had disarmed many an adult. He worked the pitch to perfection with the kid.

Wasserman gave Colin the go-ahead.

'I just wanted to go home.'

'You did tell us that you thought you might have kicked Justin's hands. Well, our lab police found bruising there, so that was a good answer. You said you kicked him more than once. Is that correct?'

Wasserman nodded.

'He scratched my back first!'

Caught off guard, Wasserman threw his hands up. *Unpredictable kids!*

'May I see the scratch? I'll bet you didn't cry.' Moitié didn't move a muscle. His voice was low and friendly.

Colin pulled his shirt up. Moitié examined the scratch and took a photo of it. 'I can see why you kicked more than once.'

It was Colin who nodded in agreement. The police seemed to be on his side.

'The next question is very important, Colin. You told us that you looked back after you got out of the pool. Where were you exactly?'

'Why is that important, Detective?' Wasserman asked, stalling.

'Part of the official record, sir.'

If the lawyer could answer, so could he. 'I was at the hedge near the side gate.'

Moitié took his time writing down that point. 'Thank you for your honesty, Colin. Last time, you said you weren't sure if it was Justin's finger because it was dark. Am I right, Colin?'

Wasserman gave Colin the go-ahead.

'Yeah. Yes,' he corrected himself.'

'Thank you. You're doing very well, Colin. It doesn't really matter if you saw Justin's finger or just his head when you turned around and looked back. Whatever part you saw of Justin means that he was all right then, he wasn't drowning. Tonight, I am sending police to Justin's house. One will stand at the hedge and the other will stand in the pool where Justin was on the night he drowned. I want the officer standing at the hedge near the gate to tell me if he can see his partner in the pool. Now, Justin, did you look back when you got to the hedge? Take your time and think hard.'

Wasserman hadn't planned for Moitié's trap or the bond the cop had established with Colin.

The police are gonna find out! Colin's tongue went dry. He tried his best. 'It was dark.'

'Did you look back, Colin?' Geoffrion asked softly.

It all happened so fast was the rehearsed answer. The boy's thoughts were single-minded. *The police will know.* Colin shook his head from side to side once. 'No,' was the whisper. Colin knew nobody could help him now. He had overheard his parents last night about the kids at school and moving. He shot a quick glance at his mother before he crumbled in on himself. He didn't even cry. His next words bounced off the floor. 'Justin deserved what he got. I didn't want to go swimming that night. He said he'd tell all his gang I was a wuss. He thought he had so many friends, but we just wanted to use his stuff. He had everything.'

With the last three words, a heavy bleakness settled in the room.

Wasserman jumped to his feet. 'This interview is over! You know very well, Detective Moitié, that Colin only meant that he had the right to push Justin back so that he could get out of the pool. He was not referring to anything more serious than a few kicks.' Wasserman motioned for Colin and Steve to leave, but the damage was done.

'Mr. Sharpe,' Moitié cautioned, 'with tests pending, I must ask you not to leave the city with Colin.' Moitié was somber. He saw a bewildered little boy across the table who was trying not to cry. Moitié hated bullies. At that moment, he hated himself.

Steve appeared beaten and broken. He had his arm around Colin.

Outside, Wasserman pulled Steve aside. 'Listen carefully. Colin is eight. Under the Criminal Code, he is not capable of forming criminal intent, *mens rea*. We're looking at assessment, psychological counselling with Family Services. No one is going before a judge or being sent to jail. Keep in mind that the father is also a suspect. Try to calm the family.'

'Whatever vulnerable, tender life my son had is broken. In his mind, he's found himself guilty. Do you get that, Harvey?' Steve walked back to his family.

Chapter Thrity-one

ROBERT DIDN'T STAY LONG at work. He walked around various offices and into the warehouse at the back, taking in the business he had founded. The sale meant forty-three people would be out of work. *I had no other choice. Sales were plummeting. I was damn lucky to get the price I did.* Next week, he'd feel hostility here too. He locked up and left for breakfast. He scanned the street for the Buick. He thought of the arena across the street because he knew there was a parking lot behind it, but gave up on that idea as paranoid. He gunned his Porsche out onto Hymus in front of an oncoming bus and swore. *Good move! Just blocked my rear view.*

Fortier wasn't swearing. He stood at the side of the arena, got back into his car and began to tail the car behind the #200 bus. At boulevard St-Jean, he saw that Tyler didn't intend to turn. With a green light, he lost his cover from the bus, but he still had the car in front of him. Tyler turned off into a strip mall. Fortier drove past that entrance and turned into the second one. West Islanders are shoppers, and the mall was crowded. He parked and began to search for the Porsche. Tyler made it easy for him. He didn't see the car but he saw Tyler himself, carrying a jacket, and standing in line for Chez Cora, the popular breakfast eatery. The place was always crowded. Fortier had his own little breakfast nook in Pointe Claire Village. Today, the line-up here served him well. The jacket had caught his attention. Tyler was the only one around with a jacket.

'Why you old codger! What are you doing here? Thought you said you hated the place.'

The speaker was carrying twins, with his wife trailing behind. 'John, Natalie! Hello!' An idea sprang to mind. 'You guys could do me a big favor, and I'll comp your breakfast.'

'Shoot!'

'I'm working for a client. I need to get into the restaurant unnoticed. If I sit with you, I won't be.'

'Thought you had retired eons ago, Mike?'

'Work on the side keeps me young.'

'Is this dangerous?' Natalie wanted to know.

'As dangerous as an omelette.'

'Cheating husband?' John asked curiously.

'Can't say. May I borrow little Trevor and carry him inside?'

'You can keep him,' John laughed and handed Fortier the boy who promptly gave Fortier a good kidney kick. Five minutes later, they were seated four tables from Tyler who was busy with French toast smothered in fruit. His eyes were trained on the washroom at the far end of the restaurant. Minutes later he got up and headed there, carrying the jacket.

'Natalie, may I take Trevor to the washroom for a minute?'

'I don't know.' Natalie was uneasy.

'John can come with me.'

'I don't like any of this.'

'We'll be back in a minute,' John assured Natalie. He was excited.

Inside the room, a line waited for toilets. An employee emptied trash into a green garbage bag. Tyler scowled. A full trash was what he needed. *Damn! I'll get rid of the gloves, but I'll have to find another drop for the oil.* The tube was heavy and would make noise when it hit the bottom of the trash can.

Fortier and his small entourage had edged their way into the room. The sinks too were crowded, and the smell of cheap soap hung in the air.

Robert unzipped his jacket pocket and balled the gloves into his fist. He bullied his way to the first available sink and ran the water over one hand while pumping paper from the machine on the wall with an elbow. He was stuffing the gloves in with the paper when a kid startled him.

'Mister! You didn't wash both hands.'

Robert froze for a second. Then he jammed the gloves and paper back into his jacket, strode out of the bathroom, paid and took off.

Fortier wasted no time. 'Take Trevor back.' He pulled out a fifty and gave it to John. 'Gotta go!'

'That's it?'

For John and Trevor, it was.

Robert threaded his way around cars. *I should have dumped this crap by now.* The first trash can he saw he'd use, but he stopped dead when he saw a tan Buick. *Fuck!* He began to run. Four rows of cars later, he spotted another of the same color. His shoulders relaxed and slowed down. *Who the hell buys a Buick the color of shit?* When he spotted a Tim Hortons donut shop at the side of the mall, he sprinted in that direction. Luck was not with him. When he got inside, he found the bathroom but there was no lid on the trash can. *I can't believe this!* He hurried out. Robert didn't know the exact moment when he felt someone was watching him. When he did, the sidewalk fractured under him. With forced calm, he walked stiffly back to his car and left the mall. He didn't look back.

Fortier knew he couldn't pick up the tail. Tyler had too good a head start. When he reached his car, he sat and made notes. Tyler had met a woman in St-Eustache. That was something to follow up. Today, he was trying to dump something, but what, was the question. Chances were that Tyler would dump the stuff. Fortier didn't have much for Henley, but Tyler's actions were suspicious. Fortier had scanned the bathroom for surveillance cameras. There were none, as he suspected. In any event, he had to speak to Henley about another car. Fortier didn't harbor regrets. Today, he had his first. *Shave off the years, and Tyler would never have gotten away.* He rubbed his arthritic fingers.

Fortier had been right. Robert had driven along Hymus and dumped the gloves and oil at Lafleurs, Montrealers' favorite greasy spoon for hamburgers and fries. The first item on Robert's agenda when he reached Roselawn was checking on the Buick. It wasn't there. He swore. The house, save for Sylvie, was quiet, but Robert knew the duo was somewhere. He felt their presence as he went downstairs. Surveying his belongings, he figured he'd need a three-bedroom condo when he made the move. When Sylvie called everyone to a late lunch, Robert was glad to get out of his lair.

Sylvie had prepared poached salmon and spinach. Henley and Jessie walked in together talking. How he wished Henley would go home! Any chance of redeeming himself with Jessie seemed impossible as long as Henley was around. They were inseparable and always had been. Henley spent lunch explaining what he had planned for Sunday and Monday nights at the funeral home. From time to time, Jessie eyed Robert as though he were her enemy. He shuffled his feet, grateful when she gave her attention to her father. 'Dad, I don't want any of

Justin's classmates to come into the room with me and Justin. Seeing them would tear me in two. They're all alive. My boy is dead.' Robert saw that Jessie's decision was final. Her voice was cold and detached. Her pupils were large with whatever drugs she was taking.

Henley nodded reluctantly.

'They can say a prayer in one of the other rooms where you have his pictures.'

'And Robert,' Jessie said dismissively, 'you can have a few minutes with Justin. After that, I don't want you in the same room with us. Justin was my miracle and I hold you...'

Robert was stunned. A small derisive smile escaped but he rose silently and left the room. He stood for a moment at the door. He ached to release his own barrage of words, but he saw that Jessie and Henley had already forgotten him.

Chapter Thirty-two

COLIN HAD A LOT TO THINK about. Most adults believed kids didn't listen. Adults were often wrong in their presumptions. At the window, he could see the pool. He wondered what Justin looked like dead. Were his eyes still open? Would he ever come back, not like tomorrow, he knew that, but like in a long time? It was easier to think of Justin than it was to listen to his mother and father fight. It was easier to think of dead eyes than to think of Justin's gang coming after him, kicking and punching him. Would they kill him too? Would his picture be in the paper like Justin's? What if his parents got a divorce? What if they didn't want him anymore? What if the police came for him? Colin didn't want to go back to bed, so he stayed at the window. Tomorrow when the kids from school went to see Justin and he wasn't there with them, then they'd all know. He backed away from the window.

Steve knew exactly what Donna was thinking. 'The kid got taken in by a pro.'

'Isn't Harvey a pro?'

'I bungled everything again. Is that what you want to hear?' He took a step closer to Donna. 'Are you and I in trouble?' His hands had fallen to his side.

'I thought you were the strong one. I don't think I know you. All the weight of this disaster has fallen on me.'

'I see.' Steve sat down and covered a fist with his other hand. 'If we'd hidden Colin's involvement like you wanted, how long do you think it would have taken for him to blurt something out to one of his friends? Our boy talks. The police would have come after him with a vengeance. Would that have been better, do you think?'

'Couldn't be any worse than it is now!' Donna noticed a puddle of sunshine had settled on the counter. 'It's beautiful outside and we can't even go out.'

'Watch me!' Steve slid the patio door open, stepped out and sat down.

Donna flew after him. 'Come back inside.'

'This is our property. The Tylers can't see us through that damn hedge. It was a fucking accident!' Steve shouted loudly.

Please keep your voice down,' Donna pleaded.

Steve jumped to his feet and kicked the chair off the patio. 'It was a fucking accident!' he shouted louder.

They were jarred by a harrowing scream from Colin's bedroom window.

'Mom! Mom! It's Colin!'

Donna and Steve flew up the stairs. Horrified, they ran into the bedroom.

Colin was hanging from his bathroom door. He had used his school belt. His back was up against the spine of the door. His shoes had fallen off, and a bathroom stool was on its side.

Susan was screaming and trying desperately to hold Colin up by his legs. Steve pulled the belt off the door with one hand. With his free arm, he held Colin against his body. Colin's head lolled to one side. Steve laid him on the floor and knelt over him. First he pried his mouth open. He pumped his chest and began mouth-to-mouth with a fierce determination.

Donna couldn't move. The strength she'd had evaporated and she crumbled to the floor beside Colin.

'Susan, call 9-1-1! Move! Don't just stand there, move!'

Robert itched to storm back into the dining room and rage against their tyranny but he couldn't afford an outburst. *That freakin' document!* After the funeral, he'd tell Jessie he was leaving her. There was nothing left for him in that house. Although it was Saturday, he called the private number of the principal buyer to tell him he should be able to meet with all of them on Saturday. Once that task was attended to, Robert felt better. Forgetting a paper trace, he'd dialed three digits of Carmen's number before he hung up. *Give her time. Carmen has to have faith in me. I should have thought of a random drop for the gloves and oil.* His thoughts stopped when his eyes fell on the obituary lying on the keyboard.

The wail of sirens and the intermittent "beep beep" of the ambulance jostled him out of any thought of Justin. The sounds stopped close by. Had Henley succumbed to stress? He could hope. That would change the whole dynamic between Jessie and him. Robert rushed upstairs to find Henley standing outside on the front stairs. 'Jessie?' Robert came close to a shout.

Taken aback by the genuine concern he read on Robert's face, Henley said, 'Not Jessie. It's something next door at the Sharpes.' The ambulance, the fire truck, the police cars, the lights were a repeat performance. The only differences, their destination and the time of day. Neither Henley nor Robert approached the Sharpe property.

The Sharpes' house was unnaturally quiet. Donna cradled a pillow against her stomach rocking back and forth. Sweat dropped from Steve's chin and the veins in his neck knotted as he worked to revive Colin. Seconds before the paramedics came rushing into the room, Colin coughed, a thin, dry, strangled cough. Steve shouted, 'Colin, come back, come back, son.' He breathed more air into Colin's mouth. The response was another cough, dry still, but louder. He kept working.

Donna crawled closer to them and fell against Steve's back and kissed it. 'I'm sorry for everything I said. If it weren't for you, we'd have lost him.'

Paramedics rushed into the room as Colin coughed again. They went to work quickly and bagged Colin, took his vitals, set him up with intravenous fluids and lifted him onto a stretcher. In minutes, he was inside the ambulance. Steve and Donna climbed in with him. Susan had followed all the procedures a few feet away. Now she ran out to the ambulance. 'Honey, get back into the house. We'll call with any news.'

'I'll wait by the phone, Mom. No other calls, I promise.' Susan saw Robert and Mr. Henley before she ran back into the house. The teenager had begun to shoulder the weight of responsibility.

Henley related the story to Jessie. Robert stood in the doorway. Her eyes were thin with pain. She asked one question. 'Is Colin dead?'

'We don't know.'

Jessie's lips thinned. 'Justin is dead. Colin shouldn't be allowed…' Mercifully, she didn't complete her thought.

Chapter Thirty-three

DETECTIVE GEOFFRION called Robert to ask for blood and hair samples. 'Mr. Tyler, this is common procedure.'

'What about Colin Sharpe?'

'We don't wish to cause you further undue pressure, but we must eliminate you as a potential suspect before we concentrate on anyone else.'

Robert's hand tightened on the phone. His knuckles whitened. *This bastard still has me in his sights.*

'Is there a chance you could come in today?'

'Couldn't this wait until after the funeral?'

'I know the wake is tomorrow. You'd be helping the investigation and the family.'

'Justin was my son too!'

'I meant you as well when I spoke of the family.'

A wave of claustrophobia swept over him a second time. How would his blood and hair help the investigation? Had he left hair near the safe? Geoffrion had wrong-footed him again. He hadn't vacuumed there. *Shit!* He recalled the paternity question. If they had his blood, they'd discover Justin wasn't his. Once that was out, Jessie would come forward. 'Detective, I have the distinct feeling I'm being harassed. I'm contacting a lawyer.' He wanted to say he knew the Henleys were pressuring the police, but he stopped short of that accusation.

'Sir, I am acting with due diligence in this case. I'll get a court order for those samples. No lawyer can help you with that.' Geoffrion was curt and cold.

'Do that then.'

Geoffrion did a good job of punishing his knuckles before he called Moitié and told him to contact the Sharpes and get his ass down to whatever hospital they were at. 'Tyler's lawyering up. Making noise about harassment. He's an arrogant prick. He thinks he can walk away from me.'

'I'm on the Sharpes.' It didn't take long for Moitié to drive to the Jewish General Hospital on Côte-St-Catherine Road. He knew their emergency room well. He flashed his badge and got information from the duty nurse on the desk before he went to find the Sharpes. *Attempted suicide!* Flipping open his cell, he called Geoffrion. 'The kid tried to hang himself. A serious attempt from what I've learned. The kid's handing us the case.'

'Two kids!'

'I did what was necessary, Jean. I had to twist the truth out of him.'

'Two kids, Moitié. Colin Sharpe tried to kill himself! In our work sometimes we can damage the lives of civilians who lose their privacy. Goes with the job, but we have to be aware of that at least.'

'Wait a minute! Don't dump a guilt trip on me. I get it, but this kid might have killed his friend. He's lying to us. Justin Tyler didn't opt to drown in his own pool. Now I feel like a shit for doing my job! And you're pissed every time the solve shifts my way.'

'Enough said. We both get it. Stay in the background. You'll pick up more from the sidelines than the front.'

'Don't need a training lesson either. We're after the same result, aren't we?'

'Thought you 'Island' guys never got upset.'

'I was born here, Detective!'

'Double checking, a fault of mine. Get over yourself.'

In Emergency, Moitié scanned the green curtains he hated that reeked of the sick and of disinfectant. He found bed 14 after popping his head into the bays of sick, startled faces. He spotted the parents before they saw him. He might not have recognized them right off, haggard and weighted down by a weariness he recognized from other cases. The only thing holding them up was their son who now was a victim himself, no matter what he had done. Sharpe had his arm around his wife, and a doctor was checking the boy's blood pressure. Colin's face was wan, but he was conscious.

Colin's thoughts brought him back to the floor in his bedroom. He remembered coming out of some tunnel that was far back behind him. A voice calling him grew louder until it was on top of him. When he opened his eyes and saw his father, a surge of life rushed through his heart. He didn't want to be dead. As soon as he kicked over the stool, the belt had cut into his neck. He'd tried to squeeze his fingers into the belt to free himself, but it was too tight. His throat was on fire. The last thing he remembered was Justin waiting in heaven to beat him up.

Colin breathed in the oxygen greedily. He heard his parents crying. They didn't want to get rid of him and they weren't fighting.

'It's alright, Son. We're here.'

'Mr. and Mrs. Sharpe?'

Too weary to fight Moitié off, they accepted his presence. 'What more do you want from us?' Steve asked.

'Mr. Sharpe, I need a few minutes. We can talk in the corridor.'

Saving Colin's life had reinvigorated Steve though the change was not perceptible from his appearance. He followed Moitié without comment and waited for him to speak.

'Mr. Sharpe, I have the medical report. I'm grateful for all concerned that the boy is still alive, but his action implicates him to a greater degree in the death of Justin Tyler.'

'You don't know that, Detective. I won't permit Colin's health to be further jeopardized. The drowning was accidental. I'm not subjecting him to any more questions. He's an eight-year-old, for God's sake!'

'By law, your son will require psychiatric care. For my file, I need answers. The Henleys have a legal right to know how their son died.'

'How much more can my son say? They scuffled and scratched and kicked. Kids do that stuff. I came forward with my son to Geoffrion to help the investigation as soon as he woke up the morning after Justin drowned. We haven't dodged anything. The police grilling my child, my wife and I arguing, Colin hearing that the kids would bully him at school, or that we might have to move away, all those pressures pushed my son to the brink. Write the drowning up as an accident. That's what it was.' Steve began to walk away.

'Mr. Sharpe! A citizen does not direct an investigation.'

'Do you have kids of your own?'

'No.'

'You don't know where I'm coming from.'

'You have your son. Your neighbors have lost theirs.'

Steve turned and left. *It's never going to end.* Donna's expression tightened when she saw Steve. 'It's alright, he's gone.' Steve sat beside Colin and took his hand. It was half the size of his. He laid his cheek against it. Donna drew her chair closer to them. His tears fell on Colin's hand.

Chapter Thirty-four

ROBERT CONTACTED DOUG Hoye as soon as he was off the phone with Geoffrion. Hoye had promised this weekend to his three kids and his wife Val who'd told him if she didn't get out of the house she feared for her sanity. Ben & Jerry's ice cream and the Old Port awaited the young family. When he heard his cell, Val let out a moan, and Hoye hesitated. He showed her the caller's name and she signalled for him to take it. 'Robert, please accept my deepest sympathies. I read the obituary this morning. I don't know what I'd do if I lost one of my little monsters. How can I be of help?'

Hoye played squash with Robert. Neither man had time for golf. 'Thank you. I need your help. I should have called you sooner. It's urgent.'

'My office tomorrow morning at ten.'

'I'll be there.'

Henley listened intently to Fortier's account. 'Of course, change the car to something upscale. Find out who she is. You know where she works. What he tried to dump is important.'

'It was something relatively small because it was in his jacket pocket.'

'Is there a chance you're mistaken, Mike?'

'I have a flat ass from years of tailing and observing. Robert was definitely trying to dump something. Sorry I lost him or I'd know what.'

'I was beginning to feel Colin Sharpe was responsible. Now, you raise my suspicions of Robert again. I'm counting on the crime lab to prove Robert got into the safe. Stay close; keep up the tail. We're in for the evening. I don't think Robert will go wandering tonight. Take it easy.'

'Will do.' A few hours later, Fortier was driving a year-old Beemer. *My old slag is more comfortable than this!* That didn't stop Fortier from peeking out his side window to see if anyone was checking out his wheels. He took a corner with a little extra speed. *Have to admit it corners well.* The Beemer was growing on him. He'd be back on Roselawn early tomorrow, sitting pretty.

* * *

Robert kept to himself and grabbed a quick breakfast Sunday morning. Henley was in the kitchen absently scanning *The New York Times*. 'How's Jessie?'

'No better.' Concern creased his face. Henley bided his time like a panther before he'd pounce on Robert.

Robert felt the hostility. 'Were you able to learn what happened with Colin Sharpe?'

'I have a few friends at the Jewish. The boy attempted to hang himself. His father revived him.'

'I wonder what went on between them at the pool. Before you say it, Douglas, I will. I should have known. I won't forget my negligence. Kids don't understand danger.'

'There's a long line of adults who don't either.'

'I have to go out for a few hours, break the tension.'

'I'm not stopping you, Robert.'

Every hair on the back of his neck rose. *Get out of my goddamn house! Go back to your fortress in Westmount and take Jessie with you! You're suffocating me!* Robert thought of Justin's last moments for a second time when he realized you could suffocate with air all around you. He didn't breathe properly till he was backing out of the driveway.

A dark blue Beemer pulled out and followed the Porsche to Old Montreal, to a law office on rue St-Paul in a converted graystone. Fortier double-parked on the chaotic narrow street. Horns blasted immediately. He flashed his old badge to the first car behind him, then slapped it on the dash and put on his hazards. He signalled three fingers to the irate drivers. He copied down the three names on the brass plaque. He tried the front door. It was Sunday and whatever lawyer Tyler had gone in to see had relocked it. Fortier hadn't caught a glimpse of the man or woman. He made a quick call. 'He's talking to a lawyer. Here are the names I found.'

'Good work! I have connections. I'll discover which one.' Henley wasted no time. He made a single call and waited. Fifteen minutes later, he had the name of one Douglas Hoye. He smiled ruefully at the coincidence of names.

'Come on in, Robert, you look like you could use a stiff drink.' Hoye led him into a very modern office that surprised Robert because the building itself was once an old house. He would have preferred a more somber setting. The pale yellow walls with striking, colorful modern artwork were too upbeat for his problems. Hoye himself was tanned, balding nicely, and relaxed behind the European designer desk. Behind him were volumes of law books in a panelled bookcase that ran the length of the wall. Robert rearranged himself in the burgundy leather armchair. Most of the night he'd been trying to decide if he were making the right decision about seeing Hoye. When the cops discovered he wasn't Justin's father, he could pretend surprise. After all, he only learned that fact a few days ago. His problem came down to the crime lab proving he'd gotten into the safe. The motive for murder lay there. That was the reason he was sitting in a law office.

'You're nervous and devastated. Tell me succinctly what the problem is. I won't interrupt you.'

Robert sat forward on the chair. 'I was in charge of Justin the night he drowned. I thought he was in bed. I didn't check on him. He and his friend snuck into the pool. They scuffled. The kid left. Justin drowned. Jessie and her father are determined to have me charged with his death. Douglas has hired a retired cop to tail me. The boy who left just attempted suicide, but that fact hasn't swayed their intent. The cops are looking at both of us because Jessie accused me of a crime in front of the lead detective the night of the drowning. To an extent, they're succeeding. I was hauled into an interrogation room under the guise of simple questioning. Everything taped, I think. Now the cops are asking for hair and blood samples.' Robert was reluctant to continue.

Hoye looked up from his notes. 'So far, from what you've told me, they can't manufacture a case. Justin's death reads accidental to me.'

'There's more.'

'Always is. Take your time and be precise.'

Robert told Hoye about the safe, about the will and the codicil and about the paternity. 'I lied to the cops about getting into it. The crime lab was up in the room Friday. I wore gloves, but there could still be a problem.' He told Hoye about the combination in the drawer and the almond oil and wiping the carpet with his hands.

'First things first. When did you discover the contents of the safe?'

'The day Justin drowned. Jessie told the cops she thinks I got into the safe. She also told them about cutting me out of her will. She didn't mention the paternity question to protect herself. The outward trappings of money are deceptive, Doug. It's a whole other world. The will wasn't a great surprise. The codicil she added didn't fool me. If Justin died, I'd get half her estate. It wasn't a probability. It was a ruse to keep me from contesting the will because I've paid all the bills.'

'Why didn't you call me when this happened? You're a smart man, Robert. The codicil is a major problem. You know what motive means, no matter how you tried to get around it. *I* know the Henleys will change the will. Let's hope the cop on your case figures that out too. But what were you thinking?'

'I hadn't done anything.'

Hoye let that sentence hang for a few seconds.

Robert broke the silence. 'There's more. I've met someone and I managed to sell the company for a decent price before the Chinese factor destroys what I worked to establish.'

Hoye was thirty-eight. He'd long ago stopped trying to figure out why couples hung together or broke up. Human beings were too complex for a template. 'I trust you haven't seen this woman since Justin's death. You did say you are being followed.'

'Once.'

'You're smarter than that!'

'Christ, I'm twisting shit-side up out here alone. I need someone. How hard is that to understand?'

'And the company sale?'

'Planned for this Saturday.'

Hoye put more pressure on his pen than was necessary. 'Have you taken Self-Destruct 101?' The comment drew a smile from both men, but it was short lived. 'Let's look at the damage. You lied to the police and that's on record. Suspects lie to the cops all the time, but lies build cases. Knowing the contents of the safe serves up motive. Seeing a woman at the time of your son's death is not a positive either.'

'There's one last thing. I wore gloves and got rid of them and the hand oil I used in case I'd left traces of it on the carpet in the bedroom. The tail didn't catch the drop, but I'd made an earlier attempt and failed. I might have been seen then.'

'Did you check to see if there were security cameras in the room?'

'In a bathroom?'

'Alright on that. Robert, you've done a better job of sabotaging yourself than Henley with his gazillion could ever have done. No murderer is this stupid.'

'Can you help me?'

'I can't do worse than you've already done. If Henley weren't involved, this boy would be held responsible. He's keeping the pressure on you, and your actions have helped him. As far as the samples are concerned, reroute all calls to me. I can't stop a court order, but an extra day gives them more time to focus their attention on this boy. Don't talk about the case with anyone! You won't feel better when you leave here. It's a misconception that lawyers ease pressure. We generally add to it. According to the second document in the safe, Justin's paternity is uncertain. It doesn't completely rule you out as his father. Have you entertained the idea that Justin might have been yours?'

An absolute stillness fell on Robert, and it emanated throughout the room. Robert didn't gasp or appear frightened. The trembling began inside. 'No, not once I saw the document.' Robert hesitated. He got up and began to pace. 'I had doubts long before I read that document. Justin didn't look like me. He was Jessie's son. There was no doubt there. I know a child can bear the physical traits of only one parent. I'd look for flashes of me in Justin. The way he carried himself, or laughed, or stood, or smiled, but I never found anything. Once Jessie and Douglas kidnapped Justin, I lost myself in my work, trying to prove my worth to Henley. When Justin was almost three, I bought him his first tricycle. Douglas had a little motorized Benz toy car sent to the house the next day. I could never compete with him.'

Robert stopped pacing. He smiled sadly, mostly to himself. 'I envied Justin, not for the things he had, but for the love that Jessie and Douglas showered on him.' Robert sat back down. 'Maybe Justin picked up on that. Doesn't matter now. He didn't like me. Spending time with me meant he wasn't with them. I stopped trying with Justin. There were times when Jessie and I were alone that I felt she wanted to be with me. There was never a time, once Justin began talking in sentences, that I ever felt he was happy to be with me. I saw only one side of that document. In my heart, I knew Justin wasn't mine.' Robert got up again and turned away from Hoye. He began walking to the door. His hands were trembling. *What if the boy was mine?* 'Doug, I have to go.' Blood rose in his cheeks. He had revealed an intimacy he hadn't intended.

Chapter Thirty-five

FORTIER HADN'T BEEN ABLE to wait for Robert. Rue St-Paul was impossible except in the very early hours of the morning. Montrealers took taxis or the metro to the famous old section of the city. He had what Henley wanted. Robert was still trying to assimilate Hoye's question when he reached the street. A young boy, Justin's age, pushed past him carrying a skateboard. Robert stood and watched him idly as he disappeared along the crowded sidewalk. What if Justin was his? The lost years and fading hope, because that's what they were when Robert sought the spark of life elsewhere, fell heavily on his shoulders. He'd given up on Justin so soon and never put up a fight for him. Whatever love he'd felt, he'd let go when Jessie threw her arms around the boy.

He knew nothing of love, the length and width, the well of it. The love his mother must have felt for him was bled by her illness, shredded and strained until she gave him up. His youth had been spent on the sidelines of his aunt's family. Jessie? He felt something in his heart had moved. He must have loved Jessie, but she too had turned him aside. Had he seen himself in the boy, he might have been a better father, wrestled love from his heart and from Justin's. He'd known the start of love, the first months with Jessie, the first few years of Justin's life and the newness of something with Carmen. Of its test and duration, he was ignorant. Jessie's scarring grief for Justin was something he'd never experienced, not even when his mother died.

He felt the first stab of loss on his way home. When he found Jessie and her father in the living room, he stood firm in his resolve. 'Since you don't want me in the room tonight with you, Jessie, I'd rather drive down to the funeral home.'

'Robert, you should be with me and Dad.' Jessie had spoken softly, pleadingly.

'To show a united family for appearances?'

'The next three days belong to Justin. Our differences should not intrude.' Behind the veiled threat, there was her lonely need.

'Alright.' Robert wanted to sit down with them, but he saw he wasn't welcome. They had the illusion they wanted of being united.

* * *

From the morning Julia Hanson called the emergency number at LCC, Justin's school, and the response from the Junior School Director herself, the work of contacting students began in earnest. The school was the fortunate beneficiary of generous Henley endowments. Although the director, Melanie Walker, knew the donations had come to an end, she remained grateful. The school owed a great debt to Justin's grandfather. Reaching the students in July was not an easy task. These affluent families travelled in the summer months to Europe and beyond. If they remained in the country, the children might be off at specialty camps or away at summer homes, in such locales as Gray Rocks, North Hatley, Rawdon, or Muskoka. The possibilities of venues were varied. One call puzzled Walker. Colin Sharpe's sister said the family would not be in attendance.

The obituary had run in multiple papers, so the school's assistant administrator had come in from holidays to field calls from parents who had learned of the tragedy. The final student tally was 38. The school arranged for a school bus, but the parents wanted to attend the wake and insisted they accompany their children. The amended plan was for the staff and the administrators to meet the children at the bottom of the hill on Chemin de la Forêt. Together, they'd form two lines of young boys, and a few girls, in school uniforms. Parents agreed to follow the children. Melanie Walker knew most of the students by name and knew what to expect. Justin's drowning would have become a survival lesson for the youngsters. Do you see what can happen if you disobey your parents? Sunday night, young brows would furrow unnaturally, excitement would nibble at the edges of their eyes. Curiosity would spike their toes to pump themselves up to see more of Justin, whose death was another world away from the young.

In the few hours before Henley's limo arrived, Sylvie prepared a buffet that no one touched. Robert sat uncomfortably beside Jessie who kept her eyes and thoughts closed for the entire half-hour drive. Henley broke the silence by reiterating what "position" he expected Robert to play once he had spent his time with Justin. 'Your main work is protecting Jessie. Don't allow any children into the room with Justin. I'll alert you to the close family friends who may have a short visit. I'll receive the mourners in the other two rooms. Justin's picture will suffice. Both rooms have flowers and memory books. I don't want a circus, but I don't wish to deny dear friends an opportunity to grieve with us.' The limo slid onto the driveway and stopped at the front of the large complex. Down the hill, the children were standing quietly with their parents. People gathered with them. Jessie let out an involuntary moan. 'I can't bear to see the children.' Her voice was strained. 'Why are people here so early? This is our time!'

'It's alright, Jessie. The staff know not to open their doors before six.'

The funeral staff stood outside, waiting for the family. Henley spoke with them while Jessie and Robert followed the signs for Justin Tyler. Each of the three rooms had portable stands with Justin's name. On the last, where Justin lay, his name was printed in brass letters. Jessie stopped at the first room and grabbed the wall for support. She could go no farther.

Robert's legs threatened to give out when he entered the third room where Justin's body was exposed in front of a wall of blue roses. *Is there a chance Justin might have been yours?* The question wound its way around Robert's heart as he neared the casket. Robert wiped away tears with the back of his hand. He studied Justin as though he'd never taken full measure of the boy. Justin lay as still as marble and as beautiful as an angel. The ache in Robert's heart was foreign. Most of his life he had reacted to his own hurt. The ache grew for the boy he never knew. Separated in death from the Henleys, Justin was just himself. That's who Robert saw, a child who might have been his, a boy he abandoned. On the last day of his life, Robert hadn't made any real effort to connect with Justin. He'd allowed the boy's indifference to be matched by his own. He hadn't even said 'good night' to him. Fractured memories ran across his brain. Robert stood very still. At the last minute, he bent over and kissed Justin's forehead. It was as cold as death. 'Good night,' he whispered.

Geoffrion was inside the funeral complex. He was there to observe Tyler. The man he saw leave the viewing room was not the man in the interrogation room. Tyler stood alone quietly in the doorway, lost in thought and grief. Geoffrion did his best to steer away from gut feelings, but he was human. Had Tyler shown any of this emotion the night his son died, he might not be there. First reaction was key for this cop. No matter what the circumstances, Tyler's first reaction was flat and suspect. What was this sudden grief, he wondered? Murderers felt grief. He'd seen it, especially those who had neatly convinced themselves of their innocence. Who was Tyler grieving for? That was the question. Their eyes met.

It was Robert who spoke. 'Could you not leave me alone for the wake?'

'I'm doing my job, Mr. Tyler.' Geoffrion saw that Jessie Henley had not gone into the viewing room with her husband. Her absence suggested that her accusation still stood.

Robert brushed past him. When he found Jessie, he whispered, 'Justin is yours now, Jess. There was never any question about that.' He added quickly. 'He loved you most—go to him.' Robert walked with Jessie until they reached the room. She left him by the door and went to her son.

Down the hall, Henley was taking charge. The children and their parents were admitted first. Easily close to three hundred people had come to pay their respects. The lines went back to the bottom of the hill. Henley had hired three security guards to keep reporters at a distance.

Jessie neither heard them nor saw any of the mourners, not even when some were admitted and accompanied by Henley into the room. She sat rigidly on the edge of her chair with one hand against Justin's cheek. Her legs were drawn tightly together. Her intelligent eyes never left Justin, but she could not have told anyone later what he wore that day. She was steadfast in this passionate singular grief. Those who saw the mother and child wept as much for Jessie Henley as they did for her boy, because they knew her soul was in the casket with her son. For the next night there was no change in Jessie. In her woe, she sat quiet and lonely.

Geoffrion did not come the second night.

The children were unhappy. They wanted to see Justin. They wanted to see a dead person. Their parents left relieved. At nine, both evenings, Henley joined Jessie and together they bid farewell to the family hope. All the while, Justin was far away from all the chaos of grief. His journey had begun the night he died. The little prince was gone.

* * *

The private funeral at St. Peter's Anglican Church on Laird Boulevard in the Town did not have the rigid guidelines or the separate camps visible to a keen observer like Detective Geoffrion. On Tuesday morning, he stood well behind the forty invited friends. Henley and Jessie and Robert all sat in the same pew. The only jarring moment occurred when the brass casket was wheeled onto a red carpet at the front of the church. When Jessie spotted the color, she saw the red floor at the morgue. Digging her nails into her father's arm, she shrieked. 'Get Justin off that carpet!' Church assistants appeared and rolled up the offending carpet and took it with them. Once it was gone, Jessie settled into a grieving numbness.

Henley said a few words for Justin. Fatigue and the finality of the moment softened family tensions. He ended his eulogy simply. He looked at Jessie, and his voice trembled as he spoke. 'If love could have kept our boy with us, none of us would be here today. Eight summers is not enough. It's not even a solid start at life. Justin was still missing some of his second teeth.'

Chapter Thirty-Six

STEVE AND DONNA SPOKE at length to a psychiatrist entrusted with Colin's care. Steve described the terrible tragedy and Colin's part in it. In the best interest of the boy, the physician decided that Colin was physically able and should go home with his parents. He advised them to keep a careful eye on their son and he set up dates and times for additional counselling. On Tuesday morning, the day Justin's casket was placed beside his grandmother Leslie's in the family mausoleum in Mount Royal Cemetery, Colin Sharpe went home.

To reassure his son, Steve had spent a lot of time explaining to Colin what Wasserman had told him. Colin listened carefully and a subtle change came over him. He sat up straight, he squared his small shoulders. 'Even if I kicked Justin? What if I kicked him a second time?' Colin asked eagerly in a hoarse voice.

'You had a right to go home, but kicking is never right, Colin. Intending to hurt anyone is never right. But you're not going to jail. Son, this terrible tragedy is over. You're home safe with us. Try not to think about what happened.'

'Maybe the kids won't think I'm a wimp if I beat Justin.'

What the hell is wrong with kids today? My father would have given me a good smack across the head. 'Colin, Justin is dead. Nobody won. Mom and I almost lost you too, son. You're not a wimp, but there's nothing here to be proud of either. If you had obeyed house rules, both of you would be fine today. Do you see that?'

'Some kids think I'm a wimp. Justin pushed me down once at school. I didn't fight back. All the kids laughed. I won't say anything when I go back to school. If Scott asks me, I'm going to tell him. He's my friend,' Colin said boldly.

The mild tranquilizers the psychiatrist had ordered were on the night table. Steve itched to slap sense into Colin. 'It's time for your medication. Remember, Colin, none of what happened makes you brave.' He handed the boy a glass of water and one pill. This abrupt change in Colin's mood worried Steve. Colin's defiance, *I'm going to tell him*, was such a rapid change from his self-destructive act of a few days ago. Steve saw that the psychological counselling was necessary and not just protocol. How could Colin be proud that his friend was dead and he a part of that tragedy? A shiver ran up Steve's back when he recalled a more chilling statement Colin had made. *We just wanted to use his stuff. He had everything.*

Colin took the pill without another word and lay back down on his bed. When his father left, he lay back and studied his ceiling. Colin pumped a small fist in the air. He was just like Superman—he couldn't die! And he wasn't going to jail!

Moitié had done some digging while Geoffrion was securing his court order for the blood samples. Moitié discovered from the boys' cell phone logs that Justin Tyler hadn't called anyone. Colin Sharpe had called *him* Wednesday night and, he figured, had invited himself over. It was the boy's second lie. *Le p'tit crosseur* (The little fucker)! Being lied to wasn't something new for him, but it wearied Moitié and raised his hackles, especially when it was a kid. He got off his chair and stretched to ease the pressure in his back. He opened one of his desk drawers and lifted out the *Criminal Code* and read a line he always disputed. *A person under 12 years of age is incapable, as a matter of law, of committing a criminal offence.* The *excuse of infancy* was the actual term of law.

He remembered he was the same age when he was confirmed, the Catholic idea of the age of reason. He knew right from wrong at Colin's age. Today, he snapped aloud, 'The age is twelve for confirmation!' He kicked over his wastepaper basket and picked it back up. It angered and astonished him what kids got away with, and their parents backed them. *Dad would have gotten the truth out of me, one way or another.* Moitié rubbed his eyes and his temples and felt better after his little rant. Colin Sharpe had tried to hang himself. The attempt might have ended fatally. He knew that. The cop in him prevailed. Just the same, he intended to get the truth from the boy. He was not about to stand idle while a little killer walked off. Moitié wasn't looking for gold bars—he was doing his job. He knew the boy was home. *I'll spot him a few days, but I'll be back with more questions when we hear from forensics.*

Neither of Geoffrion's calls was welcome Wednesday morning. Jocelyne Thibeau, chief crime technician, was thorough and hated to be bothered before she had all the evidence. The divorced mother of an eighteen-year-old son could handle Geoffrion. Anyone over forty brave enough to have her nose pierced and wear stiletto heels with tight black leather pants under her white lab coat was not about to let a career detective bully her. 'Jean, I need your samples.'

'What about the prints on the safe?'

 Her mood was good so she decided to placate the cop. 'None matching Tyler, but we did find cotton fibers, two of them. You might be looking at gloves, a dust cloth, part of a shirt. Something cheap and white.'

'I'll check into that. What about the shoulder bruising?'

'Not completed. I can say that there are at least two bruises on each shoulder, perhaps more. Unfortunately, they bled into one another. We couldn't lift any fingerprints from the body.'

'Lead you to believe they were made by feet?'

'Feet or palms or both.'

'Can't you guys tell one from the other? You're the experts.'

'Can't manufacture what's not there, Detective.'

'Thought you worked miracles, Jocelyne?'

'The book on me has been greatly exaggerated.'

'The water bottle?'

The 'spect picked it up more than once and rubbed the side with a thumb. We have a partial on the palm, a good partial nonetheless. You didn't catch that yourself?'

'No, rank beginner's error! I guess the book on me is a crock as well.'

'Lighten up. Get the samples down here. We have something,' she chimed, pleased with herself.

'The kid's nails?'

'No, too much chlorine. We do have a single dark hair found near the safe.'

'You'll have the samples ASAP.' Only two people in that house had dark hair, Tyler and Sylvie, the maid. He made the second call to Tyler. Robert told him to contact a Doug Hoye and he gave him his number. 'You could make this so much easier than going through a court order.'

'And get caught in another interrogation box because the regular room is being used? Do you think I'm an amateur? Henley is behind this undue pressure, but I see it as harassment, Detective Geoffrion.'

'No one pressures me, Sir. I'll have the court order by the end of the day or tomorrow morning at the latest.'

'I guess you'd better get to work then. When you learn that I did not hurt my son, I will expect an apology.'

'I have never apologized for doing my job.' Tyler had just given Geoffrion additional reason to keep up the pressure.

Robert hung up. A blizzard of angry fearful emotions swirled around in his chest.

Chapter Thirty-seven

WAITING FOR GEOFFRION's call colored the rest of Robert's day but he heard nothing more from the cop. He felt stuck in a tar pit. Late Wednesday afternoon, he wanted to call Carmen after he confirmed his plans for Toronto, hoping she might go with him. His cell was open when Henley summoned him upstairs, but he snapped it shut and braced himself. Whether Robert felt his end was at hand, or whether he decided to take a stand against the odds, he knew where he wanted to go. It was more a question now of who could stop him.

Jessie sat beside her father, remote and void of any emotion he could discern. 'Robert, sit. Now that the obsequies of Justin's death are behind us, we've made some decisions.'

Jessie winced. Robert saw the strain because he was looking at her and not at Henley.

'You've made them, Douglas?'

'Yes, I did. You can see that Jessie isn't up to that task and with reason.'

'What have you decided?'

'Jessie will come and stay with me until the investigation is complete.'

'I want the pool drained,' she whispered determinedly to her father.

Robert's palms dampened. 'Douglas, Jessie's your daughter, but she's also my wife. I want to speak to her alone. You owe me that privacy, and Jessie owes me some time. I've stood by and allowed you both to conduct the funeral and the investigation against me as though I were some junkyard dog waiting for scraps. I have to speak to Jessie because, from what I gather, I might not have that opportunity for quite a while.'

Henley was about to refuse, when Jessie spoke. 'I can do this, Dad.'

'I'll be outside then, Jessie, if you need me.'

'No, Douglas, I'd rather you left the house and gave us an hour. That's not too much to ask. You may own the place, but I've maintained it. Your constant presence has prevented Jessie and me from simply talking to one another or comforting one another.'

Jessie didn't argue the point, so Henley rose. He had never been dismissed and walked stiffly from the room. 'I'll be back in *one* hour.' The words sounded like a threat.

Robert waited until he heard the door close. Jessie sat rooted in silence. Robert sat across from her. 'I'm glad we have this time. Losing Justin is an agony that you'll never get over, I understand that, Jessie. If I could relive that night...'

'But you can't,' Jessie added quickly.

'I accept you'll never forgive me. The three of us, you, me and Justin were loosely tied together in something resembling a family. Justin's death has severed whatever that was. I saw that the day you told me you didn't want me in the room with you and Justin at the funeral home.' He saw Jessie's eyes tear, but he didn't think the tears were for him. 'It doesn't matter to me now whether you ever loved me. We lived very different lives. I never gave much thought as to whether I was happy. I was busy with work and your life was always full too.' His nostrils knotted up. 'This investigation shut us both down.'

'Why did you stay?' Jessie sat up, slighted and irritated. Her mouth tightened.

'In the first years, love, but less after I moved downstairs. I loved the part of you I could never have. I lost hope for us along the way. You're Douglas's girl. I was an addition.'

'I loved you.' Jessie's face softened.

'As best you could, Jess, but support and affirmation came from Douglas. Unconditional love went to Justin. Wasn't much left for me.'

'You were jealous of Justin?' she mocked.

'I guess I was. Of Douglas too, for that matter.'

'You can't just walk out, Robert, not after I've just lost Justin?' Her voice hardened into defiance and disbelief.

'You want my life for Justin's. Isn't that your crusade? You and Douglas have humiliated me and you're trying to destroy me. You think I should stand by and watch that happen?'

'What about honesty, Robert?' Jessie shifted topics again.

'Try me.' Turns in their conversation were easy for Robert because he was calm.

'Did you get into the safe?'

'At times over the years, when you were out, I did stand in front of it and tried a few combinations. I figured you hid the combination somewhere near the safe, so I searched for it. I always vacuumed that damn carpet to hide my tracks when I left. Did you memorize the combination? Why *did* you cut me out of your will? Why bother with the codicil. After twelve years, I learned I'll never see any of your money. Know what, none of this shit matters now.'

'You didn't answer the question.'

'No, I didn't get into the safe, but Geoffrion is getting a court order for my hair and blood samples, thanks to you.' Robert saw and enjoyed the alarm in Jessie's eyes. He knew the reason for it. 'Answer my question, Jessie. What more are *you* hiding that had to be locked away from me?'

Jessie stiffened like marble. Robert's blood test would expose the second document and her own secret. Her cheeks drained of what little color they had. 'You won't believe my answer any more than I believed yours. You should reconsider leaving me so soon after we buried our son.'

'For appearances, you mean?'

'To see if Colin is responsible for Justin's death. He did try to hang himself. Maybe we can settle things between us.'

'Justin drowned accidentally, Jessie.' Robert didn't want to settle things.

'I'll never accept that. He was too good a swimmer.'

'An Olympian swimmer drowned some years back at his parents' summer home.'

'I don't care about someone I didn't know.'

Stung by the threat of exposure, Jessie had no idea where the next question came from. It might have sprung from a common involuntary reflex. 'Is there someone else?' she asked pointedly, a trace of pain and incredulity in her question. Jessie turned to Robert and eyed him with a new scrutiny.

'I hope there will be, for you too.'

'Damn you.' Stunned by the finality of Robert's response, her breaths quickened. She rubbed her hands together as though she were cold. 'She's not the first, is she?'

'Haven't we hurt one another enough as it is?'

'She's not, then?'

'How about you, Jessie? Have you been my true and faithful wife? How does that go, *forsaking all others*? At least admit the irony. Sex was the one place we were good, and we managed to ruin that too.' Robert couldn't continue to taunt Jessie because he understood the implication behind every word. Justin's paternity had to stay a dirty little secret. He had to bank on her fervid need to keep it hidden.

'From the start, you knew what you were getting into.' Jessie could distort facts and she was very good at separation. It was inconceivable to her that Robert would think of leaving. She had every right to know what had happened to Justin. He was the reason for the investigation. Though Robert was its target, she felt he should understand and accept the reason for it. As her husband, she'd fully expected him to stand by her.

Robert was forthright in his response. 'I've heard that expression before, but I didn't know what I was getting into. I wasn't familiar with the Henley kingdom and its pecking order.'

'He's my father, family.'

'I'm your husband.'

'You never understood about family because you didn't really have one.'

'Not even when I had you and Justin. Jessie, come out to the pool with me. I'd like to have a last look at the water Justin loved and the water that took his life. Once you drain the pool, you'll lose another small part of him.' Jessie made a slight move. 'Come on, Jessie, come with me. Let's have some token memorial together, put aside what we did to one another for a minute.' He reached for her hand and Jessie went with him. She'd lost her fight. They stood together where the tape had been and looked into the blue water. 'Justin loved it here.'

Jessie strengthened her grip on Robert's hand. 'Don't leave me, Robert.' He heard no pleading, no forgiveness and no tears. Not even a threat, just a short sentence without any emotion.

'Douglas will probably decide to sell the house. He'll want you to stay in Westmount with him and you will. You won't come back here. You're already leaving.' It was Robert's turn to tighten his grip on her hand. 'Jess, it's time, for me and for you, time to leave without added rancor.' Seconds later, he slipped his hand from hers and left Jessie by the pool. Robert was pleased with his performance. He'd been kind, gentle, calm, non-accusatory, and at the end he'd exhibited a profound sorrow that was undeniable. Brushing aside the imminent threat she held over him, Robert stood straighter. He'd definitely been the dominant figure in the conversation. His words had been alarmingly simple. A power he'd felt with other women when it was easy to feel superior, had come to him as he spoke with Jessie. He stood at the patio door and waited for her to come back inside with him.

Jessie stayed at the pool, staring into water. She hadn't worn shoes, and in shorts and a sleeveless top, she looked very young. For as long as she could recall, her life had been a social performance without an apparent miscue. Her secret had kept her power intact. Losing it meant a loss of that power and stature. Jessie was Douglas Henley's glamorous, accomplished daughter, the golden girl with the beautiful son, the daring young woman who had titillated the wealthy enclave by going outside the gilded gates to choose a husband. What a tragic blunder it had been to put those papers in her safe and what a price she'd pay for it! When the paternity document and the blood test came to light, she'd become the laughing stock of the social circuit. Loss of face was the reason multi-millionaires threw themselves in front of trains or shot themselves in the head. That devastating shame was incomprehensible to someone like Robert who had come at life from the other end of the spectrum. Justin would have understood, Jessie felt, if she explained it to him. Justin had been a Henley.

Shielding her eyes from the distorting sun, Jessie turned to find Robert waiting for her. The burden of her secret was hiding it and living through troubled hours with the gnawing feeling that it might escape and become tawdry gossip for the Westmount elite. The secret could destroy her life. Robert had had a few days to live with the idea that Jessie could produce a motive for him murdering Justin. He had rehearsed his response to the test result, a pretended shock and sense of unmitigated betrayal that he felt he could pull off. Jessie's shock, he saw, was immediate and bare. It was odd, Robert thought, to know exactly what Jessie was thinking. She would ask her father to impede the investigation, and that was precisely what he wanted her to do. Could Henley actually abort an ongoing investigation? Did he wield that much power?

Chapter Thirty-eight

Henley did not walk up and down Dumfries and Dobie Avenues in his brown cotton pants and white shirt like some schoolboy expelled from class. He called Mike Fortier to see if he had been able to discover the identity of the woman he'd seen Robert with in St-Eustache.

'The office was an easy walk-in. You don't forget seventeen years of undercover work. Her name is Carmen DiMaggio. She's a sales rep for some company that sells security grilles. I have her business card and I pulled a favor from the grandson of an old friend. Robert has made two calls to DiMaggio. I did see them hugging and the woman did stand and watch him drive away. Is there any chance this is a business deal, Douglas?'

'Robert's company has nothing to do with grilles. He's high-end specialty gifts and he has no new stores in the offing. I'm taking Jessie home with me, but maintain the tail and keep me posted.' Henley's cheeks flushed with anger. *Robert's talking up some woman at such a time and then trying to throw something away!* Henley was livid. *When I take this evidence to the police, I want better than the Haitian cop. I want Geoffrion on the case.* There was a grim satisfaction to his anger because Robert was its target. Why had Jessie been so careless with those papers? He'd always had such pride and confidence in her, but he was unforgiving with stupidity. For that moment, his anger spread to Jessie and he felt no pity for her, then shuddered with these unsettling thoughts. The air around him was still and quiet, untouched by his turmoil. He gazed skyward into a slow-moving network of milky blue that stretched across his line of vision.

A shriek of joy tore into the quiet and startled him as he searched for its source. A young boy, no more than four, came whizzing down his driveway on a new red and white tricycle. No one was supervising the boy. Henley ran to stop him, fearing the child might ride into the street. He grabbed one of the handlebars and stopped the bike.

The boy looked up terrified at first, but hotly indignant in the next second. 'This is my bike!' he pronounced with unflinching pride and a bolt of energy. His cheeks flared and his eyes widened with youthful defiance. His hands gripped the handle bars.

For an instant, Douglas wanted to scoop the boy up and run away with him. His desperate urge was so powerful that his other hand came forward, but he let go of the bike. 'You have to be careful. Never drive onto the road. It's a great bike.'

The boy had clearly forgotten the rules about talking to strangers because he had something else to say. 'I know how to stop.' The boy was too young to know of danger.

'Good for you!' Henley walked away, but stopped abruptly a few feet on, for he heard another voice as piercing as the boy's. *I know how to swim!* Henley knew with unequivocal certainty that Justin's death was no accident. His eyes reddened with tears and he moaned audibly for the boy he had lost. Justin's death had been a betrayal of Jessie's dreams, but of his as well. Losing his grandson had denied him of his vicarious male immortality. He wiped his eyes quickly and called Fortier. 'Where are you?'

'Almost back in TMR in case Robert decides to go out tonight.'

'Good, meet me at Dumfries and Dobie. What I have to say won't take much time.' Henley looked back at the boy's house, but he had disappeared. He paced and checked his watch every three minutes. When he finally saw Fortier pulling up alongside him, he slipped into the car before it had come to a complete stop. Douglas's jaw was rigid.

'What's happened?'

'Hear me out, Mike. I have my doubts about the investigation. My grandson is gone. He was in Robert's care.' His proposition was simple and lucrative. '… I don't want anything to happen to Robert until Jessie is back on her feet.' Douglas turned to Fortier waiting for his reaction. 'It doesn't have to be you. I need a name.'

Fortier's face was grave and offended. He said pointedly, 'Don't go there, Douglas. Don't ever go there.'

The men sat in awkward silence.

'Do you still want me to tail Robert?'

'Yes.' Without another word, Henley left and walked back to Jessie's in a self-imposed contained dignity and rage.

It would have been wise for Robert to exercise restraint when he was back in his quarters, but the exhilaration of taking the lead from Jessie caused him a surge of confidence. He felt lighter, formidable really and free! Laying caution aside, he called Carmen at work. She was unavailable, so he left his message on her voicemail. 'It's Robert. Hope you're having a good day! I know it's already Thursday, but my business meeting is on for Saturday. Is there any chance you might want to come with me till Sunday? No strings, just good company. We can go slowly. Things are much better for me. You have my cell number.' He felt good about the call too. The desperation in his voice was gone. If Carmen didn't go with him, well, he'd go alone. He showered and changed. He was charged with energy.

Guilt and the sense of failure of the last eight days evaporated when he told Jessie he was leaving. He knew that she might not take him at his word because he'd caught her off-guard. Arguments and recriminations and lasting bitterness were sure to follow, but he felt he could stand outside their assault. She might be glad to be rid of him when she thought things over. He would be a constant and guilty reminder of Justin. Excluding him at the funeral home and leaving the house with her father initiated the process and indicated the way she was thinking. He thought about going back upstairs and explaining that to her, but his cell rang and he grabbed it.

'Robert, Detective Geoffrion has a court order and wants you at Crémazie tomorrow at ten. There was little I could do about this, sorry. You said you were prepared for this eventuality, right, Robert?'

Robert's lips stretched across his teeth. He was not impervious to the minefield he'd hoped to avoid.

'Are you there?'

'Unfortunately. Monday would have been more palatable. Probably another well-timed gaucherie on my part but I told Jessie that I was leaving her because she'd given me little choice. She's running scared, so I think she'll recant her allegation against me to conceal the parentage issue. Actually, she doesn't want me to leave, not now at least. Failing that, she'll urge Douglas to impede the investigation. To save face, she's hoping the case settles on Colin.'

'Was your decision to leave a ploy to have her stall the case?'

'No, it wasn't. Douglas is taking Jessie with him to Westmount. I figure they'll put this place on the market. Before I'm summarily evicted, I wanted to make the first move. Didn't expect Jessie to ask me to stay.'

Get to the test tomorrow, Robert. Once a complaint is lodged with the police, it's very difficult, actually rare, to have the complaint dropped.'

'What about Douglas's influence? I'm counting on that, Doug.' The desperation was back.

'Times have changed. The cops are afraid of lawsuits. They drop the charge against you and discover later that you're guilty, they're liable.'

'But I'm not!'

'This is an explanation. Cops don't want to take the chance you are. Henley might have a better chance of bringing his influence to bear before the case is presented to the crown prosecutor. Once he or she has it, your chances fall dramatically. He's the king. Female's the queen, and they don't waffle for the same reason—litigation.'

'Great!'

'DNA will take weeks, months in run-of-the-mill files, so Henley has time to manoeuver.'

'Doesn't change that I have to appear tomorrow.'

''Fraid not.'

'What about the codicil. I never saw the damn thing. How much can it hurt me?'

'Another piece.'

'Shit!'

My advice is to make some peace with your wife, think things over and play nice and understanding.'

'What about my pride?'

'Swallow it.' Before Hoye hung up, he heard Robert swear again and he was satisfied he'd take his advice.

Carmen listened to her voicemail, thought about the weekend and the housecleaning she could avoid. Caitlin was off to New York for a summer conference. There was the casino, but there was Robert. She wanted to see Robert.

He was shoring himself up for a retreat with Jessie when his cell rang. One glance at Caller ID and he shut both doors before he opened his phone.

'Offer still good?' Carmen played it light.

Robert's mood had changed and he wished he hadn't made the call. Fortier was still out there. His voice was tense. 'Hi! Of course it is, but if you'd rather have more time, I'm okay with that. If we're on, we'll keep things simple. I'll send the ticket to your office tomorrow and meet you at the gate. The flight's at eight. I have lots of prep to do and I may arrive at the last minute. Sorry for the bum's rush, but I want everything to go well with the sale.'

'You might be better off alone. Are you sure you want company?' Carmen had expected more enthusiasm. Her mood flattened.

'I am. It's just that I've been on the phone all morning.'

'You can change your mind, but let me know by tonight. You can email me the boarding pass. You have my business card. It'll make things easier. Sorry, I have another call.'

'I won't. See you tomorrow night.'

'Alright.' Carmen hardly recognized the harried voice on the other end of the phone. Robert was very different from the man she'd been with at the St-Sulpice. The thrill of the weekend ahead wilted. A voice Carmen chose not to hear told her to call back and cancel. The one she did hear was familiar. *I'd like to see what happens.*

The chagrin Henley harbored against Jessie fell away when he found her in the dining room, sitting forlornly at the end of the table. He could see from where he stood that her beautiful face was eaten up with grief, a mother's vulnerable grief. A small crystal glass of ice cider was untouched. Jessie's head was cradled in her hand, her fingers buried in her hair as she studied the only portrait of Justin in the room. Henley always felt there was something stilted about the casual pose. The boy stood on a dock with Lake Muskoka behind him. The mop of blonde hair he'd gotten from Jessie falling across his eyes was eerily real. The determined set of his mouth seemed more angry than casual. The stance itself was incongruous to Henley. Justin never stood five seconds on the dock before diving into the water. Looking up at the portrait, Henley expected Justin to turn and dive into the lake. He walked quietly into the room and laid his hands on Jessie's shoulders, rubbed them and kissed her cheek. 'Do you need help packing?'

'Robert's leaving me.'

* * *

Following Doug's advice, Robert steeled himself for a recanting of his own. Before he reached the top of the stairs, he was already sweating. The rapid-fire shift of emotions was taking its toll. His forehead creased when he heard Jessie's comment which meant Henley was back. A quick glance at his watch infuriated him. *He didn't even give us an hour!* And there he was, solid as a stone angel guarding his daughter. He could afford to indulge her grief for years and he would. 'Douglas, I'd like a minute with Jessie.' He had no energy for anger and spoke gently.

Jessie turned to him. 'My father doesn't have to go anywhere. You're the one who's leaving.'

'We're all under great stress. I may have spoken too quickly. Between the accident, my negligence and the investigation, my thoughts are a mess. We should both take a few days to rest and calm down. I have to report to the police for the tests tomorrow.'

Robert expected the conspiratorial look that passed between Douglas and Jessie. 'That's a squalid excuse distressing to Jessie.'

'Douglas, if you had given Jessie and me a chance to cope with this tragedy together…'

'Leave my father out of this. Justin was always safe with him.' Her words echoed across the room with contempt.

No one said another word before Jessie and Douglas left.

Chapter Thirty-nine

HENLEY HAD HIS DRIVER shut the interior window inside the limo. Jessie was on edge and shifting on her seat every few seconds. 'You have to stop the tests, Dad. I can't face the damage they'll do. I can't cope with losing Justin.' She rubbed her eyes with the ball of her fists. 'I'm not sure Robert got into the safe. He wasn't nervous about the tests, just angry. Why risk what little I have left? Colin tried to hang himself. Everything points to him, doesn't it? I've been out of my head since Justin died.'

Henley turned on the intercom. 'Richard, forget the bottleneck on Décarie. Take Côte-St-Catherine Road down to Westmount.' He flipped it off.

'Are you listening to me, Dad? It's no good reiterating what I should have or should not have done with those documents.' She raised her hands in an imploring gesture. 'It's hard enough that I know what I've done.'

'I'm listening, Jessie.' Henley was running the evidence Fortier had on Robert, wondering if he should share it with Jessie.

'Since Justin died, I've been afraid. The fear began when I saw him lying by the pool and it hasn't let up. At first, I wanted to be with Justin, but I'm afraid of dying.' Jessie shook her head sadly. 'Just not brave enough. The dread is worse at night. I'm afraid to move in bed. I still see that red floor when I close my eyes and I can smell the plastic from the morgue when I open them. Just the idea of those test results sends a nauseous wave of panic through my stomach. Please do something. I might be able to sleep if Colin is responsible for Justin. I wouldn't have to live every day knowing I helped kill my own son.'

'I fully appreciate what a good name means and the devastation caused when it's lost. Are you saying that if the police found evidence against Robert, you'd recant your allegation to avoid your own guilt?'

Jessie sat bolt upright and turned to her father. 'I've assumed there *was* nothing. What have you kept from me?' Her legs felt clammy and the stretch-limo claustrophobic. Her breaths were quick and shallow.

'I wanted to wait until I had something definite before I told you.'

'Are you saying there is nothing then, Dad?'

'It's Fortier and it's not much.'

'I don't care, tell me.'

'He followed Robert and saw him trying to dispose of something, changing his mind and probably getting rid of it somewhere else.'

'Does he know what it was?'

'No.'

'For God's sake, that's nothing.'

'Robert drove out to meet a woman.'

'And Fortier caught them together?' Her voice was thin and nervous.

'He spoke briefly to her and he's called her twice.'

'Was it sex, is that it?'

'Actually, no. We're just beginning the investigation. We don't have much.'

'You have nothing then. Robert might have been getting rid of Kleenex and decided to hang onto it. He spoke to a woman, he called her. It could have been business.'

'Why are you defending him?'

'For our inner circle, the people who count, Robert was Justin's father. I don't want that to change.'

'The results will take weeks. Why not give Fortier and the police time to investigate Robert and then I'll work at delaying the process? If we stop the investigation now, we'll never know if he was involved.'

'I can't sleep with this over my head. I'm stumbling around during the day. Justin lost his life, but he still has his name, an identity that I won't have ridiculed. I don't want to be put in a fish bowl either. I'm trying to survive, Dad.'

Henley saw Jessie was fighting a moment of panic as she gulped back tears. Her self-absorption, the fear of her own personal shame, depressed him because there was a loneliness in it that he recognized in himself. 'I'll see what I can do,' he said, resignedly.

Jessie slumped against the seat and all conversation stopped.

Thursday afternoon, Moitié told Geoffrion about the Sharpe kid having made the phone calls to Justin Tyler. 'I can talk to the kid at the house.'

'He's just home from the hospital. You don't have a smoking gun here. I want the test results. You don't have kids. Lying is a way of life

194

to most of them. The Sharpe kid was nervous and afraid he was in trouble. What we do have is cheap cotton fiber.' He checked his notes. 'I'll call the housekeeper, Sylvie Drouin. I'll use the speaker phone so you can take notes if necessary.'

Sylvie was packing more wasted food that she herself could use. No one had eaten much of anything in the past week, but she'd kept fresh food coming in case the family did eat. When Sylvie saw that it was Detective Geoffrion calling, she took one quick breath and picked up the phone. 'The Tyler residence.'

'Mademoiselle Drouin? '

'Yes.'

'Detective Geoffrion. I have just a few questions, Mademoiselle Drouin. What are your duties at the Tyler house?'

'I cook, I clean and I shop and keep the house accounts.' She tapped her foot nervously against a counter.

'Every room of the house, including the master bedroom?'

'Of course.'

'What do you use for polishing or dusting?'

'My cotton gloves and blue or white dusters.'

'Have you ever cleaned around the safe?'

'Never! Miss Henley takes care of that herself.'

'Would you pack up one pair of gloves and any white cotton cleaning material and give them to an officer I'll send out to the house?'

'I hope I've done nothing wrong. I'm very meticulous about the things I use and purchase for the house.' As she made this declaration, Sylvie ran her hand across the counter looking for dust.

'I'm sure you are. The officer will be there within the hour.'

Sylvie was trembling when she hung up. In the cleaning closet she found two white dusters and pulled out the opened box of gloves. She took one pair and counted the rest. *It's odd. I should have nine pairs and I have only eight. I suppose Miss Henley might have taken a pair.* Sylvie counted the gloves a second time and went looking for the missing pair she might have left in a room, with all the sad confusion and cooking of the last eight days. *I can't see Miss Henley cleaning this week. She could barely move. All the same, I will ask her.* Sylvie was comfortable when things were in their proper places. It was her responsibility to keep the household books. She'd feel better when the gloves were found or accounted for. It was a question of order.

Geoffrion was of the same opinion as Sylvie after the call. 'Odds are Henley didn't take the gloves, and Sylvie doesn't go to the safe. We might have found a fiber match. I knew the will wasn't news to Tyler. I knew it the day I asked him the question. This should be interesting. He's coming in tomorrow.'

'Don't discount *mon p'tit crosseur*! I haven't.'

'You should have kids. You'd know more.'

'You think? Parents don't want to see that their kids are capable of malice. You're gunning for Tyler because we can't do dick about the kid under the law. No stars if he's guilty, no coverage. Tyler is your gold case.' Moitié wasn't sure of that angle. The kid's suicide attempt was serious. In Moitié's experience, fear of discovery was a principal factor in suicides. Kids were people, just smaller.

Geoffrion ignored the jabs because they had hit the mark. He had Tyler in his sights and was secretly exultant with the promise of this big case. He was disappointed the kid was involved because the resolution would have a flat end and Moitié was the lead. If he made the case against Tyler, his reputation would rise to remarkable heights among his superiors. 'I'm still of the opinion that there's something off with Tyler, quite apart from the family treatment of him. I want to find out what.' Geoffrion was stubbornly determined he had a case against Tyler.

Both cops were cautious. The case was high profile and it was being closely scrutinized by their superiors. Failure was not in their vocabulary, but they also recognized the problems with two probables. Neither suspect was receiving the full attention of both detectives. In the end, it didn't matter how they slanted their views. A case was solved on what they could prove.

Robert's nerves knotted. The Henleys' departure hadn't produced the relief he had counted on. In fact, he felt a worsening misery. He paced, restless and irritable. He flexed his legs to keep them from twitching. Would Henley stop the goddamn tests before tomorrow? That's what he wanted to know. He needed to calm down, but his nerves were jumping. Would the Toronto sale and the hidden money go through as he'd planned, and skip the dreaded 'X' factor? The thought of tomorrow's tests dug into him. The air was dry and heavy.

Was Carmen a mistake? He needed someone, a friendly face. He wasn't above admitting that, but he felt there was a tail on him. He'd need a plan before he headed for the airport. A hot shower hadn't helped. Then Robert thought of something that would.

Sylvie had the items neatly packaged and checked her watch, hoping the police would get to the house before she was forced to stay late. Should she tell Robert? She knew he had been questioned by the police, but he paid her salary, she liked him and he deserved to know. She was about to shout down to him when the bell rang. Surely he'd hear it. Instead of alerting Robert, she hurried to the door. The hand-off to the police officer took only seconds. Sylvie walked back to Robert's door and called down, but got no answer. *How did he get out without me seeing him?* Should she leave him a note? Sylvie headed to the kitchen to write one and to fetch a glass of spring water as she always did before leaving. She had taken only a single gulp when the glass slipped from her hand and crashed on the floor. Water splashed all around her and up her legs. Robert hadn't left the house. He was outside swimming laps in the pool.

Chapter Forty

EN ROUTE, JESSIE OPENED her purse, took out an Ativan and swallowed it. Now that her father was taking care of the investigation, she could fall back into her grief, a close companion that comforted her. Along the way, she kept her eyes closed.

From time to time, Henley looked over at his daughter. With the aftershocks of Justin's death and the ongoing investigation, he still found himself amazed that the lovely creature beside him was his daughter. Under great stress and unfathomable sadness, vulnerability had added a gentler tinge to the beauty he saw in her. Her bare arms were sculpted but delicate, her hands folded like a young girl. Her face, though taut with resolve, was unlined and feminine. When he saw her take the tranquilizer, he leaned closer and whispered, 'Jessie, don't take too many of those things. They're addictive.'

'I need what help I can get, Dad.' When the limo reached The Boulevard, Jessie sat up and regarded the elegant mansions and hundred-year-old trees that bordered the street without seeing them. Pangs of abandonment had crept into her heart. She had left the home where Justin lived, where he died, where his belongings lay. A shiver shook her shoulders. A connection had been severed. She felt an anxious need to reconnect and shifted on her seat.

'Are you all right? We're almost there.'

When the limo slid to a stop on the circular driveway, Jessie's head drooped and she moaned involuntarily. She looked at the mansion sideways and said ruefully, 'This is the first time I'll go into this house and Justin won't be here either. I don't know if I can.'

'Let me help you.' Henley held Jessie under her arms. He could tell she was fighting him.

They were greeted at the door by one of the two housekeepers. The women here wore uniforms, navy pleated dresses with small white collars. One, a sturdy woman of sixty, handed Henley a pad of notes. 'Mr. Henley, these are just a few of the calls. I've left a list of the others in your study.'

Henley took the pad without comment. The call he was about to make occupied his thoughts. 'I'd like a whisky, Patricia, if you would.'

Jessie had gone up the rounded oak staircase to her room midway down the hall. Closing the door behind her, she reached into her purse for her cell and dialed Robert's number. When she had no answer, she felt a ripple of nerves. Where was he? She checked her watch. They had only been gone half an hour, give or take. She tried the house phone. Sylvie was locking the side door and was about to leave when she heard the phone and ran back for it. 'Sylvie, I'm glad I caught you. Is Robert there? I can't get a hold of him.'

Sylvie paused before she answered. 'He's here.'

'Well, he's not answering his cell. Would you get him for me?' When there was another pause, Jessie's alarm sounded. 'What's the matter? What's wrong now?'

'He's outside.'

'Go out and get him, Sylvie.' A hint of wary irritation rose in her voice.

Sylvie swallowed. 'He's in the pool.'

The desperate need Jessie had felt to reconnect with Robert, perhaps to tell him about the investigation, was lost in a confusion of horror and anger at his callousness. He could not have hurt Jessie more if he had punched her in the face. She threw her cell against a wall, gouging it and chipping the paint. Two pieces of the phone flew in different directions.

Sylvie thought about calling Jessie back to tell her about the gloves and the police but it wasn't the time. She had heard the crash of the phone and she hung up the dead line. Inching to the window, she stared out aghast at Robert who swam with force and abandon. *The next time Miss Henley calls, I'll tell her about both things.*

Jessie tried to catch her breath before she tore down the stairs and stormed into the study to find Henley sitting behind his favorite working table that he had acquired from Parliament Hill. He hadn't touched the whisky. 'Don't do any calling! Robert's swimming in the pool.' Her eyes blazed and she bit her index finger until she left deep indentations. 'Only a heartless bastard could do such a thing! He waited till we left of course, coward that he is. I can't believe it!' she wept bitterly.

Henley leaned forward in his armchair and spoke between his teeth. 'Remember what I told you, Jessie. I'll have the time while they're waiting for the results to quash any private matters if need be. I can call in a lot of favors. Justin was my grandson. I'm sorry it took this heartbreak for you to change your mind about continuing our investigation of Robert, but you've made the right decision.'

'I have to accept my negligence. One careless act on my part might have been fatal for Justin. That's my burden, but Robert has to pay for his, whatever that might be.' Jessie sank under the weight of self-reproach.

A new unease began to fill the space Justin had left behind.

When Robert got out of the pool, he lounged in his favorite lawn chair, his legs comfortably splayed. The hedge blocked the afternoon sun from most of the yard. Where it did break through, long shadows gathered and twisted with the breeze. He followed their darting shafts. *Geoffrion will never see me shit-side-up like a shadow.* It took no time for his concerns to resurface. Although it was extraordinarily balmy, he rose quickly as though a wind had come up and went back into the house. What he wanted most was Jessie's call telling him the tests were off. He checked the notepad Sylvie used and discovered Jessie hadn't called. He looked around the quiet kitchen and left. The thought of the tests picked away at him. He remembered when he was a kid, his aunt had taken the family to a rented cottage. That night he couldn't sleep. He heard small, ticking sounds through the walls and his skin itched and he squirmed until morning. Much later in his life, he realized the cottage was infested with termites.

He could hear them now, gnawing away at him. *You want to jack up my life, Jessie? Damn you, I'll play my part tomorrow and I'll walk away!* His need of Carmen was irksome. He loathed his weakness, loathed admitting that he'd needed the other women as much as they'd longed for him. Till this crisis, it had hidden under the guise of adventure. He knew Carmen wasn't boxing him in. She'd offered him an out if he needed one. Still, her importance had diminished in the swirling turmoil, and she had become a refuge. The threats ate away at him. Isolation and a hollow loneliness drained his energy. Carmen might refuel it. He had juggled secrets in the past without dropping any of them. Dealing with Carmen was easy for Robert in the midst of the mess. It was Fortier tailing him, and the ploy he'd need to lose him tomorrow. It was Geoffrion who had it in for him. It was the sale on Saturday. Most of all it was the freakin' tests and the motive they might offer up to the cops!

To calm himself, he began formulating a plan for evading Fortier. First though, he showered, shaved and threw on some clothes. He backed the Porsche out of the driveway and drove to Rockland Road and turned left toward the shopping mall. He ignored the rear-view mirror until he pulled a fast right and gunned the car into a driveway at the next corner. He knew the family and they were away for the summer. It didn't take long for a car, a Beemer, to make the same turn and drive slowly on past him. Robert wouldn't bet his life on the driver he saw, but the old guy in the car fit the size of Fortier and he was good at simple arithmetic. At least he knew now there was a tail. The idea was fact. Robert pretended to ring the bell at the house before he got back into the car and drove home. Fortier had no way of knowing that he was dealing with a master of shabby subterfuge.

As soon as Fortier saw the Porsche in the driveway, he swore as he had in the old days. Corners were always tricky. If the mark wised up, he had options. Tyler had just used one of them. 'Fucking shit!' He drove by and gave up the tail. Henley was curt when he called.

'Change the car.'

Robert lost no time when he was back in the house. He figured correctly that Fortier would back off for a while hoping he'd passed him undetected. He called Hertz, and within an hour, the driver delivered new a Volkswagen Tiguan to the door. After signing the papers, he had the driver park the SUV on the other side of the crescent and called the man a cab. Robert packed what he needed, checked the street and walked around to the rental. He popped the trunk, dropped his bag inside and shut it. All he had to do tomorrow was get to the SUV. A supposed walk was his plan. When that work was accomplished, he felt better. He checked the phone again, but Jessie hadn't called while he was out.

He spoke with Hoye. 'If they ask you anything that makes you feel uncomfortable, advise them you will not be answering questions without representation. You're there for the tests. That's it. You're okay with that?'

'This time, my eyes are open. If I need you, I'll call you.'

'Don't blink.'

Robert walked nervously through the empty house. The house seemed cavernous, and Robert's eyes, weary from lack of sleep, glistened and burned with his secrets as he passed the master bedroom and Justin's room. The tension eased somewhat when he was back at his desk going over the business papers. He had also decided which employees would keep their jobs and go with the new owners. Selection hadn't been easy because many of his people had been with him from the outset. The economic meltdown was responsible for thousands of job losses every month. His company was one of many. He didn't feel better because of that, but he had to salvage what he could. He'd done his own accounting for the sale, verified the terms of the lease and contacted the bank in Belize. Robert knew his business and he'd hired a very competent lawyer to go over his end of the sale when he received the letter of intent from the buyers. There had been work on both sides before this final meeting. He looked over at his cell when the papers were packed. Why hadn't Jessie called? His confidence sagged because he'd been so certain he'd spoken the words she wanted to hear. What could have changed her mind? It wasn't Fortier. He ran back the events of the last few hours. Then he knew. Sylvie had seen him in the pool. Now Jessie knew.

Hoye's words repeated. *Robert, you've done a better job of sabotaging yourself than Henley with his gazillions could ever have done.*

Chapter Forty-one

GEOFFRION AND MOITIÉ waited in their office with the crime tech and sent a uniform to escort Robert up. 'Jean, I have one question for Tyler. I know he has a lawyer, but I haven't given up on the kid, and I think Tyler might be of help.'

Geoffrion did not want a detour from his main suspect. 'What is it, Denis?' he asked, clearly irritated by this invasion on his 'spect and the thought that Moitié might gain ground.

'I was thinking about the phone calls Sharpe made to the vic, actually the lie he told us about them. I want to know more about the kid.'

'Don't turn Tyler off.' His command approached a threat, *don't mess with my guy!* 'If he doesn't know about the cleaning stuff the lab is analyzing, he'll think the tests are eliminatory, routine.'

'I'll keep it simple.' Both cops stopped talking when they saw Tyler.

He was dressed in a business suit that didn't camouflage the micro tense facial expressions. He was suitably nervous for a suspect.

'Good morning, Mr. Tyler.'

Robert nodded. 'Let's get to this.' He took off his jacket and slung it over a chair. He rolled his sleeve above his elbow and offered his arm to the tech. The cops watched him closely, but no one spoke. As soon as the band-aid was on his arm and the follicle taken, Robert said, 'That's it.' He turned to leave.

'Mr. Tyler, I have one question for you.' Moitié didn't give Robert a chance to respond. 'It has to do with your son, not you. I have Colin Sharpe's take on your son. Your wife, understandably, has only positive things to say. I'd like to know more, round out my view of your son.'

'My lawyer wants all questions going through him.'

'Yes, but this has nothing to do with you. You have my word. Thought you might want to help. What kind of boy was Justin?'

Weighing his options, Robert decided it was better to answer. 'He was a decent kid.'

'Was he a bully?'

'Didn't have to be. He got everything he wanted. I don't think either of you men can understand that comment. It took me a few years to know the extent of it. I mean everything.'

'Must have made him king of the hill.'

'He had the crown the day he was born. I don't know what he was like at school or with Colin. I gather you're asking because of him and their argument.'

'If you had to sum him up, what would you say?'

Robert thought for a few seconds. 'He was clever for his age, he was egocentric because of the wealth, and he was full of energy. He could manipulate. He learned that from his grandfather. He adored Jessie. He made her and Douglas happy and proud. He hated peanut butter, but he could eat a jar of honey.' At his last comment, Robert seemed lost in that memory.

'What did he bring you?'

Robert's eyes narrowed. He looked first at Geoffrion and then at Moitié. He took a step back because he found their physical presence oppressive. 'I've already spoken about our relationship. Check your notes.' He leaned over and grabbed his jacket and left. He didn't say any of the usual banalities in parting. He didn't wish them a good day or 'good' anything.

'No one told him about the pickup at the house,' Geoffrion said, smiling. 'I'll wait till I know what the fiber is before I call Miss Henley to see if she cleaned the safe with any of that material. We should know about it by Monday.'

Moitié saw that his partner was jacked. He saw his predatory sign, two fingers he tapped against his temple. 'What about Sharpe?'

'He can wait till Tuesday.'

'Since when are you determining my investigation? Have I missed some appointment you've just been given?'

'No up-staging intended, Denis, and no appointment.' Geoffrion said defensively. 'If the kid hadn't used the belt, you'd see him tomorrow, latest Monday. It's just the way things are playing out.'

'You want the big solve. You want to be first at the gate. Admit it.'

'There's that too. Luck of the draw, I got to the house first.'

'Sure.' He kept his reply to one word because this was not the time for a personal confrontation.

The cops worked well together, but Moitié begrudged his partner the extra frontline he always had on the files they worked. He'd felt it was his Haitian blood though he knew Geoffrion would never admit his racism. It was there before Obama was elected President of the U.S., and it was still there five months after. Geoffrion was a good cop— he also thought he was the better cop and he was wrong. He was ringing a lot of bells that he could not unring if the kid turned out to be the reason Justin Tyler was dead. Moitié was looking forward to Tuesday.

The ominous threat of justice served would have to wait till then.

Robert's muscles were still stiff when he got into car and called Hoye and recounted the exchange.

'That's a good sign asking you whether Justin was a bully. The neighbor is still in the mix.'

'I agree, but the results will come out.'

'That'll take time. No telling what can happen in between. Time is hope.'

'If the cops had something on me from the safe, wouldn't they have come after me by now?'

'This isn't TV. Time again, so you're not out of it yet. Keep me posted.'

'I will.' Robert didn't bother worrying about a tail. He drove home quickly and scanned his work table and desk to see if he'd left anything incriminating around. His laptop was safely in the car, he shredded the paper in the wastepaper basket and he thought briefly of not coming back if the deal went through. He'd come back from Toronto as planned. Far more than the police, he feared Henley's long arm. His investigators would follow the money trail of the sale and track him down. No one would ever know what had happened to him. At least, that was the way Robert was thinking.

Sylvie was upstairs cleaning or avoiding him. That was fine with him. He wasn't about to ask her if she had told Jessie about his swim. He decided he had the time to make an appearance at work and he drove out to Pointe Claire. On his desk he found cards from the employees and he felt worse about the sale. He called his manager into the office. 'How are things?'

'My sympathies to you and Jessie.' Ray Huston reached across the desk and shook Robert's hand. 'Here, it's been business as usual. Orders are small but steady and we're getting some promising new quotes. We're busy. That's never bad.'

'Ray, set up a general meeting for Monday afternoon.'

'Alright. Anything in particular?'

'I'm working out the agenda for it now before I leave.'

'See you Monday. Try to get some rest.'

'Sounds like a plan.'

On the drive back to TMR, Robert realized he had only added to his tension by pretending it was business as usual at work. This company was his structure and his refuge. His employees, while not close friends, were his support. This time tomorrow, he'd be on his own. The jump-start of a new beginning fizzled though he felt the sale was necessary. In less than a year he figured, the company's profits would fall by sixty percent or more. He couldn't wait around. The Fairmont Royal York in Toronto and his meeting with the buyers at the hotel was the right move. Business thoughts did not erase the specter of the test results and their potential damage. He scratched his arms and gunned the Porsche. He didn't expect a cop to be around to nail him for speeding and he was right on that count. When he got home, he changed, went for a run and cased the area. Before he left, Sylvie said hello sheepishly, confirming his suspicion, and he grunted something back at her.

He showered once Sylvie had left. Robert locked the side door she had used and left the house. He walked around the crescent, checking every car he saw. Fortier wasn't on that side of the crescent. He got into the SUV and crawled into the back. He had pushed the seats down to allow him the space he needed and he waited for thirty minutes. It didn't take long for a car to drive slowly past his SUV. Robert waited for him to make another swipe, and he did. A half-hour later, he climbed onto the front seat and drove off. In case he hadn't fooled the old bastard, he got to the airport after five and headed to the VIP lounge. The old cop wouldn't be able to say he saw him with anyone if he was still on his tail. Robert settled into a moody silence and drank two glasses of red wine.

Carmen too had lost the high buzz she'd felt driving down to see Robert at the hotel over a week ago. Robert was going to a business meeting and she was there to fill in the spaces. Twice she thought of cancelling, but she didn't. Trying to recall positive words in his last short conversation wasn't much help. However, she had a friend in Toronto who'd be thrilled to see her while he was at his business meeting. She was going business class and, behind the chaos, there was a chance! She couldn't deny that. A good look in her mirror drew a hopeful smile. She called her cab and threw caution into the summer night.

The perpetual construction along Highway 13 almost made her late. The sexy, slow entrance she wanted to make was lost. Bag in tow, Carmen galloped down the hall to her gate.

Robert saw her first and broke out in a smile. He remembered why he had asked her along. 'You made it!'

The blood ran high in her cheeks. 'Only just. The story of my life.'

Robert didn't hug Carmen or touch her. 'They're boarding.' He looked behind him, but he didn't spot Fortier because the place was crowded with arriving and departing passengers. That didn't mean the cop wasn't there.

Chapter Forty-Two

ON THE PLANE SITTING beside each other, Carmen felt awkward and Robert wasn't any more at ease with her. Stressed from a long day and a nervous rush to the airport, she felt she wasn't there and wished she hadn't come. Robert was preoccupied with the threats back home and the imminent sale of his company. Neither one had noticed what the other was wearing. Carmen had been glad to discover her plane ticket was open-ended. She could fly back anytime she chose. 'Maybe this was a bad idea,' Carmen said, breaking the silence.

A flight attendant appeared and poured them each a glass of champagne.

'You don't like champagne?'

Carmen managed a very good smile.

'As least you know I'm not a stalker.'

Carmen turned to Robert and gave him her best appraising eye, actually both eyes. 'Looking at you now, I think I could take you. So, no, I'm not afraid.'

'We can start from there. You run pretty well too, as I saw at the airport.'

'Only when I have to.'

Robert reached for her hand, and their body heat rose. His thumb caressed her palm while his fingers held hers gently. Carmen tightened her grip on his hand. The banter stopped. His thumb moved up to the inside of her wrist and traced its lines before he stopped and waited to feel her pulse. Carmen looked down at their hands and closed her eyes. His thumb moved back and forth across the top of her wrist. Fatigue, nervousness and tension drained from their bodies, seduced by the touch of flesh, soft and pliant. They didn't speak until the pilot announced their descent at Pearson International Airport. Robert leaned over and whispered, 'I meant what I said that we can keep things easy. I won't pressure you.' He knew he already had.

Carmen's breaths were short. When she found her voice, she said hoarsely, 'Where are we staying?'

'The Royal York. The meeting's there. You can borrow the rental car tomorrow while I'm busy. It'll give you a chance to enjoy the city.

My best guess is four hours.' They shared small talk on their way to Front Street in downtown Toronto.

It was almost eleven when Robert opened the door to their room. Carmen laughed, 'Two beds?' Their suite was lovely, light blue trimmed in gold with soft white lamps. The sitting room with a sofa and matching armchairs, softened by an interesting variety of plants, was as inviting as a living room.

'I told you no pressure. I want to get to know you.' Robert was good with the right words. He began to unpack immediately and lay out his work for the next day. Feeling a little lost, Carmen stood and watched him before she started with her own bag. 'Would you like an easy night? You know, just both get some sleep. We have Saturday night.' Robert changed quickly and got into the far bed. 'I have quite a day tomorrow.'

Carmen, off balance again, headed for the bathroom and changed there. She climbed into bed herself. 'I feel like a Girl Guide at camp! I was never a Guide and I never went to camp.' With that comment, she turned off the lamp and lay quietly in darkness. 'Good night!'

'Back at you.'

Carmen lay thinking that they had not spoken one word about Robert's son or what was going on in Robert's life. She didn't move, but she couldn't fall asleep either. It was pitch dark in the room, but beyond the heavy curtains, she knew there was a full moon. She'd seen it on their drive to the hotel. The first hour seemed endless. All she heard was her own breathing. Puzzled and a little angry with Robert's decrees, she arched her shoulders and tried again to find a comfortable place on the pillow. She didn't hear Robert get up from his bed and she was almost asleep when he was suddenly beside her in the dark.

'May I get into bed with you and hold you?'

Carmen pulled down the sheets and turned on her side away from him. His arm went around her shoulder and his body inched firmly against her back until she could feel his chest and hips against hers. He never spoke. Not a muscle moved, except for one, and it did not demand anything but closeness from her. To her surprise, Carmen fell into a deep sleep, lulled in no small part by Robert's warmth and quiet breathing. They woke together, stuck to one another. Carmen could not remember a time she had felt so comforted. When she rolled over, they made love, tender at first, then measured and drawn to a fierce and final thrust. Robert fell on top of Carmen and she held him there.

Carmen's brain did not surrender completely. With each thrust, it was torn and pushed from old mistakes to the possibility of new ones. Before the final orgasmic burst, they each had a single thought they could never share. Each despised their own weakness.

Before he got up, Robert whispered, 'We have tonight together.'

Carmen waited in bed till Robert had showered and before room service arrived. 'Last night was beautiful. May I ask you one question?'

A flash of anger she'd seen before surfaced. She could hardly accuse Robert of obsessive self-concern.

'Just the one. More after the meeting.'

Carmen sat up in bed, ready for a rebuke, but she had to know. 'We made love. I don't know how you did that. Do you care that your son is dead?' She saw that his patience was about to snap.

'The answer is very complicated. We can talk tonight. For now, the answer to your question is—not as much as I should.' He packed his things and left for his meeting before breakfast arrived. There was a bounce to his step. He had accomplished one of his goals in Toronto despite the question.

Carmen felt again that she didn't belong in this story—she wasn't part of it. Robert was manoeuvring her into the maze of his life, and she wasn't putting up any resistance. An ominous thought occurred. *I've allowed myself to fall for a man who might be a murderer.*

She rolled off the bed and called room service, cancelling breakfast. When she'd showered and dressed, she called Annie Nolan. The gravelly voice that answered was familiar and reassuring. 'Annie, it's Carmen DiMaggio. I'm in Toronto. Do you have time for a visit because I'd love to see you?'

'How soon can you get here and take me out of my dungeon for breakfast? I'll treat.'

'About thirty minutes.'

'Olga will have my travelling wheels on the ready.'

Carmen grabbed her purse and the chit for the car and headed down to the front desk. She knew the city well, a plus from her last sales job. From Bay Street she turned onto Lakeshore Boulevard, then to the Gardiner Expressway. From her exit on South Kingsway, she turned left onto Riverside Drive to Annie's grand old home. Annie was Carmen's kind of character. Felled by a stroke that had left her left side paralyzed and imprisoned in a motorized wheelchair, Annie fought back at that outrage with cigarettes, O'Henrys and a searing wicked sense of humor. *She must be 64 by now,* Carmen thought as she pulled onto the driveway.

Before she was out of the car, the door flew open. 'Come on in!' Annie called, waving her up with cigarette in hand.

Carmen ran up the stairs and threw her arms around Annie.

'It's so good to see you.' Carmen held onto Annie a little too long.

'Oh, oh, with that kind of hug, something's up. I've booked the Boulevard Club. Let's get my wheels into the trunk and we're off.' Annie made everything sound exciting, like a great adventure. Olga and Carmen strained lifting Annie from the wheelchair into the car. It took them almost five minutes to see that she was sitting comfortably. The trunk was big enough for the wheelchair. Annie had managed to keep her cigarette lit and began to pull away at it, hacking like someone dying of emphysema.

'Annie, there's no smoking in this rental, sorry. Your cough is worse.'

'Drat!' Annie threw the butt out the window. She didn't give a hoot about littering. Caught in the act, Carmen knew Annie would chat up the officer who might buy her story and let her off.

Carmen sighed.

'You used to be such fun!'

A doorman at the club helped Annie into her chair and wheeled her into the club. 'Well,' Annie proclaimed, 'this is a wonderful escape from another day of deadly routine in Riverside prison.'

'Would you like to eat on the terrace?'

'You mean out in the hot humid air? God, no!' She settled for a table by the closed french doors that gave them a good view of Lake Ontario and a blast of air conditioning. Once the coffee arrived with her eggs Benedict and Carmen's omelette, Annie wasted no time. 'Alright, out with it!'

Carmen told her story in detail. Annie loved a good caper. Carmen felt she'd find a sympathetic ear.

Annie listened and didn't touch her eggs. She enjoyed pretending she was quite normal about food, but she ate very little apart from her chocolate and toast with marmalade. After a hollow hacking that rattled Annie's whole body and drew the attention from anyone in hearing distance, she took a sip of coffee. She pulled and rubbed each of the fingers of her clawed hand, trying to soothe them. 'You're an idiot!' Annie didn't give Carmen one of her great 'excuse me' laughs after that pronouncement. She chose her withering glare instead and she didn't regret her words. She did feel sorry for Carmen's crimson, stricken face.

'What if everything Robert says is true? What if there is a chance for me?'

'You're a beautiful young woman…'

'Not that young.'

'Let me finish. It can't be this difficult to find one good man. If you had two noses, I'd understand, but you don't. Why are you settling for seconds?'

'He was really good to me last night.'

'It's a con. Olga doesn't just work for me. We've become great friends. That doesn't change the fact that I spend my day trying to con her with one thing or another, like finding novel hideouts for my wretched vegetables that I tell her I'll never eat. I recognize a good con job.'

'I want to believe him.'

'He knows that. I jump at adventure, but I'm not fool enough to risk the life of someone I care about. I play with my life because silly games distract me from pain and boredom, but you don't have those excuses. Your life is still ahead of you.'

'I'm hooked,' Carmen admitted.

'You're addicted like I am to my Cameos.' Their conversation continued, but the words didn't go anywhere.

When Annie was safely home, back in her wheelchair, she said gently but with resolve, 'Protect yourself. Look where vodka and tobacco have gotten me.' It was rare for Annie to admit the part she'd played in her present state. It was a sign of her deep concern for Carmen.

Forty-three

From the minute Fortier knew Tyler had made him, he took extra precautions. Thursday night into Friday morning, he cased the crescent. By now he knew the vehicles by heart, if not their owners. When he spotted the Tiguan, he knew it didn't belong. He copied the tag and called in his last, last favor to get the tag run through the DMV.

'This is not as simple as it might appear, Mike. You know this is against policy. I could have my ass kicked. I'm still a rookie.'

'The work is for a very influential man who'll take good care of your ass if necessary. I'm relying on your skills and discretion.'

'After this, the book on favors is closed.'

'Agreed.'

Officer Pierre Martin ran the tag and came up with Hertz. He called Roadside Assistance and Jeremiah Belcher took the call.

'For security purposes and client privacy, I'll need your badge number and your division for verification.'

Martin complied and waited for a name while he went back to work. Belcher called some minutes later. 'The rental is registered to a Robert Tyler.'

'Thank you.' Friday afternoon when Robert left for the airport, Fortier was waiting for him on Beverley and tailed him to Trudeau International Airport where he contacted Henley.

'Good work, but we just heard from the housekeeper. Robert left her a note for Jessie saying he'd be in Toronto for business and back Saturday night or Sunday morning. Did you manage to get inside Trudeau?'

'Far as I could tell, he was alone, if that's the next question.'

'He mentioned something to Jessie about business problems. The trip could be legitimate.'

'Why bother with the rental?'

'To lose you is my guess. Is there a chance…?'

'I'll be at Trudeau by six. I can sleep anywhere and I don't close both eyes.'

'You should have a check for this work by Monday, Mike.'

'Appreciated.'

'Works both ways. I want whatever I can get on Robert. If the woman is with him, I want to know.'

'If they're clever, they won't be walking together.'

'Get what you can.'

'Bet on it.'

As Robert walked down one of the main halls to the conference room the buyers had booked for this meeting, he had a jolt of nerves. His anxiety mingled with hope. At least he'd left that note at the house about his whereabouts, and he needn't worry about police disrupting his business. Geoffrion had not suggested he stay in Montreal. If the deal closed today, Robert would feel that something he had created mattered in hard coin. He hesitated at the door; the closure also meant the death of his dream. Jessie's face streaked across his mind's eye, and he took a step back. Straightening his tie, he took a deep breath, opened the door and walked in with a practiced confidence. 'Good morning, gentlemen!' The men, all small and seemingly the same size, rose in perfect unison to greet him, their eyes bright and inquisitive. Except for their leader, Mr. Chong, who conducted the meeting, the men wore gray suits, white shirts and red ties. Chong wore a navy tie. The air in the room was stale from hundreds of conferences that had taken place in this old Toronto landmark at a time when smoking was permitted. Old tobacco fumes had settled deep into the walls and floors, no matter how many furniture changes had been made over the years. The papers were neatly laid out for Robert, and each man had his own set. He opened his briefcase and added what he brought with him.

'Please read with caution,' Mr. Chong said. Oddly, they all kept their eyes on him and did not confer with one another as he read their contract.

'It is of great importance that we have no errors,' their leader cautioned.

Robert brought his hand to his mouth as Chong spoke. "Errors" had sounded like "arrows." *Nerves*, he told himself. Once he had finished reading the documents, Chong asked Robert a question they had never discussed. Would he be interested in heading up their

214

Montreal and Toronto conglomerate to train the new managers, and perhaps stay on if he wished? Before the question was asked, Robert had already admired the succinct work he was reading. Certainly, when the world economy was stronger, the Chinese would continue to be an economic force.

Pride flowed through him when he realized they respected him enough to want him spear-heading the operation. His heart swelled with confidence. 'That's a very tempting offer. I'm very interested. May I get back to you on Monday?'

Concealing their disappointment but understanding his move, they smiled and assented. Less than five hours since Robert had walked into the room, he had seven million dollars in Belize and the same amount in his business account in Montreal. He shook hands, collected the necessary documents and was the first to leave the room. The men knew of the loss of his son and had not proposed dinner.

Carmen drove slowly along Lakeshore in a melancholy mood. She felt a dry chill from the a/c blasting in her face and from Annie herself. Compared to Annie, Carmen was a rank amateur when it came to risks. The image of Annie at the hospital propped up with oxygen, gasping for her life, haunted her for months. And yet Annie had reached for a Cameo a day later on her way home from the hospital, despite the physician's warning. *You're opting for a slow and painful death, Annie.* She was still puffing away today, and yet Annie hadn't supported her with Robert—quite the opposite. A malaise, like Toronto's milky smog, settled in her heart.

She spotted a pink hotdog and ice cream stand at the lakeside and stopped there. Food always helped Carmen. 'Give me the works without onions, and a cherry coke,' she said to a middle-aged man who seemed to own the place. His fingernails were ringed with mustard. The foot-long hotdog was easily the size of two. The corn roll was a great match for it. Before she took her first bite, Carmen kicked a stone as she sat down at the picnic table. In seconds, flies swarmed around her head. *Neither Caitlin nor Annie has seen Robert from the inside. They're worried about me. Robert is no murderer. He had no motive. He knew he'd never get their money. I wasn't the reason. He hardly knew me.* Carmen bit into her dog, and relish spilled out the side of her mouth. *Damn! It's not cooked.* She bit off the ends and threw the rest away. Her hands were sticky, but there was no bathroom to clean off. *Just great!* Doing the best she could with her one allotted napkin, she got back into the car. A nagging suspicion would not let go of her. *What did I just read in that mystery book? One of the motives for murder was loathing? That's it. Could Robert have loathed his son enough to kill him? That's ridiculous. I'm beginning to think like Caitlin.*

Carmen started the car with a touch of her finger and promised herself that she'd find out more about Justin and Robert. Even if it was a horrible accident, Robert's reaction to his son's death troubled her. He had promised to talk about the situation and she intended to hold him to his word. Each person mourned differently, she understood that, but an absence of mourning set up alarms, thoughts of indifference or, worse, implication in the death. Carmen wasn't afraid, she was wary. The open ticket was her escape if she became frightened.

She had expected traffic and she wasn't disappointed. Congestion along the expressway was exacerbated by the annual road construction that began in the spring, as it did in every city in Canada. Carmen had the time to take in the Rogers Centre and the Air Canada Centre. She had been to an Eagles concert at the ACC a few years back. The CN Tower and the skyscrapers highlighted the most impressive skyline in the country.

After handing in the car, she ducked into a washroom in the lobby before she headed back to the suite. As soon as she inserted the card, Carmen felt that Robert was back, and he was. Champagne was cooling in a silver bucket and he was absolutely buoyant! The suite smelled faintly of shampoo and cologne and soap. Robert was beaming, sitting in the best chair with his legs crossed. He was wearing a blue suit with a faint pin-stripe. The jacket lay on a sofa. His shirt was light blue with a white collar, and he was tie-less. A broad easy smile had replaced the strain and fear of the last week. The sudden change sounded a note of additional warning for Carmen.

Robert sensed her concern. 'Before we get into anything serious, let's have a glass of champagne!' He poured the champagne with a flourish. 'I couldn't wait to tell you about my meeting. In the past week and a half, everything in my life has gone wrong. Today I made something happen, for me! Working out a fair price for a company in this economic collapse is a real feat and I did it!' He got up out of the chair to bolster his next point. 'The Henleys have tried to destroy me since Justin died. I was at the point where I felt I couldn't do anything right. Well, I can. It's one thing to build a company, to believe in yourself, to spend the best years of your life working on it. But it's validation to have a conglomerate seek you out and pay good money for all that work. I'm talking too much. Choose any place you want for dinner. I'm happy to have you with me. I can say that now because I know where I'm going, and I don't need the Henleys.'

Robert's surging mood continued to unnerve Carmen. 'That's great news, but I thought, you did promise...' She felt awkward, harping back to yesterday's news and being present for an occasion in which she had no part.

'I'm hyped. Sorry, go on...' Robert was barely listening to her.

'*Desire* is a Cajun restaurant I love...'

'You've got it!'

'Robert, I know this is great news, but you did say you'd tell me about your son. I thought that was to be part of this weekend.'

His eyes grew hard, and his smile froze in irritation. 'I did, didn't I?' That Robert's promise to tell her about himself sounded like an accusation wasn't lost on Carmen. 'Let's have another glass of champagne and save that talk 'till after dinner. Nothing should spoil this moment. I'm trying to put all that out of my mind.' On the drive to Humber Road, there was an awkward silence.

Robert was on another mental plane. He might as well have been in another car. In this air of estrangement, Carmen felt her presence was obtrusive. The weekend that had begun with a glimmer of hope had turned sour. She wondered if she had the right to ask any questions of him. He'd promised her the story in desperation, but that was long gone, replaced with a brassy confidence. Robert hadn't alluded to that new life with her. He might be going through the motions. Selling his company had set him free not just from the Henleys, but from needing her. He might simply dump her when they got back to Montreal. 'There's the restaurant!'

'The place isn't much to look at,' Robert said, parking the car. 'It's in the middle of a nondescript strip mall in nowheresville.'

'Wait till you taste the fish and then pass judgment.' If this was the end for her, so be it. Chalking up another loss wasn't new to her.

As soon as they entered the small restaurant the owner came over to greet Carmen. Peter was a Greek, a broad-shouldered man who exuded pride in his heritage and in his food. He was tall with just the hint of a belly under his dark suit. Giving all his attention to Carmen, he said he had missed her pretty smile. 'I've changed jobs, Peter, so I'm not on the road anymore.'

'My loss,' he said, bowing and backing away. 'Enjoy your dinner.'

Robert ate three mouthfuls before he gave his review. 'Impressive! Nice atmosphere too. I'll be back. My blackened mahi-mahi is delicious, the best I've ever eaten, even better than in Hawaii. I'm ravenous. It's been a while since I've enjoyed food.' His words relaxed them both and they ate with gusto. They spoke very little throughout the meal, and the Caesar salad and warm Greek bread that appeared midway through it. Finally Robert sat back in his chair and sighed contentedly. 'Well,' he said, placing both hands palms down on the table. 'You're on. What do you want to know?' The closeness and the physical attraction of the previous night were notably absent in Robert's tone. Carmen felt his dispassionate appraisal since reminding him of his promise, as though he weren't quite sure what to make of her. Carmen thought *the disconnection began the minute I walked back into the suite.*

Carmen wiped her mouth and hands with the linen napkin. Under the table she brought her knees together and held them there. Averting her eyes from his, she realized that she didn't know one thing about Robert Tyler that mattered. Everything to date had been a defence, but there was nothing solid about him. Was he truthful, loving or loyal? They had arrived for dinner early, so Carmen felt isolated without the support from the easy banter of dinner patrons. 'Maybe this isn't the time, and I have no right to ask you about your private life. We don't know each other.'

'I gave you my word.' Robert zoned in on Carmen. 'Tell me something about you first. Why did you come to Toronto? A week ago, you were afraid of me.' There was no warmth in his tone. He might have been asking a fly why it had landed on his arm.

His question made it plain what he thought of her intrusion. Carmen looked down as her cheeks flushed. She reached for the pink cashmere cardigan on the back of her chair and put it around her shoulders. She well knew and hated the primacy of males who initiated relationships and turned them off at will. Her reply would seem weak and submissive to him and out of sync to her. Carmen could never be confused with an artful dodger. 'I wanted to believe what you said about us.'

'Well then, ask away,' he said, with no attempt to conceal his smirk. Carmen's admission had not softened Robert's appraising look. He cupped the side of his head in his hand, preparing for another interrogation. 'Shoot!'

He'd chosen that verb purposely, she thought. Before she asked her question, Carmen felt a familiar succession of emotions that surfaced when she sensed she'd soon be back in the dating jungle, failure, disillusionment and anger lurking. 'Why aren't you broken up about losing your only son?' Robert's nails turned blood red as he pressed his fingers harder into the table. The question felt so out of place she regretted asking it. She hadn't felt remotely part of his life, since the meeting at the hotel. 'Look, forget it.'

'You asked and I'll answer.' His words stung Carmen with their abruptness. It was obvious Robert didn't like losing control of the conversation. 'I never had the chance to grieve for him. You already know he was in my care when he drowned, and Jessie hates me and accused me of murdering him. Some hotshot detective has it in for me regardless of the kid next door. My father-in-law has seen to that. The bastard put a tail on me…'

Carmen's heart began pounding.

'They wouldn't let me help with the funeral preparations. The day of the viewing, Jessie pulled me aside and told me she didn't want me in with Justin and her. She moved to Westmount with her father yesterday. I also made another colossal blunder. With no meds to help me through any of this, I took a swim in the pool after they left. I shouldn't have, but Jessie announced that she was draining it. I'm pretty sure the housekeeper informed on me. And Justin? I didn't have time in the early years for him because I was trying to prove myself to Douglas. Anyway, my son didn't like me much. He never wanted to do anything with me when I had the time. Not football, not hockey, none of the shit I like. When he was alone in the pool, I asked him to do a few laps with his old man and he said no.' Robert jerked and sat up rigidly. Why had he made that particular comment? The reckless words exploded in both their ears.

The easy fluency of Robert's account had already made Carmen suspicious. The last sentence caused a jet of unspoken dread between them. *Were you there when he drowned? Did Justin set you off that night? Did you …?* Carmen pulled her sweater around her.

Robert's hands went up to block the fallout. 'Don't take what I just said the wrong way!' he ordered, balling his fist and opening it again to placate her. 'I don't mean the night he died, for God's sake. Carmen! You're worse than the cops. What I just said happened a few weeks ago and more than once in the past year. I was a rotten father, but I was blocked along the way as well.' He wanted to feel grief, but his own lack of emotion surprised him. At that moment, every nerve in his body screamed and he felt nothing for Justin or the Henleys. 'Don't join the opposition! All I wanted was this one night! Is that too much to ask?' He felt guilty for his selfishness, but defiant. 'It's been hell for me and you've just brought it all back!'

Why tell me about that incident? Was it a conscious slip to test me? Carmen sat back stiffly against her chair to ward off a blow that never came. Nausea swirled in her stomach. She attempted to put up her own stop signs by changing the subject. 'I'm not proud of a few things myself. Do you think you were followed here?' Her words trembled and rang false, but that was the best she could do as a slow, heavy terror gripped her tongue. *If he killed his son, I've just become a threat to him.* The ticket and her wallet were both in her purse.

'I left a message telling them I was here on business, so I don't think I was tailed. The meeting was legit. What's wrong? You look awful. Jesus, Carmen, the only time I saw Justin in the pool that night, he had already drowned. I've been interrogated and followed all week. Don't blow this up. You're on my side, remember?'

Carmen groaned, rubbing her stomach. 'It's not you. I ate too quickly. My stomach is rebelling. The shrimp are doing a number on my stomach. It could be the lettuce. I have trouble with that some-times.' Carmen heaved for effect. 'I'm sorry. It's a bad habit and I often pay for it. Order the bread pudding and give me a few minutes in the washroom.' She grabbed her bag and ran to the washroom at the end of the corridor near the kitchen. She knew that Robert was suspicious, but she had to get away from him.

He rose from the table. 'Do you want me to go with you?' he called after her.

She kept running and waved him off.

Robert walked after her until she closed the bathroom door. Perhaps he was overly rattled. He went slowly back to the table and kept an eye on the door until he was out of range. He signalled the waiter, ordered the bread pudding and drank more wine. He saw that the restaurant had quietly filled to capacity while they sat. He checked his watch, fuming.

Carmen opened the bathroom door slowly and scooted into the kitchen. 'Please get Peter for me! This is an emergency.' She huddled by one of the stoves and hanging pots and pans until he came rushing in. 'Peter, is there a back exit?'

'Yes, next to the men's toilet.'

'Can you get me a cab and have it come round back. I'm very frightened.'

'Of course! Do you need the police?'

'No! I have to get out of here.' She stood shaking as he called. 'I need you to go back to my table and tell the man I was with that I'll be back to join him in a few minutes. Would you do that for me, Peter? I can't be with him. I have to get away.' Tears mingled with panic.

'Go outside and wait.' Peter called while shielding Carmen until she was outside. 'The taxi stand is very close by.' He kept the back door open with a wedge. Carmen rocked back and forth against the wall without being aware of her actions. She clasped her hand over her mouth to keep from screaming. It didn't matter what Robert did or did not do, she wanted to get away from him. He'd unintentionally made her a liability. She'd seen the alarm in his eyes; it was there.

Carmen kept looking at the door, expecting Robert to run after her. Her imagination ran wild. Annie had enough to cope with. She wanted to go home where she felt safer. She couldn't afford to miss work. She had a key to Caitlin's house. Relief swept over her when she saw the cab. 'Take me to the airport, please, as quickly as you can,' she said getting into the cab. 'It's an emergency.'

'Will you pay the speeding ticket, Ma'am?' the Arab cabbie asked.

'As fast as you can go without speeding.' She looked at her watch— she'd been away from the table nearly eight minutes.

Peter checked the laneway, saw that Carmen was safely away and approached the table.

'Sir, Carmen will be back shortly.'

Robert didn't believe him and jumped to his feet. His napkin fell on the floor. He rushed past Peter to the washroom, but a woman was walking in. He brushed past her. 'Carmen? Are you alright?'

'Sir, you shouldn't be in here,' the woman said disapprovingly. 'There is no one here but me.'

The room had only two toilets, and Robert could see that Carmen wasn't there. He ran to find Peter who stood at the edge of the room. 'Where is she?' His voice had risen and drew the attention of the guests.

'She wasn't feeling well, Sir.'

'Bullshit! She's not even in the bathroom. Where did she go?'

Peter was as tall as Robert and didn't back down. 'You are disturbing my customers, sir. You should leave.'

'Give me the goddamn bill! In fact, never mind.' Robert threw money on the table and ran out to his car. He slammed his fist against the steering wheel and until it hurt. 'Hoye was right. I'm a fuckup! What the hell did I just do? Carmen won't dare go back to the room. If she runs to her friend here, she might be convinced to call the police.' That prospect was intolerable to him. 'I can't leave the freakin' papers at the Royal York.' He sped to the hotel. He knew that flights to Montreal from Toronto left every hour, but not at night. He thought they ran every hour and a half. He might just have enough time to pick up his work and get to the airport before Carmen's flight left if she decided to go that route.

Although the air was still hot and humid and the cabbie didn't use the a/c, Carmen sat shivering in the back seat. *It doesn't matter if I overreacted. Robert doesn't care about his son, or about me. He scares me.* Her cell played her song. Opening her purse, she flipped it open. It was Robert. She threw it back into her purse. It began again. This time she answered. 'Robert, I want nothing more to do with you. I'm staying in Toronto for a few days. Leave me alone.'

'Don't hang up! You completely misunderstood what I said, Carmen. I never harmed my son. Why are you doing this to me? I trusted you.'

'I'm not doing anything to you. I was a pickup and I thought I could stretch that into something. I was wrong. There's no us. Leave me alone.' Carmen was trying to keep Robert from seeing her as a threat. It was the reason she had picked up the call and the reason she hung up.

Carmen was running. He knew she was lying. If he moved fast enough, he'd find her at the airport. Rabbits always ran and Carmen was a rabbit.

Chapter Forty-four

ANNIE NOLAN WAS PROPPED up in bed early as usual. The bedside table was fully equipped for the night and any emergency. She had her cell and personal phone numbers, water, the infernal cigarettes and ashtray, the night meds, her book, the remote, graham crackers and her Trident gum. Olga had left to begin the process of care all over again at home with her husband who was cantankerous and suffering from two herniated disks. Although Annie was financially secure, she steadfastly refused to have a night nurse. Every day since the stroke, almost two years ago, Olga invaded her essential privacy. The worst was being lifted onto the toilet and held there and hoisted off and lying naked on the bed while Olga dressed her. The humiliation never lessened. It hardened into a chronic, stubborn pain. 'I'd rather die in bed than have Olga watching my every move, asking me every ten minutes how I'm feeling!'

Annie picked up her cell. 'I don't care if Carmen is angry. I want to be sure she's safe.' She laid the phone against her paralysed hand and tapped in the number with the hand that worked.

On the drive to Pearson International, a sudden rain fell and, in seconds, became a squall. At the airport, Carmen paid the cabbie and hopped quickly out of the cab, using her purse as a shield to escape being drenched by the sheets of rain. Her cell began to play insistently. After shaking off the rain, she took a quick look to see if it was Robert. Hair rose on her arms. When she saw it was Annie, she took the call. Without giving Annie a chance for a single word, Carmen told her what had happened.

'Where are you?'

'I just got to the airport. I'm trying to make the next flight before Robert gets here. I'm really scared, Annie.'

'Are you out of your mind? That's the first place he'll be looking for you. Get back outside, grab a limo and come to my house. When you get here, call me and I'll give you the combination to the front door. I'll rent a car for you and you can drive back to Montreal. Tonight or tomorrow, you can decide when, but right now, get your buns out of the airport.'

'Alright.' Carmen's teeth began to chatter. She ran back outside and tried to stand under shelter. Inside the limo, the vise of nerves relaxed. She had envisioned sitting on the plane and Robert appearing above her. For the time being, he wouldn't know where she was. Her eyes filled with tears.

'Are you alright, Miss?' the driver turned and asked. He passed Carmen a box of Kleenex.

'Thanks. I'm okay.' But her tears of relief just kept coming. Annie would tell her she had to call the police. She didn't know if she dared make that call. She couldn't take the chance of going back to her place when she got back to Montreal either. Another harrowing experience had come back to her. In her second apartment, the woman across the hall was beaten by her common-law husband on a regular basis. Carmen offered her place as a refuge, told her she'd drive her to a shelter, but the Filipino woman, in her twenties as Carmen was, was too frightened to leave. 'He'll find me.'

During one of the worst beatings, Carmen called the police who traced her number and name. They knocked first at her door. The husband was arrested, but the wife did not press charges. She took off while he spent four hours in a holding cell before he showed up at the apartment. He knew Carmen had informed on him. She lived in terror each and every day for three months, running up the five flights of stairs instead of being caught in the elevator with him, checking her peephole before she ran back down the stairs to get to work. He smashed three of her car windows at different times before the trial. When she appeared in court, the wife backed down when she saw him in the hall. Carmen told the truth and the terror continued. When he was finally evicted, the super found two sticks of dynamite in the apartment.

The lesson Carmen took from that experience was that there is no protection once you become involved with abuse. Her cell rang twice in the limo. Both times it was Robert. The second time he left a message. 'Carmen, I don't think you've been fair to me. I'll have your things sent to your place. Please don't make my life worse than it already is. You misunderstood what I said.' Carmen closed her phone. Her heart thudded and her hands were clammy. Running out might have been irrational and demeaning to Robert, but that sentence, so revealing, hanging in the air, had her frozen in a state of fearful consternation. Running was the only way she could arm herself against her fear of him. His phone call had reminded her of a recurring pattern in his dealings with her. When he knew that she was frightened, and he needed her for something, he'd call with his self-deprecating tone to win her back. Well, finally she had opted out of his tangled mess.

When the limo stopped in front of Annie's, a wave of relief washed over her. *Hiding at the airport! What was I thinking of?* When she rang Annie's bell, Carmen burst out laughing. It played *'Oh When the Saints Go Marching In.' I hope Annie will be marching in on her own two legs when her time comes.*

'Carmen?' A hoarse voice called through the intercom.

'It's me, Annie.'

'Here's the combo. Press down hard on the keypad. It can be a bitch like me. I'm in bed.'

Carmen had no trouble, locked the door and scooted up the stairs to Annie. 'It's so good to see you!' Carmen sat on the side of the bed. Annie had what she loved in her spacious bedroom. War books filled the recessed shelves of two full walls. A big-screen TV hung on the wall in front of her. There was a small fridge near the bed on her good side, a phone, her cards and games, the remotes and her easy chairs.

'Don't be fooled by this room. A prison is a prison. Now, we have to see about you. I think you should stay the night, for me and for you. I need company and you need to rest.'

'Thanks, I am very tired.'

'It's nerves. I promised myself I wouldn't give you one of my sermons, but they're just too good to miss. Get yourself a glass of wine from the fridge; in fact, bring the bottle. The wine will soften the blows.' Annie rehearsed while she waited for Carmen to get back. 'Alright then, sit in that blue soft chair. You're a beautiful young woman, Carmen. You're a gambler, I know that too. I'm throwing these questions out, but just think about the answers. What kind of money do you have to show for all the wasted time at the casino? You like edgy men. I know that too. What do you have to show from those relationships? Those men look at you and never see you. Now, you might have stepped into a very dangerous situation that threatens your life. For what, some deluded dream? At best, if he's not a murderer, he's a serial cheater. What kind of relationship could you have hoped for with him? I don't want you to wake up old and bitter and cynical. I want you alive! I want you to grow up.'

'What do I do?'

'I'll take care of the rental. Drive home and go to Caitlin's. Did you tell her you were here with him?'

Carmen stared at the floor.

'Just as I thought.'

'I can't call the police, Annie. I'm not even sure he's done anything. I can't make myself a target.'

'You've done that already, but I agree with you. However, I can hire a security guard for you. I had a very good company when I first came home from the hospital because I was afraid at night. I didn't want anybody in the house, so the fellow stayed out in his car. I'll contact them. They must have an office or they can direct me to one in Montreal.'

'I can't pay that kind of…'

'Never mind that. I have money rotting in a bank or evaporating in this meltdown. If Robert was correct in believing his father-in-law has someone tailing him, you have no assurance he doesn't already know about you. Keep that in mind.'

'I took a call from him coming over here.' Carmen took her cell from her purse and replayed the message.

'That doesn't change anything. The super can take the clothes. Have no further communication with Robert. My gut tells me he'll have his hands full with this investigation. He's afraid you'll contact the police, so he'll keep his distance until more evidence against him surfaces. In that event, we have to take very special care of you. He may see you as a damaging witness.'

Carmen began to cry quietly.

'Tears are a waste of water. Grow up, Carmen. Call Caitlin and tell her you're coming. You can leave by eight. Write out your address and Caitlin's. I'm sure you didn't tell her about this. The security guard will go with you tomorrow night and fetch work clothes and whatever else you'll need. You can't show up for work in a slinky cream dress.'

Carmen put down the wine glass and hugged Annie. 'Thank you.'

'You're too much like me. That's why you have to change. I never got around to it. Wish I had. Take a shower and use either bedroom. Olga will make us a good early breakfast in the morning. I'll contact the security company. They're open 24/7 and they'll find you a rental too.' Annie was alert and spirited. She was at her best when in charge.

Carmen exhaled a sigh of relief when she was safe in Annie's guest room. Almost immediately, she was overcome with a vast grief, an engulfing sadness that held her still. It wasn't grief for the chance she might have had with Robert. The grief was the price she had paid for all her exploits. She did not allow herself the luxury of self-pity. That was too easy, but she knew for certain that Robert had never wanted her forever.

Robert was livid when Carmen didn't take his call. In the hotel room, he tossed their belongings into bags, rushed down to the checkout and bullied his way to the front of the line. 'This is an emergency. My wife is very ill!' No one objected; after all, this was Toronto where people are generally courteous. Running for the rental with both bags, his shoulders sagged under this new stress. He noticed that the streets were wet, but the rain had stopped. He kept his windows open until he reached Highway 401 and sped around eighteen-wheelers, zigzagging his way to the airport. With each passing minute, he was determined to survive the enlarging catastrophe.

Carmen had no right to invade his private life. His mistake had been letting his guard down. People rarely understood or intuited what he meant. Flushed with the high from the sale, he'd opened up to her. She had come to Toronto, beguiling him into taking her loyalty for granted—at the very least, giving him the benefit of the doubt. At the airport, once he'd gotten rid of the rental, the problems in Montreal took hold of him again and appeared more ominous. A flight was leaving for Montreal in three-quarters of an hour. *She didn't get out before me. She's here somewhere. I just have to find her.* Trying to find anyone in that jungle wasn't going to be easy. She could be hiding anywhere. He checked in and hurried to the gate, but his legs felt leaden and tired. He scanned the commuters. He saw the women's bathroom and rushed over where he caught a middle-aged woman with her hand on the doorknob. 'My wife and I have lost one another. Would you see if she's in there? She's very pretty, with dark shaggy hair, about 5'6", in a cream dinner dress with a pink sweater.'

The woman was hesitant for a second.

'I'd really appreciate the favor,' Robert said, smiling warmly. 'I don't know how we lost each other.'

'I'll see what I can do.'

Robert shifted from foot to foot, checking everyone who walked into the gate.

The woman emerged. 'She's not in here. There's only one other woman and she's sixty or thereabouts.'

'Thank you.' *Where the hell could she be hiding? She was counting on me not making the flight. I don't often guess wrong.* He left the gate and went searching. The darkness he saw outside chilled him. His throat was dry. The rush and push of people hurrying past created a palpable isolation in him. Robert stopped moving. He had hoped to clear the air before Carmen thought of talking to anyone. That opportunity was gone. His confusion knotted into a simple fact when the shock of impact struck. *She's with her friend right here in Toronto. She's scared and she's told her exactly what I said.*

Chapter Forty-five

THE SHARPES TRIED TO GET BACK to some form of normalcy after bringing Colin home from the hospital. Donna trusted Susan enough to allow her to see her friends. Susan was sufficiently frightened about Colin and her parents not to divulge anything about the family situation. Steve had gone back to work on Friday, but he had turned into himself and become quiet and unsure again. Colin seemed to be working with the therapist, Ms. Tritt. Donna was worried about the mild sedatives and anti-depressants Colin was taking. He wasn't tranquil; he was hyper most of the time.

A call before noon on Saturday, the first of three, demolished what fabricated calm Donna had tried to bring back to the family. Scott Patterson's mother was on the other end of the line.

'Donna, I just want you to know that I will help in any way I can. I've been devastated since Scott told me about Colin's attempted suicide and what went on between Justin and him. Colin must be feeling so badly. I can make food or take Colin here for awhile to relieve you, whatever you need.'

Donna's arm holding the phone seemed paralyzed. Breath caught in her throat.

'Maybe this is a bad time. I'm here if you want to talk. Are you still there? I didn't mean to upset you further.'

Donna put the receiver down and sat in the nearest chair.

Kim Patterson understood the rebuff and hung up at her end. She hadn't taken two steps before the phone rang again. Kim thought it was Donna and scooped up the receiver. 'I understand... Pardon?' Kim made no further comment while she listened to Moitié's request for an interview the next morning. 'Of course, Detective. My husband and I will be here with Scott. Rest assured that my son will have no further talks with Colin. Tomorrow then.' Kim stood uneasily for a few seconds before she marched into Scott's room and grabbed his cell phone. 'Scott, I'm taking this and I don't want you to talk to Colin. Do you understand me?'

'But why?'

'A detective is coming to our house tomorrow and he wants to talk to you.'

'But I didn't do anything.'

'I know that, Scott, but I'm telling you, no more talks with Colin. You can get going on your summer reading. Am I clear on no more calls?'

'Yeah,' Scott answered nervously, walking like a snail to the two summer books he hadn't touched.

Tension grew in the Sharpe home. Donna sat alone in the dining room, threw her head back and closed her eyes. Her face was ashen. *What has Colin told Scott? What has he said about Justin?* Colin was in the kitchen demolishing a large bag of chips. She watched dumbly. Her body ached and felt bruised. Her fatigue was heavy and she was afraid. Colin frightened her. Any censure could push him over the edge. She didn't know what to do, so she sat and watched her little boy. He was in trouble and Donna didn't know if she could save him.

The phone rang again. She got up slowly and took it.

'This is…'

Donna put the receiver down. She did the same for the third call and then she sat back down. Every siren in her body arced red. How she wished for a physical place to hide, even for five minutes, from her fear and from Colin. Any miscue from her and she could lose her boy forever. How could anyone watch another human being 24 hours a day? Steve had his work and Susan had her friends, needed distractions from the stress. Donna couldn't afford to hide, so she sat and watched her son, unable to rouse herself from her stupor. She felt she could smell the stench of this disaster and her failure in every room of the house. Since Colin's suicide attempt, she had lost her confidence just as though Colin had pulled the pin from a grenade and had handed it to her. Neither parent felt steady.

Although Saturday was his day off, Moitié hadn't availed himself of the free time. His girlfriend Nicole was his best friend and, unlike most cops who kept their work sacrosanct, he shared his with her. Her father had worked Major Crimes. Nicole understood the work. She had urged Moitié to track his own leads. 'You respect Jean and he depends on your loyalty, but there comes a point where you have to establish yourself. Jean isn't your superior. Had he caught the Sharpe file instead of Tyler's, he'd pursue it, believe me. This isn't a hotdog move. You're trying to get at the truth. There's a great temptation to fit theory and fact, especially as you're under pressure from this family and the director.'

Moitié agreed. He'd meet with Scott Patterson and his parents tomorrow at 11 a.m. In the afternoon, he'd talk to Michel Gagnon and his parents. Moitié took Sharpe's suicide attempt seriously. Steve Sharpe might have been right when he said the stress was too much for his son. Moitié felt guilt might have been the reason for that desperate act. The boy's lies had caught his attention. He set up his questions for the boys. He wanted key information about Colin Sharpe. Saturday night, he and Nicole went to their favorite French bistro, *L'Express*, on rue St-Denis.

At 10:42 p.m., Fortier called Henley. 'Robert's back. He's just got off the plane and he's alone. However, I've tried contacting Carmen DiMaggio and got no reply. She might take another flight, or she's not with him.'

'At least he didn't run. That idea had crossed my mind. Stay on him.'

'Will do.'

Sunday morning, Moitié was on Lansdowne Avenue in Westmount, standing on a very large balcony that he could see needed work. The house was large and old and dark, one of many old fossils on the street. The introductions were made quickly; a parent sat on either side of Scott. 'Scott, nice to meet you. This won't take long. Colin told me you were his best friend.'

'I have two best friends.'

'Good for you. Were Justin and Colin good friends?'

'Sometimes.'

'Did the other boys like Justin?'

'The teachers liked him 'cause of his grandfather. That's what everybody said.'

'Scott, that's not what the detective asked you,' his father said.

'Well you told me that...'

Moitié broke in. 'What about you boys?'

'When he loaned us his stuff, we liked him.'

'When he didn't?'

Scott looked at his father. 'Well sometimes he pushed us around 'cause he was tall and he never got in trouble.'

'Have you talked to Colin since Justin died?'

'Yeah.'

'Please tell me what Colin told you. It's very important.'

Scott began to fidget. His mother gave him the nod to go ahead. 'Colin said Justin didn't want him to go home that night and Justin scratched him. Colin said he,' Scott looked at his mother who silently urged him on, 'kicked Justin real hard a few times and he got out and Justin drowned.'

They all sat in silence. Scott dropped his head.

Moitié asked his next question very slowly. 'Did Colin say he saw Justin drown?'

'No, but he said he wasn't going to jail no matter what he did.'

'Did he tell you why he went to the hospital?'

Kim stopped the questioning. 'That's enough, Detective. Boys are very susceptible at this age. There's nothing more Scott can tell you.'

'Yes, Mom, there is. Colin said he was like Superman—he couldn't die.'

Moitié rose, gathered his notes and ended the interview. 'Thank you, Scott, and both of you.' The next interview didn't yield anything he could use. Moitié had to give Colin Sharpe credit. He was still hiding the whole truth. Kids talked, but Colin knew when to shut the door. Was he manufacturing facts to boost himself in the pecking order at school, or was he telling the truth, just not all of it? The scar he'd seen on the kid's neck wasn't going to disappear; his bravado might be his defence against being called a coward at school. Another possibility loomed. The kid had turned around that night at the pool and seen Justin in trouble and stood and watched him drown.

He jotted down these notes and prepared to meet with the Sharpe family Tuesday, provided nothing with Tyler exploded on Monday when they heard about the cotton fiber from the gloves.

Robert spent most of Sunday deciding to take a more active role in his own defence. Waiting around for Geoffrion to make his move or the damn tests results to come in was exacting a heavy toll. The minute his plane landed at Trudeau, he felt collapsed and exhausted, a fatigue that went to his spirit. The sale didn't much matter if he were arrested. He'd left Carmen's overnight bag at an airport claims desk with her home address. The last thing he needed was to be picked up with her bag in his cab. He could not leave the threat she posed dangling. What did Fortier have on him?

Chapter Forty-six

Monday morning, from ten feet away, Moitié could see that Geoffrion had something. He was pacing firm-footed behind his desk, talking into his ear piece and waving him into the office. It wasn't even seven o'clock. 'It's a good start,' he said, ending his call.

'The fiber matches the cotton gloves. If Miss Henley hasn't used those gloves cleaning the safe, Tyler did. Sit, Denis. It's early, but I'm about to call Miss Henley.'

'On my own time, I interviewed two of Sharpe's friends.'

Geoffrion gave his partner a steely glance. 'You want to blow through my evidence and get to the kid first. He's in your craw.'

'It was my time, Jean. It's still called initiative.'

'I thought we agreed nothing till Tuesday. That aside for the moment, what did you find out?'

Moitié put aside a verbal comeback and took out his small spiral pad and located the quote he wanted. 'I don't have a confession, but I did learn that Justin Tyler did as he pleased and was never reprimanded because of Henley's donations to the school. Here's a quote from a Scott Patterson who spoke recently with Sharpe. Sharpe told him, "…he won't go to jail no matter what he did."'

'A kid's boast, doesn't prove anything. His parents probably told him that to keep him away from belts and doors.'

Did Moitié detect a smirk? He cracked his knuckles. 'Tells me the kid did something we don't know about.'

'You're reaching, Denis. Let me make my call.' When he didn't connect with Henley's cell, he called the house and was told by the housekeeper that Miss Henley was with her father. He used the private number Henley had given him and apologized for the early call. He waited for Henley's daughter to take the receiver.

'Yes?' Jessie was fully awake.

'Detective Geoffrion, Miss Henley. Did you ever use the house-keeper's white gloves when you cleaned the safe?'

'No, never. I don't believe I've ever used those gloves for anything.'

'Mr. Tyler has said he pretended to run the combination in your presence. Did he ever use gloves on those occasions?'

'Again, never!' Jessie saw what Geoffrion was getting at and her nerves twitched. 'You've found traces of the gloves on the safe, haven't you?'

'I can't comment on that, Miss Henley.'

'What about the other tests?'

'They're high priority, but they're not in yet.'

Jessie went to her father as soon as she was off the phone. 'Dad, they've found evidence on the safe, residue or fibers from Sylvie's cleaning gloves. The bastard got into the safe. I was right from the beginning. He knows Justin might not have been his. He knew that the night Justin drowned.' Her words were hammer blows and she sank into a chair, overcome with grief and guilt. 'I'm not innocent in Justin's death, not if Robert killed him.' These last words were uttered in a strangled whisper. Jessie seemed unaware of her father's presence. He dragged a wing chair a few feet and sat down in front of her.

'Jessie, listen to me. Robert might have tried, but he might not have gotten into the safe. If he did, I see now that we have to go on that assumption. It's time for us to tell Geoffrion what Mike has discovered. As I promised, I can work on the privacy issue involved. Once the results are made public, I'll have a harder time containing the information. We can't afford to be rear-ended. Please pay attention to what I'm saying, Jessie. Open your eyes, Jess. That's better. You must recall that Mike said Robert was trying to dispose of something small. It might well have been the gloves. Are we together on this? I can make the call right now. First though, I'll call Mike and tell him to make a report of everything he has on Robert. He likes to keep everything in his head. Geoffrion will want a written report.'

Jessie clenched and unclenched her hands, trying to stem an outburst of sentiment. She looked across at her father and held his gaze. The trust between them was unspoken but understood. Her father was not judging her. He waited quietly. Her love for Justin remained absolute. Taking responsibility, she said simply, 'Make the call.'

Jessie went on, ruefully. 'I thought my past was safely buried, but it never leaves your life. It's simply locked up where someone will find the means to get at it. I know you don't want to hear this, Dad, but it was just two nights on a golf junket. He used protection, but it didn't work. I kept that document, as I've said, to keep Robert from taking

Justin if we fell apart. Funny thing is, he wouldn't have wanted Justin. Robert isn't a bad man, but I think this information corrupted what he felt for me, and the will did the rest. Everything began with me. I protected Justin from everyone but me.'

'We can't alter the past, but we can work to fix the damage. Justin still needs you to seek justice for the life that he lost. Do you have the documents with you?'

'Yes, they're upstairs.'

'Let me call Mike.'

Luc Ranger was Mike's neighbor. For two years he had promised to show Luc the shotgun he had carried as a cop although he told Luc beforehand he would never reveal how many guys he had taken down with that gun. It was a very big deal because Mike never showed that gun. He kept it wrapped in a red blanket and tied with two black belts. Well, today was Luc's fourteenth birthday. He had seen a lot of the other files that Mike had kept from all his cases, all neatly categorized, from bank robberies, to murders, to the Mafia. Mike had better stuff than anything Luc found online. In the boy's eyes, Mike Fortier was a real legend. At eleven o'clock, he stood at Mike's front door and knocked. Mike didn't come to the door. Luc pounded. Mike was deaf in one ear. After the third pounding, he tried the handle and found the door open.

'Mike!' he called out and he took a few steps inside the front door. 'Mike!' he shouted louder. 'It's me; it's Luc!' Luc was about to shout again, angrily this time because he thought Mike had forgotten all about his birthday and what that meant. Luc froze. Mike was sprawled awkwardly at the bottom of his stairs. The stairs were steep, narrow, uncarpeted and treacherous. A pool of blood had formed around the side of his head. One leg was lying on two steps. An empty brace lay beside his right hand. One arm was under his body. 'Oh shit!' Luc ran from the house to get his mother. 'Mom! Mom! Call 9-1-1! Mike fell down the stairs. There's a whole mess of blood.' Michelle ran back to Mike. Luc ran after her. 'Luc, find a blanket. For God's sake, don't move him.' She knelt at Mike's side and laid two fingers on the side of his neck to find a pulse. She tried his wrist and hiked her shoulders. 'I'm probably too nervous.' She touched the side of his cheek. 'It's warm. That's a good sign.' She wanted to put her hand in front of his nose, but his nose was bloody. When the phone rang, they both jumped.

Michelle picked up the receiver warily. 'Yes?'

'I'm looking for Mike Fortier.'

'This is his neighbor,' her voice shook uncontrollably. 'There's been a terrible accident. Mike has fallen down his stairs. I've called for help.'

'Is he alright?'

'He's unconscious.'

'Is he alive?'

'I'm not certain.'

'I'm Douglas Henley. Mike was doing work for me. Tell the paramedics to take him to the General. I'll have doctors there to care for him.'

'I'm Michelle Ranger.'

'Whatever you do, do not let them take Mike to the Lakeshore Hospital. I want my physicians to see him in a private room. I'll cover the costs.'

'The paramedics are here!'

'Put one of them on, please.' Henley made his wishes known. 'Is he alive?'

The paramedic who took the call had no idea who Douglas Henley was. 'Family?'

'No, friend. Douglas…'

'We have no time to waste, sir.'

'Then get on with it,' Henley ordered.

Chapter Forty-seven

THE DAY BEFORE, CAITLIN lugged a carry-on of hand-outs from the conference, her own bag, and laptop into her house on Wood Avenue. Out of the corner of her eye, she had spotted the Mini, but Carmen's wasn't the only Mini in the city. She didn't want it to be Carmen's. What she needed was a hot shower and some down time. Most wishes didn't materialize and hers didn't either. Carmen was sitting on her best couch and talking to a man she didn't recognize. Her nerves heated. Robert?

'Caitlin, I'm so glad to see you!' Carmen hopped up and ran to Caitlin and took the bags. 'Before you explode, sit down and let me explain...'

'I'll leave you alone.' Bruno, from security, went back to his car.

Caught unaware, Caitlin wanted to offer her best friend comfort, but her tank was empty. 'When you didn't call, I thought something was up.' Caitlin looked away from her friend.

'Is that all you have to say?'

'What else is there to say? You don't listen to anyone. Underneath your risk-loving demeanor, you must have a death wish. That or you hate yourself to the point of self-destruction.' Caitlin had finally struck a chord because Carmen was suddenly silent. They sat uneasily together for the next few minutes.

Carmen said quietly, 'Annie went easier on me.'

'That's because she doesn't know you as well as I do, or as long. You can stay here, Carm. I just don't have the energy to take on your never-ending problems.'

Carmen forced her eyes not to tear. 'Can I ask you one question?'

'Shoot!'

'What do you think Robert meant by saying that he found his son alone in the pool? Do you think I interpreted its meaning correctly?'

Indignant and fatigued, Caitlin fired back. 'You have the most irritating ability to hang onto things. What the hell does it matter what he meant? You're now living with round-the-clock-security. Zone in on yourself and think of the money Annie is wasting because of you. What does one call this—desperate insecurity? Let the police deal with Robert. I don't want to lose another person I love. Don't let Bruno out of your sight!'

'Isn't it the other way around?'

Caitlin flopped onto the couch and laughed loudly. 'You drive me crazy!'

Carmen caught sight of the photos of Chris on the antique table. Caitlin must have put those up very recently. Her brother had been killed a few years ago. 'For what it's worth, I'm sorry for what I've put you through. People change; give me another chance.'

'Get over here!' Caitlin hugged the breath from Carmen, but she didn't mind. 'You can have as many chances as you need.'

'Now I have Bruno.'

'Three cheers for you. Don't ever get in touch with Robert again.' Caitlin's last sentence was stark and cold and threatening.

'You have my word.'

The first thing Henley did after he was off the phone was to go to Jessie with the news. 'I now have to call Geoffrion and I'll ask that we meet at the hospital in the off chance that Mike can talk. We have to make a clean breast of things, and I feel that you should accompany me.'

Jessie knew all along that this time would come and she changed hurriedly. Somewhere, deep inside of her, she heard her own wordless scream of grief. In the limo, Henley took Jessie's hand. It was very cold. 'We have to be forthcoming with Geoffrion. I know you understand that.'

Henley made his call from the limo. 'Detective Geoffrion, please. This is Douglas Henley. The call is urgent.'

'Major Crimes, Detective Geoffrion.'

'Douglas Henley, Detective. Allow me to give you additional information without interruption.' Henley intended to conduct their conversation. Obstructing the investigation by hiring Fortier had already set up an unpropitious beginning. 'I have information about my son-in-law. I took it upon myself to hire a retired homicide policeman, a friend, to investigate on his own. I was about to ask him for a written report when I learned of his accident. My daughter and I are minutes away from the Montreal General Hospital. I am a director there. Could we meet at the hospital and give you the details we have to date? Ask at Information to direct you to the main conference room on the first floor. I have my physician with him. We'll go to Emergency first to check his condition.'

Geoffrion wrenched his mind from concentrating on Henley's blunder. He said, trying to control the anger and excitement in his voice, 'I will meet you there. What's his name?'

'Mike Fortier.'

'The Mike Fortier?' *The shotgun-slingin' cowboy cop.*

'The same.'

'But he must be...'

'He's seventy-nine and sharp as a tack.'

'I should be there in thirty minutes.'

'My daughter and I will be there, Detective.'

Geoffrion picked up his things and motioned to Moitié who was busy working on his interview with Colin that would take place tomorrow. 'Denis, I may have more on Tyler. The Henleys hired Mike Fortier. He's had an accident. We're meeting at the General. You coming? We're still working this file together.'

'You bet.'

Geoffrion gave Moitié what little he had. 'It burns my ass that Henley thinks he can run the investigation behind our backs and obstruct our work. Anybody else, I'd have charged his ass for this.'

'Money rules. Always has. Are they certain Fortier met with an accident?'

'We'll find out now that the Henleys have seen fit to include us.' In their unmarked vehicle, Geoffrion used the sirens.

Mike was not in ICU, he was in surgery. He had fractured his jaw and cheekbone, his right shoulder and his hip that had been shot out so many years ago. He was eight hours in surgery and would face a great deal of pain and a long rehab. Henley had been told of his injuries, and he and Jessie had gone down to the conference room to wait for Geoffrion. 'At least he's alive,' was all Henley had to say. Jessie had nothing to add. Henley flinched when he saw Moitié. He'd wanted Geoffrion's full attention.

All four people sat down stiffly. Henley had no intention of offering

241

any apology. He knew that Geoffrion would not dare to repri-mand him.

'Summarize what evidence Fortier gathered on your son-in-law.'

Moitié took out his pad and took notes. Geoffrion asked the questions.

'Robert was seeing a woman at the time of Justin's death, a Carmen DiMaggio. Fortier wasn't certain of their relationship, but the woman is listed in the phonebook. There were calls between the two of them and he met with her. Robert went to Toronto Friday night. Fortier was at the airport and saw him. She may have gone with him. Most damaging, Fortier followed Robert to a mall in the West Island. Although he was not certain what the object was, he did see Robert in a washroom, trying to dispose of something small. Robert changed his mind and tucked whatever it was back into his pocket. He got rid of it somewhere else. Fortier wasn't able to keep up with him. He does know that Robert realized he was being tailed.'

A look of satisfaction passed between the cops. They both wanted a conviction. 'You have Fortier's notes for all this?' Geoffrion asked, quietly confident.

'Old guy, old habits. He kept everything in his head. I was calling his home to ask him to make a report when I heard of his accident. His neighbor had just found him.'

'That's all hearsay. We need Fortier's corroboration. Do we know this was an accident?'

'I know only that a neighbor found him at the bottom of his stairs.'

'What's his address? We'll close off the scene and get out there.'

'Do you think there is a chance that Robert...'

'We know nothing until we follow proper procedure and investigate the scene.'

Henley nodded at the rebuke. He wasn't about to lose the last word. 'You have something with the cleaning gloves. Jessie called Sylvie. We know about them.'

'We can't discuss an ongoing investigation, sir.' Geoffrion wanted to add, *No matter who you are!* 'How truthful is the housekeeper?' Before Jessie had the chance to respond, he added, 'She might have come upon the combination. She has full access to the gloves and the house when the family is not present.'

'There was money in the safe, a definite amount. It wasn't touched. To my knowledge, Sylvie is honest and trustworthy.'

'Did you count it?'

'No, actually, but...'

'Count it to be sure. A caretaker would not take a large amount. You might be deceived into thinking no money had been taken.'

Geoffrion and Moitié left, anxious to get to the townhouse and call Carmen DiMaggio for an interview. Before they left, they spoke with the head nurse, introduced themselves and asked to be informed as soon as Fortier regained consciousness. Geoffrion turned to his partner. 'I know you're anxious to have another go at Colin Sharpe, but you can see I have something here.'

'I'll cover the townhouse with you. Nothing yet alters my view of Sharpe. You're not hearing what he told his friend, *no matter what I did.* Both subjects remain viable.'

'Fine.' Decarie Expressway was its usual treacherous bottleneck. The siren didn't help much because the expressway was subterranean. Three lanes of cars were jammed, so there was no place for the cars to move to let them through. Montreal motorists follow a simple code: *Every car for itself.* Unlike other provinces, drivers here are less likely to make way immediately for a police car or an ambulance. Once they were on the Trans-Canada Highway, the siren was a definite advantage. They drove south on St. Charles Boulevard to the row of townhouses on Elm Avenue. The homes were built high and narrow. Geoffrion had called ahead and officers were waiting for them.

He asked if the neighbor who found Fortier was around. He was told the boy was next door, waiting for them. When Geoffrion knocked, Michelle Ranger came out with her son Luc. Moitié had gone into the house. 'Good afternoon, I'm Detective Geoffrion. I have some questions...'

Luc's eyes widened as he described what he found.

'The front door was unlocked?'

Michelle took over. 'We've been Mike's neighbor for eleven years. I can't believe this has happened! I've told him often to lock up, but he steadfastly refuses to bolt his front door. I'm sure that he fell and this was an accident, but just the same, home invasions don't faze him, not even knowing an elderly couple on St. Charles was killed by three teens some years back. Mike still thinks he's *on the job*, as he likes to say.'

What else does he say?'

Luc knew and, beaming, he quoted the old cop. 'I've never met a brute I couldn't put down.'

'Did either of you see anyone going into the townhouse?'

'It's my birthday! I was opening stuff from my parents. Mike promised to show me his shotgun the day I turned fourteen. That's why I was there today.'

'Never mind that gun,' Michelle said. 'I don't want you anywhere near it. Detective, how is Mike? I should have asked that first. Before you go, there was something odd. Because of his bad hip, Mike always wore his brace, but he wasn't wearing it when he fell. He hadn't had a chance to put it on. I wonder how that happened. He even wore the brace to the bathroom. He was joking one day when he told me.'

'He's in surgery.' Geoffrion took the information and asked a few more questions before he joined Moitié. 'There's a lot of blood. Lucky Fortier's not dead. These stairs are steep. I was wondering why he didn't grab the banister to break his fall. I gather he didn't because I think he might have broken it, had he grabbed it.' Moitié was pulling at the banister. 'It's not well built.'

'He rarely if ever locked the front door,' Geoffrion told him. 'In his head, he's still a cowboy cop.'

'He had a whole room upstairs and half the basement full of files, photos and trophies and commendations. How he managed to keep all this stuff, against regulations, is one thing. The collection itself would make a great book of police history in Quebec.'

'We can't leave the shotgun here. Did you come across it?'

'No, it must be hidden. I'll stay till I locate it.'

'He fell late Sunday night or early Monday morning. Tyler was back in Montreal. Fortier's door was unlocked. Tyler could have gotten in here undetected.' Geoffrion took out his notes, found what he wanted and punched in the number. 'Mr. Henley, Detective Geoffrion, you said Tyler knew he had a tail. Did he by chance know who?'

'Robert knew it was Fortier. He'd been introduced to him a year ago and had seen him in the house the day after Justin drowned. He knew I had hired him. From there, the math was easy.' Henley weighed once more giving Geoffrion the evidence of the other document.

Carmen DiMaggio was next on Geoffrion's list. Words spoken between the sheets.

'Detective, there is another issue.'

'Yes?'

'There was a potentially dangerous document in the safe that might have provided Robert with a motive. It is a very private matter.'

'What?'

'I'll discuss it with you in person.'

Geoffrion was about to say there was no privacy in murder cases, that the innocent often suffered collateral grief, but he wanted the evidence. 'I'm on my way.'

'THE MOMENT JUSTIN DROWNED, this meeting with Geoffrion was inevitable, Jessie.' He expected her to balk, but he was surprised by her unexpected percipience.

'Secrets are never safe, not even when they're locked up.' They sat together and waited. Tears oozed from her eyes. 'Perhaps I'll be able to sleep and remember Justin's face in happier times.' The opulence of the living room, from the décor to the size of the room itself, diminished father and daughter whose vulnerable presence was at odds with the power of objects money can buy.

When the bell rang, neither made any move. When Geoffrion was led into the room, Henley rose. 'Detective, I do not want to hear about obstruction of justice. My daughter struggled with this from the day Justin died. I want your solemn assurance that this information will not be leaked to your division or to the media.'

The bitter irony of a man seeking justice for a grandson he loved and hiding the motive for his murder was not lost on Geoffrion. He ignored the fire in Henley's eyes. 'Unless it is absolutely necessary, no detective divulges information injurious to innocent parties.'

'You must go to any length to be certain it never becomes necessary,' Henley ordered.

'The file is my priority; everything else is secondary.'

Henley looked over at Jessie, but she looked away, waiting for her secret to be exposed. 'Excuse my manners. Please sit down, Detective.'

Geoffrion took out his notepad.

'You won't need it. In the event that the marriage between my daughter and Robert failed, Jessie attached a second document to her new will. It puts Justin's paternity into question. The documents had only been in the safe a few days.'

There was a moment of startling silence as if someone had just told them about the death of a friend.

Geoffrion brought his feet together, and they made a slight noise on the plush carpet. 'Paternity was never clarified?'

'It wasn't.' Henley hoped Jessie would speak up, but she continued staring out the window. 'The other man involved was out of the picture.

Jessie did not want to break the tenuous connection between Robert and Justin.'

Since there was nothing more forthcoming, Geoffrion changed subjects. 'Had Mr. Tyler done anything that prompted you to change the will and exclude him, except in the event of your son's death?'

Jessie's shoulders sagged, but she did turn and answered. 'Robert is doing well enough on his own. The Henley money must stay within the family.'

And Robert wasn't family. Geoffrion felt something akin to pity for Robert.

'Because of a situation I created, I had to see to it that Justin was protected. He was family.' Jessie had not met Geoffrion's gaze. She focused on his hands. It was remarkable that he never used them for emphasis, not even when they held his pad. All the force of his words emanated from his head. She saw that he pulled his hands closer to his body.

Henley added, 'Most people do not understand that great wealth brings with it greater responsibility.'

'It is not my place to judge, Sir.' Inwardly, Geoffrion found them both culpable. *What kind of people value money and secrets above the life of their child and obstruct the investigation into his death?*

'Keep in mind what this information means to me and my daughter. When do you expect the other test results?'

'I check in every day. As soon as they are available, I'll have them.' Geoffrion kept one question to himself. He was certain the answer was plaguing them. *Have you considered Justin might be Robert's son?* Henley walked him to the door.

Back in his office, Geoffrion took out a larger notebook and amended the evidence he had on Robert Tyler: opportunity, indifference between father and son, disinherited in favor of the son, unless the kid dies. He underlined that last point. Was that the kicker? Did Tyler know in that heated moment that the will would be changed? That was the key. Paternity questioned (both last issues recently discovered), paid for all the private schools et cetera, the cotton gloves, Fortier sees him trying to dispose of something rolled in his hand, seeing another woman. Was this enough for an arrest? Did he have sufficient motive? He opened the smaller pad and found Carmen DiMaggio. Was she the final link?

He called her workplace. '*Best Grilles*, bonjour, good morning!'

'Miss Carmen DiMaggio, please.'

'Sure, may I tell her who's calling?'

'This is a personal call.'

'Just one moment, please.'

Carole gave Carmen that scolding look she had for personal calls. Carmen's upper lip beaded with perspiration. Robert wouldn't have the gall to call her at work, not after Toronto. She trembled when she picked up the receiver. 'Carmen DiMaggio.'

'Miss DiMaggio, this is Detective Geoffrion from Major Crimes.'

Oh my God! Oh my God! Her asthma threatened to come back. 'Yes?' Both hands trembled.

'This call is in connection with the Justin Henley drowning. Would you please come to my office for an interview at the North Division on Crémazie on the corner of St. Hubert at three today?' He gave Carmen the necessary details.

'But why? I'm in no way involved.'

'You do know a Robert Tyler.'

'Yes, but…'

'This is normal procedure, Miss DiMaggio. Today at three then.'

Carmen's face blanched as her boss approached her. 'What's wrong Carmen? You don't look well.'

'I have a personal emergency. I have to go.' Carmen grabbed her purse and ran out, still visibly shaken. By the time she got inside her car, she called Caitlin. 'The police want to see me today!' she cried into the phone.

'Whoa! Slow down.'

'I can't slow down. I have to get to the police station today. Major Crimes, Caitlin! Shit! What am I going to do?'

'For God's sake take a breath and try to speak coherently.'

Carmen lost it. 'Christ! A detective wants me at his office at three today in connection with the drowning. Have you got that now?'

'Don't take this out on me. What are you so worried about? You haven't done anything. We have time to talk.'

Carmen's tears fell freely. Her shoulders felt like boards. 'What do I tell him?'

'The truth.'

'It's that sentence that made me run. If I reveal that, and Robert isn't arrested, he'll come after me. Is there any way you can come with me? I know I got myself into this, but would you please help me?'

'What about the sale of the company? If you reveal that, the police will see Robert as a flight risk. Can you make it there by 2:30? I'll meet you and we can discuss this.'

'God, I don't know how to thank you.'

'I'll think of ways. In the meantime, don't drive like a maniac. I'll be there.' If Caitlin had the time to list all the reasons Carmen should be facing her own stupid problems, she would never have left the house. Fortunately, she too was frightened for Carmen. Her worst fears were materializing. She had to watch her speed as well because she was almost as nervous as Carmen. The traffic didn't help. When she finally pulled into the parking lot, Carmen was easy to spot. Her hands were on the steering wheel and her head was resting on it. When Caitlin tapped on her window, Carmen jumped. Caitlin got onto the seat beside her. 'Carmen, just listen. You have to be forthright with everything. Apart from your fear of Robert, there is the threat of him implicating you somehow in this, or the police thinking the same thing. You ended the relationship. You have to tell them why. You didn't know he was married. Then he was leaving his wife. Then he frightened you and you ran. Tell all of it.'

'Can you come in with me? I'm so nervous. I'm not sure I can talk.'

'You're doing fine now. I'll try to go in with you. If he won't let me, you have to step up.'

'Why am I so stupid?'

'Part of your charm. Now, pull yourself together. Where's Bruno, the security guy?'

'See that black CRV?'

'Over there?'

'He's in the car.'

'Good. You have to tell the police about Bruno. Let's go. Remember, the truth.'

Chapter Forty-nine

AT THE HOUSE ON ROSELAWN CRESCENT, Robert was in his habitat, cleaning obsessively. He belonged there. He had purchased every piece in his quarters. His nervous movements had not assuaged the fear that had spread like contagion into every vein. One sentence, taken out of context, had spooked Carmen and made her dangerous to him. *How could she just turn on me like that? I trusted her. I thought she trusted me. She never even gave me the chance to explain! I kept my word and told her about Justin. I didn't give her enough attention. It's always the same shit with women. I deserved one night to celebrate the sale. The bitch couldn't give me that.* He wished he had never broken his routine with women. It was imperative he do something about her.

He called Hoye and laid it all out.

'What were you thinking of taking this woman with you to Toronto?'

'How damaging is that sentence?'

'It won't stand alone, Robert. You can try to toss it off, but evidence is gathered piecemeal unless there's a smoking gun. That sentence is another piece.'

'You mean another nail, don't you?' Robert picked up on Hoye's censorious tone. Gone were the assuring words. Hoye was abrupt. 'I fucked up. I know it. I'm sure other clients have fucked up as well.'

'Until anything breaks, and even then, call me before you say anything to anyone. Don't do the prosecutors' work for them.'

'That won't be hard. Jessie's moved out, the housekeeper's avoiding me and Carmen's run off. Am I'm going to be arrested, Doug?'

'The police are still gathering evidence and waiting for lab results. "Possibly" is the best I can do. DNA evidence will be a strong determinant. If they can prove you got into the safe, "probable" is my answer.'

'I'm screwed?'

'That's when my work begins. That's when we start to fight back. Stay away from this Carmen.'

'Got it.' For most of his life, Robert had believed that people who should have supported him had failed him. Carmen had joined that list.

After the call, there was no consolation in recognizing that he had failed himself. Hoye was wrong about one thing. He couldn't leave Carmen alone. He had to convince her that she had misunderstood his intent. That would be one less piece of evidence against him. He knew her work number from memory. He thought about Hoye, he hesitated, and then he called. Carmen wouldn't take his call at home, but she had to take calls at work.

'Miss DiMaggio has left for the day.'

'I see, thank you.' *Fuck!*

'Would you like to leave a message, sir?'

'I'll call tomorrow.'

'Have a good day then!'

So she's back. Where the hell is she? He checked his watch. Sylvie hadn't left for the day. He went up to find her. Her bag was on a side counter in the kitchen. When he turned, she was walking into the kitchen and flinched when she saw him. 'There's no need to be afraid, Sylvie. I know what you did. You gave Jessie and Douglas another reason to keep up their attack. However, I thought I had your loyalty. I do pay your salary and I paid for the pool. Jessie is about to drain it. I wanted one last swim.'

Sylvie backed into a wall. 'I didn't call Miss Henley. She called looking for you.'

'I see. Didn't you think of coming outside and handing me the phone?'

'I'm sorry. I didn't.'

'I wanted to see you before you left. Seeing as Jessie isn't here, I won't need you more than two days a week. Say Monday and Thursday. That way you can enjoy a long weekend.'

Sylvie's face fell. 'We have a verbal contract, Robert.'

'I had a son and a wife.' She'd turned on him and he felt nothing for her.

'You know I help my mother out.'

'This might not be permanent, Sylvie, but for now, I could use the extra money. I might need it for a lawyer, and you can file for unemployment for the other three days.'

Blood rushed into Sylvie's cheeks. It started around her jaw and rose to her eyes. She could hurt Robert by telling him about the gloves, but she didn't dare. Losing her two-day week wasn't an option. 'I'm under a great deal of stress. Truth is that I'd prefer to be alone.'

Sylvie suffered no qualms of doubt. She took her purse and left without another word. If Robert was involved in Justin's death, she didn't want to be in that house a moment longer. Robert followed her outside and watched her leave. A gust of wind had come up suddenly and chilled him. A dead leaf swirled in the wind for a few seconds and came to rest a few feet from him. A single leaf, dead in July. Robert stepped back into the house and closed the door. It was odd, he thought, ten days ago his guilt was palpable, but it was less now, faded. He had let go of the listed memories, his memoranda of grief. Robert poured himself a double scotch, single malt, and took it out to the covered deck. He leaned back on his favorite chair and took a good swig. It had never tasted better.

Certainly, he felt the thud of separate attacks, but his will to survive was absolute. He had come to a dull acceptance of the Henley barrage. Carmen was another issue. There the blow was unacceptable, something he had to rectify. His bleak utterance was dangerously ignorant. Had he purposely tried to frighten Carmen because she was doggedly holding him accountable and not joining him in that one celebration? The sale had emboldened him and empowered him, but one foolhardy throwaway sentence could destroy him. He didn't finish his drink. He changed and drove to Laval in Jessie's SUV. Carmen had to come home sometime, if she wasn't already there. He was hoping he might catch her arrival and work from there.

'I almost feel *I'm* a suspect,' Carmen whispered to Caitlin as they waited behind the gray locked doors to be admitted. 'I hope you can come in with me.'

Geoffrion was surprised when Carmen introduced herself and surprised to find two women. DiMaggio's dark eyes caught his attention. Everything about her seemed as fresh as the girl next door. 'And this is?'

'Caitlin Donovan, a friend. I'm hoping I can attend the interview because Carmen is very nervous and I can fill in what she might forget.'

Geoffrion didn't want DiMaggio to have support, but he changed his mind because they both appeared sincere and out of place in a police division. He wanted everything he could get. 'Follow me, ladies.' Inside the room, he pointed to a chair for Caitlin at the end of the table. Carmen was directed to sit across from him. 'Alright, let's get started.' Geoffrion turned on the recorder.

'How do you know Robert Tyler?'

Carmen looked forlornly at Caitlin. She felt humiliated. 'I met him at the casino on a Sunday, the only day I go. I had dinner with him the next night and the night after. I didn't know he was married.'

'The dates?'

Carmen opened her purse, checked her palm pilot and gave Geoffrion the dates. 'He invited me to go to Toronto with him that Friday.'

'When did you learn of his son's death?'

'I'm really nervous, Detective. I hadn't made up my mind about even going with him when he called me on Thursday. All he said was he couldn't make the trip because his son had just drowned. That's when I knew he was married. I didn't speak to him for five days or thereabouts. He suddenly showed up at my office one day to explain. I told him he should be with his family.'

'Did he call again?'

'He showed up at my apartment unannounced and insisted that I hear him out.'

'Go on.'

'This all feels so contrived now. It didn't then. He wanted a new start in life; he said with me. He was going to leave his wife, before his son died.'

'Did you see him again?'

'He said he needed someone on his side and I was attracted to him.'

'So you saw him again?'

'I went to Toronto, a huge mistake.'

'Why?'

Carmen was close to tears. Caitlin urged her on. 'He sold his company. He was on a high and was put off because I wasn't sharing it. The fact was he didn't want me there. He didn't need me anymore.' Her eyes teared. 'He'd promised to tell me about his son because I couldn't understand why he wasn't mourning him. I could see he was irritated. He said something that shocked us both. I pretended to go to the washroom and took off. I went to a friend's who has hired 24/7 security for me. I don't have that kind of money. I may have misunderstood, but I am afraid of Robert. I'm staying with Caitlin to be safe.'

'He sold his company?' Tyler had just become a flight risk.

'Yes.'

'What did he say that frightened you?'

'He spoke in generalities about his son. Then he said something particular. He had come upon his son when he was alone in the pool and asked him to do a few laps with him. His son had said no. All that struck me was, is that what happened the night he drowned? Was Robert there? That suggestion freaked me out. That's when I took off. I knew the chef. I'm a sales rep and I often eat there when I'm in the city. He called me a cab, and I left by the back door. I left my bag in the hotel. Robert tried to explain that his comment wasn't something that happened on the night his son drowned—it was a common occurrence. I was beyond fright. I don't know if he was taken aback by my reaction or by what he said.' Carmen didn't feel any better or safer at the end of the interview.

Geoffrion did not give any indication of the importance of this last point. 'What did he say about his son?'

'Generalities, mostly. His son didn't much like him. He didn't participate in any of the sports he liked. They had nothing in common. Robert was abrupt in his explanation. I felt I was intruding, though the Toronto weekend was initially supposed to be his time to tell me about his life.'

'Do you intend to go back home?'

'I do have security, but I'm frightened, especially now. Will I have to testify in court?'

'I can't give you a definitive answer, Miss DiMaggio, but there is a probability you will.'

'I can't believe how stupid I've been.'

Geoffrion smiled, relieving the tension. 'You belong to a very large club.' He believed DiMaggio.

Carmen didn't bother trying to hold back the tears.

Chapter Fifty

Before going to the hospital, Moitié had gone around Fortier's home, examining all the sites of possible entrance. If Tyler had assaulted the old cop, he had no way of knowing the front door was unlocked. Fortier had two air conditioners. Nothing had been tampered with there. Ironically, the garage was locked. The other windows were secure. He found a side-entrance door to the garage unlocked. He called forensics to dust for prints. An officer at the front of the house was instructed to tape off that door and to keep everyone but forensics out of the house. He relayed what he had to Geoffrion and told him he'd go to the hospital in the off chance Fortier regained consciousness and could at least write something of a clue as to what had happened to him. He certainly wouldn't be able to speak with a broken jaw.

He heard about DiMaggio's interview. 'A damaging statement on Tyler's part, but not any more definitive than Sharpe's *no matter what I did*. Tomorrow is my last attempt with the kid. As I hear he's feeling cocky and invincible, I might hit the big score.'

'Denis, keep in mind the kid could be boasting. After all, there's no one to refute what he says. If Fortier was assaulted, things change.'

'Agreed, but not before I have one last crack at Sharpe.'

'Have you alerted the family?'

'Not happy about it, but they'll be prepared with their lawyer, the therapist and parents. I might have to stand. I've agreed to do the questioning at their home.'

'A fair concession. I'm calling the lab to see what's up there.'

'If Fortier gives up anything, I'll fill you in.'

Though neither cop would own up to the truth, each was in a race to the finish line.

Fortier lay in recovery. His eyes opened a few times and closed. His mind was wrapped around bales of wadding and inside those was colossal pain, not intermittent pain, but dull unrelenting pain that threatened to break through the wadding that barricaded it. Everything but his eyes felt enclosed in cement, tight and dry. He felt the dryness in his throat first, a desert dry, red and fiery. He tried to swallow, tried to force a swallow with his jaw. Fierce pain shot like a blow torch from his jawbone to his hair, but he couldn't swallow. The nerve block, which should have cut the pain for six to eighteen hours, had stopped working within two hours. Fortier could vaguely make out a voice, but it seemed far away.

'Mr. Fortier, you have a morphine pump in your left hand. Use it as often as you want.'

Someone was pulling at his hand. He hadn't heard what the nurse had said. She was speaking into his near-deaf ear. Whoever it was pumping his thumb, he was too tired to open his eyes. He tried to moan, but that worsened the pain. A jet of vomit shot up the back of his throat and began to drown him.

Doctors rushed to the bed to pry some of the gauze from the side of his mouth and suction the vomit that had gone up into his nose as well. 'We have it under control, nurse. Keep his head raised.' The nurse wiped Fortier's mouth gently. She felt his forehead with the palm of her hand and went for a cold wet facecloth. Her touch brought Fortier back thirty years. The familiar touch of a gentle hand ignited a distant memory. Such humane and generous actions from a nurse had saved his life so many years ago, had brought him back from the dead. Fortier had never read Proust, but he would have agreed with him if he had.

Fortier knew then instinctively where he was. He was in another fight. He went to the one part of his body that moved, and pumped the morphine. No matter what had happened, he wasn't going out on a gurney. He put his confusion aside and began to fight the pain, taking its blows, one by one. He kept his eyes closed and he pumped till he fell asleep. He needed energy.

Moitié waited patiently outside recovery until a physician had the time to speak with him. Moitié identified himself.

'Mr. Fortier will survive, but he's looking at a great deal of rehab.'

'Is he awake?'

'In and out. His jaw is wired shut, so he won't be talking.'

'I have only one question and I had a pad in mind. We want to know what happened.'

'Give him a few hours.' He read Fortier's file. 'He'll be eighty on

Friday. After a fall like that, and the drugs, confusion is not uncommon.
I suggest you come back tomorrow or the day after.'

'I'll give it one try tonight. Fortier's a fossil, but he was one of ours, a legend actually.'

'Then we're on the same side. We'll take good care of him. Law enforcement tries to stop violence; physicians work to repair what you miss.'

Moitié waited for four hours and had to call it a day. He'd be back after his interview with the Sharpes.

Robert had found a convenient place to park half a block away from Carmen's apartment. Jessie's SUV was good camouflage. His fingers quietly drummed the steering column. He had decided against music; he had to keep his eyes peeled. He cracked his fingers and sat apprehensive and daringly excited. However, time began to stretch out and took its toll on him. He hated waiting, especially for someone who didn't want to see him. He remembered sitting on the orange sofa, fresh and clean in his best shorts and T-shirt and white socks and sneakers, waiting for his aunt to come and get him. Hope faded when he caught her dutiful tight glance when she arrived. He thought of the funeral home where Jessie had ordered him to wait in the halls until she allowed him a few minutes with Justin.

His heart began drumming in a wild rhythm. 'Damn!' He ran his hand roughly through his hair. A few nights ago, Carmen had slept with him. Now he was cowering on the street to get in a few cautionary words. A searing anger began to fester. *Who the hell does she think she is? She thinks she can pronounce on my life!* He crossed his legs and shook his foot for the next ten minutes. He looked in the mirror and the image he saw was not the image of a murderer. He saw a victim. Carmen was deceiving herself if she thought she could just walk away. He forced a laugh. *She owes me 800 bucks, more. I paid for air fare. She's smarter than I thought. I would have bet the bank I'd see her on the plane.* A Honda Accord pulled up in front of him. Two little brats stared out the back window at him, the boy making faces. When the mother left them in the car as she rushed into some house, the kids got braver. Now the girl was sticking her tongue out till it touched the back window, and the boy was stretching his eyes.

It was after seven, and Carmen wasn't back. These rug rats would remember him. He started up the SUV and began to pull out when he saw the Mini. He sat tight and forgot the brats. Carmen wasn't alone, a blonde was with her. They hurried into the apartment. Another car pulled in beside the Mini. The driver didn't get out. Robert didn't move. He waited, but not long.

Caitlin saw Carmen's bag first. It was sitting in front of her door. 'Carmen, calm down. Look, Robert didn't bring it here. It was delivered by UPS. Hurry in and get what you need. Don't think and you'll be fine.'

Carmen froze. 'What if I have to testify?'

Caitlin took her friend by the shoulders. 'I'm here to support you, Annie is covering your back with Bruno, but you got yourself into this. Grit your teeth and get on with it. You wouldn't listen to me or Annie. Get your stuff.'

Carmen went at her packing with a vengeance. 'I can't see myself getting up at six every morning and travelling over an hour to get to work.'

'If Robert doesn't come near you, in a few days, with Bruno, would you feel safe enough to come home?'

Carmen took her cosmetics from the bag Robert had sent. 'That's it, I guess. Let's get out of here. Right now, I don't feel safe. I can't say what I'll feel in a few days.'

Caitlin helped carry the two bags and they put them in the tiny back seat and drove off. A CRV followed them close behind.

Has she already gone to the cops? If not a cop car, a friend, a brother? Who? He pulled out, gave the kids the finger and followed the CRV, careful to keep a safe distance. About fifteen minutes into the tail, he reached a decision. He stopped following them. It was better for him to go to her work. He could just walk into the office like a customer and ask to see her. After all, what he wanted to say to her wasn't going to take more than a few seconds. One way or the other, he would get that time with her. Robert knew rejection better than most. He also knew how to get around it. The bitch was arrogant. She'd wanted his attention in Toronto. She was looking for a reason to leave in a huff. Well, he'd see how well Carmen could bear the truth about herself and what could happen to her if she threatened him.

Hadn't Justin paid dearly for his rejection? Had he loved him, the kid wouldn't have had to sneak out to swim. He'd still be alive. Each day that passed distanced him from his memory of the boy. One day, he'd struggle to recall his face. An unsettling thought occurred. What if Justin had been his son? Robert shut that thought down.

Chapter Fifty-one

ON TUESDAY, BEFORE the first light of sun had seeped through the partially closed wooden shutters, Robert was in the shower. For his confrontation with Carmen, he wore a dark blue summer suit and carried a briefcase. He intended to park in the visitors parking near the front and get inside before he was recognized by whomever was in the car tracking Carmen. As he backed out of the driveway, he was pleased to have had the house to himself. He used Jessie's SUV. He didn't think about Fortier. He kept the window down for a few minutes, but the air felt heavy, almost sluggish. By 8:15 a.m., he was a few minutes from her office. He watched the minutes pass. At 8:40, he drove onto the property of Best Grilles and parked up front in the visitors' parking.

He grabbed his bag, got out of the car wearing shades and headed for the front door. He walked inside unobstructed. The building was a standard one-level. At the receptionist's desk, he received a warm smile and he asked to see Carmen DiMaggio. He could see Carmen at a printer at the other end of the rectangular room, but she didn't see him. 'Is there an office where we might meet?'

'Why, yes.' Carole led him into an empty office. The boss was out with a client.

'I'll wait here,' Robert said politely. He was grateful that Carmen hadn't seen him. He sat with his back to the door, so she wouldn't run the minute she walked into the room.

Carmen's legs felt leaden as soon as Carole told her a man wanted to see her and pointed to the office. *I am going to be called as a witness. God, don't let it be worse than that!* She left the printing there, straightened her hair, took a few deep breaths and reminded herself that she'd done nothing wrong. She was exactly three steps inside the room when Robert turned around.

'I have only a few things to say. Don't leave this room, please. You owe me a few words.'

'How did you get in here?' She wanted to say, *How did you get by Bruno?*

'I walked in the front door.' He could read the tangle of emotions that coursed across her face. What he desperately needed was confirmation that she would not involve herself in his life. 'I hope your bag arrived safely. Promise me you won't take something you misunderstood and make my life worse than it already is. You won't ever see me again, but if you do anything to harm me, I'll keep you in court until you lose this job. You may not have much, but I'll go after every scrap until you have nothing. You may have enjoyed your gratuitous voyeurism, but this is my life. It's not a slot machine. Do I have your word?'

Robert's lips were bloodless. A shaft of light from the verticals caught him in the eyes and he moved. Words didn't come. She couldn't offer him the comforting illusion of her loyalty and she wasn't a good liar. She stood in a shocked daze.

A slow awareness crossed Robert's face before it became a shrieking alarm. 'You've gone to the police already?' Robert hissed incredulously, crowding Carmen. His entire face was an ugly grimace. Carmen smelled his mouthwash.

Tormented by a guilt she didn't understand, she did answer with safer words. 'I didn't!' she pled in her defence. 'A detective summoned me to his office. I had no choice. He knew all about me.' Carmen backed toward the door.

Robert froze. 'Detective Geoffrion?'

'Yes.'

'What?' he asked brusquely.

'Yes,' Carmen said louder. 'I had no choice.'

His question was slow and threatening. He had moved closer again and bent his head closer to hers. 'What did you tell him?'

Carmen's neck oozed perspiration. 'I answered his questions.' She recognized the banality of her response.

'You know what I'm asking. Did you tell him what I said in Toronto? Did you screw me, Carmen?'

Carmen had her hand on the doorknob. Her top lip began to twitch.

'You did, didn't you? Fuck!'

"I also said I might have misunderstood,' she said white-faced.

'Like he cared a damn, once he had that. I meant every word I said, Carmen. Now it's your turn to be afraid!' Robert's eyes smoldered as he pushed past her and strode out of the office. She sank into the nearest chair. Quite apart from her momentary terror and the shell game that appeared to be Robert's life, she saw with absolute clarity the damage her words had done if he were innocent.

Carole crept into the office. 'Are you alright? I thought he was a customer.'

Carmen rubbed her eyes as if they were sore before she was back on her feet. 'It's personal. Please, keep it that way, Carole. I don't want people in the office to know anything about this. It's very unprofessional.'

'I won't say a word.'

'I have to get out for a minute, but I'll be right back.'

Robert had regained his composure or a good facsimile of it when he walked the short distance to the SUV and drove off undetected by Bruno. He punched in Hoye's number, but had to wait till he got on the line. Robert angrily told him what had transpired at Carmen's office. Before Hoye got a word in, he continued. 'I want you to sue her for libel. Get the papers ready by tomorrow morning!'

'Are you finished?'

'I'm just beginning with that bitch!'

'You can't libel anyone with the truth, you know that.'

'You can fuck up her life and frighten her with a suit and drag her into court, can't you?'

'Get a hold of yourself. How would Geoffrion and Moitié see the suit as anything other than harassment? If this case goes to court, regarding that Toronto statement, it'll be your word against hers. That's the time we attack her credibility and her reasons for deliberately interpreting more than you intended. She was a pick-up who felt jilted because she wasn't getting enough of your attention that night. We can work that angle. For God's sake, stay away from her. You've probably walked yourself into a restraining order.'

'That's just what I need to hear. She goes to the police and I get served!'

'Anyone in your position feels helpless, frustrated and angry, but you can't allow those emotions to dictate your actions. Stick with the truth; she didn't go to the police. They called her. The tail, remember?'

'He's the least of my problems now.' Robert swore loudly.

'Whoa! Watch your language. I'm not the enemy.'

'She probably told the cops about the sale. Douglas will learn of it in no time.' Robert swore again.

'Don't run! You probably have surveillance cops on your tail now. We can't do anything until they make a move.'

Suddenly, Robert was utterly exhausted. 'There are moments when I can't believe this is my life or how I got here.'

'I'll put out my feelers and see what I can learn. Nothing from the tests yet. Take it easy and lay low. That's an order.'

Carmen ran over to Bruno. Beyond tears, she was angry and she focused her anger on him. 'Bruno, the man who just left was Robert. Didn't you see him? How did he get by you?'

Carole was taking in the scene from the boss's window, though she couldn't hear anything because it was closed with the a/c.

Bruno was out of the CRV in a flash. 'I'm sorry. I saw him, but he looked like a customer. I was expecting a Porsche.'

'What was he driving?'

'A Lexus SUV.'

'Sorry for taking this out on you. I thought I was secure.'

'He won't get by me again. You have my word.'

Carmen hurried back into the office in time to catch Carole scuttling out of the boss's office. They didn't speak to one another.

As best as she could, Carmen tried to get back to work, but her nerves were jittery. *What do I do now? Do I call that detective? Robert's going to sue me!* Caitlin would know what to do. At the moment, with many employees forced into a three-day week, she tore into her work with a vengeance. She needed this job. There was no afternoon break, so she couldn't call Caitlin till after five. Her whole body was sweaty and chilled with the damn a/c. She wanted to open a window and get out! A call came in, and a good sale buoyed her flagging spirit. Once she had written up the quote and final figures, Carmen slumped into a puzzled fear of her present situation and what to do about it. Could Robert drag her through court? Would she lose her job as a result? There was something else. The derision she'd heard in Robert's tone caused her once again to fear him personally. He'd never utter those threats out loud. He was too smart for that.

On her way to Westmount, she got hold of Caitlin. Her voice wavered as she related Robert's visit.

'I'm not angry with you anymore. This is serious. We'll discuss your options when you get here. Only one stands out for me. You have to call the detective who questioned you.'

Chapter Fifty-two

WHEN MOITIÉ TURNED onto Rockland Road, he was eager and enthusiastic to meet with Colin Sharpe. This case had two legs, he saw that, but he was not about to cut the young limb out of the investigation. He had purposely dressed as casually as the dress code permitted. From experience, he knew that subjects who had discovered that the law couldn't exact justice from them wanted to talk. They were cocky; they'd beaten the cops and the system. He parked in front of the house and glanced over at the Tyler house before he walked to the Sharpes' front door and rang the bell.

Steve Sharpe opened the door. 'I'm very disappointed you felt the need to be here, Detective,' he said with undisguised resentment, regarding him as though as he was a ghoul. 'Follow me.' He'd clung to his angry contempt. Moitié wondered whether Sharpe's target was him personally or his job. Sharpe led Moitié into the dining room, a large, narrow room with one of the longest dinner tables he'd ever seen. Harvey Wasserman sat on Colin's right, the woman he took for his therapist on his left, Donna Sharpe directly across from her son and Steve himself sat at the head of the table while Moitié was still standing.

Moitié let the snub work to his advantage. He walked around the table to Colin and extended his hand to the boy. 'I'm very happy to see you looking well, Colin.' The boy had worn a polo shirt with its collar raised to hide the livid red scar.

Colin's was the only bright face in the group. He got to his feet and shook hands. What boy would not relish being the center of attention? He sat back down when his father motioned with his head. Moitié saw the large glass of orange juice in front of Colin and nothing prepared for the others. He walked around and greeted them, ignoring their dour faces, and sat down on the other side of the table. He took his time taking off his jacket and refrained from using his notes or openly recording the session. If he learned something significant, the therapist wouldn't lie on the stand. As backup, he had the recorder on inside his jacket, which he folded carefully and laid on the table to his left.

'I guess we can begin. Your father and Mr. Wasserman have told you that I'm not here to arrest you and no one else will either. I need your help.'

Colin sat up eagerly and pulled his collar up.

'I know that you didn't drown your friend, that what happened that night was an accident. You kicked Justin a few times, even if they were hard kicks so that you could go home and not get into trouble.'

'That's right,' Colin admitted proudly.

'It's the bump on Justin's head that's bothering me. You didn't kick him in the head, so he must have done that to himself. I just can't figure out when.' Moitié held Colin's attention with his best easy smile.

Colin jerked forward like kids in class when they know the answer to the teacher's question. 'He did it himself,' Colin said before Wasserman could stop him.

'Just a second, Colin,' Wasserman said, but there was no stopping Colin. He had forgotten his parents again.

'I didn't do it! He hit his head on the side of the pool when he tried to grab me.' Colin was defiant.

Ms. Tritt, a slender young woman, efficient and brimming with confidence and optimism, had convinced the Sharpes that Colin should tell the truth for his full recovery as long at it did not implicate him. No one was looking for a thrashing argument before Moitié arrived, so the family grudgingly accepted her counsel.

Undetected, Moitié had moved closer to Colin. Adrenalin burned in his veins. 'That's what I thought too, Colin. I guess he hurt himself after you left. Well, thank you…' He began to get up from the table.

Colin stretched across the table and held him back. 'No! I was there. I kicked him the second time and he dove under the water to try to grab me again, but he hit his head on the side of the pool 'cause he said a real bad word when he came up holding his forehead. He was coughing too.' Colin darted a quick glance at his father before he regarded Moitié.

'That's when you ran?'

'Yep.'

Moitié looked at the angry faces, eyes that scorched his with derision. 'Was he in trouble, do you think?'

'I don't know 'cause I left.'

'Thank you, Colin. You left, I understand. Before I go, I've been wondering about one small thing. It's not important, but you told me that Justin called you that night to go to his pool. I found out that you called him. I guess *you* wanted to go over to his place.' Moitié rose and picked up his jacket.

Steve and Donna and the therapist sat rigidly.

Colin sulked. He didn't like being caught in a lie. He forgot about his collar and grabbed the juice. He was about to say something else, but Wasserman stopped him. Moitié walked back to the front door alone, carrying his lanky frame easily. Sharpe caught up to him. 'Detective, leave us alone. How do you sleep at night?' He despised the cop. *He's nothing but a tan suit wrapped in a badge.*

Moitié didn't counter or look back at Sharpe or his double mahogany front door. He did a slow shamble back to his car. He uttered only one word, 'Huh!' He had another piece. *If Justin was in trouble, Colin might have not run. Le p'tit crosseur may have stood there and watched Justin drown.* Inside his car, he took out his recorder, rewound and played back what he had. The quality was not the best but he could hear every word. The techs could clean up the tape. There wouldn't be any cinderblock cell for the kid, but Moitié might get closer to the truth for the family. Geoffrion was at the hospital and he drove there to meet him. At the point where the pressure of time was beginning to take a toll on both cops, Moitié's brain was issuing an order. *Don't fold on the kid!*

Geoffrion was pacing, waiting to speak to a doctor. He was tapping his notebook against his thigh. Fortier had to come though his ordeal with some memory of what had occurred. Earlier, Geoffrion had learned the techs hadn't found a print match for Tyler among the many they had been able to lift. He didn't hold out for prints inside the house, particularly on the walls. He hated waiting for anything, especially the final test results. He wished this were a TV cop show. Tyler would be sweating in an interrogation room. He wasn't in the mood for his cell when it rang. He wanted the go-ahead from the physician. 'Detective Geoffrion.'

'This is Carmen DiMaggio.'

He heard the tremor in her voice. 'What can I do for you?'

Caitlin urged her on. 'Robert Tyler came to my office to warn me to stay out of his life. He figured out I had talked to you.'

'Did he threaten you, Miss DiMaggio?'

'He said he'd drag me through the courts till I lost my job and whatever else I owned.'

'When did this confrontation occur?'

'At my office. He walked right in and my security guard didn't pick him up. He was in a different car and dressed like a customer.'

'Are you in fear of your safety?'

'Yes. I'm still at my friend's.'

'I suggest that you take out an order of restraint.'

'Is there any way you could contact him and tell him to stay away from me and my work?'

'Miss DiMaggio, this is an on-going investigation. I am reluctant to approach Mr. Tyler until I have a warrant. If you have told me the truth…'

'Of course, I have!'

'Then Mr. Tyler cannot charge you with libel. His lawyer knows that. I doubt that he will file a suit against you. He was probably blowing off steam. I am glad you have security. Speak to the men. I assume you have two officers, one relieving the other. Get to know them by name.'

'You can't help then?'

'I'll send a patrol car to drive by your office a few times a day, but I doubt the security officers your friend hired for you will miss him a second time. They're professionals.'

Carmen was devastated. She had expected Geoffrion to call Robert at least or arrest him for harassment. 'I regret speaking to you, Detective.' *What about protecting me and my job? I pay taxes.*

'If I had been forced to get a subpoena, Miss DiMaggio, I might have deduced you were involved in the case.' DiMaggio might be an important witness. He didn't want her to suddenly forget what Tyler had said. 'Give me the address of the friend you're staying with. I'll see to it the street is patrolled.'

'I'm very frightened.'

'The patrol car will be at your office tomorrow morning. Here is my personal cell number. Feel free to use it.'

'Will I ever feel safe enough to go home?'

'For the short-term, stay where you are. Keep the security officer with you at all times. Keep me apprised of any new development.' Geoffrion had his smaller piece. He felt a little better.

Carmen felt worse. 'Can you believe this? I have to take out a restraining order. Geoffrion is more interested in the whole case than he is in protecting me! I'm just a spoke in his wheel.'

'You can stay here as long as you want,' Caitlin said without further comment. Caitlin feared for her friend, but she was also troubled. Carmen had created this crisis, against her better judgment, against advice. Such crises had three parts: the chase, the prize and the fallout. Caitlin knew Carmen better than any other friend, but no one comes close to understanding another human being. She understood Carmen's need for the chase. The disconcerting aspect picked away at her. Was there a remote chance that Carmen was enjoying the fallout, the attention and the stress? That possibility was too grim to consider for long.

'You haven't said that boring cliché, *I told you so*, but you're thinking it.'

'What I am thinking is that you have a place to stay. Annie said when I called her that she'll give you two weeks of this security, you'll get the restraining order, you have the detective's number…'

'And a patrol car three times a day.'

'You have support, Carm. Be grateful for that.'

'I guess I wanted sympathy, but I don't deserve it. I know that.'

'I can spare a spoonful.'

Carmen smiled nervously. 'What if Robert didn't kill his son? What if he's just an arrogant, self-serving, adulterous prick? He'll have it in for me for a long time.'

'I'll wager that a month from now, he won't remember your name.'

Chapter Fifty-three

Henley had been to the hospital, but Mike was sleeping most of the time and cursing the pain the few times he opened his eyes. It was not time to ask him questions. He stopped in at his office on McGill College Avenue and conducted business before he drove back to Westmount. Jessie was home. He could hear soft music as he approached her room. He found her lying on her bed, staring at the ceiling, blank with grief. Normally assertive and not given to sensitivity, he wanted his daughter up and back into the business of living and adapting. 'You'll feel better if you take a shower and dress, Jess.'

'I'm thinking of taking some time and travelling abroad, Marseilles, I think. I can't talk to my friends. Some of them are beginning to think I'm rude, but I have nothing to say and nothing that I want to hear from any of them. I want solitude.'

'You'll be taking yourself with you.'

'I know I'll be quite alone. Justin is dead, Robert is gone and the house too. I can't imagine ever walking into that house again.'

'The guilt you're feeling will travel well. Travel won't give you absolution, if that's what you're trying to find. It won't offer any reassuring words or answers. Retreats never do.'

'I thought nothing could touch my family, especially Justin. He was young and strong.' Her voice was belligerent. Her pampered life had deceived her. A wave of color rose in her neck and travelled up to her forehead in red splotches. 'I thought we were safe.'

'No one is ever safe.'

'I thought I was a decent person.'

'You still are.'

Jessie sat up and buried her face in her hands. 'Oh, Dad!'

Henley reached over and held her. 'You have to stay and fight for Justin. You have to forgive yourself. You can't do that if you run away.'

Henley had struck the right chord. 'How is Mike doing?'

'Hanging in there like the old warrior he is. After you shower and eat something, how about going to the hospital with me? He'd appreciate that, I think. We have to find out how this happened, if Robert did this. We've always been a team. Let's see this through together.'

'I'll try, Dad.'

'That's all I need. Now, get in the shower because my beautiful, blonde daughter can stink like the rest of us!'

'Give me an hour.' Jessie grabbed her robe and walked into her bathroom.

'That should do it.'

Geoffrion saw Moitié before his partner saw him. From the clip of his walk, he knew he had gotten something from the interview. 'What did you get from the kid?' He admired Moitié; he was a formidable partner. He had come to his decision and had held firmly to it without wavering or defence or apology. Cops who could defend opposing views and work toward a common goal were good together.

Moitié gave him a brief, succinct account. He made no attempt to grab the file.

'So Tyler hit his own head and the kid was there.'

'You got it.'

'Question is, how long did Sharpe hang around?'

'Just what I've been thinking, and add another thought. If Justin cursed when he hit his head, I'm wondering if Robert Tyler has been lying to us. What if he saw the whole thing?' Geoffrion mused.

'You mean if he saw Sharpe leave, saw an opportunity?'

'Exactly.'

'We're back to parallel tracks.'

'With a slight curve on my file. Tyler threatened DiMaggio at her office.'

'Physically?'

'Libel, legal shit that he knows won't fly, but that might have been camouflage. Second consideration, if he assaulted Fortier…'

'You haven't questioned him yet?'

'Waiting to get the go-ahead. We can do that together.' The men were conversing when a doctor finally made an appearance.

'You must be the detectives waiting to interview Mr. Fortier.'

'Detectives Geoffrion and Bertrand, Doctor.'

'He's strong as an ox. He's stopped using the morphine pump. We took out the drains, so he is a little more comfortable, but certainly not pain-free by any means. You know he can't talk because of the wired jaw. So don't get your hopes up. He thinks he's been shot.'

Geoffrion had done his prep work on "the legend." 'That's what he would think. He was shot different times on the job. The night of this incident, it was dark. His injuries are reminiscent of what he got on the job.'

'Mr. Fortier will be eighty in a few days. Isn't all that a very long time ago?'

'Fortier kept meticulous records, files, photos, press clippings and his shotgun. He's looking for a publisher, so his mind would be focused on that period in his life. At the time of this incident, he was doing private work.'

'For Douglas Henley? We're old friends. I wondered what the connection was when he called.'

'May we go in?' Geoffrion pressed.

'Of course, but don't overtire him. I have strict orders from Mr. Henley to give him the best care.'

'Understood.'

'Follow me.' The detectives followed the doctor to a private room. The curtains were drawn, but the room wasn't dark. A nurse Henley must have hired sat near the head of the bed. Geoffrion and Moitié saw that the hospital hid VIP rooms like this one from Joe Public. Both chairs were burgundy leather, the bed was wide and the sheets were the purest white cotton he'd ever seen, with a Cape Cod-blue blanket. The night tables were new as well. The whole package was the stuff of movies, nothing he'd ever seen in Montreal hospitals. 'Different world,' he said to Moitié.

'Different people.'

Fortier opened his eyes when he heard their voices. He groaned. The nurse spoke up. 'You'll have to come to this side because Mr. Fortier is deaf in that ear.'

'Nurse, will you wait outside, please?' Geoffrion said.

The nurse was middle-aged, stocky, sturdy and quick on her feet. She was out of the room in seconds. 'Call me if he needs help.'

'Mike, I'm Detective Geoffrion. This is Detective Bertrand. Raise your index finger if you can hear me.'

A thick, crooked finger rose.

'Good. I have a pad. I'll pull this table tray over the bed and I'll hold the pad for you to write whatever you can. Alright?'

Mike didn't bother with the finger. He gave a slight nod of his head. He trained his piercing pale blue eyes on Geoffrion.

'Nobody shot you. You fell or were pushed down the stairs.'

Mike's beefy hand took the marker and scratched one word on the pad. 'What?' His letters were poorly formed and lopsided, but there was no mistaking what he'd written.

'Luc Ranger, your neighbor, found you. You weren't shot, but the fall down the stairs was bad.'

A confused and angry grimace gripped Mike's face. He took the pen and wrote, 'Go ...'

'We know you were tailing Robert Tyler. Douglas Henley told us.' There was no point of mentioning obstruction at this late date. It was Henley, no doubt, who swore Fortier to secrecy. 'The thing is, Mike, Luc's mother said you never went anywhere without your brace. You were barefoot when you were discovered at the bottom of your stairs.'

Fortier attempted to lean to his side, as much as his injuries would allow, to catch every word.

'You leave your doors unlocked, so anyone could have gotten into your home. Listen carefully, Mike. Why did you get out of bed and leave your brace behind?'

Mike had held onto the pen so tightly that Geoffrion thought he'd break it.

Moitié could tell the old cop was trying to remember. His eyes were worried slits. The cops waited. 'Take your time, Mike,' he said loudly.

He printed one word again. 'Noise!' The letters were haphazard, but clear.

'In the house?'

Mike stabbed the pad.

They all looked at one another.

'I know you had a long list of enemies years ago, that there were even contracts on your life. Have you received any recent threats?'

'No!' Mike took no time with this word.

'Anybody in your complex who has it in for you?'

This stab tore through three sheets. 'No!'

'What about Robert Tyler?' Geoffrion asked.

Mike stabbed the pad. His face was mottled red. As far as he was concerned, Tyler was their man.

Both cops were quiet. There was a flicker of hope. Geoffrion asked so loudly that Mike tried to back away. 'Sorry. Did you see Tyler in your house?'

Their hopes were quickly dashed. 'Dark.'

'You're not in the phonebook.'

'Douglas from there…'

'He contacted you from the Tyler house?'

A nod. The mood was suddenly buoyant. 'Mike, I've typed up an account of your work on Tyler that Douglas Henley gave me.' He took the report from his case. 'Would you sign it for me?'

'Not dead!' Mike broke the plastic marker with one hand.

Moitié leaned into his partner and whispered, 'The old bastard wants to go after him himself!'

'Of course you're not going to die! You know I need this copy for the official record. If there is a trial, you'll be called.' Geoffrion handed Mike a pen. 'My wife gave me this. Go easy on it.'

Mike complied reluctantly. *If I weren't laid up, I sure as hell wouldn't need papers to get the truth out of Tyler. These guys are sissies!* That thought gave Mike a small, perverse satisfaction. He began to plough through his head trying to remember details of the night he fell.

Chapter Fifty-four

ROBERT SENSED MENACE ALL around him. He was alone in the house, yet the Henleys still dominated every room.Henley, he knew, was seething with controlled anger. The man was vain. This tragedy happened to other people, not to his family. Justin's death had chipped away at his strength and Henley hated weakness. How he must loathe having to wait for the slow-grinding process of the law to puzzle out what had occurred that night! He threw himself down on Jessie's king-size bed and laughed. And Jessie? All the coddling, all the love, all the lavish gifts, nothing bestowed on her could save Justin from the water in his own pool! And Carmen DiMaggio? He had been taken in by her apparent innocence, but she'd taught him the lesson he'd learned from the Henleys. Never trust anyone. He never would again. Running? Henley was probably hoping he would. He even knew the plan. One day he'd simply disappear. Robert knew he could follow the mystery fiction route and leave a letter with Hoye: *If I die or disappear, go after Douglas Henley.* He wasn't a fool. A letter wouldn't help. Henley would see to it that no evidence ever established a direct line to him. Robert was safer here with that patrol car outside his house. He'd seen it of course. He laughed heartily.

Rolling over on his side, he regarded his reflection in Jessie's wall mirror and smiled at his image. He liked what he saw. Handsome men, like beautiful women, didn't have to work on such banal things as character. It wasn't fair, but neither was life. Robert would start again, and this time he'd go at life differently. No one would push him to the outside of his own life again. In the immediate, there was urgency to this self-justification because Robert could feel bands tightening and cutting off his circulation.

Steve and Wasserman left after Colin's interview. Ms. Tritt had gone out for a walk, but was due back in half an hour. Donna stood outside Colin's bedroom. Colin sat at his computer, completely engrossed in some game, laughing infectiously at something on the screen. To Donna, he looked like the boy who had gotten away with what bullied children could only dream about. A twitch in her legs brought about an involuntary retreat. Turning away, she caught sight of Susan at the front door. 'Hold on there!' Donna tore down the stairs. 'Are you going out again?' Her fear and irritation made her ready to explode.

'There's nothing to do here. I'm going to the mall. Anyway, you don't need me for anything.' There was an angry tone to her voice.

'Of course I need you here. You could be a little kinder to your brother and to me for that matter. Keep an eye on him and relieve me.'

'Don't you get it? Colin's not going to hang himself again. Why would he? He's the center of attention and he's loving every minute of it. He has you and Dad scared shitless to call him on anything...'

'Watch your language!'

'He has a therapist who listens to his every word, and a lawyer. He knows the cops can't touch him. His friends are all calling. He's never been happier.'

'That's very cruel and heartless, Susan. Colin could have died.'

'Well, he didn't, Mom.' Susan shouted to emphasize that point. 'This is the first time you've noticed me in over two weeks!'

Donna was stung. 'You're not a child, Susan.'

'That's why I can go to the mall,' she answered, insufferably self-righteous.

'Susan!'

Susan dismissed her mother with a backward wave-off. Tears stung her eyes as she ran from the house. In seconds, her face disintegrated into a look of frightened resentment.

Donna had come out the front door with a mind to run after her, but she hadn't the energy, and grabbed the railing for support. She couldn't leave Colin. In her heart, she accepted Susan's indignant protests. When was the exact moment she had lost her grasp, lost the balance she had brought to her family? It wasn't the night Justin drowned. It was the night Colin tried to hang himself. Desperate to forget, Donna tried to block her mind from the merciless memory.

'Mrs. Sharpe, are you alright? I came back early,' Eva Tritt asked, standing at the bottom of the stone steps.

'I'm tired.'

'No doubt. I can take care of Colin. Why don't you get out of the house for an hour?'

'I will.' Donna freshened up quickly, took her purse and drove up Rockland Road to the high-end mall, hoping to catch Susan who was walking. She caught sight of her five blocks up, pulled ahead of her and waited. Susan was oblivious, plugged into her iPod. Donna got out of the car and stepped into her path.

Susan stopped dead, on the edge of tears and dreading at the same time that one of her friends would spot them.

Donna threw her arms around Susan. 'You're right about everything you said, but you have to know that I love you. You're still my baby girl, but you're also the first child and I depend on you, too much lately. Please forgive me.'

'Mom, it's okay that Colin's your favorite. I'm fourteen and I have friends, but what I don't get is that you don't know Colin as well as I do. I hate his guts most of the time, but I get him. Why don't you?'

Donna pulled away hurt. 'What do you mean?' Her legs were shaking and she tried to steady herself.

Susan's tears mingled with bitter laughter. 'He's a wuss, Mom. You and Dad think he might have killed Justin! In his dreams! He can't kill a spider. He ran after their scuffle. I'm sure he's faking about the rest.'

'But why, why would he do that? Why would he hang himself?'

'He got scared he'd gone too far. He really thought he'd go to jail. I don't think he understood what he was doing when he hanged himself, that he could die, I mean. He knew I was in my room, and the door was open.'

Suddenly, there was a deliberate silence. Then Donna whispered to herself. 'He could have died.'

'Mom! He didn't. When he found out the police couldn't touch him, the little shit went for broke.'

'How do you know these things?'

'Come on, open your eyes. Why did you leave him just now?' Susan asked hopefully.

'I came to find you and Eva came back early.' At times, relief is only intermittent. Donna took what she could get. 'If only you could be right about this.'

'I think I am. At times, I love the little shit too. Go back, you'll feel better.'

'How did you get to be so wise?'

'A good mother?'

Donna smiled. 'Have some fun time with your friends.'

Henley had his driver let them off at the corner of Ste-Catherine and Guy. 'We could both use a good walk together up to the hospital.' He took Jessie's hand and she didn't pull away. Montrealers and tourists were out in full force carrying shopping bags and cameras. Cars snaked along Ste-Catherine, some to show off their wheels and others trying to get from 'A' to 'B.' Pedestrians, as usual, jaywalked, darting between cars without the slightest consideration for traffic lights. Henley and Jessie fought their way across the city's main street, headed up to Sherbrooke and up the hill towards the hospital. When they stood on the hospital steps, Henley turned and looked at the city. 'It's a beautiful place to be in summer! How about dinner with your old man at *L'Epicier* after we see Mike? If you'd like, we could drive to the mausoleum before.'

'Let's see how I feel after we visit Mike.' Jessie wanted to be close to her son, but the mausoleum sealed the reality of Justin's death. It was a cold place without hope.

'That's fair.'

The hospital had that sour smell of illness clinging to the walls. Disinfectant added its own acrid odor and curled Jessie's nostrils. Henley noticed it less because he was often there for board meetings. They wasted no time getting to Mike's room. It was Jessie who first heard the agonizing low growl, a terrible moan of utter pain. Douglas knew its source immediately. A nurse hurried from the room and came close to crashing into Jessie. 'I'm so sorry.' In the next second, she recognized Douglas Henley. 'Mr. Henley! It might not sound like we're doing everything we can for Mr. Fortier, but he's still refusing pain meds, and the pain worsens the second day. I'll be back.'

Jessie stopped at the door. 'I can't go in.' Her cheeks whitened. 'Mike's going to survive. Try to understand, Dad? An old man lives, but Justin dies. Is that fair?'

'He was helping us, Jessie. It's a frightening world and it's not just, but little boys die.'

'They shouldn't, Dad.'

'Alright, stay by the door; you might change your mind.' Henley was aghast when he saw Mike so visibly changed. He looked ninety, much smaller than the barrel of a man he'd hired, yet he fought the restraints of the bed and the pain like a raging bull. His eyes were stained red from lack of sleep and the throbbing stabs of his injuries. Silenced, Henley watched Mike thrash his good arm against the bedrail and jerk his head from one side to the other. Henley held out a desperate hope that this awful event would not signal a final, unrelenting physical descent for the old bear. He didn't want his friend to trudge that long road to oblivion on his account. 'Mike! It's Douglas Henley,' he shouted on his good side.

The thrashing stopped. Mike blinked and tried to focus on Henley. His good hand was moving urgently as though he were writing. Henley was slow on the pickup, and Mike growled, and began to write in the air again.

'You want a pen?'

Mike blinked hard.

Henley reached into his pocket for his Mont Blanc and searched the room for paper. He took the breakfast menu, already filled out by someone, and turned it over. He grabbed his wallet and put it behind the paper for support. He pulled over a chair, handed Mike the pen and held the wallet and paper for him.

Mike's eyes lit up with restless enthusiasm as he wrote the first word. 'LIGHT.' He held the pen in his fist and wrote badly again in capital letters. 'GREEN LINE MOVED.'

Henley felt his spirit sag. Mike was hallucinating.

Mike banged the expensive pen against the bedrail. 'MOVED. SHOES.' He simulated a walking motion with his fingers.

Jessie had been listening and crept into the room. 'Dad, what's he writing?'

'Mike's not thinking clearly. It's probably the effects of the anesthesia.'

Mike banged the pen again on the bedrail, and the top flew across the room.

'Let me see.' Henley handed Jessie the menu. Jessie mentally reran the gesture Mike had made with his fingers and looked at the words on the paper. Her voice was a low shriek. 'Get Geoffrion down here!'

Mike grunted through the metal in his mouth. *She understands!*

Chapter Fifty-five

GEOFFRION WAS BUSY on the phone bothering the lab. Moitié was in his office, quietly going over all his notes on Colin Sharpe. A gloom had begun to settle in on both men. As the days passed, though the men didn't share their thoughts, each began to worry that he might not find the definitive evidence to close the file. Moitié reread his notes on the last interview. Something wasn't right. In spite of his age, Colin Sharpe had proved to be a formidable suspect, but the change in the kid in the last meeting troubled Moitié. From the beginning, the kid's fear, blundering, pauses, movements, all rang true. Then he knew what bothered him. Colin Sharpe enjoyed the last interview. Moitié chewed on his last thought. His fingers drummed the side of his desk. The victim was uppermost in the cop's mind. Moitié never forgot that he took up the victim's fight for justice. That burden was his.

The devastation of Justin Tyler's death had left its scars on the Sharpe family. Moitié had not been concerned about them, not at first. He and Geoffrion shared common goals, not the least of which was their passion to close files. In one area, Moitié differed from his partner. The gold stars for the quick solve and the adulation from their peers that came with it, on some occasions fell second to the voice in his heart. Justin Tyler hadn't died alone. He had taken with him his mother's heart, her marriage, and his grandfather's hope. It had also taken the young family next door, devastating the parents and destroying an eight-year-old kid. The cop in him realized he wanted the truth, and that rarely had anything to do with justice.

He left the building quietly and quickly and broke procedures by calling the Sharpe house first and advising them of an official visit. The Metropolitan was the usual snag, but he was on Rockland Road in twenty minutes. Donna answered the door. 'My husband's not home and Colin's with Ms. Tritt.'

'Mrs. Sharpe, this is an unofficial visit. It's you I'd like to see.'

'I'm not really prepared.' Donna began to back away from the door.

'I'm here for you. I hope you can give me the time to understand that. Nothing you say will be recorded. In fact, I'll do most of the talking. All you have to do is listen. You have my word that this visit is off the record.'

'Well…' After what Susan had said, Donna did want to learn what she could. She couldn't damage the family by listening. 'Come in. No one will hear us in the dining room.' Donna made herself a promise to hold her tongue and she sat across from Moitié, kneading her hands.

'As you know, Colin won't be charged. The official ruling will be accidental. Neither Detective Geoffrion nor I believe that Justin's death, where Colin was concerned, bore any malice aforethought. Two families have been devastated, theirs and yours. In the interest of Jessie Henley, I need the truth. In your interest, you need the truth. Your son is embellishing his part in this tragedy, as young boys will do. You're his mother. If you don't manage to get the truth from him now, the lie will grow. His character will change and you'll lose him, maybe even to the penal system in the years ahead. I have to know if he saw Justin in trouble and because he became frightened, he ran. I can close the file then if that was the situation and that's the end of it. If he ran home before he saw anything amiss, we look elsewhere. If you want the son you raised back, you'll get the truth from him. Here's my card. If I don't hear from you in a few hours, I'll know everyone involved in this tragedy has lost. The investigation will continue. Adults can live with lies. I don't think good kids can. That's all I have to say.'

Moitié's card lay in the middle of the table.

Donna fought tears and kept her eyes on the card.

Moitié was struck by the enormity of human carnage. He spread his hands on the table and rose. 'Whatever you decide, remember that I did at least follow one code today, *to serve and protect*. I can show myself out.' Out of the corner of his eye, he saw Mrs. Sharpe pick up his card. He closed the front door and walked over to his car. He looked back at both luxurious houses built with gray stone, small fortresses. *Stone, high-tech alarms, money and power didn't protect either one of their boys.* He drove back to his office and waited there for the call. In his human book, any kid under ten, even *le p'tit crosseur*, deserved a second chance. In his murder book, if the kid left his friend in trouble, he had the solve. His tactic was a winner either way.

Geoffrion was running down the stairs to the main floor and almost knocked Moitié over in the process. Both men used the stairs to stay fit. 'Where have you been?'

'What's up?' Moitié asked, dodging the question.

'Looks like Fortier figured out who attacked him. You coming?'

Moitié checked his cell. 'Sure.'

'Waiting on a call?'

'Played a hunch, and yes, I'm waiting on a call.' Moitié caught the heavy steel door that Geoffrion had thrown open and ran after him. 'So?'

Moitié would have preferred to wait for the call before he said anything, but no cop broke codes that dealt with partners. He gave him the facts, and Moitié sensed his partner's disappointment.

Geoffrion recovered quickly. 'Well, good luck! If the case breaks your way, at least I'll nail Tyler for assault and intent if they have what I need for an arrest.' He used the siren. 'We'll know soon enough.'

'Watch your speed. We don't want to take out a pedestrian. Don't need the paper work.'

'Alright!' Geoffrion said irritably. 'Shit! I would have put money on Tyler. I could smell him for the murder.'

'You may still have him. Sharpe's not a sure thing.'

'You're very close.'

'Slow down! You almost hit that van.'

'I'm pissed!'

'Get over it.'

'You went right for the kid's jugular. Nice piece of work, I admit. I'm going to park out front and leave the lights flashing.'

'It's a tow-away zone.'

'They wouldn't touch a cop's car.' He left their cards and cherry on the dash. 'There, official police business.' He slammed the door and ran into the hospital with Moitié at his back. Henley was standing guard outside Fortier's room and ushered them inside. Jessie rose, her face a mask of shock and fear. The detectives greeted Fortier.

'I better explain,' Jessie said. 'Mike was able to get across to us what he saw the night of the attack.'

Mike banged on the bedrail, directing Jessie to stand beside him. It was his find, after all.

'That night, Mike said he saw moving green lines and he made a walking gesture with his fingers. That's when I knew.'

The cops knew not to interrupt. 'I bought new trainers for Robert and me for night runs. Mine have florescent pink lines around the shoes. Robert's have green lines. That's what Mike figured out he saw that night, green fluorescent lines. Robert must have worn the trainers.' There was no elation in Jessie's voice. Her grief had fallen to another level.

'Uh huh,' Mike growled loudly with pride.

'Was he aware of this feature?' Geoffrion wondered if Tyler had disposed of the shoes after the attack.

'I mentioned it when I gave them to him, but I don't think Robert was paying much attention. That was a week before Justin died.'

A cell rang and startled everyone. Moitié grabbed his, but the call wasn't for him. It was the lab. Geoffrion walked out of the room to take the call. 'Shoot, Jocelyne!'

'You have the source of the contusion on the forehead—we gave you the fiber and the safe. Still working on the shoulder bruising. It's tough going. One new addition, the DNA. Robert Tyler is the birth father. Are you there, Jean?'

'Keep working on the bruising.'

'Like I'd stop!'

'Stress, sorry.'

'Get back to your case.'

Geoffrion leaned into the room. 'May I speak to you both out here?'

Henley and Jessie joined Geoffrion. Moitié stood at the door, keeping a watchful eye on Fortier.

'Miss Henley, we have the DNA results. Robert was Justin's father.'

Jessie covered her mouth with both hands to smother her scream. She began to falter and Henley caught her in time. Her face grew small and taut. Her eyes were slits, boring into Geoffrion's. 'You should arrest me for murder as well. I had eight years to learn who Justin's father was and I did nothing. I thought that document would make certain I never lost Justin in a divorce. Instead,' her voice was steely and bloodless, replete with self-hatred, 'it was the reason he died.' She pulled away from her father and began walking aimlessly down the hall. Then she began to run as though the hospital had caught fire.

Henley took off after her.

'Sir, we don't know that for certain,' Geoffrion called after him, slamming his heel into the hard floor. 'All I need now is for them both to blow this file. Denis! No call yet?'

'Nothing. You were only out in the hall a few minutes.'

'We need back-up and warrants. The first was dated.'

'What about the Henleys?'

'Henley will see to his daughter. We can't waste time. As soon as we have the warrants, we'll bring Tyler in. Call ahead for them, will you? Dammit! It's the Henleys who've kept us both in the back seat of this case. The goddamn rich and their insatiable need to control!'

Moitié didn't point out the ironic humor of his partner's tirade. 'I'll do the driving. I like living—you make the calls. We need surveillance here. It's a long shot, but we can't afford to take a chance. Tyler must have figured out that Fortier survived the fall.'

Chapter Fifty-six

Henley was chagrined and winded when he lost sight of Jessie. He ran straight out the front door to the limo, but she wasn't there. His thoughts were rushed and confused. Standing anxiously at the side of the limo, he tapped the roof of the car. *The mausoleum!* He got inside and slammed the door. 'Get to the mausoleum and forget speed limits!' Trying to speed anywhere in the city was a no-go. 'Use the horn and side streets, for God's sake! Jessie's in a bad way. Your job depends on how fast you can get me there!'

When the limo roared sharply onto chemin de la Forêt, it caught the shoulder of the road, and cinders flew around behind it. It came to an abrupt stop, and Henley threw open the door with such violence that it threatened to come off its hinges. He ran past the funeral complex into the cemetery. His shirt was plastered against his chest and arms. When he was deep in the bowels of the cemetery, Henley began to know the scorching pain of losing a child, his only child. Because he had not understood the depth of it, he had hoped that Jessie might marry again and have another child. She was still young. The young were resilient and moved on. Now, the horrible specter of losing his only flesh and blood tore at the very core of his heart. He couldn't lose Jessie. She was all he had. Without her, nothing mattered. As he ran, he wiped off sweat that rolled into his eyes.

He ran up the steps to the family mausoleum, coughing and gasping. The white marble structure stood on its own property, surrounded by trees and lush green shrubbery meticulously maintained. Two pillars stood on each side of the door. He didn't have the remote with him and he wracked his brain trying to remember the combination. He knocked the side of one of the pillars. A marble square opened and he punched in what he thought was the code. The door didn't move. He frantically rapped his temples with his palms and tried again. This time the door slid slowly to across the inside wall. 'Jessie?' Henley did not recognize his voice. 'Jessie?' he called again. He tried to rush inside the mausoleum, but his feet felt like marble and he was afraid.

He was able to grab the side of the door and he pulled himself inside. Tears mingled with sweat. His eyes burned. The room was dark, still with the void of death. He felt for the light and whispered her name again. 'Jessie?' His shut his eyes when light filled the somber marble crypt. He'd find her with Justin, under his casket sealed in glass. He opened his eyes and gasped. His knees buckled. He let out a cry of utter relief. Jessie wasn't there. She was still alive!

But, where was she? Henley was not often wrong. His nerves began to tighten with a new force as he ran back to the limo after locking the mausoleum. Off balance, he scrambled for ideas. *She wouldn't have gone to the hospital chapel. Was she huddled alone on some park bench?* A slow recognition came to him in the sounds of her footsteps running from his house and they pounded at the back of his brain. He was shouting as he ran. 'She has my Smith & Wesson. She doesn't know that I took out the clip to protect her after Justin died!' He stopped running, grabbed his knees and moaned. 'She's gone home for a reckoning! God! Please!' He stumbled and fell and got back up and ran until he was at the limo. 'Get to TMR! Go!'

He called Geoffrion. It was almost a full minute before he came on the line.

'Detective Geoffrion.'

Robert had driven to Old Montreal in the early afternoon to see and place a bid on a penthouse in the M9 Evolution condo project. When he made his new start, he'd want a private terrace. Robert had had a decent day. His business was in order. Earlier, in Pointe Claire, he had guaranteed five employees their salaries for the next six weeks during the transition. The others, he said, should begin to look for work elsewhere. He wasn't going to bother Hoye with nothing happening. Yet the minute he turned onto the driveway of his house, he was back in the vise of waiting for that knock on the front door. Every phone call, every sound had become ominous. Hoye had been right about DiMaggio. He would tear her apart in court. DiMaggio was done. When he saw the driveway clear, he breathed more easily. He parked outside and stole a quick glance at the Sharpe house. A quiet gloom had settled over both houses.

The first thing he did when he got into the house was to check phone messages. There were none. It was good to have the house to himself. He headed to the kitchen for a swig of orange juice. An alarming jab caught him between the ribs when he spotted the opened bottle of vodka and a crystal glass with an untouched drink. He backed out of the room. His breathing was short and shallow. Was Henley here? Robert didn't move. Had he sent someone? He didn't dare call out and disclose his location. The door to the basement was closed. Sylvie wouldn't drink on the job. She needed her two days. Could he make a run for the front door? *The living room! I didn't look inside.* Robert turned around without a sound. The back door was out of the question. He'd be running into a trap there. Mowed down where Justin died, fitting! He took one measured step at a time, trying not to make a sound. When he reached the edge of the living room, he stopped short, afraid of whom he might see.

'It's only me, Robert. I've come to talk.' Jessie's mouth was twisted in a rancorous smile. The revolver was hidden beside her. 'You need that vodka. You look dreadful. I'll wait.'

Robert's shoulders sagged in relief. He shrugged and went for the drink. He drained the glass and poured himself another before he joined Jessie. 'I'm surprised you've come alone,' he said sardonically, trying to establish an ease he didn't feel.

'For some things, I don't need my father.'

'Have you come to evict me?' He tried a smile that didn't work. She ignored his question. 'Mike Fortier survived.'

'What?'

'He fingered you. Maybe I should say, he footed you.'

'What?'

'The shoes, the ones I bought you, the ones you wore that night. There are fluorescent green lines. He saw them that night, and I tied them to you.' Jessie took a sip of vodka.

'They're popular shoes, aren't they? It could have been anybody.'

'Robert, don't play the fool. We don't have much time. It's just you and me.'

'What do you care about Mike Fortier?' A slow assertive aggression rose in his tone.

'Robert, I want our business done before the police and my father get here. You're right, Mike's not that important.'

'You think I'll make some grand confession because *it's just you*

287

and me?' he asked sarcastically, pouring himself another drink.

'It's you, me and this.' Jessie slid the Smith & Wesson out from under her purse. 'Did you know that women, on the whole, are better shots than men?'

Robert's eyes widened with dread as he sat up. 'Are you nuts?'

'I'll make this easier for you. I blame myself as much as I blame you for Justin's death. I had the affair and I put the documents in the safe, and you found them.'

His sarcasm and aggression were gone. 'Jessie, I didn't…'

'Ah, but you did. The police matched the fibers from the white gloves you used. Dad and I figured that out with their calls to Sylvie and me. We don't have time for lies.' Jessie pulled the slide back and cocked the Smith & Wesson. She knew to fully depress the trigger for the gun to discharge.

Robert swallowed hard. He knew why she had come. He'd never have to face the police or Henley because neither of them would leave that room alive. His nose began to run. 'Alright, I read the documents, but I didn't…'

A single tear rolled down Jessie's cheek. 'The DNA results are back. Justin was your son. He was yours and you killed him to get back at me.'

Robert lost all care for his own safety. *He was yours…* He stood unsteadily. 'You spoiled, greedy, arrogant, conniving, reckless bitch! How dare you ask me about *my* infidelity? Look at what your own has cost you. You didn't even bother to find out if I was Justin's father. *You've* ruined our lives! I just paid all the bills and stayed in the background.

'You kept every cent you owned, you kept the house, you disinherited me, but at least, all that money was yours. You took my son from me!' Each of those words cut like a razor. 'You stole every day of his living years from me because you didn't think that I was his father. You kept Justin from me even in death, but he was mine. He came from me and I had no time with him!' Robert was shouting at Jessie and crying. Spittle dripped from the side of his mouth.

The revolver was steady in Jessie's hand. 'He was my son too and you killed him.' Her tone was flat.

Robert sat back down, laughing through his tears. 'After the way you've treated me, I watched you suffer and I was glad, Jessie. I wanted

you to hurt. I wanted you to fall apart.' Robert began to laugh hysteric-
ally, sniffling loudly, wiping his nose with the back of his hand and
laughing. 'Look at the place you've brought us to. Take a good look
and wallow in it. You deserve your guilt. I hope it chokes you.'

Jessie's face twitched with every barb, but she was undeterred.
'Geoffrion probably thinks your motive was money. But it wasn't that
at all, was it Robert? It was about revenge and hatred.' Jessie locked
eyes with Robert. 'I need closure. I have to hear the words.' She was
beyond grief and tears.

'Jessie, I …' *Keep her talking*. She was sitting so still he wondered
if she was capable of moving. Still, he'd never get to the revolver before
she discharged it. He backtracked. 'I never laid a finger on Fortier. He
tailed me to the airport and he was there when I got back. I had had
enough. I went home and changed. I found his address in the kitchen
and I drove out to his place. I wanted to offer him more money to
leave me alone. I sold the company. I'm flush. His junker was in the
driveway. I rang and I knocked three times. I tried the door. The damn
thing was open. I took two steps inside and called him. I couldn't find
a light switch. I bumped my knee on some table that fell over. Next
thing I knew, he was falling down the stairs. I didn't wait around.'

'He's almost deaf.'

'How the hell could I remember that?'

'We have no more time, Robert. For once, do the noble thing.
Admit you killed our son.'

'Jessie…' He couldn't get another word out of his mouth.

She stood slowly. She curled her finger around the trigger and
levelled the revolver.

Chapter Fifty-seven

DONNA HAD FULLY RECONCILED herself to the challenge of regaining her child. She knocked on the bedroom door and asked Ms. Tritt to cut the session short for that day.

'But, Mom, we're at a good part.'

Ms. Tritt wasn't any happier.

'You can both catch up in the next session.' Ms. Tritt smiled obligingly. Colin pouted. Donna walked her out and came back and closed the door to Colin's bedroom. 'Colin, get away from the computer and sit on the bed.' He stomped over to the bed and plunked himself down. 'I want you to sit there and listen and don't interrupt me.' Colin began to pull at the comforter. 'Leave that alone.' He pushed it away.

'But…'

'Not another word. This good time you've been having is over. I haven't liked the boy I've seen in the last while. He's not the son I love.' Colin drew in a breath to say something, but he didn't. 'Your friend is dead—you almost died. You lied to us. You called Justin to go for a swim. You fought. You were lucky you didn't drown, swimming in the dark. You should be ashamed of disobeying the rules, ashamed of lying to the police about the call, and ashamed of boasting to your friends. You tried to hang yourself, Colin! You're not Superman. Susan found you and Dad got you down in time. You were just lucky a second time!'

Colin's small chest deflated and his head dropped. The toe of one foot began to dig into the carpet.

'I know you better than anyone else. You're not telling the whole story. If you don't tell me what happened after Justin hit his head, you'll still be my son, but I won't ever love you the same way. I can't love anyone I can't trust.'

Colin's shoulders began to heave.

'Now, it's your turn. I'll listen.'

'I'll just be a wuss again.' Big, perfectly formed tears fell like crystal balls down Colin's cheeks.

'It takes courage to tell the truth. You won't be a wuss. You'll be a brave person. That kind of son I can love with all my heart.'

Colin dropped his head again and wrung his hands. 'Justin hit his head and he swallowed too much water and he said a really bad word and then…'

'And then what, Colin?' Donna knew his nose was beginning to run.

Colin's words came out in a block of sound without punctuation. 'I couldn't help him he'd pull me under 'cause he was bigger than me and and he'd beat me up for sure if he got out of the pool 'cause I kicked him then then it was real dark so I ran but but then I thought I saw Mr. Tyler at the window in the kitchen but I don't know for sure maybe that was another day then maybe Justin could come back from the dead and still get me so so that's when I hanged myself so he wouldn't find me.' Colin's eyes bulged and he gasped because he hadn't taken a single breath. Then he hung his head and his shoulders began to heave.

Donna rushed to the side of the bed and held onto Colin and he held onto her and cried like the child he was. Colin did not yet know that he had lost his childhood the night Justin drowned. Justin's death had subsumed that irrevocable, tender loss. In time, Donna hoped, Colin would forgive himself for leaving his friend to die. He'd be older then and might even succeed in believing he had done more that night than run. That was how adults survived. No one could ever bear the truth. He would work around it; pad it till it was soft enough to be borne.

Some time later, when Colin had cried himself to sleep, Donna slipped out of his room and made her call to Moitié. Robert Tyler was part of that call.

Henley and Geoffrion were rushing to Roselawn Crescent, each from a different direction. Moitié was waiting on a courier with the arrest and search warrants at the North Division. The call from Donna Sharpe came in on his private cell. Before he picked up, he opened his drawer and turned on the recorder. 'Detective Bertrand.'

Donna didn't take time to plan her words or to squirm around their story. It was time to reconcile, and work through the challenge of the truth. Her only addition was punctuation and the pauses that went with it.

Moitié had only seconds to nod with smug satisfaction that he'd been right about the kid's involvement in Henley's death. At the mention of Robert Tyler, he gritted his teeth. 'Mrs. Sharpe, thank you for your cooperation. In your opinion, do you think your son saw Robert Tyler?'

'I don't know what Colin saw. He doesn't either. It was dark and he was frightened.'

'I'll need your signature for the official statement.'

'I'll sign it. My family needs to struggle back to some form of normalcy.'

'I wish you good luck.'

'Thank you.'

Moitié's solve slipped off the desk with the mention of Robert Tyler. He expressed his letdown as soon as he was off the phone and recorder. '*Ostie d'tabarnak!*' He gave his desk a good thump. In the next second, he called Geoffrion. 'The warrants are here. I'm leaving to join you. I got my call…'

Geoffrion snorted, adding a few colorful words of his own. Had the Henleys been up front from the outset, he might have… How convenient money was! The Henleys had obstructed his investigation from day one and kept him off pace. 'That's just great! Accidental with mitigating circumstances or a no solve. If I can't get to Jessie Henley in time, there's no telling what Tyler will do to her. Even with the siren, I'm four minutes away.'

Robert didn't take his eyes from the barrel of the revolver. His body was slippery with sweat. Nothing but the barrel and the hand that levelled it at him crossed his mind. Not the idea of a lunge that might save his life, not the hidden money in Belize, no life flashes, no bargains and no regrets. There was a discordant look to Jessie's beautiful hand holding the Smith & Wesson. He'd seen that hand extended in reception lines and ruffling Justin's hair. It didn't seem right. He tried to focus his mind on dying, but it stuck to the sight of her hand.

Jessie spread her feet apart. 'Your son deserves the truth. I promise that no one but you and I will ever know it.' Her voice crackled with contempt.

Robert didn't flinch. 'I've never been much good with the truth. Our life was a lie.'

Each word, caught in the space between them, seemed distilled, full of the import of a dying declaration. There was no time for comfort or treachery.

'Can I stand, Jessie? I don't want to die sitting in a chair.' When Jessie didn't respond, Robert managed to get to his feet. "I asked Justin to go for a swim when we got home. 'Don't feel like it,' he said. I wanted to tell him right then that he wasn't my son, but he ran up to his room."

'Hurry.' Jessie jerked in a sudden shiver.

The last seconds rushed away from him. With time gone, Robert thought he might fall. 'I had some orange juice and went out for some air that night. I heard a splash in the pool. I saw Justin fooling around. I never saw Colin. I told Justin to get out of the pool. He knew the rules. I held out my hand, but he went under to avoid it, and it hurt me. He wasn't even mine! I was so angry with you, Jess, angry with your selfish secrets, resentful of you and the years with Douglas, that when Justin surfaced close to me, I dunked him under again, only once,' he whispered wretchedly, 'to teach him a lesson. I went back inside because I figured he'd get out of the pool after that.' Robert covered his eyes, and his head shook from side to side. His voice cracked. 'I left him there, Jess. I thought he was okay. He'd didn't cry for help. I thought he was giving me his usual silent treatment. It was dark. I didn't know! I didn't know!' he wailed. A minute passed before Robert spoke. His voice was thready. 'When you called, I checked his room. I figured he was there. Then I turned on the pool lights and ran out back and found him. I carried him out of the water. I tried, I tried with everything in me to bring him back, Jess...' Robert's eyes had gone dark with utter despair.

Click! Robert grabbed his chest and fell to his knees.

Click, click, click, click, click. Robert saw Jessie point the gun at her own head and discharge it. The Smith & Wesson fell to the floor. Jessie stood there, motionless as stone. The room was unnaturally quiet. He crawled over to her as she fell forward and he caught her in his arms. 'No matter what happens now, I beg you to forgive me for not knowing, Jess.'

She didn't pull away from Robert. She wept with him, dropping her head on his shoulder. Contempt and recrimination, even revenge, dissolved in the face of unfathomable grief that would haunt their lives forever. They hung onto each other and to the memory of the son they had unwittingly destroyed.

* * *

Henley had gone around to the back of the house and let himself in. He found them together in their embrace. Geoffrion arrived seconds later. Henley opened the door for him.

Jessie turned to both men before they made any move towards her. Her face was raw with pain and knowing. The truth, she had learned, was sad and unforgiving. It had spread her anguish. Her careless action had defined and precipitated the loss of her only son. When she finally spoke, Henley and Geoffrion knew her words were unalterable. 'Our son died accidentally.'

Robert closed his eyes, still traumatized by the barrel of the Smith & Wesson. Humbled by Jessie's generosity, he was appalled and shamed that he had left his son in the dark of night, thrashing in the water until it claimed him. Robert knew now with a leaden certainty that Justin was reaching out for his help that night, not avoiding him.

Epilogue

No one person killed Justin Tyler. Everyone close to him had a hand in his death.

Geoffrion and Henley left the inseparable couple and walked out of the house to wait on Moitié. Neither man spoke. Henley stood erect and looked up at the sky. Far in the distance, he saw the horizon was already pink. The slow-rolling white clouds above him were clean. The breeze was warm and clammy and stuck to his face and hands. The moon was already full-face, and, from where he stood, Henley could make out the smudges that tainted its cheeks. The earth rotated in its usual path, unperturbed by the flaws of man and his small tragedies. He was saddened and exhausted. When he looked back at the house, he hid the rejection he felt and straightened his back. Without bothering to address Geoffrion face to face, he said, 'Jessie wouldn't lie, Detective. I know my daughter. Justin was her world. This turnaround has taken me by surprise. I'm not often wrong about people.' That was as far as Henley went with his admission.

'There are still the facts we have, sir. Your daughter is not a crown prosecutor.'

Henley whirled around to Geoffrion. His face was twisted in an effort to manage his anger. He was not about to cede control to this cop. 'You've been in the death business. You, better than I, know how truth, perhaps never absolute or complete, finally outs itself. Robert thought he was going to die. Jessie got the germane facts out of him. I have no doubt of that. The safe, the gloves, that night… What the hell does that matter now? He didn't drown the boy! Isn't that what you were after?'

Moitié pulled into the driveway and picked up the warrants on the passenger seat. Geoffrion walked over to confer with him. Geoffrion spoke quietly. He was angry and arrogant. 'I had Tyler on motive, opportunity and suspicious actions following the death. I had him in my crosshairs! The two of them are in there,' he pointed to the house, 're-united, for shit's sake!' When the solve wasn't his, Geoffrion wasn't a generous cop. He rubbed the side of his nose, something he did when a case turned on him.

Moitié hid his triumph well, except for an undeniable twinkle in his deep brown eyes. Jean had taken the best part of the case for himself, and he'd end up with a B&E aggravated assault. He claimed his solve. 'I was right all along, Jean. You told me to lay off the kid.' He'd get the nod this time from headquarters and he deserved it.

'I still have doubts,' Geoffrion persisted, 'but the boss will tell me to back off. The rich and the rules they make up along the way! If Tyler was anyone else, I'd have him in a holding cell, but that won't wash with the 'big boss.' Miss Henley had what she thought was a loaded weapon. She probably discharged it, but that won't go anywhere because neither Tyler nor she will admit what really occurred when they were alone.'

'Suck it up, Jean. Look at the facts. If you believed you were seconds from dying, would you lie? Would you be brave enough to take that chance? Some facts you'll never get to. You know the routine. That's part of the game we play.'

Geoffrion ignored the questions. 'Tyler will answer for Fortier. Let's take him down. By the way, you did *good*.' He acknowledged his partner with little enthusiasm. Geoffrion was accustomed to winning. Second place didn't sit well with him. He'd feel somewhat better slapping the cuffs on Tyler.

'The next case might be the one you've been looking for, Jean.' Sometimes Moitié could hear his partner's unspoken thoughts.

'Shit! Thought this was it!'

'It was for me.' Moitié fought an urge to gloat. He wasn't a kid. He and Geoffrion were a team. It hurt to lose a solve you had lined up. He'd lucked out.

'Right,' was all Geoffrion could manage at that moment. Seconds later, he turned to Moitié, extending his hand. 'Great work, Denis.'

'Thanks. I mean it, Jean. The Henleys boxed you in most of the way.'

'The case is still open in my head.'

'Figured as much.'

Alone, huddled together beside a massive couch, the tenuous lifeline Jessie had extended to Robert began to shred. The link was Justin and he was gone. Jessie spoke first, relieving Robert from the awkward after-moment. 'If I hadn't immediately accused you, my father wouldn't have hired Fortier. He wouldn't be lying in a hospital bed.'

Robert took her face in his hands. 'In your place, I would have done the same. I'm not innocent, Jessie. Work aside, I take no pride in myself. You acted out of love. I acted out of rejection.'

'Is there forgiveness, do you think?'

'No, not really. I hope there's redemption though. That's a beginning.' Robert helped Jessie to her feet when they heard the men coming back inside.

Geoffrion wasted no time. 'Robert Tyler, I have an arrest warrant for you, Sir.' He read Robert his rights and the charge against him. Robert reiterated what he had told Jessie.

'Robert told me the exact same thing half an hour ago,' she said. 'Is this arrest necessary?'

Henley walked off. He had no intention of assisting Robert.

'We have photos of the scene. We can better verify your account about the table you knocked over at the division.' His case had turned, but Geoffrion intended to keep the file in the bottom drawer along with the other unsolved cases. He remained unconvinced about the circumstances surrounding the death of Justin Tyler.

'Are the cuffs necessary?'

'Procedure, sir.'

'Jessie, please call Doug Hoye. His number's on my desk.' It wasn't long before Robert was back inside an interrogation room, this time, waiting on Hoye. Three hours later, the lawyer was driving him home.

'You're not out of this mess, Robert. Fortier was one of theirs, but I'm not talking about years behind bars this time.'

'I accept my part.'

'You should.'

As Hoye turned into the driveway, the first thing Robert noticed was that Henley's car was gone. His heart fell. Jessie must have gone with him. 'Thanks, Doug.'

'You'll get my invoice.'

'Fine.' Robert had one letter he wanted to get off before he poured himself a stiff scotch and flopped onto the nearest chair. His nerves jumped when he saw Jessie in the living room.

She didn't approach him. 'I told my father I wasn't going back with him. I broke his heart. All our hearts have been broken one way or another. I don't want to run away from myself or my memories. It's time I stood on my own.'

'Do you want me to leave?'

'No. Justin was our joy and our loss. I want to fill in the parts of him you never knew. I need you to share the grief and the guilt with me. I can't do that alone and I think you need me to shoulder you through that last night.'

Robert's tears came with a sudden rush. 'I do, Jess,' he whispered with the agony he'd bear every waking minute for years to come.

It was a trembling, desperate, complicit peace they made with one another.

Henley saw to it that Mike Fortier was eventually transferred to a posh suite at the Mount Sinai Convalescent Home in Côte-Saint-Luc. He spent many evenings with the old man listening to his stories. Mike's recovery sped forward when Henley announced that he had found him a publisher.

Once Colin stopped boasting, and that occurred with his mother beside him when he was on the phone, most of his friends lost interest and stopped calling. He began to worry about the purple scar on the front of his neck, but Donna told him she had something special to hide it when school started. She herself worked on a letter of sympathy that she dropped into the mailbox next door. Four days later, a note was left in her box. *Thank you, Jessie.* Spoken words between the families would come in time.

Carmen picked up a registered letter a week after Robert's arrest. She read its contents in her Mini. *Carmen, My behavior was unforgivable. I won't offer excuses. I'll only say that my words about you on those first few nights were true. What came afterward was a product of a weak man and my situation. I wish you the best. You deserve better than the man you met at the casino. As a brief aside, my son died accidentally, but I live with my negligence. Be well, Robert*

Carmen called Annie Nolan immediately to thank her and tell her she could stop the security watch. As usual, Annie was brief and on point. 'You have a new beginning. Use it well.' A few minutes after the call, her cell vibrated across the empty seat. 'It's me. I was wondering if you wanted to do breakfast on Sunday. Then I remembered the casino.'

'Breakfast sounds great, Caitlin. I feel like French toast and sausages.'

'Really?'

'Absolutely. I heard from Robert. I'll bring his note with me.'

Henley threw himself into work, but that was nothing new. Forgiving Jessie and accepting her rejection of him and the path she had chosen didn't come easily for Henley, so he stubbornly stayed away. Jessie needed some space—well, she'd have it. In private moments, he admitted to himself that he grudgingly admired her independence, but it didn't help his need of her. He was lonely but far too proud to admit this weakness, as he saw it. Five months later, Jessie called him.

'You're going to be a grandfather again. We're having a little girl, Dad. Would you mind if we chose Leslie, Mom's name?'

Henley drove over that night. He didn't use the limo. His daughter was back! A new life was coming into the family. But Justin was lost forever. His hands gripped harder on the steering wheel. Fortier's words rang in his ears. *Don't go there, Douglas. Don't ever go there...*

Acknowledgements

A great sense of excitement preceded the writing of *The Red Floor*. With the two Miami books, I expected the Miami police to be friendly and open. That's American! I felt that we, in Quebec, are somewhat reticent to open our doors wide. I could not have been more wrong. I was taken aback by the warm welcome and the committed enthusiasm of every professional I visited. At the end of my research, the only fear I had was writing a book that might not equal the excitement I felt in the field research. It is with gratitude that I introduce them.

Lieutenant Detective Jean Bissonnette of Major Crimes welcomed me at Place Versailles with a lengthy, informative interview, a tour of the interrogation room, the video room beside it and the holding cells. I left with his private cell number and the offer to call him anytime with additional questions. A day later, he called me to set up another interview at the North Division that would serve as the setting for my book.

Although the Division was dealing with the sad and combustible events in Montreal North, Lieutenant Detective Denis Jr. Bonneau called to set up the interview. On the edge of my seat, I listened to his intriguing interrogation techniques and I followed him to the 14 cells (the common cell, the padded cell, the separate cells), the intake desk, the video surveillance room and the photo and finger-printing room in the basement of the imposing building. I was doubly relieved to be there only temporarily.

At L'Édifice Wilfrid-Derome, I waited quietly in a protected area for the Chief Coroner, Me Gilles Éthier. What I recall most from our long interview is the respectful and gentle manner in which Me Éthier spoke of the dead and his mission to close their files with human respect. It was in the morgue, precisely in the external examining room, where I found the title of my book.

For the case-law on minors, I was indeed fortunate to listen to the expertise of Victor A. Carbonneau, an attorney-at-law. Victor had also worked with the R.C.M.P. He discussed at length the problem of my fictional case while I took notes every time we spoke. As the book moved along, new questions arose that he answered with an attorney's precision.

Robert Menard, a former sergeant-detective in the Montreal Police Department, the undercover cop who brought down the Montreal mafia boss, Paolo Violi, regaled me with his nail-biting stories of city crime in Montreal 30 years ago. He was such a dominating presence that I felt he was a good base for one of my fictional characters in the book.

Any procedural errors in *The Red Floor* are mine, and I blame my Uni-Ball pen.

I owe particular thanks to some usual suspects:

To Gina Pingitore, thanks from the heart for your continuing enthusiasm and long hours of proofing draft after draft. I couldn't do it without you!

To David Drummond, what an eye-catching cover! Thank you.

To Margaret Goldik, your expertise in the latest style guides keeps me sharp and keenly focused on details. Your incisive editing and close reads tighten the screws of the book. Thank you.

To Irene Pingitore, our last-word proofer, thanks for those great pick-ups!

To Kathy Panet, thank you for a good read.

Gina Pingitore, Rose Strati, Maggie Baxter, Shirley Shum, Kathy Panet, Rose-Anna Starr, Lucie Day and Hille Vires: You all make each signing a good day! Many, many thanks.

To Mary Tellett, my sister, thanks for being my support in Toronto.

To Louise Morin, *merci* for your friendship, your acumen and your time.

To Hélène Fortin, *merci* for being my accurate French resource and my friend.

To my readers, you make the books worth writing!

To Montreal: Thank you for being my home and my first love.

To Leslie Gardner, my London agent: I am deeply indebted to you for the time and the effort you have so generously given me.

Most of all, thank you for giving it to me straight because you have brought out the best in me.

David Price was my guide for the first five books in the Caitlin Donovan series. David was there at the beginning.

To Véhicule's sales reps, thank you for your interest and hard work.

To marketing manager, Maya Assouad, I greatly appreciate all your efforts on my behalf.

To my new editor and publisher, Simon Dardick, thank you for warmly welcoming me on board. I am delighted to be an author with Véhicule Press with its wonderful staff and its excellent reputation. I am grateful for the fine editing and comments and the germane and critical suggestions. I value your enthusiasm, your trust and your commitment.

Véhicule Press